# A KILLING MIND

## LUKE DELANEY

MIX
Paper from
responsible sources
FSC
FSC C007454

made and from independently certified FSC paper to ensure
responsible forest management.

HarperCollins*Publishers*

HarperCollins*Publishers* Ltd
1 London Bridge Street,
London SE1 9GF

www.harpercollins.co.uk

This paperback edition 2018
1

First published in Great Britain in 2018 by
HarperCollins*Publishers*

A catalogue record for this book is available from the British Library

ISBN: 978-0-00-758579-3 (PB b-format)

This novel is entirely a work of fiction.
The names, characters and incidents portrayed in it are
the work of the author's imagination. Any resemblance to
actual persons, living or dead, events or localities is
entirely coincidental.

Set in Meridien by Palimpsest Book Production Limited,
Falkirk, Stirlingshire

Printed and bound in the UK by CPI Group (UK) Ltd, Croydon CR0 4YY

I'd like to dedicate this book to my brothers and sisters: Kirsty, Cathy, John and Alex. Thanks for always being so supportive, funny and caring. You're a pretty cool bunch.

Luke Delaney

# 1

William Dalton was glad to be alone in the lift that jerked and rocked its way from the platforms in the depths of the Borough Underground station towards the streets of Southwark high above. The shiny metal walls of the large steel box reflected his image from all sides. There was no way to escape his own dishevelled appearance. Only eighteen years old, but the ravages of crack cocaine and living without a home had taken a heavy toll. His white skin had taken on a yellow tinge, his blue eyes were faded and sunken, his fair hair unkempt and tangled. At least with the lift to himself he didn't have to worry about disapproving or pitiful looks from the more fortunate or worry that it was his odour that made them contort their faces or cover their noses with sweeter smelling hands.

The steel cube jolted to a stop and the doors scraped apart. Quickly he moved through the ticket area, nodding to the guard he recognized from previous days and nights, and used his treasured Oyster card to open the barrier and head into the freezing night streets of this ancient part of London. He moved as fast as he could along Marshalsea Road, only looking up occasionally to check for any possible threats. The money he'd earned from a hard day's begging in London's West End was carefully hidden in the crotch of his underpants; the last place anyone would put their hands – or so he hoped, although he knew other beggars desperate for cash would not hesitate to search *everywhere*. The only other serious risk was gangs of drunks or groups of feral youths who might decide to kick him to death purely for entertainment, but it was late and the night was bitterly cold – like only January can be – so the streets were practically deserted.

As he scuttled towards his current home – an abandoned garage at the back of a low-rise residential block – he was oblivious to the faded detritus of Christmas hanging from some of the lampposts, and the torn, dirty streamers and decorations that adorned the windows and doors of the flats he passed, fairy lights forlornly trying to cling to a happier, less bleak time. He turned into Mint Street and was soon at the garage that served as home. He could have stayed in the West End, but that would have meant sleeping on a bed of cardboard in a shop doorway till he was kicked awake by frustrated employees or owners. He moved some corrugated metal sheets aside and slipped into the garage, pulling them back into place behind him as he took a small torch from his pocket and surveyed the interior, relieved to see his few possessions were still where he'd left them. With a sense of urgency, he turned on both his camping lantern and a battery-powered outdoor heater. Its effectiveness was minimal, but it took the bitterness from the air and provided a comforting, almost homely glow. He rubbed his hands and began to search the garage for food he'd been given by donors who wanted to help but didn't want to give him cash. On a night like this he was grateful for the food and was soon devouring a packet of biscuits as if it was his last meal.

After he'd retrieved the cash bag from its hiding place he settled down to count his daily earnings on the old broken car seat that served as his sofa, the foam protruding from gaping wounds in the vinyl cover. He pushed another biscuit into his mouth and tipped the money next to him on the seat, pushing the coins around with the tips of his fingers, satisfied at a glance that he had enough to take to his dealer tomorrow to replenish the supply he was about to use. He wiped the mix of saliva and crumbs from his lips, gathered the coins back into the bag and carried it to the wall at the back of the garage. His fingers traced the outline of a loose brick – his *secret* brick – and began working away at the edges until they gained sufficient purchase to pull it free and lower it to the ground.

Listening hard, he slid his hand into the hole and searched inside the cavity until his fingers touched the plastic bag he'd hidden there. He lifted it out and then replaced the brick before heading back to the sofa and making himself comfortable. As delicately as if he were handling surgical instruments, he removed the contents and placed them in a neat line in front of him: a tiny clip-seal plastic bag containing three small waxy rocks of crack, a glass pipe to smoke them with and a lighter to heat them.

Carefully he set one of the rocks on the end of the homemade pipe, placing the other end between his lips and raising the lighter towards the translucent pebble – not rushing, enjoying the moment before his world changed, for a few hours at least, from rank misery to ecstasy. But as he drew his thumb firmly over the flint of the cheap lighter to produce a spark, his head snapped around. He was sure he'd heard a noise outside. Not the normal wild noises of the night he'd grown used to hearing – the screech of a catfight or the scavenging of a fox – but something different. The clumsy noise that only another human would make.

For almost twenty seconds he sat frozen in place, his head cocked so that his ear pointed towards the entrance. He was beginning to doubt he'd heard anything, until suddenly, terrifyingly, the sound came again: unwary feet tripping over something on the ground. Another homeless person? Another drug addict? Someone who'd followed him or who'd been watching the garage, waiting for his return? Someone planning to lay claim to all his prized possessions – maybe even the garage itself? In a panic he scrambled for the six-inch kitchen knife he kept under the sofa, squeezing its thick rubber handle hard – the feel of it in his palm calming him and making him feel stronger and less vulnerable. He reminded himself he'd been surviving on the streets since he was sixteen and had yet to be seriously turned over or battered. If someone was coming for him, he'd give them what they deserved.

He moved silently towards the entrance of the garage, hoping to startle his would-be attacker by suddenly calling out: 'I don't know what the fuck you want, but I've got a serious fucking blade. You fuck with me, I'll fucking cut you up, man.'

His bold words made him feel more confident and stronger, but it was a fragile power, fading by the second as his words met with silence. Again he started to question whether he'd imagined the noise, or whether it might have been a stray dog looking for an easy meal. But until he could be sure there was nothing out there, he knew he wouldn't be able to relax and enjoy the blissful escape he had planned.

Forced on by the need to know, he began to pull back the makeshift front door, continually cursing under his breath until he was able to look out into the night, the darkness illuminated slightly by the glow of the city's light. It had begun to rain; freezing pellets of sleet lashed his face, stinging his skin and making it hard to see as he peered through squinted eyes. Blinking rapidly, he wiped the water from his face with a sweep of his hand and looked up to the starless sky, opening his mouth to catch a few drops on his tongue – like he used to do when he was a child.

A smile began to spread across his lips until suddenly it was smashed away as something hit him hard across the back of the head – the blow powerful enough to crack his skull and knock him semi-conscious to the ground, but not enough to kill him. His befuddled mind was struggling to work out what could have happened when he became aware that he was moving; someone was dragging him backwards across the ground into the garage. There were no sounds of exertion; whoever it was seemed able to move him with ease. He felt his lower legs being dropped to the floor and moments later he heard the scrape of the board being replaced across the entrance, the noise of the rain outside fading to a quiet hiss.

After a few seconds he'd recovered enough to slightly open his eyes and was immediately aware that someone was circling him, first one way and then the other, like a tiger moving in on his prey. He tried to move but instantly felt a kick to his stomach that made him double up with pain. As he lay clutching his belly and trying not to vomit, his assailant crouched by his side and a gloved hand reached out to seize a handful of hair in a vice-like grip. His head was twisted around until he was looking into his attacker's face, but the features were hidden in the depths of his hoodie so all Dalton could see were shadows, as if his torturer had no face at all. Even so, there seemed something familiar about the figure crouched next to him, although in his swirling confusion he couldn't make a connection between this nightmare and anything that had existed in the real world.

After an age of silence, Dalton managed to draw sufficient breath to mumble, 'Who are you? Want do you want?'

The reply came from deep within the darkness where a face should have been as the attacker, by some sleight of hand, produced a vicious-looking knife – long and thick, with a serrated edge like the lower jaw of a piranha. He held the blade close to Dalton's face. 'I want them all to know – I want them all to know who did this.'

'I don't understand,' Dalton whimpered – his eyes fixed on the knife. 'Did what?'

The attacker's hand moved fast, the knife slicing deep into Dalton's neck, opening a gaping wound through which the air in his lungs rushed out, mixing with the pooling blood. But the man who would soon kill him had been careful not to sever the carotid artery. He didn't want him to die. Not yet. For now, he wanted silence. He wanted Dalton to be alive so he could see the terror and horror in his eyes before he allowed him the blissful release of death.

'It's time,' the voice from the shadow told him. 'Time to show them all.'

# 2

Detective Superintendent Featherstone entered the main office of the Special Investigations Unit in New Scotland Yard and made his way to the goldfish bowl of a room that belonged to Detective Inspector Sean Corrigan. He opened the door without knocking and tossed a pink cardboard file marked 'confidential' on to Corrigan's desk to grab his attention. Sean flicked the file open before looking at Featherstone, who'd slumped into the seat opposite clutching another pink folder, and then his eyes returned to the file where he was confronted by crime scene photographs of William Dalton – his throat cut and face disfigured with dried blood congealed around his gaping mouth. He flicked through the first few photographs, making a special note of the victim's hands, from which the fingernails had been removed, leaving behind bloody stumps. Sean winced and looked away for a second.

'I hope he was dead before he had his nails pulled out,' he said.

'And before he had his teeth removed,' Featherstone added, making Sean look up. 'The blood and swelling in and around his mouth was caused when our killer extracted some of his teeth using a combination of knife and, most probably, pliers – too early to say for sure; nothing was found at the scene.'

Sean nodded to show he understood. 'Who was he?'

'William Dalton,' Featherstone answered. 'Eighteen years old, homeless and addicted to crack. Home was a disused garage in Mint Street, Southwark – that's where he was killed. He sustained a significant injury to the back of his head, and then there's the damage caused by removal of the teeth and fingernails, but that wasn't what killed him. There were two distinct wounds to his neck and throat: his throat was cut – straight through the trachea – which wouldn't necessarily have killed him, but the second wound sliced open his carotid artery. He bled to death, or at least that's what it looks like. Won't know for sure until the post-mortem.'

Again Sean looked down at the photographs and then to Featherstone. 'Unusual and significant injuries,' he admitted, 'but why give Special Investigations the case? He could have been in debt to a particularly nasty drug dealer. Maybe they tortured him to find out if he had any drugs or cash hidden away. Teeth. Fingernails. All looks like torture.' He didn't tell Featherstone about the images the crime scene photos had conjured up in his mind – a madman stabbing and pulling at the victim's teeth and nails, his face contorted with the effort, yet in control. Unafraid. Calm.

'Firstly,' Featherstone explained, 'Assistant Commissioner Addis is aware of the case and has insisted that you take it on. His apologies, by the way. He's away at a conference in Bramshill, otherwise he'd have briefed you in person.'

'And . . . ?'

'And,' Featherstone told him, leaning forward and tossing the other file on to his desk, 'this isn't his first kill.'

Sean tentatively opened the new file and was again greeted by crime scene photographs: a young woman's body lying on the wet ground behind a large wheelie bin. Other photographs showed close-ups of wounds similar to those William Dalton had suffered: teeth and fingernails traumatically removed. He also noted that her clothing appeared to have been pulled and torn and assumed the worst had happened, but again he said nothing, knowing that Featherstone would start talking soon enough.

'Her name is Tanya Richards,' Featherstone obliged. 'Twenty-three years old. A known prostitute. Ran away to the big smoke from some shithole in the Midlands a few years ago. Soon discovered the streets aren't paved with gold and started using heroin. Prostitution paid for the drugs. Not an unfamiliar tale.'

Sean acknowledged this with a nod.

'Her body was found not far from where she lived,' Featherstone continued. 'She had a room in a dump of a flat in Roden Street, Holloway. When she wasn't there she was working the streets around Smithfield Market during the night – looking for punters. He left plenty of DNA, only it's not on file, so looks like he has no previous.'

'Could the DNA be from a punter?' Sean asked.

'Unlikely,' Featherstone answered. 'Looks like she was on her way to work when she was attacked. Judging by the contents of her handbag, she was careful.'

'Condoms?' Sean guessed.

'Yeah,' Featherstone confirmed, 'and plenty of them. Also we found semen smeared on her abdomen that matches that found inside her, so everything points to it being the killer's.' Featherstone shook his head. 'Strange thing to do – wipe himself off on her belly.'

'He was marking her,' Sean said before he could stop himself – drawing a concerned look from Featherstone. 'Raping and killing her wasn't enough,' he tried to explain. 'He wanted to mark her.'

'Why?' Featherstone asked.

'That,' Sean answered, 'I don't know yet.' He turned his gaze back to the photographs, wishing he could be alone without being disturbed by Featherstone's clumsy observations. His understanding of this killer was coming together

9

faster than in any of his previous cases, as if the year-long gap since his last significant investigation had sharpened his instincts and senses. He needed this killer more than any of his team could possibly understand.

While his mind was engaged with the faceless killer who'd turned his fantasies into reality, using the helpless Tanya Richards as a conduit for his warped desire, Sean threw out a question to keep Featherstone occupied: 'Was the same knife used on both victims?'

'Hard to say,' Featherstone admitted, inhaling deeply before continuing. 'Neither victim was stabbed – slashed, but not stabbed. Makes it difficult to be certain. Maybe the post-mortem will help.'

Sean started flicking through the file with an increased sense of urgency. Something told him every second could be vital. 'When was she killed?'

'More bad news, I'm afraid,' Featherstone answered. 'Only ten days ago. This one's not a once-a-year killer, Sean. He's running hot.'

'I didn't hear anything,' Sean told him. 'Didn't see anything on the news.'

'A prostitute and heroin addict murdered in London,' Featherstone explained with a shrug. 'Not exactly front-page material. The first murder got a mention on the local news – nothing more. They'll be all over it now though, that's for bloody sure.'

'But the fingernails and the teeth,' Sean frowned, 'that must have got the interest of the media?'

'Ah.' Featherstone cocked his head to one side. 'Would have, only the MIT who picked up the Richards case had the good sense not to mention the fact she'd had her nails removed. They let on some of her teeth had been pulled out, but kept quiet about the nails.'

'To eliminate nuisance callers claiming responsibility,' Sean said.

'Exactly,' Featherstone confirmed. 'Had we let it be known her nails were removed too, the better crime journalists out there might have started getting suspicious. The MIT reckoned they could explain the teeth away as a pissed-off pimp pulling out her gold teeth for their cash value.'

'Sensible,' Sean appreciated their thinking, 'but why mention either?'

'Trying to drum up some sympathy,' Featherstone explained. 'Not easy getting the media interested in a dead prostitute, or the general public for that matter. It was hoped that by making it clear she suffered, we could tug on a few more heartstrings – loosen a few lips.'

'Doesn't seem to have worked,' Sean replied.

'No,' Featherstone admitted, sounding sad and worn out by yet another violent death few would care about.

Both men were silent for a while before Sean spoke again. 'Unusual,' he said. 'Looks like it has to be the same killer, yet we have a male and a female victim. So, unless he's bisexual, the motivation can't be entirely sexual, despite the fact the female victim was raped.'

'Dalton doesn't seem to have been sexually assaulted in any way,' Featherstone added, 'but again, it's too early to say for sure.'

'So what's his motivation?' Sean directed the question at himself rather than Featherstone. 'If killing *is* his motivation, then he's a very dangerous and rare animal. A killer who kills because he likes it rather than to cover his tracks or out of panic – that's about as bad as it gets.'

'Rare like Sebastian Gibran?' Featherstone asked, dragging a ghost from the past into the small, warm office. 'Remember him?'

'I'm not likely to forget him, am I?' Sean sighed, memories of the most dangerous killer he'd ever dealt with swarming into his mind.

'He was something else though, wasn't he?' Featherstone reminded them both. 'Pure bloody evil, that one.'

'Evil?' Sean answered. 'Not sure that exists. He was just wired differently.'

'You mean wired wrongly?' Featherstone checked.

Sean ignored the question. 'He had everything anyone could ever want, but it wasn't enough. Killing made him feel like he was some sort of god – that taking life was his entitlement.'

'Do you think we could have another Sebastian Gibran here?' Featherstone sounded concerned. 'The last thing we need is another Gibran on the loose.'

'I doubt it,' Sean reassured him. 'Gibran was . . . exceptional. A one-off. This one's profile should be more straightforward. Gibran constantly changed his method so we wouldn't make a link. This one has varied the sex of his victims, but he's already showing a strong dedication to a particular method. And taking the teeth and fingernails – almost certainly souvenirs. Gibran only took memories.' He glanced down at the files on his desk, the brutal crime scene photographs staring back at him. 'All the same, we have a very dangerous individual on our hands.' He drew a breath. 'Ten days between the murders?'

'That's right,' Featherstone confirmed.

'Not good,' Sean replied, shaking his head. He chewed his bottom lip, deep in thought for a few seconds before continuing. 'Maybe we'll get lucky. Maybe he'll slow down for a while – use his souvenirs to relive the killings – keep his urges at bay.' The image of a faceless man touching, smelling, tasting the extracted teeth and fingernails flashed in his mind.

'You don't really believe that, do you?'

Sean shrugged.

'Anyway,' Featherstone tried to look on the bright side, 'it'll be good to have a proper Special Investigations case again. Can't have been much fun, being loaned out to other MITs these last few months.'

'Don't forget Anti-Terrorist, Special Branch and anyone else who was short of manpower,' Sean reminded him.

'Indeed,' Featherstone agreed. 'Nothing Addis could do to stop that happening. Can't justify detectives sitting on their backsides doing nothing, not in this day and age.'

'No,' Sean admitted. 'I suppose not.'

'Still,' Featherstone perked up again. 'Your unit's back now – with a proper investigation.'

'So it would appear,' Sean said, but without any cheer, although inside he felt himself coming to life – adrenalin and ideas, memories and anticipation beginning to flow through his body, sparking the darkest areas of his being that had lain dormant for months. Dark areas that he knew were dangerous to him and everything he'd achieved in his life, just as he knew that the answers tended to lie hidden in that darkness. Answers that could help him catch a killer before he claimed more lives.

'Speaking of investigations . . .' Featherstone appeared to change tack, 'you should know that this will be my last.'

Sean leaned back in his chair. 'Oh,' he managed to say. He liked and trusted Featherstone. With him gone, there would be no protective buffer between him and Addis. Worse still, Addis could put someone else in charge of overseeing Sean and his team. Addis's own man or woman. His own gamekeeper. 'How so?'

'Time for me to call it a day, Sean,' he told him. 'I've done more than my thirty years. Could have gone a couple of years ago. Was clinging on in the hope of making it to Commander, but it's pretty clear that's not going to happen. Every time it looks like it might, I get passed over by some graduate on accelerated promotion. Who gives a fuck if they don't know their arses from their elbows, right?'

'Will you be replaced?' Sean asked.

'You mean will you get a new boss?' Featherstone smiled, sensing Sean's concern. 'Who knows? That's Addis's call.'

'Great,' Sean moaned.

'You'll survive,' Featherstone assured him. They were silent for a while before he spoke again. 'I was meaning to ask: how's DS Donnelly getting on?'

'Dave?' Sean asked, confused.

'Since the shooting,' Featherstone added. 'Not an easy thing to take a life.'

'If he hadn't shot Goldsboro,' Sean reminded him, 'Goldsboro would have shot me. Dave's got nothing to feel . . . guilty about.'

'We don't all process these things the same way,' Featherstone told him. 'We don't all have your . . . clarity of thought.'

Sean knew what he meant: if it had been Sean who'd pulled the trigger and killed Jeremy Goldsboro – the suspect in their last major investigation – he would have felt no guilt. It would simply have been something he had to do. 'Well, the inquiry concluded it was a justifiable shooting. I think we've all moved on.'

'Good,' Featherstone replied, though he seemed less than convinced. 'Well, speaking of moving on,' he added, getting to his feet, 'time I wasn't here. Good luck with this one.'

'Thanks,' Sean replied.

'Oh, one last thing,' Featherstone turned at the door. 'Addis wants Anna Ravenni-Ceron to work alongside you on this one. Given the nature of the killings, he feels the input of a psychiatrist would be useful. Since you've worked with her before, he thought best to stick with her.'

Sean felt an instant stab in the heart and a tightening in his stomach. He'd barely seen her in over a year, but his feelings about Anna remained confused. The only stability in his life came from his family and his job. Anna was a threat to both. 'Fine,' he answered without elaborating.

'Regular updates would be appreciated,' Featherstone told him as he left. 'And watch out for the press.'

Sean's eyes followed Featherstone across the main office and through the exit before he took a single photo from each file and slumped back in his chair – looking from victim to victim. The more he looked, the more he was sure the killer's motivation was the act of killing. For some reason he felt compelled to kill.

Again Sean found his thoughts turning to Sebastian Gibran. He threw the photographs back on to his desk and cursed under his breath. 'Shit.'

David Langley sat at his desk in the manager's office of the Wandsworth branch of Harper's Furniture store. Forty-two years old, six foot tall and muscular, he looked fit, tanned and handsome in an everyday way, short brown hair pushed back from his face to show off his deep green eyes. The office was hidden away from the customers who patrolled the showroom outside looking for bargains in the seemingly never-ending 'All must go!' sale, the office was crammed with cheap, utilitarian furniture, filing cabinets and computer equipment. The Christmas decorations had been removed from the showroom on 2 January, but a few tattered and depressing remnants still hung in the office.

Anyone who looked in through the office's only door would have seen Langley facing forward, typing away on his keyboard like a man hard at work. He'd strategically positioned his desk so that no one could sneak up behind and look over his shoulder at the computer monitor. If they had, they would have seen that instead of checking stock levels or placing orders, he was searching the internet for news of last night's murder of a homeless man in Southwark. To his intense frustration, only the local press carried any mention of the killing. The removal of the victim's teeth seemed to have generated some interest, but there was no mention of the missing fingernails. He assumed that detail had been deliberately withheld by the police, so they could eliminate

15

crank callers claiming responsibility for his unique handiwork. Planning and carrying out the killing had been sweet enough, but now he craved the fear and awe that only media attention could give him.

Disgusted, he gave up the search for in-depth coverage – the coverage he deserved. He told himself he shouldn't be surprised his greatness had not been recognized. Only a blessed few were gifted enough to see in these two early works the blossoming of his special talents. But he had no doubt that his legacy would surpass everything that had gone before – even if he had to rub their faces in it before he was truly appreciated.

Almost without thinking he began to type the names of some of the gifted few into the search engine – those serial killers who had achieved fame on a global scale. He bit his lip to suppress his rising jealousy and anger. Why should they have been given so much coverage when he received so little? Could it be that the police had failed to make the connection? Fools! How easy could he make it for them? What would he have to do to make it more obvious? Cut out their eyes as well?

Though he tried to resist, it wasn't long before he typed in the name of his most revered and hated rival: Sebastian Gibran. Several years had passed since Gibran had been sent to Broadmoor, but barely a month went by without yet another documentary devoted to him or another true-crime paperback trying to explain his compulsion to kill or speculating how many victims he'd claimed. Most pundits came to the same conclusion: the final tally would never be known. So varied were his methods of dispatching his victims, some would inevitably have been attributed to others, some would remain forever unsolved.

That was where he and Gibran differed. That's what made his work superior. Where Gibran tried to hide his crimes, or at least his responsibility for them, Langley was proud of his work. He wasn't afraid of the police or anyone else knowing these murders were the work of one man, and he knew the day would come when he'd be caught or, better yet, surrender himself to custody before he was cornered. After all, what was the point in creating such a storm of infamy if he could never stand in front of the world's press and drink in the acknowledgements that he was the best ever? The most feared ever.

Unlike Gibran, who had settled for terrifying individual victims, he would terrorize an entire city. The world barely knew of Gibran until his capture, but soon everyone in London would be living in fear of David Langley. He would be the new bogeyman – the vampire in the night – the were-wolf in the forest – the monster under the bed. His power would hang over the city like a vast black cloak. Soon no one would be talking about Sebastian Gibran any more.

The door burst open without warning, making Langley jump in his seat as his fingers scrambled to close down the browser and open an accounts file. 'Christ's sake, Brian,' he complained as he recovered – his accent tainted with a trace of London. 'Don't you ever knock?'

'Why?' Brian Houghton asked, his beady eyes sparkling with mischief behind his thick, heavy-rimmed spectacles. 'You watching porn again?'

Langley couldn't stand his short, chubby assistant manager. Houghton's jovial, over-familiar demeanour inevitably gave rise to thoughts of slashing his throat, maybe taking a pair of pliers to those nasty yellow teeth of his. Ever since he was a teenager, he'd been entertaining similar thoughts about any number of people who'd crossed his path. Then those thoughts had turned into visions – signs of what he was destined to be. And now the time had come to act.

'I won't tell if you won't,' Houghton continued cheerfully. 'Just remember to clear your search history. I hear the area manager's a real bitch.'

'She is,' Langley sighed, disinterested. 'I've met her. Listen, did you want something?'

'I need a bit of paperwork from the cabinet,' Houghton explained.

'Then don't let me hold you up,' Langley told him, losing patience.

'Yeah, sure,' Houghton shrugged and made his way to one of the tall cabinets before nosily pulling a drawer open and searching inside. 'So,' he asked, turning back to Langley. 'Is it true then? Did you almost get the sack for banging some young assistant?'

Langley winced at the memory. It had been embarrassing and beneath him. How dare they insult him with their innuendos and accusations. 'She was twenty-three,' he replied through gritted teeth.

'Sounds young to me,' Houghton leered. 'Fair play to you, I say, but head office frown on that sort of thing. They don't like the managers messing around with the junior staff.'

'Like no one at head office ever does it,' Langley complained, the bile of jealousy and hatred rising in his throat.

'Yeah, but that's head office,' Houghton crowed. 'Law unto themselves. Besides, I heard it wasn't your first *misdemeanour*. Like the young ones, do you? Can't blame a man for that.'

'Perhaps you shouldn't believe everything you hear,' Langley warned him.

'Just saying. I've heard the rumours.'

'Rumours are all they are,' he insisted.

'If you say so,' Houghton smirked as he pulled some forms from the cabinet and slammed it shut.

'You've only been here two weeks,' Langley reminded him. 'Maybe you should wind your neck in.'

'Fair enough,' he grinned. 'I'll let you get on then.'

'You do that,' Langley snarled as he watched Houghton trail from the room. Once he was alone he took several deep breaths to calm himself before reopening his browser, the screen instantly filling with the unsmiling face of Sebastian Gibran staring back at him.

Geoff Jackson parked his battered old Audi saloon in the visitors' car park outside Broadmoor Hospital and immediately checked his phone for missed calls from his editor or network of informants that included everything from pimps to politicians. The display told him he was in the clear. He stepped from the car wincing at the various pains that stabbed at his body as he tried to stretch them away – looking over at the building site that would soon become the new hospital, spelling the end to the foreboding Victorian building that could never look like anything other than a prison. He'd heard it was going to be turned into luxury flats or something. He could only assume they would be sold to wealthy ghouls with more money than sense. 'About fucking time,' he muttered under his breath as he lit another cigarette – squeezing in one last smoke before entering the sterile smoke-free zone that Broadmoor along with every other building had become. He needed something to calm his excitement and fear before meeting the inmate he'd come to interview.

He pulled his trench coat tight around himself and walked across the wet and freezing car park under a leaden grey sky heading for the reception building. It seemed to him that every time he'd been here the weather had been as bleak as it was today. He tried to imagine Broadmoor in the sunshine, but somehow he couldn't. After having his authorization letter for the visit scrutinized he was fed through several layers of security, including passing through a scanner and having a full and thorough body search before being led to an interview room and being told to make himself comfortable and wait. Thirty minutes later he checked his phone for the umpteenth time and was about to call for assistance when the door swung open and a large muscular man in his mid-thirties wearing a white nurse's uniform filled the door-frame eyeing him and the room suspiciously. After a few seconds he finally spoke.

'You here to see Sebastian Gibran?'

Jackson swallowed involuntarily before speaking. 'Yes. Geoff Jackson, from *The World* newspaper.'

The big nurse merely nodded as he stepped further into the room, breaking right to reveal the man walking directly behind him – his hands secured to the restraint wrapped around his waist in soft leather bindings secured to his posey belt and handcuffs. He reminded Jackson of a prisoner on death row being taken to his execution, only unlike the deliberately overfed and sedated fatted cows of America's final solution, the man in restraints looked athletic and strikingly strong. Like a leopard in human form. Jackson had heard about his strength before, but now, up close for the first time, he could actually feel it. Following Gibran into the room was an equally powerful-looking man, only this one wore an HM Prison uniform – such was the dilemma that was Broadmoor. Was it a hospital or a prison?

'You have authority to interview this Broadmoor patient?' the big nurse asked rhetorically.

'I do,' Jackson replied searching for his paperwork.

'That won't be necessary,' the nurse assured him, keen to move on. 'And you have agreed to this interview?' he asked the man in restraints.

'I have,' the man answered, his cold, black eyes never leaving Jackson. His voice was calm and assured.

'Mr Jackson,' the nurse told him, 'I strongly recommend that you have myself and Officer Brenan here throughout the interview – in the best interests of everyone.'

'No, no, no,' Jackson argued. 'The agreement was that the interview is to be conducted in private. I'm a journalist and therefore anything I'm told is journalistic material and subject to journalistic privilege,' Jackson reeled out the well-practised spiel. 'This has all been arranged and agreed in advance with the hospital directors. The agreement was for the interview to be conducted in private – as I'm sure you have been informed.'

The big nurse took a deep breath as he looked back and forth from Jackson to the prisoner in restraints. 'Very well,' he submitted, 'but we'll be right outside watching everything on CCTV. If you need us, we'll get to you fast.'

Jackson swallowed hard as he noticed the concern in the big nurse's eyes. 'Fine, so long as there's no sound on the monitor,' he managed to say while hiding his fear, 'and no bloody lip readers either.'

The nurse ignored him. 'In order to allow this interview to be conducted with no hospital staff present it has been necessary for the patient to consent to wearing restraints at all times. That consent has been given.' He looked at the man in the leather handcuffs, who gave a single nod. 'Sit down please,' the nurse ordered. Gibran did as he was told and slid into a seat opposite the spot where Jackson remained standing, his eyes never leaving the journalist – studying him. 'I'm going to remove your hands from the waist restraint now,' the nurse explained, 'and secure them to the table fastenings. If you resist in any way we're authorized to use whatever force is necessary to make you compliant. Do you understand?'

'I understand perfectly,' Gibran answered politely, turning his wrists as much as he could to make it easier for the prison officer to release them. After a nod from the nurse, the officer stepped forward and released one arm, securing it to the table then doing the same with the other, before stepping back a little too quickly, betraying his fear.

'He's all yours, Mr Jackson,' the nurse told him, 'but remember – don't get too close or touch the patient in any way. And under no circumstances are you to give him anything whatsoever. All items the patient receives must be

21

submitted to the hospital staff first for clearance. Do I make myself clear?'

'I know the rules,' Jackson answered, trying to sound confident and in control, despite his pounding heart.

'Very well,' the nurse said, turning on his heels and leaving the room, closely followed by the prison officer. Jackson watched the heavy door being pulled shut and listened to the key turning heavy locks and he knew he was now alone with arguably the most dangerous killer of modern times.

'Sebastian Gibran,' Jackson struggled to speak, barely able to believe that he was alone in the room with Britain's most notorious serial killer. 'Thank you for seeing me. I can't tell you how much it means.'

'Geoff Jackson,' Gibran ignored Jackson's platitudes. 'Chief crime editor for *The World*,' he continued, referring to the red-top newspaper Jackson worked for.

'Britain's most read,' Jackson couldn't help himself saying, although he regretted it almost immediately.

Again Gibran ignored him, his black eyes searing into Jackson, probing him, until he suddenly smiled and seemed to relax – inhaling the tension in the room and replacing it with an atmosphere of cooperation in that way that only the truly powerful and self-confident can. 'Well, I should congratulate you on getting permission to see me, Mr Jackson. You appear to have succeeded where many have failed – and, believe me, many have failed, although I would never have agreed to meet them anyway. Half-baked novelists and playwrights looking for titbits to shock and scare the poor unsuspecting members of public. Can you imagine anything more tedious?'

'I know a couple of the directors here,' Jackson explained. 'Promised I'd show this place in a good light, if I was allowed to meet you.'

'I see,' Gibran nodded.

'You said you wouldn't have seen the others who wanted

to meet you,' Jackson reminded him. 'So why me? Why did you agree to meet me?'

'Because you have a pedigree, Mr Jackson,' Gibran told him. 'You've earned the right.'

'Please,' Jackson told him, shaking the confusion from his head. 'You can call me Geoff.'

'No,' Gibran consolidated his control. 'Mr Jackson will do for now.'

'Erm,' Jackson wavered slightly, 'if that's what you're comfortable with. You were saying – I have a pedigree?'

'You interviewed Jeremy Goldsboro – correct?'

'Yes,' Jackson answered. 'Yes, I did. While he was still at large and the police were looking for him.'

'That must have taken great courage.' Gibran's eyes continued to scrutinize him. 'To meet a killer. Alone.'

'It was a great story,' Jackson tried to explain. 'A killer with a cause. A man of the people trying to fight back for the little man.'

'Only it was a lie,' Gibran reminded him. 'He killed for his own satisfaction. Tell me, Mr Jackson, would you have still met him if you'd known he was really just a vengeful, jealous killer and not the man of the people he pretended to be?'

'Probably,' Jackson admitted.

'Why?' Gibran demanded.

'It would have been a great story in any case,' Jackson explained. 'Perhaps even better. A unique insight into the mind of a coldblooded killer while he was on the loose and killing. It would have been huge anyway.'

'And if you'd ended up becoming one of his victims?' Gibran asked.

'Wouldn't have happened.' Jackson smiled. 'Whether I'm dealing with a killer with a cause or a mindless killer, it makes no difference. They're not going to hurt me.'

'Why?' Gibran pushed.

'If they're talking to me, it's because they want publicity,'

Jackson answered. 'Why kill the person who's going to give them what they want?'

'Because not everybody does what's expected of them,' Gibran argued. 'In some people the urge to kill overpowers everything else. Perhaps you should remember that.'

Jackson paused before answering. 'Would you have?' he asked. 'Would you have killed me, if we'd met when you were free?'

Gibran leaned back in his chair, his restraints straining and creaking under the strain. 'Maybe,' he smiled, 'but that's because I'm mentally ill, Mr Jackson. That's why I'm in here and not prison.'

'Right, OK.' Jackson nodded.

A silence spread between them before Gibran spoke again.

'So what is it you want to ask, Mr Jackson? I should remind you that I can't talk about the murder and attempted murder I was charged with.'

'The uniformed cop and the woman detective,' Jackson clarified.

'Exactly,' Gibran confirmed. 'I may one day be deemed mentally healthy and fit for trial. It would be foolish of me to hand my enemies a stick to beat me with.'

'By your enemies, you mean the police?' Jackson asked. 'Or more specifically Detective Inspector Corrigan?'

For a second all the fury and anger that burned deep inside Gibran flashed in his eyes, but he immediately dragged it back under control. 'Corrigan is irrelevant,' he dismissed the man who'd caught him. 'What is it that you want me to tell you about, Mr Jackson?'

Jackson cleared his throat before he began. 'Well, some people – quite a lot of people actually – believe you have committed many murders. That you are in fact one of the most prolific serial killers there's ever been in this country.' Gibran went to speak, but Jackson held his hand up to stop him. 'Obviously I'm aware that even if this were true, you'd

24

hardly be likely to tell anyone about it. But perhaps you would give me your thoughts on what it would be like if you *were* a serial killer. What do you think might motivate such a person? What would be going through their mind? How would they kill and not get caught? No need to mention any specific crimes that *may* have happened. We could keep it more . . . generic.'

Gibran considered him in silence for a few seconds. 'I see,' he eventually responded. 'And what would you do with such . . . information?'

Jackson shifted in his seat before answering. 'My intention is to serialize the interviews in the paper. One a week. Maybe more. We'll see how it goes, but I believe readers will be fascinated.'

'Even though I'm not discussing details of *real* crimes?' Gibran queried.

'Trust me,' Jackson smiled. 'The readers will fill in the blanks for themselves. It's your . . . unique background that will sell it. The fact you're locked up here in Broadmoor won't hurt either.'

'And how do you profit from all this, Mr Jackson?' Gibran asked. 'To increase your standing with your editor doesn't strike me as sufficient motivation for a man like you.'

'No,' Jackson agreed, once more squirming uncomfortably. 'The pieces in the paper would be largely to draw people in. A few weeks after they stop I'll release the book of our interviews. The bigger picture. What it's really like to be someone like you.'

'Someone like me?' Gibran questioned, leaning in as close as the table and restraints would allow. 'How could you or your readers ever know what it's like to be me?'

'They might,' Jackson argued. 'If you tell them.'

Gibran leaned back in his chair before changing tack. 'Why do you want to write a book about me when you've already had one published? One that contained a great many unsubstantiated allegations, I may add.'

'Allegations made by the police,' Jackson explained. 'Not me. I was just reporting on the investigation, working on what the police gave me. There was no opportunity to put your side of things across. But there is now – if you want to.'

'And why would I do that?' Gibran asked. 'Why should I care what the police or public think I am or what I've done? What makes you think they're anything to me?'

Jackson knew Gibran would never be enticed into cooperating by the chance of helping others understand what he was. Gibran existed to satisfy himself and no one else. Jackson knew his psychological profile well. Gibran was as pure a sociopath as had ever allowed themselves to be caught – totally incapable of feeling remorse or guilt. He'd most likely been that way since the day he was born – a killer created by nature or God. Not some sorry case of a normal man turned into a monster by tragic circumstances of child abuse or mental illness. He'd had a privileged background and an apparently happy childhood, although even then he probably knew what he really was. He was well educated and went on to have a successful career, a wife and children, yet it had all been a smokescreen, cultivated to provide cover for the real Sebastian Gibran: a psychopath who killed for the pleasure of killing.

The only way to persuade such a man to play ball would be to convince him that doing so would benefit him.

'Do it for yourself then,' Jackson told him. 'Do it for your own . . . *amusement*.' Gibran said nothing. 'You would be able to see the final manuscript before it's published,' Jackson tried to persuade him.

'If I was the type of person you think I am,' Gibran responded, once more changing the subject without warning, 'why would I have to kill? Tell me, Mr Jackson: why would I feel compelled to kill?'

'No,' Jackson answered, the excitement swelling in his stomach. 'You tell me.'

'Because, if I was like that,' Gibran explained, 'it would be in my nature to kill. It would be as instinctive to me as breathing is to you. I would have to kill to live. I could survive without it, but I wouldn't be alive. I wouldn't kill to satisfy some sexual urge, or because voices in my head told me to, or because I'd grown to hate a world that had spited and tortured me. I'd kill simply because it is in my nature to do so. That is, if I was the person you think I am. You see, Mr Jackson,' he continued, leaning into the table, 'people like that aren't mere human beings. They're superhuman. Gods amongst mortals. It is their right to take the lives of inferior beings at will. Is it not a basic principle of evolution that the superior branch of a species eventually brings about the extinction of the inferior strain? Read Friedrich Nietzsche's Superman philosophy, Mr Jackson. *Since God is dead it is necessary for the emergence of the Overman, who is to replace God.'*

Jackson stared at Gibran, opened-mouthed, before recovering his senses. 'I'll look it up,' he answered. 'Sounds very . . . interesting.' Jackson blinked unconsciously as he cleared his mind. 'So . . . how would a person like this select their victims?' he asked. 'Would they be attracted to a particular type of person? Do their victims unwittingly draw these . . . Overmen to them?'

'To the Overmen, everyone is a potential victim, Mr Jackson. But enough for one day,' Gibran insisted, his mouth suddenly smiling – his teeth straight and white despite years of incarceration in a mental hospital. 'I've enjoyed our chat. Make another appointment and we can speak again. But for now, could you do me a favour and summon my *protectors*.' He pointed with his chin to the intercom attached to the wall. 'I'm afraid I can't quite reach.'

'Of course,' Jackson agreed, getting to his feet while trying to control his excitement at having potentially hit the jackpot. 'And you can be sure I'll make another appointment.'

'Well then,' Gibran closed the interview. 'Until next time.'

* * *

Sean took one last hard look at the two photographs he'd selected from the files. One from each murder scene – both showing full-length body shots of the prostrate victims lying flat on their backs, arms limp and straight at their sides. He suspected they were dead or as good as dead before the killer set to work removing their teeth – stretching his victims out before him to make the task easier. Or was there some other reason for the positioning of the bodies? Some ritual act of the killer or killers? He shook the thoughts away before they led him to a path he could end up following for hours – trying to get an early glimpse of the man he was now hunting. That was how it happened. He'd woken that morning just another man. A detective investigating serious, but not unusual crimes. Crimes that any good detective could handle. Over the last few months, investigating those everyday crimes, he'd grown calmer; happy to be at home with his family, working to earn money to pay for the mundane things all families need, leaving it all behind when he left the office instead of being haunted night and day by the crimes he was investigating. But the instant Featherstone had handed over those two folders, all that changed. Now he was a hunter of men again.

Already he sensed there was something about this killer. Something that made Sean feel their destinies had been set on a collision course. He took a deep breath before snatching up the files and heading to the office next to his where his two deputies, DS Sally Jones and DS Dave Donnelly, were both staring intently at their computers, swearing and moaning as if they were competing with each other in a profanity contest.

Sean rapped on the open door and instantly their fingers froze over their keyboards as they looked up in unison. 'I've got something for you,' Sean told them.

'Saw you with Featherstone earlier,' Sally told him. 'Please tell me he gave us a proper investigation. I can't stand working with Anti-Terror again. It's doing my head in.'

'Hear, hear,' Donnelly agreed. 'I'm sick of being shunted around like a stray dog. We need our own job.'

'Well, we've got one,' Sean announced, 'and it's a bad one.'

'Go on,' Sally encouraged him.

'I haven't got time to repeat myself,' Sean answered curtly. 'Get the team together and I'll brief everyone at the same time.'

Donnelly looked out into the main office and shook his head. 'Only about half the team here, boss. Rest are busy running errands for the world and his wife.'

'It'll have to do for now,' Sean told him. 'The rest will have to catch up as and when they can.' He spun away and marched to the whiteboards that dominated one side of the room, quickly followed by Sally and Donnelly. As Donnelly called everyone to attention, Sean swept the boards clear of any information relating to other investigations and began to pin up photos of the two victims before writing their names above them. Once he was happy with his display, he turned to the gathering audience of detectives and took a deep breath.

'All right, everyone,' Donnelly made one last call for attention. 'Listen up.'

'Ladies and gentlemen,' Sean addressed them, 'we have a new case.' A few nodded their heads in quiet satisfaction; although nobody spoke, Sean could sense their relief. 'Two victims. One male. One female. Killed ten days apart. The first – Tanya Richards – was a known prostitute and drug user. The second – William Dalton – was a homeless beggar; he too was a drug user. Both were young. Both were vulnerable. Neither deserved what happened to them. We all know how unusual it is for a killer to vary the gender of their victims, but these two are definitely linked. The killer has a very distinct modus operandi and has been kind enough to leave us his calling card.'

'Which is?' Sally asked.

'He takes some of their teeth and most of their fingernails,' Sean explained, causing his audience to wince.

'Jesus,' Donnelly said for all of them. 'Before or after they're dead?'

'Probably after,' Sean told him. 'They weren't restrained in any way, so they would most likely have been incapacitated in order for him to do what he did. The relatively small amount of blood from the wounds to the mouth suggests their hearts had stopped or were close to it.'

'Trophies?' Sally asked.

'That would be my guess,' Sean agreed. 'Something to help him relive his crimes.'

'Where were they killed?' DC Alan Jesson asked.

'Both outdoors,' Sean continued. 'The first in Holloway, North London, and the second in Southwark, Southeast London.'

'Then the killer's a Londoner,' Sally added.

'Probably,' Sean agreed, 'or at least they know London well. Killers like to know their surroundings,' he reminded them. 'It makes them feel . . . comfortable.'

'Any signs of sexual assault?' the tall and well-spoken DC Fiona Cahill asked.

'The first victim was almost certainly raped,' Sean confirmed. 'Too early to say with the second. His post-mortem is tomorrow and his clothes are already being processed by the lab, so we should know more then.'

'Maybe they both crossed the same drug dealer,' Donnelly argued, his bushy moustache twitching as he spoke. He could always be relied on to look for the simplest solution.

'That's what the MIT who initially investigated Tanya Richards' murder thought. Drug dealer or pimp,' Sean answered. 'But they couldn't find anything.'

'Now we have another murder, though,' Donnelly reminded him. 'If we can find a dealer they both used, then we'd have a link.'

'Maybe,' Sean admitted without enthusiasm. 'We'll look into it, but I don't think so. Doesn't . . . feel like that sort of case to me.'

'So what was his motivation?' DC Paulo Zukov asked in his thick London accent, his sharp blue eyes peering from a gaunt, unattractive face.

'Well,' Sean thought out loud, 'very few stranger attacks result in murder. Most are fights between males that go too far and someone ends up getting killed, but that's certainly not what we're dealing with here.'

'And?' Zukov prompted, trying to hurry him along.

'And,' Sean continued, 'sexually motivated attacks where the killer only kills in order to cover his tracks, to get rid of the main witness, i.e. the victim. Or – and this is much rarer – where the motivation is the killing itself. Usually committed by someone with extreme mental health issues, although occasionally, very occasionally, by someone of sound mind who just can't stop themselves. Someone for whom killing is in their nature.'

'Like Sebastian Gibran,' Donnelly mentioned the toxic name.

'Yes,' Sean agreed. 'Like Sebastian Gibran.'

Sally looked at the floor, her hand automatically going to the place on her chest where her blouse hid the two scars where Gibran's attack had marked her for life.

'You all right, Sally?' Sean asked, his eyes narrowing with concern.

'Yes,' she lied. 'I'm fine. Haven't heard that name for a while, that's all.'

'To go back to the teeth and nails,' Donnelly intervened, saving Sally from any more unwanted attention. 'Why take them as trophies? Bloody hard to get out. If he wanted a body part, why not cut off the fingers or ears? A good knife or pruning scissors and he could have had the job done in seconds. Pulling teeth must take time and effort.'

Sean had been giving it some thought. 'It's possible he has experience of extracting teeth and wanted to stick to something he was familiar with.'

'A dentist?' Donnelly questioned.

'Unlikely,' Sean told him. 'Someone who tried dentistry and failed is more likely. We'll have to check it out anyway, but I think the reason he took the teeth and the nails is because he wanted something durable – something from their bodies, but also something that would last. Something that could last forever.'

'Jesus,' Donnelly said quietly.

'Other body parts would eventually degrade,' Sean explained. 'Even if he kept them in a fridge – especially if he's constantly getting them out to spend time with them. They wouldn't last long.'

'He could freeze them,' Zukov suggested. 'Could last for years if he did that.'

'No,' Sean dismissed the suggestion. 'Not personal enough. A lump of frozen meat wrapped in something like clingfilm – that would never be enough for him. When he holds his trophies in his hands he needs to feel them, to have them right there with him. Nails and teeth are perfect for that. He can handle them as much as he wants and whenever he wants and they'll never degrade to nothing. Or—' Sean stopped, momentarily lost in his own thoughts.

'Or?' Sally tried to bring him back.

'Or,' he continued, 'he did it simply because he liked it. He liked pulling their teeth and fingernails. It made him feel . . . good.'

'How the hell could doing that make *anyone* feel good?' Zukov asked.

'He's not like you,' Sean warned him. 'He doesn't think like you, any more than you think like him. He's different.'

'You mean us,' Sally said. 'He doesn't think like us.'

'What?' Sean asked, confused by her words before another question saved him.

'Why not take some of their hair?' Cahill asked. 'Hair's personal and non-biodegradable and a lot easier to remove, so why not take hair?'

Again Sean had considered it. 'Too gentle,' he answered. 'Too compassionate. Parents keep locks of their children's hair. Lovers keep locks of each other's hair. It's a sign of affection and caring.' The connection he felt with the killer was growing stronger as he expanded on each theory. 'He wants us to know he feels no compassion. Wants us to know how strong he is – mentally – that he's capable of anything. For this one, it's all about the violence – and he wants us to know it.'

'Killers in the past have eaten parts of their victims,' Sally reminded them. 'It's a way of keeping them forever – as if they've ingested the victim's soul. Any obvious reason why he didn't consume something at the scene? It would have certainly been a statement of his violent intent.'

'That's not his mindset,' Sean answered without having to think about it. 'Yes, plenty of serial killers – if that's what he is – have consumed a part or parts of their victims, but it's not usually out of violence or anger. For them, it's an act of love. They want to be *one* with the victim – keep them alive and with them forever by consuming them.'

'Love?' Donnelly asked disbelievingly. 'Hell of a funny way to show love.'

Sean paused, wondering how to explain. 'You're a parent, right, Dave?'

'Aye,' Donnelly answered in his gruff voice with an accent part East London and part Glaswegian – the city where he'd spent that part of his life before joining police.

'Remember when they were young and you used to play with them and hold them and tell them you were going to *gobble them all up*?'

33

'Aye,' Donnelly replied, shaking his head, 'but that was different.'

'No,' Sean insisted. 'Psychologically, the same. But not for this one. He doesn't feel compassion or love for them and he doesn't want them to live forever inside of himself. He wants them dead. He wants to destroy them.'

'Why?' Sally asked. 'Why such strong feelings of violence and hatred towards strangers?'

'Who says he hates them?' Sean corrected her. 'Maybe they're simply a means to an end.'

'What means? What end?' Sally pushed him.

'I don't know,' he told her honestly. 'Not yet.'

'Great – another paranoid schizophrenic off his meds,' Donnelly said, dismissing anything more sinister.

'No,' Sean explained. 'There's no frenzy to these attacks. They're controlled and planned. This isn't someone hearing voices in their head or seeing demons on the train. I don't sense mental illness here, or at least nothing a court would recognize as such.'

'Then we're looking for someone who's made the conscious decision to select victims and kill them,' Cahill asked, 'but with controlled violence?'

'That's what these photographs say to me,' Sean agreed. 'And I reckon we've got about ten days to find him before he kills again. I could be wrong, but he doesn't look like he's going to become a sleeper. Now he's started, he'll keep going, probably at about the same pace or faster.'

'Do you think he's killed before? Sally asked.

'Possibly,' he admitted. 'We'll have to look into it – anything that looks remotely similar will have to be checked. But I think Tanya Richards was his first. He tried something new and he liked it. It didn't scare him or freak him out. It was probably everything he hoped for, maybe more and he needed it again – and quickly, hence . . .' he turned and tapped a photograph of William Dalton '. . . ten days later he strikes again. It's a drug to him now. He needs it.' He looked around at the quiet, stoical faces – all eyes on him, waiting for ideas and leadership. He let the responsibility sink in before speaking again.

'All right,' he stirred his team, 'we've all done this before. We all know what an investigation like this means and how to get a result.' A few heads nodded. 'Dave,' he turned to Donnelly. 'You sort out the door-to-door. Dalton was living in a garage, so maybe he was something of a local celebrity. People might know him more than usual.'

Donnelly nodded. 'Want me to do the same for Richards?' he asked. 'Not sure I want to trust some other MIT's findings.'

'Fine,' Sean agreed. 'They won't like it, but do it anyway.'

'They'll survive,' Donnelly shrugged.

'Sally,' Sean continued assigning tasks: 'track down Dalton's friends and family, will you? Chances are they don't know he's dead yet. He was a heavy drug user working the West End. Let's find out what his associates can tell us about his lifestyle. They might have some useful information, as might his family – especially about how he ended up homeless. There's a crucial piece of information hiding somewhere waiting for us. We dig and dig and dig till we find it. Don't second-guess what could be important and what's not.

'We know he had an Oyster card and used it regularly, so let's get it interrogated and see where and when he's been moving around. Fiona . . .' Cahill looked up from the notes she was scribbling; 'Take care of it, OK.' Cahill nodded her agreement. Sean turned to Jesson. 'Alan: Dalton moved around the West End most days and travelled back to Southwark most nights, most likely to Borough Tube if he was living off Mint Street, so we'll have CCTV coming out of our ears. Get hold of British Transport Police and tell them to preserve all CCTV from those areas and routes until we can give them something more specific once we've looked into his Oyster card.'

'BTP. Done,' was all Jesson said in his Liverpudlian accent.

'As I'm sure you all understand, the original investigating team will not be happy about losing this case,' Sean reminded them. 'No MIT wants to lose a job like this, so if you come into contact with them, keep it nice. No rubbing their faces in it, please. We need them onside and cooperative. Don't want them holding back any information to make things difficult for us. I'll do my best to smooth things over with them and I expect each of you to do the same.

'That's it for now,' Sean told them. 'Get yourselves organized and ready to go. Dave will be office manager and will put you into teams as soon as he can and give you your individual tasks. OK – let's get on with it.'

As the meeting broke up, the team moved quickly back to their desks gathering phones, notebooks, pens and anything else experience had taught them they might need, chatting loudly and excitedly to each other as they did so. Sean drifted back towards his office followed by Sally, while Donnelly remained in the main office and started barking out orders.

Sean paused next to him as he passed and quietly spoke in his ear. 'Keep them on it,' he told Donnelly. 'Two victims is enough.' Donnelly merely nodded. As soon as he entered his office, Sean started putting on his coat and filling his pockets with the detritus from his desktop.

'Going somewhere?' Sally asked.

'Ugh,' Sean grunted as he looked up, suddenly pulled out of his own thoughts. 'Yeah,' he rejoined the world. 'I need to go out.'

'Where?' Sally pushed.

'The scene, of course,' he told her.

'The MIT will be all over it,' Sally reminded him. 'Maybe we should leave them to it and take control of their exhibits when they're done.'

'No,' Sean replied firmly. 'I want our people on it. I want DS Roddis and his team. No one else. Roddis is the best.'

Sally didn't argue. 'OK. Want some company?'

'No,' Sean told her. 'I'll go alone. Stay here and help Dave.'

'Fine,' Sally reluctantly agreed. 'If that's what you want.'

Sean sensed her doubt. 'But . . .?'

'So long as you haven't decided to try and solve this one all on your own,' she voiced her concern. 'It's been a long time since we had a proper investigation. I know what you're like, Sean. You're hungry for this, I know you are, but we're a team, remember? We work as a team we solve this quicker. You try and do it alone, it could be . . .' She let her words trail off.

'Could be what?' he asked, puzzled.

'Dangerous,' she said with conviction. 'For you and everyone around you.'

'Don't worry about me,' he tried to reassure her. 'We're a team – I get it. It's early days and there's much to do. We just need to divide and conquer until things are moving, is all. You're more use to me here, helping Dave, than you are trailing around after me.'

'Thanks,' she replied sarcastically.

'That's not what I meant,' he tried to recover. 'Look, I'll be back soon and I'll tell you everything I find. OK?'

'Fine,' she relented.

'I won't be gone long,' he insisted as he brushed past and headed across the main office before disappearing through the door.

David Langley returned home to the small rented flat in the wrong part of Wandsworth that had been his home since his wife decided he'd had one too many 'encounters' with other women and had thrown him out. Where low-rise estates dominated and danger was never far away. The bitterness he felt towards her and at having to leave the family home burned deep in him like a stove of hatred. He blamed her for the failure of their marriage. She'd enjoyed pushing their sex life to the boundaries of near torture in the early years, but as he tried to push even further she had suddenly turned conservative and uninteresting. No wonder he'd looked elsewhere.

He grabbed himself a beer from the fridge and drank it quickly before taking another. The drab walls of the flat began to close in on him, making him feel trapped and depressed. He decided to phone his ex-wife, who still lived in their smart terraced family home in upwardly mobile Earlsfield. Maybe she would let him speak to their two children instead of constantly trying to poison their minds against him. So what if he'd forgotten he was supposed to pick them up or take them out a few times? He was busy providing for them, wasn't he?

He punched the number into his phone and listened to the ringing tone as he waited for it to be answered. There was a click, followed by a familiar voice.

'*Hi. This is Emma, Charlie and Sophie Hutchinson.*' Hearing her use her maiden name for *his* children as well as herself started his blood boiling. How dare she? '*We can't get to the phone right now, so please leave your name and number and we'll get back to you as soon as we can. Bye.*'

'Pick the phone up, Emma,' he demanded. 'I know you're there.' He waited a few seconds; nothing. 'I said, pick the phone up. I want to speak with my children.' Still nothing. 'Stop being a bitch, Emma and answer the damn phone. You can't stop me speaking to my own children. I have a right to speak to them whenever I want.' He was met with more silence. 'Fine,' he shouted into the phone. 'Have it your own way. I'll be speaking to my solicitor first thing in the morning. Who's paying for that bloody house you live in anyway?' He slammed the phone down. 'Fucking bitch,' he cursed to the empty flat.

Painful memories of the day she made him leave the family home swept back into his spinning mind – him blaming her for his infidelities while she screamed at him to get out, calling him a complete loser. 'Loser,' he repeated the insult she'd thrown at him. 'I'll show you who's a fucking loser. I'll show everyone.' He breathed in deeply and felt himself begin to calm as images of his victims washed over him, leaving him feeling powerful and in control. He chastised himself for not having mastered his temper. Control was everything. If he was to achieve his ultimate goal, he needed to put aside everything from his past – including his children and lost wife. He needed to let them go.

Calm once more, he knew he needed to feel strong again. Needed to relive the moments when he was at his most powerful. He returned to the fridge, opened the freezer compartment and removed a plastic box containing all that was now precious to him.

The first thing he took from the box was a transparent freezer bag that contained what looked like oversized playing cards. Again he took a deep breath before removing the items and spreading them out before him. Photographs of his victims, taken while they were alive. Tanya Richards leaving her flat. Tanya Richards walking to the tube station. Tanya Richards sitting on a bus. Tanya Richards walking the streets close to Smithfield Market. William Dalton begging in the West End. William Dalton walking into Tottenham Court Road Underground station. William Dalton walking out of Borough Underground station. William Dalton entering the garage he called home.

He arranged the cards carefully and neatly before retrieving two more small freezer bags from inside the plastic box and placed them side by side on the table. Again he took a deep breath to steady himself before emptying the first bag, which was marked with a number 1 in permanent marker. The nails and teeth slid out in front of him – the teeth rattling on the table like dice, whereas the nails sounded like tinkling rain-drops. He picked up a few of the nails and dropped them into the palm of his other hand. They were still coated with cheap red nail varnish that blended perfectly with the traces of her blood. He hoped they would never fade. It may be necessary to repaint them if it did.

As he held the nails he could picture them as they had been when they were attached to the young woman's slim fingers. They'd possibly been her best feature. That and her crystal blue eyes that were yet to be destroyed by whatever drug she was addicted to. He remembered her eyes staring into his in disbelief as she realized he had come to end her existence. He sighed almost happily at the memory before delicately spilling the nails from his palm back on to the table.

Next he picked up the teeth one by one and dropped them into the palm of his hand. Molars with gold fillings and other lesser teeth that showed little decay or staining. As young teeth should, despite her lifestyle. He pinched one of the molars from his palm and held it up to the light as if he were examining a diamond – slightly twisting and rotating it as he took in every detail of the tooth – every curve and peak – every scratch on the enamel. Finally he held it under his nose, closing his eyes as he inhaled deeply – each trace of its dead owner bringing exquisite memories of pulling them from her jaw flooding back. How he wished she'd been fully alive and conscious when he'd gone to work on her, but it would have been all but impossible to perform the extractions on a struggling victim.

Satisfied with the relics of his first victim's death, he ritually placed all the items on top of the clip-seal bag and put them to one side. His back straightened as he took hold of the other bag – glancing at the photographs of the living William Dalton before sliding the seal open and allowing the odour of its contents to rush at him. To the uninitiated, the scents were barely detectable, but to him they were as vivid and raw as the smell of a zoo – animalistic and pungent.

He carefully tipped the contents on to the table and shifted them about with the tips of his fingers – ensuring each item had its own space to shine before picking up one of the larger fingernails that he assumed must be a thumbnail. It, like all the others, was in poor condition. The dark dried blood, mixed with the dirt that had built up over months of not being able to clean himself properly, had left the nails looking much older than they were. They looked as if they'd been taken from a body that had been buried for years – brittle, broken and jagged at the tips. But they were no less precious to him. He'd enjoyed killing the prostitute more, but the homeless man was still an experience beyond most people's stunted and dull imagination. In any case, it was important that his second victim was a man so the police and media would know he wasn't some perverted sex offender. They needed to understand he was much, much more than that.

He swapped the nail for a clean-looking molar, although the root was stained with the victim's blood – the sight of it ignited images of the nearly dead homeless man lying on his back and gurgling on his own blood as it slipped down his throat. The memory pleased him and made his muscles tense as he remembered the power he'd felt as he crouched over the dying man. It was as if he was absorbing the victim's energy, becoming more powerful with each new kill.

Without knowing why, he was suddenly overcome with the urge to taste the tooth, to engulf it in his tongue and roll it around his mouth. Wary of sucking the blood and odour away, he made do instead with delicately placing the tip of the tooth against the point of his tongue and holding it there – his eyes closing with the pleasure of it as his entire body became aroused. Removing the tooth, he cursed his body's physical reaction and knew that others would use it as evidence that his actions were driven by sexual needs. But he knew they were not. Yes, he'd ejaculated inside the dying prostitute and done things to the dying homeless man, but they were not sexual acts. His body had simply become so electrified by the power he felt that it was overwhelmed with every sensation – as if he was feeling every emotion and physical feeling a person could ever have, only he was feeling it all at the same time. It was too much for any person to control – even one as strong as he was. Ejaculating in and on his victims had merely been an emergency release – to allow him to regain control of his own growing power. Still, he knew he needed to do better in the future and suppress his body's crude needs when in a heightened state of stimulation. It was either that or risk forever being branded as a sexually motivated killer, which would undermine everything he was trying to achieve.

Using a breathing exercise he'd picked up from a yoga video, he tried to calm his tense body and relax. The killings had left him feeling invincible, but it was gratifying to know he remained in complete control of his own body.

After a few minutes of sitting in silence, he picked up the photographs and mementoes, placing them neatly in their bags before packing them tenderly into the plastic box that he returned to the freezer compartment of his fridge. As he closed the door he was already debating what type of person he should choose next.

He sensed her unhappiness, how confused her feelings were. 'You don't have to do this,' he told her. 'You don't have to do this for me.'

'No,' she answered. 'I want to.'

'OK,' he agreed, then tried to move things on: 'I could use you anyway. This new one,' he explained, 'feels . . . complicated. Anything you can tell me about him will help.'

'No doubt Addis will give me a copy of the file,' she went along with him. 'Once I've read it, I'll give you my thoughts.'

'Good,' he told her, then struggled with what to say next. 'It'll be nice to see you again,' he managed, immediately wincing at his own words.

'It'll be nice to see you too,' she answered.

He touched the screen to end the call and stared at the phone for a while before sliding it back into his jacket pocket. Climbing from the unmarked car, he made a beeline for the two uniformed officers who were guarding the tape that marked the cordon. He spoke to the tall female constable who was clutching the crime scene log. Sean held up his warrant card so they could both see.

'DI Corrigan – Special Investigations Unit. This is officially my scene now,' he told them.

The constables looked at each other, confused. The woman spoke for both of them. 'Sorry, sir. The DCI from the MIT is inside with forensics. DCI . . .' she looked down at the log, 'DCI Vaughan.'

'Like I said,' he reminded her, 'it's my scene now.' He pulled a business card from his warrant card and handed it to her. 'No one in or out without my permission,' he insisted. 'You call me before letting anyone in. I don't care if it's the Commissioner – you call me first. Understand?'

The female constable gave a shrug of resignation before answering. 'Whatever you say . . . sir.'

Sean awkwardly covered his shoes with a pair of forensic foot protectors he'd pulled from his pocket and ducked under

45

the tape before heading to the garage some forty metres away where he could see figures in blue forensic suits working under the spotlights that lit the scene. As he drew nearer he noticed a figure standing in the dark observing the activities. The man wasn't wearing a forensic suit, but stood in a long dark coat, his back to Sean, although his feet too were covered with protectors. Once Sean was within a few feet of the man, he turned to face him. His face appeared tanned, despite the depths of winter; he was in his early fifties, but handsome, his physique stocky and powerful. Sean noticed some of the grey strands of his hair reflecting the streetlights.

'DCI Vaughan?' Sean asked, holding up his warrant card.

'Yes,' Vaughan answered in a London accent – his demeanour immediately telling Sean he was dealing with another career detective and not someone racing through the ranks on accelerated promotion. 'And who might you be?'

'DI Sean Corrigan,' he told him. 'Special Investigations Unit.'

'DI Corrigan,' Vaughan smiled knowingly. 'I've heard so much about you I feel I already know you. So what's SIU doing here?'

Sean felt uneasy, knowing that he'd been talked about by people he didn't know. He preferred to be anonymous. 'This murder's linked to another,' he explained. 'That makes it SIU's.'

'No one's told me it's linked,' Vaughan argued. 'And no one's told me to hand over my investigation to you or anyone else. SIU's not needed here. Me and my team will have this wrapped up in a few days, tops. We know how to hunt down bastards like this. Why don't you save yourself for something a bit more exotic and leave this to us old-fashioned by-the-numbers detectives.'

'I can't do that,' Sean told him. 'Orders of Assistant Commissioner Addis. SIU are to take over this investigation.'

'Addis hasn't told me about SIU taking over anything,'

Vaughan growled. 'Until he does – the investigation stays with me.'

'He left it to me to tell you,' Sean explained. 'Addis wants SIU to take over and Addis gets what he wants. And you don't want to get on Addis's wrong side. Believe me – I know.'

'I don't take kindly to DIs marching into my crime scenes and telling me what's gonna happen,' Vaughan continued to dig his heels in.

Sean didn't have time to argue, but neither did he want to alienate Vaughan and his MIT. He needed them onside and cooperative. He couldn't afford to have anyone with-holding some important fact they'd discovered – deliberately or otherwise. 'I understand it's a difficult situation,' he said in a conciliatory tone, 'but my unit was set up to deal with exactly this sort of investigation. I know you and your team could find whoever did this, but the fact is I have access to things you don't, which means I've a better than decent chance of finding him sooner – before he kills again. That's what we all want, isn't it?' Vaughan looked him up and down – weighing up Sean's words. 'All I need is full cooperation. I need everything you've found to date and in return I promise you'll get full credit for what you've achieved.' Still he sensed Vaughan wasn't satisfied. 'If we need any help I'll come straight to you. Fair enough?'

Vaughan sighed in resignation. 'Very well. Fair enough, but no airbrushing us out of what's been done.'

'Of course,' Sean readily agreed, 'but I need the forensic team to stop whatever they're doing and prepare their exhibits for transfer.'

'You want them to stop?' Vaughan questioned his wisdom.

'Like I said,' Sean reminded him, 'I have access to things you don't – including a specialist forensics team who know exactly what I expect from them.'

'If you insist,' Vaughan agreed, unconvinced.

'And I'll need all the paperwork you have so far. Door-to-doors, witnesses spoken to. Anything you've generated – in order and filed properly, so I can find what I'm looking for.'

'It will be,' Vaughan assured him.

Sean moved on. 'I understand the body's been removed to the morgue at Guy's?'

'It has.'

'Good,' he said, knowing that it would fall under the care of his most trusted pathologist – Dr Simon Canning.

'Your forensic team on their way?' Vaughan asked.

'No,' Sean told him. 'They're briefed and preparing, but no point starting now. Better to start afresh in the morning, when your people have packed up and gone. Just make sure everything's secure till then.'

'Very well,' Vaughan answered, but Sean had already started to drift away – looking out across the streets and the park close to the garage where William Dalton came to his violent end.

Vaughan noticed it. 'You want to take a closer look at the scene?'

Sean looked at the houses and flats around the scene – full of light and life – children awake, meals being prepared, people walking home across the park, the smell of heavy traffic thick in the freezing air, its sound a constant hum in the background. It wasn't right. 'No,' he told Vaughan. 'This isn't how it was.'

'Excuse me,' Vaughan asked, confused.

'Nothing,' Sean realized he'd been speaking out loud. 'I'll send a couple of my people over to your office tomorrow to pick up whatever you have.'

'It'll be ready,' Vaughan assured him.

'Good,' Sean told him and turned to leave. 'I need to be somewhere.'

'One thing,' Vaughan stopped him.

'Which is?'

'If you ever decide you've had enough of the SIU, give me

a call, will you,' Vaughan told him. 'I wouldn't mind that job myself some day.'

'I'll keep it in mind,' Sean replied before heading off back to his car, fully aware that Vaughan wouldn't be the only one who'd like his job and that Addis wouldn't hesitate to replace him if he ever looked like he'd lost his special edge.

Anna Ravenni-Ceron entered the private members' club in St James's Park, close to New Scotland Yard, and was led to a large dark dining room where Assistant Commissioner Robert Addis sat in full uniform looking as trim and tidy as ever – his peaked cap and brown leather gloves perched on the edge of the table next to him. He sipped water from a crystal glass as he read from an open file he held expertly in one hand.

'Excuse me, sir,' the hostess murmured discreetly, making him look up. 'Your guest has arrived.'

'Anna,' he smiled, but remained seated and made no effort to shake her hand. 'Please, have a seat.'

'Thank you,' Anna told the hostess as she seated herself on the straight-backed chair that had been pulled out for her. Slim and elegant with a head of unruly wavy black hair caught and tamed into a mass of swirls and ringlets, her dark brown eyes stared from a pretty oval face, studying Addis as he waited until the hostess had left before speaking again.

'I'm glad you could make it on such short notice,' he told her. 'You'll understand this isn't the sort of thing I'd want to discuss over the phone.'

'So you said.'

'Being the head of the Specialist Crime Operations can make one somewhat . . . cautious.'

'No doubt,' she agreed, before realizing she was being more assertive and questioning than she'd been with Addis in the past. If she didn't play the game better he would pick up on the subtle change and become suspicious. He might even deny her access to the investigation and with it her chance to help or protect Sean. 'Face-to-face is preferable,' she lied.

'Good,' Addis relaxed somewhat. 'Good.'

'Is this the new case?' she asked, her eyes indicating the file in his hand.

'Yes,' Addis told her, closing the file as if she'd somehow spied on its contents. 'Have you heard anything?'

'Only what you've told me,' she lied again. 'Two young adult victims. No apparent links between them. DI Corrigan and the SIU will be investigating . . . Which makes me wonder what you want from me.'

Addis handed her the file, which she accepted. 'Same as always, Anna.'

'I see,' she said, trying to hide her disappointment. 'You want me to look like I'm helping profile the killer, but really you want me to keep an eye on DI Corrigan and report back to you?'

'No,' Addis smiled condescendingly. 'I *want* you to assist in profiling the type of person we're looking for – not merely look as if you are.'

'I understand,' she replied, a hint of frustration in her voice, 'but you also want me to *observe* DI Corrigan? Correct?'

'You make it sound as if I'm asking you to spy on him,' Addis said without a hint of irony.

'Aren't you?' Anna asked.

Addis leaned back in his chair and watched her for a long few seconds before answering. 'We've discussed this before, Anna. DI Corrigan is an asset not just to the Special Investigations Unit, but the Specialist Crimes Operations. Indeed, he's an asset to the Metropolitan Police Service. He has a rare and special talent, which is why I have personally seen to it that he became day-to-day leader of the SIU. But these cases are by their very nature high profile, constantly under the glare of the media spotlight. I can't allow serious mistakes to be made during such investigations. I need to see any such mistakes coming before they actually happen.'

'But Sean— DI Corrigan is an outstanding detective and investigator,' she reminded him. 'Yet I can't help but feel you're expecting him to make a mistake, sooner rather than later.'

'I'm not talking about him missing or overlooking some vital piece of evidence,' he explained. 'He's as thorough as he is instinctive and imaginative – as I'm sure you're aware. It's almost as if he can *think* like the very people he's trying to find and stop.' He let his words hang in front of her, the silence pressurizing her to say something.

'He's simply able to combine years of experience with an excellent and active imagination,' she tried to argue. 'Nothing more than that. It's a trait I've seen in other detectives.'

'Yes,' Addis agreed, but his eyes had narrowed to slits and his voice lowered to a hush. 'But with Corrigan it's much more than an active imagination. I leave you psychiatrists to decide its precise nature, but what I do know is that in order to make whatever it is work, he needs to tread a very thin line. He needs to be very close to the edge.' He paused to take a sip of water. 'Perhaps it's only a matter of time before he falls from one of those edges.'

'Then move him from the SIU,' she told him, though she knew Sean would be furious if he found out she'd suggested as much to Addis. Much as she valued their friendship, if she had to sacrifice it to protect him, she would. 'Before he puts himself in harm's way again. It's within your power.'

'I can't do that,' he replied. 'As I've said, Corrigan is an asset. A valuable asset. Police officers are paid to make sacrifices – to take risks. They just need to be controlled – which is why we are having this conversation.'

'You don't care if he puts himself in danger, do you?' she accused him. 'So long as he solves the high-profile cases quickly. Right?'

Addis ignored her question. 'Do you accept my offer?' he asked briskly.

Anna sighed, but knew she had no choice. 'If it helps catch the killer, how could I say no?'

'Good,' Addis smiled, satisfied. 'Then I look forward to your reports. Can I get you something to eat? To drink?'

'No,' she told him, getting to her feet clutching the file he'd given her – feeling like she needed to shower and change her clothes. 'I have to be somewhere.'

'Of course,' he nodded. 'Please. Don't let me keep you.'

'Goodbye, Robert,' she replied, and headed for the entrance and the fresh, cold air she desperately needed beyond.

Addis watched her all the way. He hadn't missed the difference in her attitude. She'd been more questioning than during their previous meetings. He would have to do what he always did the second he had the slightest doubt about anyone's loyalty. He would assume she could no longer be trusted. Perhaps she'd been too close to Corrigan and his team for too long. She was supposed to be helping the gamekeeper, but maybe the poacher now had her allegiance. He decided the best way to be sure was to play along with her – for the time being.

Geoff Jackson was working at his desk in the huge open-plan office of *The World* newspaper when his editor appeared over his shoulder.

'Sue,' he acknowledged her and swivelled in his chair to face her.

'Well,' Dempsey asked him, sitting on the edge of his desk. She was tall for a woman – her slimness making her appear taller, with short blond hair that augmented her attractive face. At fifty-one she'd lost little of her appeal to men and knew it. 'Did you get the interview?'

'Yeah, I met him.'

'And?' she pressed.

'And,' he mimicked her, 'it was very interesting.'

'I bet it was,' she said. 'But what did Gibran tell you? Did you get him to talk about the murders the police think he committed?'

'No,' Jackson deflated her. 'Nothing that specific. He's too smart to talk about something he could be charged and tried for. We kept it more general – what goes through the mind of a killer, that sort of stuff. It's good, though – even if I say so myself. Good enough to be our lead story. I'll have it polished and ready to go for tomorrow's edition. I'll email it to you when it's done.'

'Fine,' she told him, springing off his desk, 'but it won't be front page. Not without him confessing to something.'

'I agree,' Jackson replied, surprising her somewhat. He rarely agreed to anything without a fight. 'I was thinking more centre-page spread – with a leader to it on the front. Lots of old photos of Gibran, his victims, DI Corrigan – that sort of thing, in amongst the interview. As I do more interviews we can run more centre-page spreads – build up a serialization.'

'Do I sense a book in the making?' Dempsey asked.

'Maybe,' he evaded, knowing she would be aware that was his plan, but that she wouldn't care.

'Fine,' she smiled and was about to walk away when she remembered something. 'By the way – have you heard about the Mint Street murder?'

Jackson leaned back in his chair looking slightly confused. 'I wasn't even a journalist back then,' he answered, 'but I'm aware of the case. Most good crime reporters are. Some crazed teenager killed a young courting couple with a knife. Can't recall his name . . .'

'Jesus, Geoff,' Dempsey told him. 'Not the murder from the eighties. Another one. A new one.'

'What?' he asked, surprised that a murder could have slipped past him. The Gibran interviews had distracted him from current affairs.

'Some homeless guy,' Dempsey explained, immediately deflating his interest. Who cared about a homeless man meeting his end? 'Probably connected to the murder of a female prostitute about eleven days ago,' she continued, reigniting his interest.

'Linked?' he asked suspiciously. 'Linked how?'

'Both had their throats cut,' Dempsey answered, but that wasn't enough for Jackson.

'And?' he pressed.

'And,' she told him with a trace of relish in her voice, 'they both had a number of teeth pulled out or cut out or something.'

Jackson felt the surge of excitement he always felt when he could smell a big crime story brewing and this one sounded like it had real potential. He hadn't had a killer who'd captured the public's imagination since he covered the story of the Jackdaw – a name that he, unbeknown to the rest of the world, had bestowed on the killer. 'Anybody covering it?' he asked urgently.

'Bill Curtis,' she replied. 'One of your own.'

'Curtis,' he muttered under his breath. He wasn't about to let a junior reporter like Curtis have what could be the crime scoop of the year.

'I would have put you straight on it,' Dempsey explained, 'but you were off meeting Gibran. Maybe you could get Curtis to give his expert opinion on this new killer,' she teased him before walking off.

'Very funny,' he answered with a grimace, grabbing his phone and checking his messages and missed calls. He'd been so wrapped up in the Gibran interview it had been hours since he'd looked at his mobile. There'd been several missed calls, including one from Dempsey and one from Curtis. 'Shit,' he cursed. He tapped the screen to call Curtis back, shaking his head at Dempsey's attempt at being funny – *Maybe you could get Curtis to give his expert opinion,* but even as he repeated her words to himself in his head a smile began to spread across his face. 'Sue, my friend,' he whispered under his breath, 'you're a genius and you don't know it.' He heard the scuffling sounds of the phone being answered.

'Bill Curtis speaking,' the reporter answered curtly.

'Talk to me, Bill,' Jackson demanded. 'I want to know everything on these murders. Everything.'

Sean sat alone in his office, poring over the crime scene photographs, studying every square centimetre of each one then swapping it for a corresponding report, searching both for something that might have been overlooked. Something he might have missed. But to his frustration he could find nothing he hadn't already seen. He was about to go through the whole procedure again when Sally knocked on his door, entered without being asked, and slumped exhausted into the chair on the opposite side of the desk. He looked her up and down. 'You look tired.'

'I'm fine,' she lied. 'Nothing a dose of caffeine won't fix.'

'You find the family?' he asked.

'Was easy enough,' she told him. 'Dalton had a long and illustrious criminal record, going back to his early childhood. His mum and dad, Jane and Peter, still live in the family home in Lewisham. Neither had seen William in a few months, but they were pretty devastated when they got the news.'

'They've lost a child,' Sean reminded her. 'Doesn't matter to the parents what that child may have become. He'll always be their boy.'

'I know,' Sally agreed. 'Anyway, they tried repeatedly to help him turn it around, but ultimately he chose drugs over them. If we need them to formally identify the body, they will.'

'We do,' he confirmed.

'Apparently, he has an older brother: Sam,' she continued. 'He tracked William down to the West End, found him on the streets begging. When he tried to get William to go with him, stay at his place for a while and get cleaned up, the lad wasn't having it.'

'Some people don't want to get clean,' Sean reminded her. 'They prefer their own version of reality.'

'Well, he sure did,' Sally said. 'None of the family knew he was living in a disused garage,' she continued. 'Or at least, they didn't until now.'

'OK,' Sean sighed. 'Find the brother and talk to him. He probably knows more about the victim's life than the parents. Siblings usually do when a brother or a sister go off the rails.'

'Won't be a problem,' she told him. 'Parents gave me his address.'

'And see if the parents will give us a decent headshot photograph,' Sean continued. 'Have some of the team hit Oxford Street and show it around. We're going to need the homeless community to talk to us, but I don't want to alienate them by using a mugshot of a victim taken while he was in custody. Let's not create a them-and-us feel when dealing with them.'

'Got one here,' Sally told him and pulled a photograph of a smiling William Dalton from her jacket pocket, taken shortly before the ravages of crack took hold and he ran away from home. 'Parents let me have it. Had a feeling we'd need one.'

'Good work,' he acknowledged. He checked his watch. 'It's late, Sally. Why don't you go home? You can start fresh in the morning.'

'Trying to protect me?' she accused him. Ever since Gibran almost took her life, Sean had been treating her differently to anyone else on the team; he couldn't seem to help himself.

'No,' he argued. 'I know you can handle yourself. But you look tired.'

'We're all tired,' she reminded him, 'and we're going to get a lot more tired before this is over. No,' she said, dragging herself to her feet. 'Now's a good time to hit the West End. It'll be reasonably quiet and the homeless will be settling into doorways. Easier to talk to them when they're static and not trying to hassle tourists for coins. I'll stir up some unwilling volunteers and see what we can turn up.'

'OK,' he reluctantly agreed. 'If you're sure.'

'What about you?' she replied. 'Gonna try for home – see Kate and the kids while you have a chance?'

Again he glanced at his watch – more to make a point than to check the time. 'Too late for that,' he told her. 'For the kids, anyway.'

'So what are you going to do instead?' she asked. 'Not sit here all night driving yourself insane reading reports, I hope?'

'No,' he agreed. 'Thought I'd check on Donnelly and the door-to-door team, and then maybe . . .' Sally's scrutinizing gaze stopped him finishing.

'And then maybe what?' she pressed.

'I thought . . . as I'll be in the area,' he tried to convince her, 'I'd take another look at the scene.'

'At the scene?' she questioned him. 'At this time of night – alone? Despite the fact you were there earlier?'

'That was the problem,' he tried to ease her concerns. 'Earlier, it wasn't right. There were too many people around, too much traffic, too many lights on in the houses and flats. Too much . . . *life*. It wasn't how it would have been when Dalton was killed. And the place was crawling with forensics. I couldn't think. Couldn't get a feel for what happened.'

Sally sighed deeply. 'Be careful, Sean,' she warned him. 'It's been a while since we had a case like this. Maybe you should ease yourself into it – go through the normal motions of an investigation rather than trying to look into that crystal ball of yours. Don't put yourself under too much pressure to solve this one by yourself. Don't get isolated, Sean.'

'I don't have a crystal ball,' he told her, getting to his feet, 'and I won't get isolated. You'll know what I know.' He grabbed his coat from the stand and began the ritual of filling his pockets with the phones, Maglite and a few other items he thought might be useful. 'I need some time alone at the scene at the right time of day or night. I need to see it like he saw it.'

'Feel what he felt?' Sally asked accusingly.

'I want to analyse the scene as the suspect would have seen it, that's all,' he lied.

'Fine,' she gave in.

'Don't worry about me so much,' he told her as he brushed past on his way out. 'Worry about finding whoever we're after before he kills again. I'll text you later,' he promised, then headed off across the main office and through the exit.

Dave Donnelly sat alone in the Lord Clyde pub in Clenham Street just around the corner from the Mint Street crime scene, sipping a pint – not his first – and nibbling on a sandwich. He'd long ago abandoned the idea of eating the chunky chips that had accompanied it. The pleasant effects of the alcohol came all the quicker on an empty stomach, but they couldn't stop the images of Jeremy Goldsboro, better known to the public as the Jackdaw, racing through his mind: Goldsboro pointing the shotgun at Sean until a bullet from Donnelly's gun smashed him backwards. That should have been enough, but the Jackdaw had raised his shotgun again, leaving Donnelly no choice but to pump two more shots into his chest to end the stand-off. The memories brought bile flooding into his mouth. He swallowed it down with another mouthful of beer just as DCI Ryan Ramsay entered the sparsely populated pub. Spotting Donnelly, he made his way across the room and took the vacant seat across the table.

'Drink?' Donnelly offered.

'No,' Ramsay told him. 'I won't be staying long.'

'Fair enough,' Donnelly shrugged and raised his glass. 'Mind if I do?'

'Go ahead,' Ramsay replied, uninterested.

'So what d'you want to talk about?' Donnelly cut to the chase. 'Why did you ask to meet me?'

'Thought we should have a chat,' Ramsay said, as if it was nothing. 'It's been quite a while since we last talked.'

'You mean when you asked me to pass you insider information

about SIU cases?' Donnelly reminded him. 'When you asked me to give you information about Sean Corrigan?'

'Information that you never gave me,' Ramsay countered.

'I'm not in the habit of talking out of school,' Donnelly warned him.

'You wouldn't be talking out of school.' Ramsay's voice took on a persuasive tone. 'I'm a DCI, remember? I can get the information I need from the same places you do.'

'Then what do you need me for?' Donnelly asked.

'Details,' Ramsay told him, leaning in closer. 'Those little extras Corrigan might be holding back and perhaps a few details about Corrigan himself.'

'And why would I tell you?' Donnelly demanded.

'Because we're both getting close to retirement, Dave,' Ramsay reminded him. 'You want to try surviving on a sergeant's pension? Got any kids at university?' Donnelly said nothing. 'Listen. I can get us both a very nice gig in our retirement. All you have to do is work with me on this, give me what I need.'

'Oh aye,' Donnelly stared at him with deep suspicion. 'And what would this gig be?'

'I can't tell you,' Ramsay insisted. 'Not yet. But it's not working as an investigator for some shitty company or as a glorified security guard. It'll be good work and not too taxing. You won't do better.'

'I'll think about it,' Donnelly told him.

'You do that,' Ramsay said quietly. 'I hear the whispers about you and Corrigan. You owe him nothing.'

'I said I'll think about it,' Donnelly repeated, irritated.

'Well, don't take too long,' Ramsay warned him. 'There are other detectives on the SIU.'

'What's that supposed to mean?' Donnelly asked, though he knew exactly what was meant.

Ramsay ignored the question and got to his feet. 'Stay in touch,' he told him.

Donnelly watched him make his way to the exit. No sooner had he passed through the door than DC Zukov entered. Seeing Donnelly, he made straight for him, sliding next to him on the bench and eyeing his food and drink jealously.

'You all right, Dave?' he asked unpleasantly.

'You want something to eat or drink?' Donnelly replied, ignoring Zukov's sarcasm.

'No,' he answered. 'Still got work to do, you know. I'll get something later – when I'm finished.'

'Suit yourself.'

'Was that DCI Ramsay?' Zukov asked with suspicion.

'Aye,' Donnelly answered warily. 'Didn't know you knew him.'

'Our paths have crossed a couple of times,' Zukov shrugged. 'What was he doing here?'

'Same as most people in here,' Donnelly tried to dismiss it. 'Having a drink.'

'Why not use a pub nearer to London Bridge?' Zukov pushed.

'Too busy, maybe. How the fuck should I know?'

'Only asking, Sarge. Only asking.'

'Aye,' Donnelly moved on. 'Never mind. How's the door-to-door going?'

'Maybe if you helped knock on a few doors yourself, you'd know,' Zukov told him.

Donnelly stared at him in contemptuous silence for a while. 'I'm here to supervise, remember? Not wear the soles of my shoes out. That's your job.'

Zukov scowled. 'You'll be needing a lift back to the Yard then?'

'Don't worry yourself,' Donnelly told him. 'I'll walk to London Bridge when we're done and get the rattler home from there. Anyway, you were about to tell me how the door-to-door's going.'

Zukov shrugged. 'Plenty people have seen Dalton around over the last few weeks. Plenty people know of him, but no one really knew him. We're not getting anything about the night he was killed, other than one of the night staff at Borough Underground says he recognized him from the photo. Says the victim came home most nights between ten and eleven and is pretty sure the night he was killed was no different.'

'So it looks a sure thing he used the tube and not the bus,' Donnelly told him. 'Thank God for small mercies. CCTV from the stations and the route he used will be easy enough to track. If he'd been jumping on and off buses it would be a nightmare.'

'The Underground staff have been told to preserve the CCTV footage for the last week,' Zukov assured him.

'Good,' Donnelly replied, taking another sip of his beer. 'Keep at it. Hopefully someone will come up with something useful.' His phone chirping and vibrating on the table stole his attention. He read the text. It was from Sean. 'You better get back to it,' he advised Zukov. 'The boss is on his way.'

'Corrigan?' Zukov asked.

'Who else?' Donnelly replied. 'And that's DI Corrigan to you.'

Zukov didn't move – a troubled expression spreading across his face. Donnelly couldn't tell whether it was real or fake.

'Well. What you waiting for?'

'There's something I've been meaning to ask,' Zukov explained, 'about you and the guv'nor.'

'Oh?' Donnelly asked and immediately regretted leaving a gap for Zukov to walk through.

'I've heard things, you know.'

'Aye,' Donnelly said, sensing trouble. 'Like what exactly?'

'Like you and he aren't getting along too well right now,' Zukov told him. 'Since the Goldsboro shooting.'

Donnelly couldn't help but tense at the sound of someone else saying that name, but he tried not to show it. 'Bollocks,' he replied. 'You shouldn't listen to any of that shit.'

'Some people say,' Zukov continued regardless, 'the shooting didn't have to happen – that the guv'nor manipulated the situation so you'd have no choice but to shoot Goldsboro. He created the circumstances and you pulled the trigger.' Zukov let his words hang in the air.

'And that's what you think, is it?' Donnelly asked after a few seconds.

'I don't think anything. I'm only telling you what I've heard.' Zukov paused for a second. 'I'm one of the senior DCs on this firm now,' he reminded Donnelly. 'If there's a serious problem between the DI and his DS, then it could impact on the rest of us. I'm just trying to look out for the rest of the team. I'm sure you understand.'

Donnelly swallowed his seething resentment at Zukov's veiled threats, but what hurt more was that it was the truth. He cursed Sean every hour for making him take a life and constantly thought of other ways they could have taken Goldsboro down without killing him. Again and again he kept coming back to the same conclusion: Sean had wanted it that way. Things had happened exactly as Corrigan wanted them to happen. Donnelly may have been the one pointing a gun at Goldsboro, but it felt like it was Sean who'd pulled the trigger.

Conscious that Zukov was waiting for an answer, he told him, 'You worry about doing your own job,' he warned him. 'I'm still the senior DS and it's my job to look after the team – not yours. You clear on that?'

'Yes, Sarge,' Zukov smiled unpleasantly. 'Enjoy your supper,' he said as he got to his feet and headed for the exit, leaving Donnelly alone with his drink and his thoughts.

Sean approached the two young uniformed constables who'd drawn the short straw and been left to guard the scene. He held up his warrant card for them. 'DI Corrigan,' he identified himself. 'Special Investigations Unit. This is my crime scene.'

The tall, fit-looking young man who was holding the Crime Scene Log looked down to check the information in his book. 'Will you be going into the scene, sir?' he asked nervously.

'Yeah,' Sean answered. 'I need to take a look at something.'

'No problem,' the constable told him, and made an entry in the log book.

Sean nimbly bent under the tape like a boxer entering the ring and immediately began to walk towards the garage that was now lit by a solitary mini-floodlight. Halfway there he suddenly stopped and turned through three hundred and sixty degrees.

'Where did you come from?' he quietly asked the trace of the killer that would forever remain at the scene like an ethereal fingerprint of violence that could never be scrubbed away. 'Did you walk straight towards it? Did you walk across the same ground I'm walking across now – feeling unstoppable – feeling like a god? Or did you skirt around the outside of the park and come up behind him?' He waited a few seconds for the answer to come, but he neither heard nor saw anything, so he continued his walk to the garage, trying to feel the killer's presence, his mind, with every step, until he reached the brick and corrugated-iron shell that William Dalton had called home.

The forensic team had pulled the metal sheet back across the entrance as best they could, but the floodlight penetrated deep inside, illuminating the squalor Dalton had lived in and the violence that had claimed his life. Sean peered through the gap in the makeshift front door. 'Is this what you did?' he asked the ghost of Dalton's killer. 'Did you move quietly up to the garage and look through the gaps, watching him for a while before you somehow lured him into your trap? And how did you do that?' He looked down at the floor inside and instantly found what he was looking for: the bloodstains from the crime scene photographs. In real life, they looked far less vivid. There was a small patch of blood

63

at the entrance and then what appeared to be a smear mark for several feet that connected to a much larger bloodstained area where Dalton had his throat and carotid artery sliced wide open, causing him to bleed to death in seconds.

Sean remembered the report said the victim had almost certainly been hit over the back of the head. The photographs of Dalton's matted, bloody hair around the wound flashed in his mind. He pulled at the sheet of metal that had served as a door, the noise loud and grating – screaming through the stillness of the bitter night. He froze for a few seconds as he looked around. Surely someone would have heard the metal being pulled away? 'Or at least you must have thought it would have been heard,' he whispered. 'You must have thought it would attract unwanted attention, that someone might look out of a window and see you . . . yet you didn't walk away. You did what you came here to do.' He thought silently for a while, seeing the killer standing in the darkness – calm despite the frightful noise. No sense of panic or fear. Just a determination to kill. A shiver ran down his spine, partly because of the cold, but mostly because of the dawning realization of the type of killer he was hunting. This one was as calm and careful as he was vicious. Those were always the most difficult to catch.

Again he pulled at the metal sheet, once more filling the night with that terrible grating sound, until the gap was big enough to fit through. He took a couple of steps back to the floodlight and switched it off, unclipped his mini-Maglite from his belt and clicked it on.

Alarmed by the sounds coming from the scene and the sudden darkness, the constable Sean had spoken with earlier called out, his voice full of concern: 'You all right there, sir?'

'I'm fine,' Sean shouted back. 'I need to look at something without the light on.' He headed to the garage entrance and stood peering into the darkness with only his small torch for illumination. He remembered there had been a camping lantern at the scene and figured it would have given off about the same amount of light. Now he was seeing the scene as both killer and victim had seen it.

He shone his torch at the pattern of blood on the ground – the cone of light tracing it from the small stain by the entrance to the larger dried pool deep inside the garage. He walked on, careful to avoid the area where the killing had taken place, while also watching every step he took, shining the light on each area of ground before placing his foot down, until he reached a patch from which he could see everything he wanted. Again he traced the blood smear from the small stain to the large pool and back again as the scene that had played out here became clearer and clearer in his mind.

'You were hit on the back of the head by the entrance and then dragged inside where he sliced across your trachea and carotid artery. The cut across the throat was survivable, but the cut to the artery was not. The pressure in the artery would have caused death through blood loss, but . . . Shit,' he cursed as he lost his way and his thoughts became confused and tangled. He took a few deep breaths to clear his mind, then started again.

'You're not thinking like a homeless teenager,' he reprimanded himself. 'What was he thinking? What was going through his mind?' He thought back to the crime scene reports. There was evidence the victim had been preparing his crack pipe, though he never got to use it. 'What would keep an addict from his drug?' he asked softly. He took a few more deep breaths while the image of the victim began to form in his mind as if he was watching him on CCTV footage. He could see Dalton, eagerly but carefully preparing to get high and forget the pointlessness of his life.

'You live your life in fear,' Sean found himself quietly saying. 'You don't feel safe anywhere. You only escape the fear when you get high, which is what you were planning on doing, but something disturbed you. You heard something outside, didn't you? Something anyone else could have ignored, but because you live in fear you had to be sure it wasn't a threat – had to make sure no one was waiting for you to pass out stoned when you'd be at your most vulnerable. So you went to take a look outside.' He walked back to the entrance and looked out into the night just as William Dalton had.

'It was raining hard that night,' he reminded himself. 'It must have been difficult to see properly with the rain driving into your face in the dark. Did you call out – demand to know if someone was there? But no one called back, did they? Did you move further from your shelter to try and see better – playing right into his hands? He used your fear to lure you into his trap, didn't he? And when you stretched too far into the darkness, he hit you hard – not hard enough to kill you, but enough to knock you down, to leave you confused and disorientated while he dragged you back inside. Did he close the entrance before he did the things he did to you? The report said it was open when the body was found, but he could have left it like that when he went.' He thought back to the original crime scene report. 'You had a camping lantern, but there was no mention of any light being on – so it was never turned on or he turned it off when he came in . . . or when he left. Was that why he wasn't afraid of being seen – because it was dark in here?' Another thought crossed his mind as he searched with his torch for the lantern, quickly finding it. He walked carefully towards it and crouched next to it, shining his torch close as he examined the on/off switch. It was set to on. Clearly the batteries had gone flat by the time the body was discovered. Sean nodded as he thought it through. 'Batteries are expensive. You would have used the lamp sparingly, but you needed light to prepare your drugs and then there was the noise outside. Your fear meant you kept it on when you went to look, but when he dragged you inside he left it on. Because he wanted to see. He had to see everything. And when he left, he left you in light – because he wanted the world to see.'

He remembered the words of the crime scene report and the photographs. There was no evidence of the victim fighting back – no defensive wounds or arterial blood-spray patterns on the walls. 'So you were too badly injured to fight back, or he was too strong. Strong enough to pin you to the floor while he cut through your throat and carotid artery. Did he hold you still while he watched the life drain from you? And when you were dead or near-dead, he took your teeth and nails – so he could relive killing you over and over again.'

Without realizing it, he suddenly switched point of view from victim to killer, as if in the moment Dalton died he left his dead body and entered the murderer's very much living body. For a few seconds he was sure he could feel the excitement and power the killer had felt coursing through him, making him feel more alive than he'd ever been.

'You raped the first victim, but your crimes are not sexually motivated,' he said, almost too quietly to be audible. 'Your excitement spread through every inch of your body, didn't it? You became aroused by this great thing you had just done, but the tension in your body was too much, wasn't it? You needed a release, so you raped her while she lay dead or dying.' He closed his eyes for a second and allowed the images of William Dalton lying dead on the ground to flood in. His clothes appeared to be fully intact, his genitals unmolested. 'Did you feel the same almost uncontrollable excitement when you killed for the second time? Did you need to release? But this was a man . . . Shit,' he suddenly cursed. This one was coming to him too fast. Thinking like him was almost overwhelming, but at the same time it was intoxicating and seductive to follow the conscious and subconscious steps of a killer towards what most would consider to be madness, but what to them was a transformation into something greater and more powerful. He drew in deep breaths to regain his focus – to regain his own voice. To take back his own mind.

'OK,' he told himself, trying to think like a detective and not the killer he hunted. 'No matter how hard you tried to keep clean, you would have been a fucking mess. Your hands, sleeves, everything would have been covered in the victim's blood. Blood has a nasty habit of getting everywhere, but once you cut through his carotid artery you had to deal with arterial spray too – blood spraying out under pressure from a heart trying to stay alive. You must have been covered in it – warm and wet on your skin like slick hot oil— Fuck!' he chastised himself for drifting back into the killer's mind.

He gave himself a few seconds to regain his composure. 'You must have been a mess. You couldn't have casually walked on to the tube or a bus like that, and even if you had a car nearby, you wouldn't have risked walking to it covered in the victim's blood. No. You plan too much. Somehow you got clean or clean enough to slip past a casual look. So you took water with you or knew where to find it or had something with you that would cover your blood-soaked clothes until you could get home and get clean. But what about your wife and family, or your parents? They would have noticed something.' He thought for a second. 'So you live alone. The bloody ones always live alone.' He paused for a few seconds to allow his observations to settle into something more solid in his mind. The first sketching of a mind-map that he knew, one way or the other, would eventually lead him to the killer of William Dalton and Tanya Richards.

He took one last look around the inside of the garage – at the squalor of Dalton's life and the bloody hell that was his death. 'What do you want?' he asked the killer. 'You're not just killing because you can't stop yourself, are you? You're trying to . . . you're trying to achieve something. But what?'

He clicked his torch off and walked into the darkness that waited for him outside.

# 4

Next morning Sean was in his office at New Scotland Yard, a takeaway black coffee steaming on the cheap wooden desk that had snagged more than one pair of trousers. Engrossed in typing up his findings on the virtually obsolete computer he refused to allow IT to replace, he was unaware that he had a visitor until a sharp knock on his doorframe alerted him. Somehow, without looking up, he knew who it would be. Maybe he'd subconsciously detected her perfume. His entire body froze with tension when he saw her standing in the doorway.

'Anna,' was all he could say.

'Sean,' she replied, looking at the floor for a split second to avoid his eyes.

'Been a long time,' he told her.

'You've not had an investigation that needed my input,' she reminded him.

'You mean one that Addis wanted your input on?' he replied. 'Your input about me.'

She walked into his office and took a seat without being asked. 'We've talked about this, Sean. My loyalty is to you. I'll only tell Addis what we agree he should be told. I'll keep him off your back while you try to find whoever committed these crimes – and maybe I can help you with that too.'

He watched her for a while before answering – taking in every breath, every minute movement and involuntary twitch of her body. 'Perhaps you can,' he eventually said. 'This one's certainly a bit different.'

'I read the file,' she told him. Sean raised an eyebrow. She saw it. 'Addis,' she explained.

'Naturally,' he replied. 'And what do you think?'

'I think he's a vicious killer who needs to be stopped,' she answered.

'That's your professional opinion?' he asked with a smile.

'Part of it.' She returned the smile.

'And the rest? I'd be interested in hearing what you think.'

'You mean you'd be interested in seeing how far behind you I am?' she accused him.

'That's not true.' Or at least, it was only partly true. He did want to hear her thoughts.

'Well,' she began, 'he's certainly high on the violence score, but low on the rage score.'

'Meaning?' Sean asked, although he believed he knew the answer.

'Meaning you can almost certainly rule out mental illness,' she explained. 'He's not raging over his victims – there are no multiple stab wounds, for example. He's very precise. If he's mad at the world, he has a very calm way of showing it. Murderous, but calm. And he's not concerned about leaving his DNA at the scene, so it's unlikely he's killed before or been convicted of any crimes.'

'Could he have killed and gotten away with it?' Sean asked, although he was sure he hadn't.

'It's possible,' Anna agreed. 'He may have used a completely different method. But I doubt it. He's used the same method twice now, which means he likes to stick to what works – what he's comfortable with.'

'Interesting,' Sean told her.

'Interesting enough,' she said, 'but nothing you hadn't worked out.'

'You've flagged things I hadn't considered,' he lied. 'You're the psychiatrist – not me.'

Anna didn't believe a word. 'I'm glad I could add something,' she smiled.

'He raped the first victim,' Sean quickly moved on. 'Yet his second victim was male. What's he thinking?'

'I don't believe he's sexually motivated,' she explained. 'There were no obvious signs of sexual activity with the male victim, but he may well be more of a sexual predator than he thinks. Certainly, when the opportunity presented itself, he took it.'

'She had no defensive marks,' Sean reminded her, 'so he raped her when she was dead – or almost.'

'Or he threatened her into submission, or he's strong enough to totally overpower her,' Anna argued.

'So what is he?' Sean asked. 'A rapist or a necrophiliac?'

'Neither,' Anna answered. 'His reason for attacking wasn't to have sex with them – dead or alive. That was merely a byproduct.'

'A release?' Sean shared his own idea.

'His excitement would have been intense,' she agreed, knowing what he meant. 'It would have manifested itself in some physical way.'

'You mean he got so excited he became sexually aroused?' Sean cut to the point. 'He needed to orgasm to calm himself down?'

'I believe so.'

'So we should be looking more closely for signs of sexual activity with the second victim?'

'Yes,' she told him, 'but you were already going to – weren't you?'

'I was considering suggesting it,' he admitted. 'Though Roddis and his team would probably have done it anyway.'

71

'I'm not sure I can help you, Sean,' she told him, shaking her head. 'You're always at least two steps ahead of me – ahead of anyone. Anything I can see you've already seen.'

'You're not going to start telling me I can think like them and all that shit?' he pleaded.

'Well?' she asked. 'Can't you? Isn't that what happens?'

'I don't think like them,' he said, his voice betraying his frustration. 'I can *imagine* what they might be thinking – there's a difference.'

'Is there?'

'Why don't you tell me?'

Before Anna could answer, Sally walked into the office and slumped into the one vacant chair, too tired to notice the tense atmosphere. 'I wish I still smoked,' she announced. 'A ciggie and a coffee would go down very nicely round about now.'

'What you got for me, Sally?' Sean ignored her plea for vices of the past.

'Well, the victim's Oyster card is being examined today, so we should know his movements soon enough. And we've seized the CCTV from Borough tube station. The transport police are going to find out what train he used and seize the CCTV from that too, so if he was being closely followed we might get something. It was late and the station was pretty quiet. Could be our best bet.'

'Then he didn't follow him,' Sean killed off any optimism. 'He waited for him. He's too smart, too careful to get caught following either victim on CCTV. But check it out anyway. You get anything from your trip to the West End last night?'

'Nothing that sounds like it's going to help,' she admitted. 'We tracked down plenty of his so-called friends and associates from the street. He was well known and well liked, but nobody has any idea why this happened to him. There were lots of sightings on the day and night he died, but he headed for home alone. No one knows what happened.'

72

'Can they say what tube station he used?' Sean asked.

'Some reckon Tottenham Court Road,' Sally told him. 'We'll know for sure once the Oyster card is examined.'

'OK, fine,' Sean agreed distractedly, suddenly aware of an absence in the room. 'You seen Dave this morning?' he asked Sally.

'No,' she shrugged. 'Haven't seen him since yesterday afternoon.'

Sean thought about his other trusted second in command for a few seconds, remembering how in the past he was virtually always the first one into work every morning. Since the Goldsboro shooting, he was usually the last. 'If you see or hear from him,' he told Sally, 'let him know I need to speak with him, will you?' Sally nodded as Sean's mobile began to ring. He checked the caller ID and answered.

'Andy,' he began. 'What you got for me?'

'Early, peripheral findings only,' DS Roddis from SIU's specialist forensic team told him. 'The Crime Scene Log tells me you've been to the scene, twice, so I doubt I'll be able to tell you anything you haven't worked out for yourself. Why wasn't I given this scene when it was fresh? It doesn't help that I've had to contend with another forensic team trampling over most of it and making off with exhibits.'

'Exhibits that will be handed over to you,' Sean tried to calm the unlikeable perfectionist that was Roddis, the best at his business Sean had ever known. 'And the murder wasn't connected to a series until it was too late. If we're unlucky enough to get another scene, you'll get it before anyone else steps foot in it.'

'Except you,' Roddis accused him in advance.

'I'd be interested in your observations,' Sean encouraged him. 'And I want you to look for a couple of things the other forensics team may not have considered.'

Anna gave him a knowing look.

73

'Such as?' Roddis asked, intrigued. He'd worked enough investigations with Sean to know to expect surprises.

'Semen. Probably close to where the body was found, but could be anywhere in the garage or just outside it.'

'You think he sexually assaulted the victim?' Roddis asked, confused by Sean's suggestion.

'No, but it's possible he felt the need while at the scene. To reduce his heightened state of excitement.'

'The *need*?' Roddis questioned. 'A killer masturbating at the scene when no sexual motivation is suspected? I've seen defecation, urination, killers that like to eat and drink from the victim's fridge, but never what you're suggesting, not when the crime isn't sexually motivated.'

'Let's just say this one's possibly confused,' Sean told him. 'Let's not assume there was no sexual element to his motivation and let's look for traces of semen.'

'If you really think it's worth it,' Roddis climbed down in the face of Sean's irritation. 'But it won't be easy – not at a scene of this type and not after it's been trampled over.'

'I know, but just do it for me, will you?'

'Very well,' Roddis conceded. 'And the other thing?'

'There was a lot of blood at the scene,' Sean reminded him. 'He was in close proximity to the victim when he cut through his carotid artery, meaning he must have had a significant amount of blood on him.'

'One would imagine so.'

'Which means he needed to clean up,' Sean continued. 'At least enough to get him past casual looks. There's no water supply in the garage, so chances are he brought his own, something he may have chosen to dispose of after he'd used it – a plastic bottle, anything. Check inside the cordon – further afield too – for anything he could have used.'

'Why you so worried about finding it?' Roddis asked. 'All it'll give us is more DNA and fingerprints. We already have plenty.'

74

'It'll help paint a picture,' Sean explained. 'It'll show he planned it. That he's organized and careful – premeditating. If he tries to plead diminished responsibility, we'll be able to disprove it.'

'So be it,' Roddis sighed. 'We'll look for your water bottle. Anything else?'

'No,' Sean told him. 'You find anything interesting or unexpected, phone it straight through to me. Understand?'

'I understand,' Roddis answered.

Sean ended the call and threw his phone back on to the desk where it immediately started chirping and vibrating again. 'Christ,' he complained, snatching it back up. He didn't recognize the number but answered anyway. With an investigation like this, he'd be getting a lot of calls from numbers his phone didn't recognize and he'd have to risk answering them all or miss something potentially vital. 'Hello,' he said, withholding his name until he knew who he was speaking to.

'DI Corrigan?' a man's voice asked.

'Who's calling?' he probed.

'PC John Croft,' the man answered. 'The Coroner's Officer.'

'You're speaking with DI Corrigan,' Sean told him. 'What have you got for me?'

'Dr Canning will be doing the post-mortem on your victim, William Dalton, later today. I've had a message from him asking if you'll be there.'

*My victim*, Sean thought about Croft's expression. Was that what Dalton was – another of his victims? 'Yes,' he said after a slight pause. 'Tell Dr Canning I'll be there.'

'About eleven a.m. then,' Croft told him, and hung up.

'The post-mortem?' Sally asked.

'Yeah,' he answered.

'Want some company?'

'No. I'll go alone. You're better off staying here and keeping everybody on it.' As he spoke, his eyes scanned the main office through the Perspex wall. 'Where the hell is Dave?'

David Langley paced the showroom floor of the furniture store. Head office had given him the grand title 'manager', but since they refused to supply him with a team of sales assistants to command – just an 'assistant manager' who was more trouble than he was worth – most of the time Langley was reduced to the role of a glorified salesman. There was a time when that would have bothered him, but now he knew it was simply something he had to put up with while he laid the foundations for his true purpose in life, his reason for being. He congratulated himself on possessing the strength of character to continue the charade of working in the furniture store until the time came to reveal his legacy to the world. The fantasies that had begun as a young teenager were now becoming a reality. He had everything planned, culminating in a final act that would see him seize complete control over the endgame. Something no one could imagine or predict. Not even Corrigan.

The automatic doors at the entrance to the shop slid open with an electric *whoosh*, drawing his attention to the attractive, dark-haired woman in her early thirties who casually drifted into the shop. He took in the fitted jacket and tight jeans that showed off her trim figure. No doubt another bored, wealthy housewife – plenty of those had moved into the area over the last two decades. She didn't look old enough to have children, not for this part of London anyway. He'd had plenty of success with the bored ones in the past and fancied his chances with her, but at the same time he found himself looking on her as something other than a potential conquest, evaluating her instead as a possible victim. It would be risky; dangerous, even. This was no homeless loser or prostitute whom no one cared about; this woman would be missed and mourned, and her family would push the police hard to find her killer – not to mention the press, who would be all over it. For that reason alone, taking her life would be worth it. She would give him ten times the publicity he'd gained from killing the druggie and the whore.

He began to walk towards her as she moved between coffee tables, watching the pulse twitch in her slim, tanned neck – imagining slicing through her perfect skin until he cut through her carotid artery, pinning her to the floor as the warm, red blood emptied from her in intermittent sprays until the flow subsided with her dying heart and finally she lay lifeless. He imagined she'd smell of expensive perfume and cosmetics.

'Can I help you with anything?' he asked, flashing his practised seductive smile.

'Hi,' she smiled back, her eyes making momentary contact before returning to the coffee tables, but it was enough for him to tell she was interested. His nostrils flared at her scent. It was as he'd imagined, but warm too. 'I need a coffee table,' she explained in an accent that suited her appearance perfectly. 'Ideally something I can take away today and won't have to build. You wouldn't believe how difficult it's been to find anything. Everywhere's saying eight weeks until delivery.'

'You should buy online,' he told her with a smile. 'Probably shouldn't have told you that, but how could I lie to you?'

'Not my thing,' she replied. 'I like to see things in the flesh, so to speak, before I commit myself.'

Hearing her say 'flesh' fired a bolt of excitement through his body. 'Well, you're in luck,' he continued. 'We have plenty of good-quality tables and most are in stock, so if your car is big enough you can take one away today.' He gave a shrug. 'Trouble is, most retailers don't keep stock any more. Takes up too much space. Costs too much money. They don't like to build anything unless they know they've got a buyer lined up. But not here. We know not everybody wants to wait for weeks and weeks.' He allowed a few seconds' silence between

77

them, until her gaze returned to him. 'Please. Take a look. Ask anything you like. If you buy today, I can probably do you a special deal – if you promise you won't tell anyone.'

'I don't know,' she told him. 'I'm not really seeing anything that grabs me.'

'Let me guess,' he tried to keep her interested. 'You've recently moved to the area and upsized. The table from your old house or flat isn't big enough and you've got friends coming around to help you celebrate moving into your new home, so you need a coffee table to fill that annoying space today? Am I right?'

She cocked her head to one side and smiled. 'That's . . . very clever,' she replied.

'So what if it's not for life?' he spoke in the code of illicit suggestion, hoping she would respond in kind. 'So long as it works in the short term, who's going to know? Once it's served its purpose, you can get rid of it, replace it with something more permanent, but in the short term it'll give you exactly what you're looking for. Something to bridge the gap – without costing a fortune.' He stood with his hands on his hips to augment his powerful physique – his chest inflated and triangular while his waist tapered away. He felt her eyes flick across his body. 'Personally, I'd recommend this one,' he said, resting his hand on the most expensive table in the shop. 'It's the best we have – a little more expensive than the others, but I'm sure you would appreciate the quality.'

'Maybe,' she replied shyly, a slight croakiness in her voice, a degree of dilation in her pupils. The flushing of her skin let him know she was interested even if she didn't know it yet.

'But,' he blurted out cheerfully, 'what's the best way to test a new coffee table?' The woman looked confused. 'By using it,' he explained. 'There's a great coffee shop along the street. You may know it – Bob's Blends? Bit of a locals' favourite.'

'Like I said,' she answered nervously, although he could sense her excitement too at his obvious interest, 'I'm kind of new to the area.'

'Then you have to try the coffee,' he smiled. 'I promise you'll be a convert. Why don't you take a look around' – he was speaking fast now, denying her the chance to say no – 'while I go grab us a couple of coffees. Don't tell me what you usually have – let me surprise you.'

'I don't want to put you to any trouble,' she tried to back away.

'You're not,' he assured her in his most cheerful tone – his smile friendly, but his eyes serious and flirtatious. 'It'll be my pleasure.' He felt her slipping away. 'You know what?' he said, trying to sound genuinely excited. 'I just remembered: we have some really nice tables in the storeroom. They're old stock, due to be taken away, but they're great tables. If you wanted one of them, I could do you a really great price and deliver today. I could even drop it round myself.' He gave her a few seconds to understand what he was really saying. 'Got to be worth a look – don't you think?'

He watched her lips – her pupils – the tone of her skin – the pulse quickening in her neck – everything. If she went for it within the next few minutes he'd have both her trust and her address. Maybe he would indulge in a brief affair with her until the time came to slit her throat. He watched her mouth begin to open as the answer formed, but it wasn't her voice that he heard – it was the all too familiar voice of his area manager.

'David,' she ambushed him, making him curse himself for having not kept an eye on the shop entrance. 'A word please.' Her voice was sharp, as if she was scolding an unruly dog.

He took a step back, before recovering from the surprise and answering, 'Of course.' Turning to the customer, he apologized: 'Sorry to keep you – I won't be a minute.'

The area manager had set off towards the far corner of the

shop, indicating she wanted privacy. Where she was concerned, this was never a good thing. Reluctantly, he followed.

Jane Huntingdon was younger than him, but had been an area manager for more than a year and was clearly destined for higher things. He'd wanted the job she now had, but the company passed him over in favour of her. A clear signal he would never progress and would do well to hold on to what he had. In so many ways she looked and sounded like the customer he'd been trying to seduce, only she was formally dressed and had short blond hair.

'What the hell are you doing, David?' she demanded, her eyes looking over his shoulder at the customer. 'Haven't you learnt anything?'

'I was trying to sell her a coffee table,' he lied. 'That is my job.'

'Bollocks,' she cut him down. 'I heard you offering to *personally* deliver to her home. I know what you were trying to do.'

'I was trying to make a sale,' he insisted.

'You're a salesman, not a delivery driver.'

'Store manager,' he told her. 'I'm a store manager – not a salesman.'

'I don't care what you call yourself,' she replied. 'What I care about is your conduct while you're at work. Jesus, if it's not female staff members, it's female customers.'

'I'm a single man,' he tried to argue. 'I can do what I like.'

'Maybe if you'd changed your behaviour, you wouldn't be single,' she told him.

He knew what she was getting at. 'You have no business bringing my wife and children into this,' he warned her. 'That has nothing to do with you.'

'Look,' she relented somewhat, holding her hands up. 'That wasn't my intention. You're right: you're a single man and you can do as you like – but not here. Not in the store. This is not your private *pulling* place. It's work. You understand?' He said nothing, merely stared blankly into her blue eyes. 'After your last transgression, you can't afford any more mistakes.' Still he didn't answer. 'Listen, David, I've fought for you more than once at central office. There are others who'd gladly see the back of you, but you do a decent job here and I believe everyone deserves a second chance. Don't blow it – that's all. Do you hear me, David?'

Again he didn't answer. He didn't trust himself to speak, not while his mind was flooded with images of the blood flowing from her neck, images of cutting and pulling the teeth from her pretty mouth. It took an act of will to remind himself that killing her would have too much of an element of vengeance. His work was about so much more than petty human emotions – no matter how extraordinary her warm, viscous blood would feel as it covered his hands.

'Do you hear me, David?' she repeated, her voice raised.

'I hear you,' he managed to answer, pulling himself back into the world. 'I hear you.'

'Good,' she said. 'I'll check back with you later in the week. In the meantime, make sure you keep your social life and work life separate. OK?'

'Fine,' he replied, managing to fake a slight smile. 'It won't happen again.'

She dismissed him with a shake of her head. 'I'll see you later,' she said, and headed for the exit – watched all the way by Langley as he studied every inch of her body.

When she was gone he spun around, hoping to find the customer and pick up where he'd left off, salvage something from the day. The store was empty; she was gone. 'Fuck,' he swore under his breath as the anger swelled, making his head hurt. He needed something. He needed something soon. Something to allow the thoughts in his head to become reality instead of beautiful images of what could be. He needed to feel skin and flesh in his hands as a sculptor needs to feel wet clay. Needed to feel blood run between his fingers as an artist needs to feel paint. He needed another victim.

Donnelly stirred late – his eyes flickering open, then closing again as they registered the grey winter light seeping in through the windows. Through the fog of the previous night's drinking he began to realize he was not alone in his bedroom and that it was his wife who'd opened the curtains and was now talking to him. Though he couldn't yet make out what she was saying, he could tell from her tone that she was lecturing him. Slowly her words came into focus.

'Dave,' she pleaded. 'You've got to get up. You're late for work.'

'Jesus, Karen,' he complained. 'What time is it anyway?'

'Getting on for nine o'clock. I've got to get Josh to school. The others have taken themselves off. Christ,' she moaned as she got closer to him. 'You stink of booze. Where were you last night?'

'Eh?' he bought himself some thinking time. 'Just had a few beers with the boys,' he lied. In fact he'd remained drinking in the Lord Clyde until it came time to head off for London Bridge Station – stopping at the Barrow Boy and Banker en route for a couple of scotches – then catching a train home, only to stop at his favourite pub in Swanley, Kent, for more shots. By the time he got home it was all he could do to walk. 'We picked up a new case,' he elaborated on his lie. 'Looks like a bad one. Thought we'd grab a few while we had the chance.'

'Looks like you had a few too many,' she pointed out. 'What's happened to you lately?' she asked. 'You always used to be up with the birds. Now you struggle to get up at all. You sure you're OK, love?'

'Aye,' he tried to laugh it off. 'I told you. Just not as young as I used to be, eh?'

'Maybe you should lay off the booze for a bit,' she suggested.

'Aye,' he played along. 'Maybe.'

'Right,' she announced. 'I'm officially out of time. I've got to go. Fix yourself something to eat and get cleaned up,' she ordered. 'And then take yourself off to work or Corrigan will have your head.'

'Don't worry about Corrigan,' he tried to reassure her. 'He needs me more than I need him.'

'Not like this, he doesn't,' she warned him. 'We've been married a long time and if there's one thing you've taught me about the police it's that no one is indispensable – not even you. Plenty more detective sergeants in the sea, I should imagine. I'll see you later.'

Donnelly grunted a reply as he watched her stride from the bedroom. For a second he considered going back to sleep, but knew if he did he'd be out for hours. Instead he forced himself to sit up and swing his legs over the side of the bed, grimacing and groaning with every movement. He rubbed his face with both hands, feeling the stubble 'Jesus,' he complained and stood on unsteady feet, the nausea of the morning after the night before taking its revenge.

He headed downstairs in his old T-shirt and boxer shorts, flicked the kettle on and thought about eating something to counteract the lingering effects of the alcohol, but couldn't stomach the idea of food. A wave of nausea hit him and made him close his eyes, but the darkness allowed images to invade his mind – images of bullets ripping through Jeremy Goldsboro, pinning him to the side of the van until he slid to the floor spitting blood. Donnelly snapped his eyes open. 'Fuck,' he cursed his own memories. 'Leave me alone,' he found himself pleading. 'Leave me alone.'

He checked his watch and winced at the time. His mobile would soon be ringing with people wondering where the hell he was. He needed to get straight and he needed to do it quickly, but he couldn't eat and coffee alone only inten-sified the tremors in his hands. His eyes wandered to the kitchen cupboard where the spirits were kept – a cupboard that until recently had rarely been disturbed other than at Christmas. He told himself it was self-medication, safer than antidepressants, but in his heart he knew what he was becoming. He opened the cupboard looking for the vodka – much harder to smell on the breath than scotch. A shot or two of the clear, oily liquid and he'd be good for a few hours. Even with a few drinks on board, he could do his job better than most. Mouthwash and mints would disguise the truth well enough until he could find a reason to be out on enquiries and head off to a pub close to his home. But this wasn't going to be another routine day helping other teams and units with their enquiries; this was a new murder investigation, so the pressure would be on and people would expect him to be visible and vocal – the old Dave Donnelly.

'Shit,' he cursed and reached for the vodka, his fingers connecting with the glass of the bottle then recoiling – the magnitude of what it meant cutting through his clouded mind. The last time he'd taken a drink first thing in the morning had been a stag do over twenty years ago. This was different. This would mean losing himself – possibly forever. 'No,' he told the room, and shut the cupboard door. 'No.'

Sean walked along the sterile corridor that led to the morgue at Guy's Hospital. It wasn't an easy place to find, hidden away from the main hospital complex, out of sight from the public and staff alike – neither of whom wanted to be reminded of the grimmest possible outcome for a loved one or a patient. But he knew the route well, having walked it many times in the past. He paused for a few seconds outside the large rubber doors at the entrance, took a deep breath, then entered.

Inside the morgue, six sparkling metal trollies were lined

up in two banks of three. Two had bodies on them, hidden under clean, pressed, green hospital sheets, whereas the others were empty. Only two sudden deaths today for Dr Canning to explain. People who died of obvious natural causes, the old or terminally ill, were not deemed suitable for his special attention. Sean saw Canning hunched over the naked body of a young white male, his face close to the dead man's skin. Satisfied, he straightened up and began to scribble notes on the pad held in his hand.

Sean recognized the corpse, though as ever it looked different from the crime scene photographs – less garish and vivid, and somehow less real. Like a yellowish, rubber imitation of a real, living person.

'I see you've met William Dalton?' he asked loudly enough to distract Canning from his examination.

'Indeed,' Canning answered, glancing up from his notes. 'I heard this one was yours.'

'Yes, it was passed to SIU because of the probable link to another murder.'

'Tanya Richards,' Canning confirmed. 'I've read the file, but haven't seen the body. She hasn't been buried yet, so I should be able to take a look before she heads off to a better place. In the meantime, you certainly have an interesting one here. A rather unfortunate end for a rather unfortunate young man.'

'Yes,' Sean agreed. 'Yes, it was.'

They both remained silent for a few seconds, paying their last respects to the victim. Then all emotions were set aside in order to find the evidence that would catch and convict his killer.

'What have we got so far?' Sean asked.

'What we have so far is unusual and rare. Most of the dead I've seen with their throats cut were victims of organized crime. South American drug gangs are particularly fond of cutting throats, but it's rare in this country. I can't remember ever seeing it in a domestic murder scenario or anything of that nature.'

'It's too cold for that,' Sean told him. 'Domestic murders are hate-driven or anger-driven, which means uncontrolled stabbing, or strangulation, but slitting a throat is cold and precise. Not an act of anger. Not rage, or at least not as we know it. But it's not gang stuff either. Something else.'

'Interesting,' Canning said. 'And the removal of the teeth – also something I've only ever seen in gang-related deaths. West African, usually. Bit of a habit from the old country they brought over here with them: if someone's double-crossed you or stolen from you, punish them by taking their teeth – and use the gold ones to settle the debt.'

'Nice,' Sean winced.

'But I fear that's not what we have here,' Canning said.

'No. I doubt William Dalton had any gold teeth.'

'I'm sure you'll check with his dentist anyway?' Canning grinned.

'Naturally,' Sean admitted, allowing himself the briefest of smiles. 'And the removal of fingernails,' he brought things back to the grim reality in front of them. 'First time I've seen that.'

'Same here,' Canning told him, tilting his head to study the dead man's hands. 'Judging by the fraying of the soft tissue that attaches the nail to the finger, it's clear the nails were pulled off as opposed to being cut away. Most likely used a pair of pliers – no doubt the same pair he used to extract some of the teeth, although there are also clear signs of a bladed instrument being used to cut away sections of the gums to make extraction easier.' Canning moved to the victim's head and opened the mouth to better show Sean the internal wounds. 'Do you see?'

Sean moved in closer, unclipping the small torch from his belt and shining the beam of light into the unholy sight that was now William Dalton's mouth. Deep cuts to swollen gums and gaping holes marked the places where he'd once had teeth. 'I see,' he said, and clicked off the torch.

'Clearly, your killer isn't the squeamish type.'

'Psychopaths rarely are,' Sean reminded him.

'I suppose not. You think he might have some link to dentistry? Even for a psychopath, the removal of healthy teeth isn't easy to accomplish – either physically or mentally.'

'I don't think so,' Sean answered. 'Perhaps if he'd only taken the teeth I'd consider it more likely, but with him taking the fingernails as well . . .'

'But you'll check anyway,' Canning said, with another grin.

Sean nodded and gave him a faint, sad smile.

'Your initial thoughts then, Inspector?' Canning asked. 'If he has no special *affinity* for teeth, or nails for that matter, why did your killer go to such lengths to take them?'

'Souvenirs,' Sean told him.

'But surely there must have been easier souvenirs to take? The victim's personal belongings, for example.'

'Not intimate enough for this one,' Sean explained. 'He needs the ultimate reminder of his victims – parts of their body. At the same time, he wants something he can keep forever. So he took their teeth and nails.'

'I see,' Canning nodded, keen for Sean to continue with his insights.

'At the same time, he's showing us his strength,' Sean added. 'Showing us what he's prepared to do to achieve what he wants. Where he's prepared to go. A challenge, if you like.'

'A challenge to you?'

'I don't know. Maybe. Or maybe to someone else.'

'Someone else?' Canning pressed, intrigued.

'The lack of defensive marks interests me,' Sean said, keen to move on. 'Neither victim had a single mark.'

'In each case a blow was administered to the back of the head,' Canning explained. 'Not with sufficient force to kill them, but enough to render them unconscious or to incapacitate them while the killer inflicted the fatal wounds.' Sean shook his head and frowned. 'Something bothering you, Inspector?'

'I don't know,' he replied. 'That just doesn't feel right.'

'What exactly?' Canning asked.

'This one wouldn't want them unconscious,' he explained. 'He'd have wanted them to know what was happening, to know that he was going to kill them. He would have wanted to look into their eyes and see the terror. Ideally, he would have wanted them to be alive when he took their teeth and nails. He wanted them to feel his power.'

Canning cleared his throat. 'Have you considered that he might have inflicted the fatal wounds just as they were coming to?'

'It's a possibility,' he answered, sounding unconvinced. 'But why the first wound to the throat? It wasn't necessarily fatal. Why take the trouble to cut through the front of the throat and then follow up by cutting through the side of the neck and the carotid artery? Why not administer the fatal wound straight away?'

'Maybe it was the other way around,' Canning suggested. 'Maybe he killed them quickly with the severing of the carotid artery and then slit the throat.'

'But in that case, why slit the throat at all?' Sean asked himself more than Canning.

'He derived pleasure from mutilation?' Canning offered.

'No,' Sean dismissed it. 'The mutilation to the fingers and mouth was coincidental, a side effect of removing his trophies. Mutilation after death's not what this one is about.'

'Certainly it would have been difficult for either victim to have screamed or cried for help once the trachea had been dissected. Maybe he wanted their silence.'

Canning's words set Sean's mind on fire as he cursed himself for not having seen it himself – the victims trying to scream, to call for help, but only able to make sickening gurgling sounds as the air from their lungs mixed with the blood from their wounds.

'That's why no defence wounds,' he announced. 'He cut their throats so he could watch them struggling in fear for as long as he dared until it was necessary to kill them. They had no chance to recover from the shock and horror of what was happening to them and fight back.'

'Fight-or-flight instinct,' Canning nodded. 'Even the gravely wounded can inflict significant damage once the body's flooded with survival endorphins. But surely that contradicts rather than explains the lack of defence wounds?'

'Their hands' – Sean turned to him, seeing it clearly in his mind now. 'Their hands would have been clawing at their own throats. They were too busy trying to stop the flow of blood to fight back. He wanted to watch them. Watch them in silence.'

'And before the fight instinct took over,' Canning went on, 'he cut the carotid artery, giving them only seconds to live.'

'He watched the life drain out of them,' Sean continued, 'and then he went to work on their teeth and nails.'

'Interesting,' Canning admitted. 'But you realize it's all guesswork – I'll never be able to say for sure which wound was inflicted first.'

'No,' Sean accepted. 'The crime scene should help though: blood-spray patterns, footprints in the blood, anything else we can find.'

'Build up a picture, eh?'

'Try to, at least,' Sean told him. 'If you just give a jury a long list of evidence, you'll lose them.'

'Not sure that would be the case here,' Canning argued. 'The viciousness of these attacks would keep most juries interested, not to mention his distinctive modus operandi.'

'I suppose,' Sean reluctantly agreed.

There was a moment's silence, then Canning spoke again. 'Does it worry you?'

'Does what worry me?'

'That he wants to leave you in no doubt that the crimes are his.'

'It does,' Sean admitted. 'It tells me he wants the world to take notice of him and that'll he'll never stop until it does.'

'Why does he want the world to take notice of him?'

'Don't we all?' Sean answered with a question. 'But that's too general – not specific enough to him. I don't think killing is the thing that drives him. I think it's a means to an end. The way he can achieve whatever it is he's trying to achieve.'

'Are you sure?' Canning asked doubtfully.

'No,' Sean shook his head. 'Not really.'

'Well, one thing we can be sure about,' Canning told him, 'is the type of victim he seems drawn to. Young and vulnerable.'

'Victims of society become the victims of killers,' Sean explained.

'Indeed,' Canning agreed sadly.

'And there'll be more of them,' Sean warned. 'Unless I can find him and find him quickly.'

'Then you'd better get on.' Canning turned to his tray of torturous instruments and removed a lethally sharpened scalpel. 'And so had I.'

# 5

Back at his desk, Sean carefully read through statements from Dalton's friends and associates – those who'd seen him on the day he died and those who had not – hoping to find some piece of information that could put him on the tail of the killer. He was confidant that he had formed an accurate sense of the killer's mind, but that wasn't going to give him a name and address. His instincts alone were never enough. He needed solid physical evidence too.

There was a single loud knock on his open door and he looked up to see Addis standing in the doorway, a folded copy of a newspaper under his arm. Immediately recognizing this as a bad sign, he sat bolt upright. 'Sir.'

Addis entered and placed the newspaper on Sean's desk, opening it at the centre pages and smoothing it out. He took a seat and waited in silence while Sean took in the double-page spread beneath the headline *Broadmoor: The Mind Map of Murder*. A large photograph of Sebastian Gibran, taken shortly after his committal, dominated the pages along with smaller photographs of other infamous Broadmoor residents. A small picture of a grim-faced Geoff Jackson appeared next to his byline. He sighed deeply inside. Jackson, he thought to himself, what the hell are you up to now?

Addis heaved a sigh. 'I suppose we should be thankful he didn't mention you by name. Neither I nor the Commissioner approve of having the names of Metropolitan Police officers spread across the pages of national newspapers.'

'Why would they mention me?'

'You caught him, didn't you?'

'In a way,' Sean agreed, 'although he was more handed to me than caught.'

'Don't underestimate the part you played,' Addis told him. 'Which is why the likes of Jackson have an unhealthy interest in you. He may yet try to drag your name into this – according to the final paragraph, this is merely the first of a series.'

'Gibran wouldn't be too happy if he dropped my name in.'

'Why not?' Addis asked.

'He feels the way I caught him was somehow unfair, that I wasn't worthy of catching him.'

'The strange mind of Sebastian Gibran,' Addis said, shaking his head. 'Well, catch him you did. And now he's giving interviews to *The World* from bloody Broadmoor.'

'How the hell did Jackson get access?' Sean asked. 'Gibran's always refused to cooperate with journalists.'

'Through his lawyers, I'm told.' Addis saw the look of suspicion on Sean's face. 'I have a lot of contacts,' he explained. 'Not much I can't find out with a couple of phone calls. Anyway, he agreed to meet Jackson. Some nonsense about how he *respected* him for having the balls to meet with that murdering bastard Jeremy Goldsboro while he was still at large.'

'Well,' Sean acknowledged, 'that did take some balls.'

'Maybe,' Addis waved a dismissive hand, 'but whatever the reason, Jackson has access to him now and there will be further interviews to follow.'

Sean shrugged. 'So long as he's not interfering in anything current, why should we care if Jackson wants to spend his time shuttling backwards and forwards to Broadmoor? Might actually be doing us a favour – keep him out the way of our new investigation.'

'And if Gibran starts talking about his own case?' Addis asked. 'Starts making accusations of wrongdoing by the investigation team? Apparently, he continues to maintain that crucial evidence was planted at his home address by the police. What if Jackson splashes that all over his rag?'

Sean's face remained deadpan. 'Is he, though – talking about his own case?'

'No,' Addis conceded. 'Not yet.'

'And he won't,' Sean insisted. 'He can't. As soon as he starts arguing lucidly about his own case, we can push to have him declared sane and tried for murder and attempted murder. He's too smart for that.'

'I hope you're right,' Addis told him. 'But once Jackson finds out about these new killings he's unlikely to leave it to some junior reporter. He'll be all over it. If only the MIT South hadn't let it be known that Dalton's death was linked to another murder.'

'The media would have found out soon enough. We need them onside for press conferences and appeals,' Sean reminded him. 'So long as we can keep Jackson at arm's length, there won't be a problem.'

'I suppose so,' Addis admitted, buoyed by the chance to increase his own public profile. 'And what about the current investigation?' he asked, changing tack. 'Any significant breakthroughs? If he kills again, people will start to get concerned. Especially if he moves away from prostitutes and the homeless to someone who actually . . .'

'Who actually *matters*?' Sean finished for him.

'You know what I mean,' Addis frowned.

'It's early days,' Sean moved on. 'The MIT in charge of the first investigation had no idea what they were dealing with so went off in the wrong direction – chasing down pimps, dealers, loan sharks.'

'What are we dealing with?' Addis asked, his eyes narrowing.

'Someone who's as organized as he is vicious. Someone who's probably been waiting for this moment for a long time, and now that it's here it's as good as he imagined it was going to be and he won't stop. The first two killings were ten days apart and there's no reason to think we have any more than eight days until he feels the need again. We may get lucky, but I doubt it. Other than that, it's all in my report.'

'I've read your report,' Addis told him, 'and I'm aware of the killer's viciousness and timescale, but what I want to know is: what do you think?'

'I'm not sure I understand,' Sean lied.

'I'm sure you do,' Addis insisted. 'After all, it's the very reason you're here, isn't it? Your instinct. Your imagination. Tell me: why do you think he's doing this?'

'His motivation?' Sean was reluctant to give away too much. In time, Addis would learn everything he believed he knew about the killer, but he was conscious of the need to drip-feed the information. If Addis knew how quickly he could read a killer, fathom out his reasoning and desires, it would put him and his team under pressure to wrap up cases in no time at all. He needed Addis to believe it was a slow, step by step process; that it took time to evaluate and justify his observations and profile the killer.

'Not just his motivation,' Addis made himself clear. 'His *reason* for killing.'

'It's too early to go beyond saying he's vicious, organized and careful – and that's he's most likely on a constrained time cycle.' He waited for Addis to react, but those lifeless blue eyes merely stared back at him like the sky shining through an empty skull. 'It's too early for me to say more.'

'I see.' Addis decided to let it go – for now. 'Then perhaps Anna can help you. I have a lot of faith in her.'

The mention of her name made Sean's whole body tense. 'She's better than most,' he managed to say.

'She seemed to help you in the last investigation,' Addis reminded him.

'I bounced some ideas off her,' he replied, considering the unpleasant idea that Addis knew he'd turned her around and that now, instead of reporting to Addis about him, she'd be reporting to him about Addis. Maybe Addis was now playing them both. 'But she didn't solve anything,' he said, maintaining his mirage of indifference to her. 'Psychiatrists, criminologists, psychologists – they don't solve crimes. Never have done. Never will. Detectives solve crimes.'

'That's as maybe,' Addis told him, barely disguising his irritation that Sean had said detectives instead of police, 'but it is my wish that she assists you, so assist you she will.'

'Fine,' he shrugged.

His business concluded, Addis got to his feet. 'Well, if your theory is correct, you don't have long till he kills again – so I'll leave you to get on. Any media work or appeals you need doing, let me know. I'm aware you have an aversion to handling that side of things yourself. But get this solved quickly, Sean,' he warned. 'We don't want another Sebastian Gibran on our hands.' He spun on his polished heels and was gone.

'We'll never have another Sebastian Gibran,' Sean said under his breath. From the corner of his eye he saw Donnelly enter the main office looking dishevelled in his cheap suit and coat, tie hanging loose around his neck and unkempt moustache bushier than ever. He'd looked like that ever since Sean first met him, but what gave him cause for concern was the missing spring in Donnelly's step. Despite his size, he always used to move like a much lighter, fitter, younger man, but now it was as if he carried the weight of the world on his back.

Sean moved to the doorway and stood staring into the main office, waiting to catch Donnelly's eye as he headed slowly towards his own office. Eventually, he was so close he couldn't avoid Sean's gaze any more and was summoned into his office by a jut of his chin. Sean returned to his chair and waited for Donnelly to reach the entrance to his office.

'You want me for something?' Donnelly asked without entering. He sounded irritable and annoyed.

'I want to know where the hell you've been,' Sean told him. 'This is no time for you to be going AWOL.'

'I wasn't. I went straight from home to check on the door-to-door. I get off the train at London Bridge anyway.'

Sean didn't believe a word of it and knew that a quick phone call could prove Donnelly wrong, but he could see no value in stirring up conflict or embarrassment when he could least afford the team to be fractured in any way. 'Fine,' he played along, 'but the door-to-door teams will be OK without you from now on. Paulo can keep an eye on them. I need you for other things.'

'Like what?' Donnelly asked grumpily.

'When I know, you'll know,' Sean told him. He would have said more, but the desk phone began to ring and Donnelly took the opportunity to slip away while he grabbed the handset from its base. 'DI Corrigan.'

'Detective Inspector Corrigan,' Geoff Jackson replied with barely disguised glee. 'Still on the same number, I see. Haven't they given you a shiny new office away from the Yard?'

It had been a long time, but Sean recognized his voice immediately. 'Jackson. What do you want?'

'There are a couple of things I think you can help me with,' Jackson answered in a friendly tone, despite the fact he knew Sean despised him. 'Why don't we start with these murders I hear you're investigating. Sounds interesting. Very interesting.'

'You know nothing about what I'm investigating,' Sean insisted.

'I know they're linked,' Jackson replied.

'So what?' Sean argued. 'We're making no secret of that. You know nothing other than what you've been told by us.'

'I know he pulled their teeth out,' Jackson persevered, 'but something tells me this isn't some drug turf war. We're talking about a serial killer who takes his victims' teeth. Sounds like something the public have a right to know about.'

'I'll decide what's in the public's interest for them to know,' Sean told him. 'Not you.'

'Come on,' Jackson encouraged. 'Give me something the other hacks don't know. Something exclusive. I promise to show you and the SIU in a good light.'

'You seriously think I'd trust you?' Sean asked, his voice full of disbelief. 'Go to hell, Jackson.'

'Well then maybe you can help me with something else?' he quickly said before Sean could hang up.

He took the bait. 'Like what?'

'I take it you've seen today's edition of *The World*?'

Sean looked down at the newspaper Addis had left on his desk, still open at the centre pages. 'No,' he lied. 'Why would I want to read that garbage?'

'To take a look at the centre-page spread,' Jackson told him, 'my interview with Sebastian Gibran. Thought you of all people would be interested in seeing what he has to say.'

'Gibran's got nothing to say that could interest me,' Sean answered. 'Unless he wants to confess to any other murders. He's locked up in Broadmoor, bored out of his brains, looking for cheap thrills – and that's what you are to him: a cheap thrill.'

'I don't think so. If you read the story, you'd see for yourself.'

'Listen,' Sean warned him, 'you don't know what you're dealing with. Gibran's dangerous. More dangerous than you can imagine.'

'Why, Inspector,' Jackson mimicked sentimentality, 'I didn't know you cared.'

'I don't,' Sean told him, although it wasn't entirely true. He disliked Jackson and knew he was potentially dangerous to any investigation, but he admired his guts and tenacity. If Jackson was a detective, Sean would want him on his team. 'But if he pulls a razor blade out of his arsehole during one of your little chats and cuts your throat, I'll be the one clearing up your mess. Literally.'

'I'm no fool, Corrigan,' Jackson replied. 'If he tries anything, I'll see it coming before he has the chance.'

'Now you're lying to yourself,' Sean said calmly, 'as well as to me.' There was a longer silence between them than Sean could ever remember. It was enough to let him know that, underneath all the bravado, and despite the bravery he'd shown in the past, Jackson was genuinely scared of Gibran.

'I thought maybe you'd want to get involved,' Jackson told him, recovering his composure. 'Seeing as you're "the cop who caught the killer". Help foster better relations between the Met and the media. Would be a great fucking story.'

'Take care, Jackson,' Sean replied and hung up. He stared at the phone for a moment then headed to Donnelly's small office next door.

'Grab your coat,' he told him.

'We going somewhere?' Donnelly asked, looking like a man who had no wish to go anywhere.

'North London MIT,' Sean explained. 'We need to speak to them about Tanya Richards.'

Sally walked along Oxford Street with DC Fiona Cahill at her side. At twenty-seven, Cahill was ten years Sally's junior and happy to follow her lead and learn from her experience. She even copied the way Sally dressed, although she was much taller and naturally more elegant, with her hazel hair cut short. Each woman carried a photograph of the smiling William Dalton in her coat pocket, but so far they'd had little luck in finding anyone who wanted to talk about the dead man. They'd spoken to more than a dozen homeless people, almost all of whom had openly told them they knew the victim, but no one could help them with his movements or suggest who would want to hurt him. Sally sensed their suspicion of the police, despite the fact they were trying to find a homeless man's murderer. Many of the West End's visible forgotten lived in anonymity and wanted to keep it that way.

As they crossed the junction with Bird Street, Sally saw a catering van parked up. From the open side-hatch a white woman in her mid-forties, not much taller than herself, stood dispensing hot drinks and sandwiches to a small gathering of the homeless, most of them men. Clouds of steam swirled from their boiling cups and disappeared into the freezing London sky. When they saw Sally and Cahill pulling out their warrant cards, the entire group immediately turned their backs and took a few steps away.

'DS Sally Jones,' she told the woman at the serving hatch. 'And my colleague, DC Cahill. Special Investigations Unit, Metropolitan Police.'

'I may not have known who you were,' the woman smiled, 'but I could tell what you are and why you're here.'

'Oh?' Sally asked.

'Word spreads fast,' she explained. 'Faster than you can walk anyway.'

'And you are?' Sally asked.

'Izzy. Izzy Birkby, from the charity Reach Out. We do what we can to help – hot drinks and sandwiches, sometimes just someone who'll listen. We don't lecture them or try to get them to rejoin society. There are enough people doing that. We don't judge. I assume you're here about poor Will.'

'Yes,' Sally replied. She held up the picture. 'Is this the man you know as Will?'

'Man?' Birkby raised an eyebrow. 'More of a boy, don't

you think?' Sally said nothing, but carried on holding the photograph out for the woman to look at. 'Yeah. That's him,' she confirmed, 'although he didn't look like that when he was living on the street. You'd be surprised how quickly being homeless changes the way a person looks.'

Sally had been in the job long enough not to be surprised, but she let it go without comment. 'How well did you know him?'

'Pretty well,' Birkby explained. 'For a few months, at least. We always try to look after the young ones – especially the drug users. Once they get high, they forget to eat and then they don't last very long out here.'

'You knew he was taking drugs?' Cahill asked.

'Of course,' Birkby admitted, surprised by the question. 'A lot of our customers are drug users.'

'Did you try to get him to stop?' Cahill asked. 'Or tell someone who could have helped him?'

'Like I said,' Birkby reminded her, 'we don't judge. If we start putting pressure on them they'll shy away and we won't be able to help them at all. We can't allow ourselves to get too attached to them either. A lot of young people don't make it out of here. We can't afford to fall apart every time one doesn't.'

'Soup and sandwiches, right?' Sally nodded.

'Right,' Birkby answered. 'Soup and sandwiches.'

'What can you tell us about him?' Sally asked. 'Anything at all could be useful.' Birkby looked nervously at the homeless huddle. 'You don't have to be afraid of betraying anyone's trust,' Sally told her. 'William's dead now. All we want is to find whoever killed him.'

Birkby took a deep breath and nodded, as if she'd come to a decision. 'He appeared on the street a few months ago,' she began. 'Was a bit of a loner at first, but soon realized it made him vulnerable, so began to team up with others to go begging. He seemed a nice kid, you know, but the drugs had got a good hold on him. Crack, I think. He got kicked out of a couple of night hostels for using drugs, so decided he'd rather sleep rough and be left to his vices than be told what to do.'

'But he didn't sleep rough in the West End,' Sally reminded her.

'No,' she acknowledged. 'Some of the weaker ones make easy targets for muggings or cops looking for easy drugs arrests.'

'And he was one of the weaker ones?' Cahill asked.

Birkby shrugged.

'Looks like someone found out where he was staying,' Sally said. 'Did he tell people where he was living?'

'No,' she replied. 'He told me south of the river, but didn't say anything more specific.'

'What about anyone from the homeless community?' Sally asked, looking over at the dishevelled figures eating and drinking. 'Could someone have known?'

'Maybe.' Birkby called across to two of the younger men in the group. 'Tom. Archie.' They both looked in her direction. 'These guys knew William. Maybe they can help.' The two young men, wearing layer upon of layer of clothes to defend against the bitter cold, shuffled forward. Little could be seen of their faces aside from their eyes, peering through small gaps in the mixture of hats and scarfs they wore.

'What's up?' Archie asked, shuffling from one foot to the other to keep warm.

'These are detectives,' Birkby explained. 'Trying to find out why someone attacked William. You guys knew him pretty well, right?'

'I guess,' Archie shrugged.

'William didn't sleep in the West End,' Sally took over. 'Do you know where he went?'

'Nah.' Archie shook his head. 'Said he had a garage over by London Bridge. He never said where.'

'And you?' Sally asked Tom. 'Did he tell you where?'

'No, man,' Tom mumbled, looking anywhere other than at the detectives. 'Never showed anybody. Never told anybody.'

'People're saying he must have been followed,' Archie said, fidgeting where he stood, the fear sharp and real in his eyes.

'Nobody knows that,' Sally told him.

'Yeah, well, people are scared,' Archie continued. 'People are saying he killed a woman in the same way. A prostitute or something. Took her teeth just like he did with Will. People are saying he's evil – that he's hunting people like us, like we're some kind of animals – that the teeth are his trophies. Some people are saying he's not even a man – that he's something else – something no one can stop. Not even the police.'

'All right,' Birkby interrupted. 'That sort of talk's only going to make people more afraid.'

'People couldn't be more afraid,' Archie told her. 'We don't have safe places to go. We don't have doors we can lock. We're easy prey, man. Easy prey.'

'I understand your fears,' Sally explained, 'but there's no evil out there – just a man. A man who pretty soon we'll catch. Until then, everybody needs to be extra vigilant and look out for each other. Keep your eyes open for any strangers who don't fit in, anyone acting suspiciously and make sure you report it.'

'Have there been?' Cahill asked. 'Have there been any strangers hanging around?'

'There are always strangers in the West End,' Archie told her.

'Any that concerned you?' Cahill pressed. The two men merely shrugged and looked at the ground.

'Anyone you can think of who we should be speaking to?' Sally asked. 'Someone who knew William better than most.'

'Yeah, sure,' Archie answered without hesitation. 'You

should speak with Jonnie. He and Will did stuff together, you know.'

'You got a surname?' Cahill asked.

'Dunno,' Archie answered, scratching his head through the multiple layers. 'Everyone just calls him Jonnie.'

'Freyland,' Tom suddenly blurted out. 'His surname is Freyland, but I ain't seen him around for a couple of days. Not since that shit happened to Will.'

'Is that unusual?' Sally asked.

Tom shrugged and looked into the sky. 'I guess.'

Sally and Cahill exchanged knowing glances. 'Then I think we'd better find him,' Sally said, pulling several business cards from her coat pocket and handing them out to her audience of three – giving extra cards to Archie. 'Spread those around for me,' she told him. 'If anyone thinks they know something or knows where we can find Jonnie, get them to call me. Understand?'

'OK,' Archie answered unenthusiastically.

'I'm trying to do the right thing for Will,' she explained, finally making eye contact with him. 'I only hope you are too.'


Sean and Donnelly arrived at what used to be the old Metropolitan Police Cadet school. The place had long since been taken over by various support services and police units, including the Murder Investigation Teams for North London. They drove on to the parade ground that was only ever used now for passing out ceremonies for recruits who'd successfully made it through the famous Training School in Hendon and parked. Both men had strong memories of marching around the hallowed ground, watched by proud friends and family.

'Fucking hate this place,' Donnelly moaned. 'Reminds me of training school.'

'Didn't like it here?' Sean asked.

'You joking?' Donnelly sneered. 'All that polishing shoes,

103

starched shirts and short hair. All that yes, sir, no, sir bullshit. Fucking couldn't wait to get out.'

'I kind of liked it,' Sean told him. 'Didn't at first – found the discipline and petty rules tough, but I got over it. Enjoyed it in the end.'

'How the hell did you manage that?'

'I embraced it,' Sean answered. 'Made sure my shoes were the shiniest, my uniform the best pressed. Got fitter and faster than anyone else. Stopped fighting the system. I took a break from all the shit of the world outside and focused on doing the little things well.'

'All the shit of the world?' Donnelly mocked him. 'You must have had a fucking shit childhood if Hendon was an escape.'

Donnelly had no idea how close to the bone his remark was. Sean felt himself tense at the mere mention of his childhood, ugly memories of his abusive father invading his mind like a marauding horde, all those hours he'd endured, locked in his father's bedroom while his mother pretended not to know what was happening. Quickly he fought to rebuild the walls that kept the darkness and demons at bay and allowed him to live almost like any other person. He swallowed the anger he felt towards Donnelly for having mentioned his childhood, albeit without knowing what it meant to him. 'It's a state of mind, that's all,' he answered. 'Like most things.'

'Not sure about that,' Donnelly replied and heaved himself out of the car. Sean gave himself a few seconds to let the last remnants of his childhood memories fade away before following suit. They headed across the parade ground towards the low-rise building where the North London MITs had their offices. Once inside, they searched the corridors until they found the team they were looking for.

Sean stopped the first person he came across: 'I'm looking for DCI Morris.'

The young male detective glanced at Sean's warrant card, which now hung flapped over his jacket's breast pocket. 'She's in her office,' he answered, pointing to an area partitioned off with Perspex, much like the office Sean occupied at the Yard. 'I think she's in.'

Sean thanked him and headed across the main office.

'Look at the size of this place,' Donnelly complained jealously. 'If we can get out the Yard, maybe we can get a decent-sized office too.'

'You want to travel from Swanley to Hendon every day?' Sean asked.

'No, but there must be a police building somewhere south of the river we can use.'

'You want to go back to Peckham?'

'I was thinking Bromley,' Donnelly answered as they reached the open door to the office.

Sean took a look inside and saw a woman in her early forties sitting at her desk. He knocked on the frame.

'Yes?' she said, eyeing them with a degree of suspicion.

'DCI Morris?' Sean asked.

'Yes,' she repeated herself and brushed her short, almost black hair from the side of her attractive, but stern-looking face. He guessed she was on accelerated promotion – just passing through on her way to better and bigger things. At least she'd have added heading up a Murder Investigation Team to her CV.

'DI Sean Corrigan,' he told her. 'SIU.' He let Donnelly speak for himself.

'DS Dave Donnelly – from the same.'

'I know who you are,' she replied, looking directly at Sean to let him know she was addressing him and only him. 'I've seen your face in the newspapers – after you caught the Jackdaw.'

'We didn't catch him,' Donnelly jumped in. 'I killed him.'

'Yes,' she stuttered slightly. 'I remember.'

'That was quite a while ago,' Sean told her, keen to move on. 'I haven't been in any newspapers since then.'

'I have a good memory for faces,' she explained. 'I take it you're here about the Tanya Richards murder,' she got down to business. 'In which case you'd better come in and take a seat.' They accepted her invitation and sat in the chairs on the opposite side of her desk while she leaned back and watched their every move until they were settled. 'I'm not happy about losing the investigation,' she told them frankly. 'It was an interesting job – a bit different from the normal rubbish. It had potential.'

Potential, Sean thought. She meant potential to get her noticed. 'As soon as it became apparent it was linked to another murder it became a matter for the SIU. A murder series would stretch a local MIT too much,' he told her. 'Believe me – I know. These things are best investigated by a central unit.'

'We could have handled it,' she argued. 'We were making progress.'

'You were concentrating your efforts on finding her pimp,' Sean reminded her.

'He's not been seen since the day she was killed. A prostitute is tortured and killed and her pimp disappears – I'd say that's good reason to concentrate on him as the prime suspect.'

'Understandable,' Sean agreed, knowing diplomacy not conflict was the best way to get what he wanted, 'and he still needs to be spoken to.'

'If you can find him,' she said. 'Mehmet has a history of going underground when he knows we're looking for him – and that's a pretty regular occurrence.'

'Much form then?' Sean asked.

'A lifetime of it,' Morris told him. 'Everything from rape and attempted murder to false imprisonment and blackmail. I wouldn't be too quick to dismiss him as a suspect.'

'He'll be spoken to,' Sean assured her, although instinctively he knew Mehmet wasn't his man. 'Tell me about the scene.'

'Haven't you seen the report?'

'I've seen it,' he answered, 'but I want to hear what it was like from somebody who was actually there. You did go to the scene, didn't you?'

'Of course,' Morris assured him.

'And the body was still in situ?

'Yes.'

'What did you see?'

'I saw a young woman who'd been horribly murdered. She'd had her throat cut almost to the bone and the side of her neck sliced open, causing her to bleed to death. Her fingernails and some of her teeth had been removed, and there were clear signs of sexual assault.'

'Such as?' Sean pressed.

'Her skirt had been pulled up and her underwear ripped off. Her legs were apart when she was found.'

'So,' Sean added, 'he killed her immediately after he raped her or she was already dead.'

'Surely he raped her while she was alive?' Morris said. 'Rape is a crime of power and humiliation. He'd want her alive when he did it or what would be the point?'

'You're assuming the attack was sexually motivated,' Sean told her.

'It has all the hallmarks,' she replied, waiting for him to agree. 'You don't think it was?'

'Maybe not,' he admitted.

'Then what?'

'I don't know,' he told her. He could see no point in sharing his true thoughts with someone who was no longer to be involved in the investigation. 'Not yet.' He quickly moved on. 'And he made no attempt to cover her?'

'No,' Morris confirmed.

'Then he felt no compassion for her,' he explained. 'No

guilt or mercy. If he had, he'd have repositioned the body and at least pulled her skirt down.'

'Or he panicked and ran,' Morris suggested. 'Maybe he was disturbed.'

'This one doesn't panic,' Sean said before he could stop himself. He kept talking to prevent her from coming back at him with any questions. 'The scene report said she had her mobile phone and some cash on her?'

'Yes,' Morris confirmed, spreading her hands apart to show her confusion. 'So?'

'Just going back to your pimp theory,' he explained. 'Did it not seem strange to you that he'd leave her phone and cash behind? It would have been second nature to him to have stripped her of anything of value.'

'Whether she was killed by her pimp or some sexually motivated madman, it's possible they were disturbed, panicked and ran,' she argued. 'But of course you don't believe that could have happened.'

Registering her irritation, Sean reminded himself that he needed her absolute cooperation and that wouldn't be forthcoming unless he could get her onside. 'You could well be right,' he said. 'I'm just considering all the possibilities at this stage.' He moved on swiftly: 'I understand she also had a wound to the back of her head.'

'Significant, but not fatal. It would have almost certainly knocked her unconscious, or close to. There were traces of blood at the entrance to the alley where she was killed. It looks like he waited for her to get level with the alley, then hit her in the back of the head with a blunt instrument. The blood on the ground would indicate she fell to the floor. He then bundled her deeper into the alley where he continued his attack behind a large wheelie bin used for commercial rubbish from the restaurants that back on to the alley, hidden from view of anyone passing along the street.'

'Could she have been dragged, maybe by the feet, deeper into the alley?' Sean asked.

'It's possible,' Morris agreed, 'but the ground was rough, so we didn't get any clear smear marks – just more traces of hair and blood. Inconclusive.'

It was enough for Sean to be convinced she'd been dragged feet-first into the alley, but he kept his conclusions to himself. 'And no witnesses?'

'No,' Morris confirmed. 'Nothing.'

'Friends and family?' he continued.

'Her family have disowned her,' Morris explained. 'Wouldn't even identify the body for us. We had to get one of her prostitute friends to do it instead.'

'Have any of her friends been able to help?' Sean persevered. 'Any of her working girl pals given you anything useful – a regular punter who was giving her trouble or obsessing over her? Anyone have a grudge against her?'

'Not that they're saying,' Morris answered.

'Did she owe anyone money?' Sean continued for the sake of appearances. He was sure that she'd been killed purely to satisfy a need to kill. 'Fallen foul of any dealers?'

'No.' Morris leaned further back in her chair and began fidgeting with a pencil. 'Nothing.'

'This Mehmet character,' Donnelly joined in, 'the one you've yet to speak to – have any of the other girls said she may have fallen foul of him?'

'They're too scared of him to say anything,' Morris told him. 'If we can find him and lock him up for a while, maybe it'll loosen their tongues.'

'If you can find him?' Donnelly asked unhelpfully.

'He's circulated as wanted,' Morris assured him, defensive.

'He's our problem now,' Donnelly reminded her, unnecessarily confrontational.

'So it would appear,' Morris replied, trying to keep her cool.

'And letting the press know about the removal of the victim's teeth,' Donnelly continued to push aggressively. 'That your idea?'

Morris hesitated. 'We . . . I thought it might help generate some sympathy for the victim – encourage people to come forward if they knew more about her ordeal.'

'Should have kept it quiet,' Donnelly told her unpleasantly. 'Now we'll have the gutter press all over it.'

'I know my business, Sergeant,' Morris bit back. 'We withheld the information about the fingernails, but felt we had to do something to stir people's consciences.'

'It was a mistake,' Donnelly rudely insisted.

Sean could see things were sinking towards an all-out trading of insults and stepped in. 'I think we're all getting off track,' he said, looking directly at Donnelly. He turned to Morris: 'I would have done the same about the teeth, and Mehmet's a worthwhile suspect. You can be sure we'll be speaking to him. Your team's done a good job.'

'You don't need to tell me that,' Morris answered. 'I know we did. I'm not some wet-behind-the-ears DC. I'm a DCI. Perhaps your *sergeant* should remember that.'

'We're under the usual time pressures,' Sean told her before Donnelly could make things worse. 'We're playing catch-up and don't always have the time to be as . . . polite as we'd like to be.'

'I've moved on,' Morris replied, trying to sound like it meant nothing. 'We've landed a domestic murder – some heroin addict killed his girlfriend and toddler while he was out of his head. So if you just tell me what you want . . .' She held her hands apart to let them know she was finished.

'Everything,' he answered. 'Forensic reports, statements, door-to-door questionnaires, CCTV footage, her Oyster card details, if she had one – everything. Get it all packed up and I'll have some of my team come over later and pick it up.'

'It'll take time,' she argued. 'I'll need at least until tomorrow.'

'Time is something I don't have,' he told her, getting to his feet. 'I need it by this afternoon.'

'Fine,' Morris reluctantly agreed.

'Thank you,' Sean replied and moved towards the door with Donnelly in close pursuit.

Once they reached the relative safety of the parade-ground-cum-car-park, Sean stopped and turned on Donnelly. 'Do you want to tell me what all that was about?' he demanded. 'She's a bloody DCI, for God's sake, and you're talking to her like she's a probationer.'

'Who cares?' Donnelly replied, as if it had been nothing. 'She's another bloody desk jockey on accelerated promotion. Probably never investigated anything in her life.'

'You don't know that,' Sean reminded him.

'Bollocks,' Donnelly argued. 'If she was a career detective we'd have heard of her. You were thinking the same.'

'Thinking it and making it fucking obvious are two different things,' Sean explained. 'I told you, we need them onside – not pissed off with us and dragging their heels about co-operating.'

'She won't hold anything back,' Donnelly assured him. 'She hasn't got the balls. The pen-pushers never do.'

'Just—' Sean began, but stopped himself. 'Don't do it again, OK. Why're you so pissed off all the time now, anyway?' he asked, although he was sure he knew the answer. He would have liked to hear it from Donnelly's own lips, though. Only then could it be dealt with.

'You really don't know why?' Donnelly asked, the muscles in his face tensing.

'No,' Sean answered untruthfully. 'So why don't you tell me?'

Donnelly seemed about to reply but then thought better of it. 'Forget it.'

'Tell me,' Sean pushed.

'I said, forget it,' Donnelly repeated and stamped off towards their car.

'Christ's sake,' Sean mumbled under his breath as he followed. Now wasn't the time, but sooner or later they'd have to deal with the infected wound that threatened not just their work, but their friendship.

David Langley waited at the gate of his children's school in Wandsworth, checking his watch and willing the end-of-day bell to sound out before his ex-wife arrived. He wasn't technically allowed to collect the children without her permission, but as far as he was concerned he was their father and if he wanted to see them, no one could stop him. If he was lucky, she'd be late and he could take them to his flat for a while. She'd be panicking, of course, but it would be her own fault for being late. The thought of her afraid made him feel genuinely happy.

After checking his watch for the umpteenth time, he allowed his eyes to wander over the gathering mums, many of whom stirred more primal feelings in him than simple happiness, but his enjoyment was cut short as he saw his ex-wife Emma cutting through the small crowd heading straight towards him – her expression a mixture of fear and anger. He straightened to his full height as she closed the distance between them.

'What the hell are you doing here?' she launched straight into him. 'You're not allowed to collect the kids without my permission.'

'I was only passing,' he lied. 'I saw you weren't here and thought I'd wait until you arrived.'

'Don't lie to me,' she warned him. 'All you ever do is lie.'

He felt the anger surge through him. How dare the bitch speak to him like that. 'Listen,' he told her, almost jabbing his finger into her chest. 'They're my kids and I'll see them

112

whenever I want. Not you or anybody else can tell me when I can and can't see them.'

'Oh yes I can,' she reminded him as their scene began to attract attention from the other parents. 'You seem to have forgotten the terms of our divorce. You see them every other weekend. You want to see them any other time, you need my permission. If I have to get a court order, I will.'

'What happened to you?' he asked. 'You used to love me. We used to be a family. When did you turn into such a bitch?'

'When I realized who you really are,' she answered. 'Or should I say when I found out *what* you really are.'

'This again,' he complained, rolling his eyes as if it was a trivial matter. 'It always comes back to this.'

'It wasn't just that,' she reminded him, 'but it was the final nail in our coffin.'

'You never used to complain,' he sneered at her. 'You liked it as much as I did.'

'I don't want to talk about it any more,' she told him, looking over her shoulder at the watching parents.

'Afraid people will find out about your *tastes*?' he asked as he stared into the watching faces.

She closed her eyes, took a calming breath. 'I grew up. I calmed down. We had children, but you . . . you were getting worse. You were scaring me, David.'

'Don't be ridiculous,' he dismissed her fears. 'It was only a bit of fun.'

'It wasn't fun any more,' she whispered. 'Things were getting out of hand. You were . . . you were becoming dangerous.'

'I knew what I was doing,' he assured her, smiling slightly. 'I would never have hurt you.'

'You did, though, David,' she told him. 'You were hurting me.'

He stood in front of her with his mouth open, as if waiting for the right words to come out, but none came.

'You need to go now, before the children see you. Before I tell my solicitor.'

He stared into her eyes, wondering if she could see the burning hatred in his own. He'd once thought she was the perfect woman for him. One who would not only indulge his tastes, but who actually enjoyed them. Someone he could have a family with. But he'd been wrong. Underneath, she was weak and timid like everyone else, too afraid to be all she could be – scared of playing with fire instead of excited by it.

'Fine,' he agreed loudly, storming past her, his shoulder hitting her hard enough to knock her into a half spin, drawing looks of disgust and disapproval from the other parents. He didn't care. As he marched through them his mind was on fire with things he'd like to do to his ex-wife. If only he could show her his new power, she'd know how extraordinary he was and how she'd been little more than a stepping stone on his journey to becoming more than most other men would dare dream of. But he knew that the power growing inside him would be too much for her; unleashed, it would surely kill her, as it had all those it had so far touched. Her life meant nothing to him now, but his children mattered – his son and daughter were his seed, one day they might carry on what he had begun. And for now they needed a mother – so her life would be spared.

Sally entered the canteen at New Scotland Yard, which by police canteen standards was not half bad. It was light, bright, clean and had a great view. The food was largely edible too. She ordered a filter coffee and stood scanning the other customers – an eclectic mix ranging from uniformed cops bristling with equipment and firearms to plain-clothes detectives trying to look like anything other than cops. She spotted Anna sitting alone at the far end of the canteen staring out of the window while a mug of what she assumed was herbal

114

tea cooled on the table in front of her. For a moment she considered taking her coffee back to her office and leaving Anna alone to her thoughts, but decided that after all Anna had done for her following Gibran's attack, the least she could do was make sure she was all right. She paid for her coffee and headed over to where Anna sat. 'A penny for your thoughts,' she said.

Anna looked up, slightly confused, as she drifted back to the real world. 'Sorry,' she apologized. 'I was lost in thought.'

'So I could see,' Sally replied as she took the seat opposite. 'Mind if I ask what thought you were lost in?'

'Oh, things,' Anna tried to dismiss it. 'Nothing specific.'

'Must be a bit strange,' Sally encouraged her to talk, 'being back on another murder investigation after all this time?'

'A bit,' Anna admitted.

Sally could see that wasn't what was really on her mind 'Being back with *Sean*.'

'Oh dear,' Anna replied with a slight smile. 'And I thought no one had noticed.'

'I don't think anyone else has.'

Anna's smile grew wider then suddenly vanished. 'It's all too complicated,' she said. 'Dangerous. We're both married. He has children. Nothing can ever happen.'

'And has nothing ever happened?' Sally asked.

'No,' Anna blurted, then: 'Well, almost nothing. A long time ago now, in my office, we kissed. Things got a bit carried away, but we stopped. Nothing since then.'

'You've wanted to, though?' Sally pressed. 'He's wanted to?'

'Yes,' Anna answered truthfully, 'but nothing has and nothing will. Sometimes it's so . . . confusing being around him. Distracting.'

'Distracting from work?' Sally asked.

'Distracting from everything,' Anna admitted. 'I think it is for him too, which he can ill afford right now.'

'Sean's fine,' Sally reassured her. 'I've seen the way he looks at you, but once he's got the scent of an investigation not much knocks him out of his stride. He can do that – compartmentalize things. No matter how much is going on around him, he can always focus on the case, albeit sometimes to the detriment of everything and everybody else. He's not the easiest person to be around.'

'I know,' Anna agreed. 'Maybe that's why I feel the way I do about him?'

'Because he's an obsessive workaholic who'll steamroller over anything or anybody to catch a killer?' Sally asked sarcastically.

'Not exactly,' Anna smiled. 'It's just there's a certain *honesty* about him. An intensity. He is what he is and he doesn't care what people think about him. He can put on the charm and play the game when he has to, but he's always . . . always . . . real. He's the realest person I've ever met, although I know he's hiding something – something he doesn't want anyone to know.'

'Let sleeping dogs lie,' Sally warned. 'If he wants you to know, he'll tell you. Don't go digging. He'll see you coming and the barriers will go up.'

'I know,' Anna told her. 'I know.'

'You want to help him and that's understandable,' Sally said. 'You're a psychiatrist. But maybe you should walk away from this. Walk away from this investigation and walk away from Sean. Go back to your nice life and forget about everything, Perhaps it would be best for everybody.'

'It's not that easy,' Anna tried to explain. 'There are things with Addis I can't walk away from.'

'You owe Addis nothing,' Sally replied. 'You owe us nothing. Don't take this the wrong way, but with or without you, we'll catch this one. You don't need this.'

'It's not that simple,' Anna answered, knowing she couldn't tell Sally the truth. 'Things are complicated.'

'Complicated how?' Sally asked, her voice tinged with suspicion.

'Complicated in that there are people who expect certain things from me,' Anna tried to explain without giving away the full facts. 'People who I don't want to let down.'

'Like who?' Sally wanted to know. 'Addis?'

'No,' Anna insisted. 'Not Addis.'

'Sean then?' Sally pressed.

'Everybody,' she managed to say. 'I'm afraid of letting everybody down.'

'You won't let anyone down,' Sally told her – her suspicions fading quickly. 'No one's expecting you to magically give us the suspect's name and address. That's Sean's job,' she joked. 'But if you're determined to stay, we'll have a better chance of catching him quickly. So why don't you make a start by telling me what sort of a person you think we're looking for.'

'Well, he's violent and vicious,' she began, 'but very much in control. There's nothing to suggest rage. Any mutilation was limited to what was necessary to kill them or to take their nails and teeth as trophies.'

'So you agree with Sean then?' Sally asked. 'The nails and teeth are trophies?'

'Almost certainly.' Anna took a sip of her tea. 'The two crime scenes were very similar: both were public places, albeit not well frequented. Yet he spent quite some time with his victims, and for that he needed privacy. At the first scene he had to create it by dragging her into an alley and then hiding her behind a large bin. Perhaps he found it unsatisfying, because the second attack took place in a far more secluded place where he could be alone with the victim without being too worried about being disturbed. I believe he'd really like to be alone with them in the place he felt most comfortable and in control.'

'Which is where?' Sally asked.

'His home,' Anna told her.

'So why not lure them back there?' Sally questioned. 'One was a prostitute and one was a homeless drug addict. Wouldn't have been too difficult to get them to go with him.'

'I agree,' Anna answered. 'Which indicates there must be some obstacle preventing him. Perhaps he doesn't live alone – he might have a girlfriend, or a wife and children. Or he does live alone, but in a flat with shared entrances and staircases where the risk of being seen is too great.'

'So why doesn't he snatch them off the street and drive them out into the woods somewhere?' Sally asked. 'Then he could have all the time he wanted.'

'Abduction's difficult,' Anna reminded her. 'A high-risk strategy. He's not comfortable trying it yet.'

'Yet?' Sally repeated.

'I wouldn't rule it out completely. He may graduate to that in the future, but for now he appears to be honing his tactics. The garage worked well for him. I believe he'll stick to what works for him: identifying victims who frequent places that offer him a reasonable degree of privacy.'

'So he selects his victims in advance?' Sally asked.

'He certainly did with the second,' Anna answered. 'And possibly the first, to some degree at least.'

'If he's stalking them, it could help us find him.'

'Possibly,' Anna replied, as if it was of no great importance, 'but what I find really interesting is he's careful and a planner, yet he takes no precautions to prevent leaving DNA at the scenes. It's almost as if he wants us to find it. DNA puts it beyond doubt. Proves it's him.'

'And why would he want to prove that?'

'Because he wants the credit,' Anna explained. 'I've done plenty of post-sentence interviews with convicted killers, dozens of profiles, and one thing almost all of them have in common is that they don't think they're ever going to be caught. They don't give a moment's thought to what will happen to them after conviction. They're too trapped in the moment. But I think this one is different. I think he's given careful consideration to life after the killings stop. If he's going to be locked up for the rest of his life, he might as well at least be infamous – be treated like something *special*. There'll be books, documentaries, fan mail. Everything he needs to sustain him during his life behind bars.'

'So he wants to be caught?' Sally asked.

'Not exactly. It's more a question of making plans for when the inevitable happens. His actions may bring about his arrest and conviction quicker than if he'd not had such a strong method or left his DNA, but perhaps to him it's worth it.'

'So he's killing to become famous?' Sally tried again.

'No,' Anna answered again, 'or at least not quite. Taking a life is a traumatic thing – even for most psychopaths. Whatever's driving him to kill is something more compelling than the prospect of fame.'

'Such as?'

'I don't know,' Anna admitted. 'Not yet.'

They were silent for a while until Sally spoke again. 'It's like having the old Sean back,' she said, leaving her statement to float without explanation.

'Really?' Anna said.

'You didn't see him this last year or so,' Sally explained, 'covering for other units and dealing with everyday rubbish. He was so flat. Bored. I thought he might pack it all in.'

'And now?'

'He's back,' Sally told her, failing to hide the concern in her voice. 'Full throttle again. Keep up or get left behind. Once he gets that scent back, you know what he can be like.'

'Quite obsessive, I seem to remember,' Anna replied.

'Quite obsessive!' Sally exclaimed. 'There's an understatement. It's like he needs to be chasing after these types of killers, the real sickos.'

'And that worries you?' Anna asked.

'Not so much that,' Sally answered.

'Then what does worry you?' Anna probed, her eyes meeting Sally's.

Sally took a deep breath. 'I'm worried he wants to put himself alongside this killer. One-on-one. Just the two of them. I can't help thinking that's what he wants. That's' what he's working towards.'

'Why?' Anna asked bluntly.

'Because he's done it before,' Sally answered, her face as serious as Anna had seen it. 'First with Gibran, which he was lucky to survive. Really lucky. Then the same thing with Thomas Keller and again with Jeremy Goldboro – only that time he took Donnelly along for the ride. Sean needs to be protected from himself sometimes. Don't tell me you've never noticed.'

'I've noticed,' Anna admitted.

'And do you know why?' Sally asked. 'Do you know why he has this need to face the killers alone?'

'I think,' Anna explained, 'he feels he can learn more from being alone with them. Can learn more about them. He wants to see them in their own environment, before police stations and solicitors are involved. He needs the contact to be personal.'

'Why?' Sally demanded. 'Once they're caught, they're caught. Why isn't that enough for him?'

'Because it's not about the one he's facing,' Anna answered. 'It's about the next one he has to find.'

'I don't understand,' Sally admitted.

'He's learning,' Anna told her. 'Learning from the one in front of him so he can better understand and therefore catch the next killer. Building up a portfolio of profiles in his mind. It gives him the tools – or so he believes – to catch them and catch them quickly.'

Sally took a few seconds to let it sink in.

'Then he is a danger to himself.'

'Sean will always be right on the edge,' Anna told her. 'It's the way he is.'

'You should tell someone,' Sally said. 'You're a psychiatrist. You should warn Addis that there's a significant risk to Sean while he's on the SIU.'

'I already have.'

'What?' Sally asked, disbelief choking her voice.

'I warned Addis during the Jackdaw investigation.'

'And?' Sally demanded.

'I was told Sean was an asset. Property of the Metropolitan Police, to be used in any way necessary to get results.'

'Does Sean know?'

'Yes,' Anna assured her. 'I told him.'

'What did he say?'

'He said he didn't care – so long as he was left alone and still in charge of the SIU, he didn't care.'

'Great,' Sally replied sarcastically.

'Doing what he does makes him who he is,' Anna explained. 'Having that taken away from him scares him more than facing any killer. Can you imagine him, not living on the edge any more – living a normal life. Do you really want to do that to him?'

'At least he'd be alive,' Sally argued.

'Physically,' Anna agreed, 'but what about the rest of him? I don't want to see him become a shell of himself. Do you?'

Sally knew Anna was right. If she protected Sean in one way she could be killing him in another. 'No,' she answered. 'No, I don't want that.'

'Then work with him,' Anna told her, 'and with me. Together we might just be able to keep him safe.'

Sean arrived home late. His two young daughters were asleep in bed, and he could hear soft noises from the TV in the lounge, which meant Kate was still up. He shut the door behind him, careful to lock it before emptying the contents of his pockets on to the small table in the hallway and wrestling out of his coat and jacket which he threw over one of the hooks of the cluttered hat stand. Relieved of his burdens, he headed to the kitchen and grabbed a beer from the fridge. Truthfully he would have preferred to be alone – to sit in the quiet semi-darkness of the kitchen and think the day through – just let everything settle in his mind until he was ready to attempt sleep and give his subconscious a chance to think of things his waking mind could not. But he knew that wasn't an option. Kate would have heard him come in and she'd be waiting for him to go in and join her, so she could talk to him about everyday things and he could pretend he was interested.

As he entered the lounge, Kate looked up from her laptop as if he'd only popped out a minute ago. Her eyes quickly returned to the computer screen. 'You're late,' she greeted him.

'Not that late,' he argued and sat heavily on the sofa. He took a long swig from his beer. 'Gonna get a lot later.'

'The new case?'

'Uh huh.'

'I heard about it, on the radio. In the papers. It doesn't sound good.'

'It's not.'

'I'm afraid I didn't have time to make anything for dinner,' she apologized. 'Four teenagers ploughed their car into a skip lorry. We worked on them for hours, but two didn't make it.'

'It's OK,' he assured her. 'I'm not hungry.'

'We make a right pair, you and me,' she smiled. 'You with your murder victim and me with my fatal accident. We don't exactly do normal jobs, do we?'

'Who wants a normal job?' He took another swig of beer.

'Want to talk about your new case?' she suggested. 'It might help.'

'Help what?' he shrugged.

'Help you unwind. You seem very tense.'

'Nothing to talk about,' he insisted. 'Just another violent lunatic with a point to prove.'

'Sounds like the sort of case that got you into trouble last time,' she reminded him, 'and the time before that and the time—'

'There were . . . circumstances,' he cut in. 'I got ahead of the investigation and ended up having to make the arrests myself. It's usually much more controlled than that.'

'The last one wasn't arrested though. He was shot, killed. And the one before that almost killed you.'

'It won't happen again,' he promised, though he knew he couldn't guarantee anything – not once he knew the killer was close. Not once he had a chance to be alone with him and look into his eyes with nobody else around – to bring it down to a personal duel between hunter and hunted. 'I'll make sure the arrest is planned and organized – use the TSG or something, but it won't be me. Don't worry,' he tried to reassure her. 'I'll keep my distance.'

'You?' she said accusingly. 'Keep your distance? I'm not sure you know how to.'

'I've told you,' he replied calmly, 'there were extraordinary circumstances. I had to be there at the end. This time it'll be different. I'll be more careful.'

'Careful? Sean, we both know that's not in your nature, is it?' He could only offer a shrug in reply. 'It's just . . . cases like this are the ones that drag you back into dark places, Sean.'

'Cases like this are my job,' he argued.

'But you've been so much better this last year, when your job hasn't involved chasing around after madmen. Can't you move to another MIT?'

'And go back to investigating domestic murders and kids stabbing each other over whose turf is whose?' he asked. 'I don't think so.'

'Then move to the Anti-Terrorist Branch or Flying Squad,'

she suggested. 'Anything to get you away from these madmen.'

'I don't want to move to SO13 or the Flying Squad. I like what I do. Being the DI on the SIU is the best job in the Met. I'm not going to leave it.'

'But it's not good for you,' she insisted. 'It changes you. I can see the difference. You're becoming distant again, pulling away from me and the kids. Because your mind is no longer with us, is it? It's with him – this bloody lunatic you're after. You didn't see the kids at all yesterday and you didn't remember to call to say goodnight. It's the first time you've forgotten to do that in ages. Before, even when you were late, you at least called. There's something about this type of case that obsesses you.'

'So what if it obsesses me? It's only for a few weeks. I catch the killer and I come back to you. And nobody else dies.'

'I know you, Sean.' She sounded exasperated now. 'I know your childhood. I don't think these investigations are good for you.'

'It's got nothing to do with my childhood,' he lied.

'I'm not so sure,' Kate disagreed. 'I sometimes think you treat each of these madmen as if they were your father. It's your way of striking back at him.'

'My father wasn't a killer,' he reminded her.

'No, but he was almost as bad.'

'What happened to me as a child helps me find them,' he told her calmly. 'It's a tool I use, that's all. And if it helps me catch them quicker than other people can, I'm fine with that.'

'We don't know what lasting effect the traumatic events of your childhood have had on you, Sean,' she warned him. 'Using your mind to catch these evil bastards is only going to increase the chances of you having to relive those events, and that won't be good for you. It won't be good for any of us.'

'I rarely think about my childhood, and I don't think about *him*. I went through all the doctors and shrinks when I was younger. I'm fine now.'

'You never finished a single treatment – you told me that yourself.' He avoided her gaze. 'You joined a boxing gym instead, and then the police.'

'Yeah, well,' he replied, staring into his beer. 'It worked.'

'Things like that don't just go away,' she told him. 'They hide inside us, waiting to drag us down.'

'Not me,' he snapped, annoyed at having to talk about the darkness of his past. 'I'm in control.'

'But these people you go after, Sean – a lot of them will have endured a childhood like yours. Their psychology is closer to your own than perhaps you want to admit. I see the way it affects you and I think it's dangerous. Doesn't matter how many of them you lock up – your childhood won't change.'

Her words made him feel suddenly dizzy and disorientated. Was that what he was doing – hunting his own father over and over again? Did he think that if he kept saving innocent people then eventually he'd save himself – save the scared little boy he used to be? No one had ever put it to him like that, and it had never occurred to him until now that that might be the case.

'You all right?' Kate asked, leaning towards him and resting a soft hand on his shoulder – her dark eyes full of fear and concern.

'Yeah,' he managed to say, knowing that if he didn't respond, her worries would only intensify. 'I'm just tired,' he lied, 'but I hear what you're saying.'

'Good.'

'Let me get this one finished, and then I'll think about it.'

'OK,' she smiled, her straight white teeth shining from her caramel skin. 'Come to bed. Let's get some sleep. I've an early shift tomorrow.'

125

'You go,' he answered, lifting his beer – hoping she couldn't detect the pounding in his chest. 'I'm gonna finish this and chill out for a bit. Let my mind settle.'

'Don't be long.' She leaned down and kissed him on the cheek. He could smell her skin cream and feel her unruly ringlets brush against his face.

'I won't,' he promised and watched her spring to her feet and glide from the lounge. Once he was alone he let out a long breath before finishing his beer in one go, resting his head back on the sofa and staring at the ceiling. He needed to push the night's thoughts away – bury them where they'd lain for years – deep in the dark pit of his soul where not even he could find them, where the memories of his father rotted in his private hell. Keep the instincts, he told himself, forget the fear. *Keep the instincts – forget the fear*. Over and over he repeated the mantra silently in his head until he was sure the demons were back in the cages of his consciousness. He shook the stiffness from his neck and headed for the stairs and restless, haunted sleep.

# 6

The following morning Sean was once again the first one into the office. He sat himself down at his desk, the crime scene photographs of Tanya Richards' murder spread out in front of him in no particular order. A few hours' sleep, a shower and clean clothes had revived him somewhat, but he knew by midday the tiredness would come sweeping back and with it the aches and pains as well as bouts of dizziness and nausea. He'd have to remember to eat something or things would get worse, but for now he made do with an occasional sip from a Styrofoam cup of black coffee. His mind was too occupied to think of anything other than the images of the lifeless young woman laid out in front of him.

The more he stared at the pictures, the more he was convinced the attack hadn't been sexually motivated – despite the fact her killer had raped her.

'You planned for the killing,' he spoke softly to himself, 'but there's nothing to indicate you planned for the rape. You brought something to knock her unconscious with and something to cut her with, but you didn't bring anything to make the rape easier or safer for yourself. No condom. No lubricant. She was a prostitute and yet you had unprotected sex with her. If you'd planned to rape her, I think you would have protected yourself – so what happened?' He leaned back in his chair in silent thought for a while before once again hunching over the photographs of the semi-naked victim lying in a great red pool of her own blood. 'There was a lot of blood,' he continued. 'It must have been all over your clothes and hands, same as with Dalton, so you must have been prepared for that. You wouldn't have risked walking out of the alley with blood all over you – someone might have seen you. So you must have brought something to wash away the blood or cover your hands and clothes, all of which would have taken planning and preparation.' He drummed his fingers on the desktop. 'Was that it?' he asked, lifting one of the photographs and leaning back in his chair as he studied it closely. 'Her blood on your hands, warm and thick like oil paint. Did you taste it – put your bloodied fingers to your lips and taste it? Did the smell of it remind you of warm copper? Was it all too much – did it set your body on fire?' His eyes darted among the photographs lying on his desk. 'You'd have had a bag to carry the things you needed. Something everyday that wouldn't be noticed. A backpack?' He swapped the photograph he was holding for a pen and scribbled a reminder to himself on his notepad to look for someone carrying a bag when checking CCTV. It wasn't much, but any filter would help when it came to searching through hours and hours of footage.

Again he returned to the crime scene pictures, his head in his hands to help shut out the rest of the world and intensify his concentration. 'How are you selecting them?' he asked the killer as if he was interviewing him in person. 'What draws you to them? They were both young. Vulnerable. Perhaps you thought they wouldn't be missed?' He thought silently for a few seconds then broke off, shaking his head with frustration. His questions weren't getting him anywhere. 'No,' he corrected himself. 'These were all matters of convenience, nothing more. Something else must have drawn you to them in particular – what was it?' Again he pondered in silence. 'Richards was female and still reasonably attractive, whereas Dalton was male and showing the effects of crack addiction. They have no obvious similarities, so . . .' He squinted his eyes and allowed the answer to come. 'You weren't drawn to them,' he concluded. 'There was nothing about them that drew you, other than the fact that they were convenient. That's all you were looking for, wasn't it? For them to be vulnerable and convenient. That's all you needed. But when will you want more? When will you feel confident enough to move on to bigger and better things?'

After allowing himself a few minutes for his thoughts to settle, he tried. 'So you were looking for convenience, but how did you find them? How did you find Tanya Richards and William Dalton? Did you know them?' He considered it briefly but dismissed the idea. 'No, I don't think so. How then? Did you see them while you were going about your normal life and decide they would be the ones? Did you then watch them – follow them – learn everything about them and then kill them?' Again he considered his own question. 'No. Why invest the time in watching and following them? Why increase the risk of being noticed? No,' he told himself. 'You knew where to look for people like Tanya and William so you just cruised the streets until you found them, didn't you? Then all you had to do was follow them until a chance came your way. You trailed Tanya until you saw the alley and took the opportunity to drag her in there. Dalton was even better. He led you to his makeshift home, all hidden away and quiet and dark. I bet you couldn't believe your luck, could you? Finally you could be properly alone with someone and live out all your dreams without having to constantly look over your shoulder. You think you're so clever, don't you? Striking like lightning – keeping your knife and whatever else you need with you, so there's no need for preparation – waiting, hoping for the chance to kill. There's no connection between you and the victims or their lives – only their deaths. Well,' he warned the man he hunted, 'I'm going to find you anyway.'

A loud knock on his doorframe made him look up to see Sally standing at the entrance.

'What is it?'

'I've got an update for you, on Dalton's lifestyle.'

'Can it wait?' Sean replied, loading his pockets. 'I need to be somewhere.'

'I suppose,' Sally shrugged. 'Where is it you need to be in such a hurry?'

'The Richards murder scene. I need to see it.'

'Won't be much to see there now.'

'The alley will be there and the wheelie bins – that's all I need. I want to see where she died.'

'Fair enough,' Sally didn't argue. 'Mind if I tag along?'

He looked up from patting his coat pockets, as if she'd suggested something extraordinary. 'No, thanks. I'd rather see it on my own.'

'Why?' she pressed. 'Two sets of eyes are better than one.'

'I need you here,' he replied, trying to think of any reason she shouldn't go with him. 'I need you to look at whatever lifestyle findings the original MIT in the Richards case found out about her. Compare them to what you've found out about Dalton. They should be with the other stuff we collected from them yesterday. If we're lucky, there could be a common denominator – a name that comes up twice. You know the drill.'

'Fine,' Sally reluctantly agreed.

'Anyone needs me, I'm on my mobile.' He was halfway out the door when a thought struck him and he turned back to Sally. 'Keep an eye on Dave,' he told her quietly. 'When he eventually turns up. He wasn't at his best yesterday.'

'I noticed,' she replied. 'Hasn't been for some time.'

'Yeah, well, talk to him if you think it'll help. He won't talk to me.'

'I'll try,' she assured him as he walked across the main office. 'I'll try.'

David Langley drove across Southwest London heading towards an area where he knew he had a good chance of finding what he was looking for. He cruised through the wealthy streets of Putney, hungrily eyeing the slim, immaculately groomed young mothers in their uniform of skinny jeans and Converse sneakers. But he hadn't come for them and knew he wouldn't find what he wanted in the well-heeled streets of SW15. He headed out of central Putney and up the hill to the heath, then cut across towards Roehampton – a strange netherworld on the outskirts of West London that backed on to Richmond Park and was home to some of the ugliest tower blocks to be seen anywhere. The low-rise blocks weren't much better and the entire area was dotted with betting shops, cheap grocer's and takeaway food shops. The major franchises had so far stayed well away from Roehampton.

He parked in a side street on the opposite side of the road from a sprawling estate, giving himself the widest possible view of the comings and goings. The area was dominated by a large playground, although any young children had been kept away by the bitterly cold weather leaving only a small gathering of threatening-looking teenagers huddled in hoodies, who had clearly taken control of this particular patch. Once upon a time the playground had been covered by CCTV cameras, but it had become a game for the local youths to repeatedly smash them until the council gave up repairing or replacing them and left the old broken cameras hanging lifeless from their perches.

The hooded youth at the centre of the gathering caught his attention. The others seemed to hang on his every word, while the members of the outer circle took on the role of bodyguards, moving in fast to stop anyone who came too close, either turning them away or allowing them forward depending on whether they received a shake or nod of the head from their leader. Once each swift, illicit transaction was completed, the intruder would be hurried from the inner sanctum. Langley was streetwise enough to recognize a drug dealer when he saw one. He would be a worthy victim – his teeth and nails suitable additions to the collection. Another victim no one would miss or mourn. But he would be hard to catch alone and in the right place.

Langley was still weighing his options when a far more enticing prospect wandered into view: a young woman in her late teens or early twenties, slim with long blond hair tied in a bunch on top of her head, wearing a grey and pink tracksuit and pink training shoes. She approached the group of youths, who jostled and laughed at her until the leader gave a nod and she was permitted to enter. Langley checked all angles to make sure he was alone, then reached across to the passenger seat, tossed aside his coat and picked up the high-spec Nikon digital camera with a 100–400mm super telephoto lens attached. Hurriedly removing the cap, he pointed the camera at the group – low magnification at first, but as soon as he'd located his target he zoomed in on her.

He could see her clearly now. The effects of drug abuse from a young age were clearly visible through the lens, but she was still attractive, although the way she dressed and moved suggested she'd never strayed too far from her estate aside from the odd shoplifting spree in the West End or maybe a cheap holiday in Spain. She appeared to be arguing with the leader, or pleading with him – it was hard to tell which. Langley wondered why the transaction was so slow and animated. He expected money and drugs to be exchanged quickly or not at all, but this was something different. Something wasn't right.

Fascinated, he watched the sad little drama unfold. Something the leader said reduced her to a still silence. The leader waited a few seconds, then repeated whatever he'd said. This time the young woman stood with her hands on her hips, looking left to right and back again – as if she was considering what he'd said. Eventually, she nodded in agreement. The leader got to his feet smiling broadly as his minions began to giggle and nudge one another.

Leaving the safety of the group, with the young woman following close behind, the leader made his way to a nearby shed that housed some of the estate's many recycling bins – used by the local residents for dumping almost anything over than recyclable items. The pair disappeared from sight behind the shed, but Langley kept the lens focused on their last position. He was in no doubt what he was witnessing – sex for drugs. It only made him want her more – to pin her to the floor and cut through the arteries in her neck – watching as her slick, warm blood spilled from the gaping wound. He'd hold her still as she grasped wildly at the wounds in her neck and throat until finally her hands would slip to her side as she lay twitching and death took her.

He imagined her blood on his hands as he slowly rubbed them together, enjoying the texture of the viscous liquid as it turned his skin crimson. He would lick some of the blood from his hands before cleaning them, just as he had done on the previous two occasions – savouring every second the metallic flavour danced on his tongue . . .

Suddenly he realized he was becoming sexually aroused. Disappointment at his own weakness went some way to calming him down. He could not afford to make the same mistake with this one as he had with the whore. No matter how alive he felt, he must not touch her like that. If he did, the police and media would defile his legacy by putting it about that he was just another pervert, acting out his sexual fantasies. He knew he was much, much more than that.

After a few minutes the leader and the girl reappeared in the viewfinder of his camera. The leader adjusted his flies while she wiped her mouth with the back of her hand. Too bad that she valued herself so little in life, but perhaps he could make something of her in death. He pressed the trigger on the camera and held it down, snapping continuous shots of the couple as they walked back towards the group. The leader pointed backwards over his shoulder at the girl and spoke to one of his laughing cohorts, who fished in his jacket pocket for something too tiny for Langley to see. He handed the item to the girl, who snatched it from his palm and walked away quickly.

To his surprise and elation, she began to walk in his direction. If she'd headed back into the estate, he could never have hoped to follow her. In a place like that strangers would be spotted immediately and either identified as police to be watched closely or as potential victims. He saw her scuttle warily behind a row of closed-down shops and waited a few minutes, checking for CCTV cameras, whether council-installed or private. Seeing none, he started the engine and rolled his car slowly to where he'd last seen her. The passage she'd walked through was big enough for a car and led to a small car park at the rear of the shops. Cautiously he drove in, stopping near the only other vehicle, a burnt-out ruin.

If she saw him, he would simply ignore her, spin around and drive away like a man who'd taken a wrong turning. But he needn't have worried; she wasn't waiting for him, ready to point an accusing finger. In fact he couldn't see her at first and was beginning to wonder whether she'd cut through the car park to get somewhere else. It was disappointing, but he knew enough about her now to find her again. Drug addicts were very predictable in their habits. If he needed to find her again he had only to wait for her to come to the playground for her next fix.

He was about to leave when he saw her slumped in a doorway at the back of one of the shops, eyes closed, with a crack-pipe clutched in her limp hand. It would have been the easiest thing in the world for him to walk up to her now and cut her neck open, but he didn't have his tools with him. More importantly, it wasn't how he'd imagined it. He wanted her to know what was happening, like the others had known. He wanted to be able to look into her eyes and see her horror and terror as she struggled to cling to her miserable, pointless life.

Another time, he promised himself.

Sean pulled up close to the alleyway in Holloway where Tanya Richards had taken her last breath. He climbed from his car and looked up and down the street. It was quiet, even at this time in the morning. The only remaining signs of police involvement at the scene were a few scraps of cordon tape hanging from a streetlight and a bollard either side of the entrance to the alley. Sean could hear the rumble of traffic coming from the nearby Holloway Road. He imagined the victim hurrying along the street, head bowed, perhaps smoking a cigarette and playing with her mobile phone – correcting himself when he remembered that it had been found in her jacket pocket. If she'd been using it when she was attacked, they would have found it by the entrance to the alley. 'No, if he'd been following you, you would have sensed it and had your phone ready to call someone. Maybe even the police? But he couldn't have waited for you in the alley unless he knew you were going to walk past it. Unless he knew . . .'

Suddenly his mind ached with the possibility that the killer hadn't simply trawled the streets of London looking for victims. What if he'd already selected them? Watched them and followed them – learnt everything he needed to know about them so he could plan his ambush more accurately. He'd previously discounted the possibility, but now he was suddenly sure he'd been wrong. His thoughts flashed to the second victim, William Dalton. He hadn't been followed to the garage the night he died. The killer had been waiting for him.

Sean wandered into the alley, imagining the killer hitting Tanya Richards over the head with something like a hammer or metal bar. In his mind's eye he watched her fall to the ground, saw the madman grab her by the ankles and drag her deeper into the alley. 'You're strong,' he spoke softly to the faceless killer. 'To drag a grown woman across this sort of ground you must be strong. But it took you time to get to this point, didn't it? You searched the streets until you saw her, but you didn't kill her then – you watched her.' In his mind the faceless killer sat astride her chest and pulled the evil-looking knife from his pocket, holding it in front of her face. 'But you didn't watch her merely to learn what you needed to know; you watched her because it was important to you – why?' He continued to watch the vivid replay of Tanya Richards' murder. The dark figure drew the knife long and deep across her throat, opening a hideous wound that gaped, bled and foamed. He saw the shock and disbelief in her eyes, just as the killer had. 'It was important to you because it made you feel as if you . . . as if you knew them somehow . . . and killing someone you know is so much more personal . . . more intimate than killing a stranger, isn't it?' The possibilities roared in his head. 'Jesus Christ, did you speak to her? Did you try to get to know her? Did you make contact with her and with William Dalton? The chances of catching him quickly seemed to increase tenfold – a hundredfold. He'd broken the first rule of stranger attacks: he was no longer a complete stranger. Sean felt his excitement rising and needed to regain control.

Slow down, he told himself. You don't know he contacted them. You made an assumption and assumptions are dangerous. Perhaps he didn't contact them or speak to them . . .

'No, you watched them and followed them, didn't you? So . . . so this is the game you play,' he accused the madman 'You're clever,' Sean admitted, 'but I'll find you. I always do.' He took a few moments to consider his adversary – the evidence he'd left and the beginnings of a trail that must ultimately lead to his capture and downfall. 'But why do I get the feeling you want me to?'

\*    \*    \*

Donnelly pulled up in Mint Street just as Zukov appeared from the stairwell of a block of low-rise flats, clipboard tucked under his armpit while his hands grappled with his vaping device. He was aware of Donnelly's car stopping next to him, but didn't acknowledge it. He continued to ignore the fact he had company even after Donnelly was out of the car and standing next to him, fishing in his own pockets for a pack of cigarettes, tapping one free and lighting it with a disposable lighter.

'All right?' he asked, exhaling a plume of smoke.

'Yeah,' Zukov replied, taking a deep drag on his vaping pipe. 'You?'

Donnelly eyed the vaping pipe with a look of disgust. 'Better off sticking to the real things,' he warned. 'God knows what's in them pipes.'

'I'll take my chances,' Zukov answered curtly.

'Aye,' Donnelly moved on. 'Whatever. How's the house-to-house going?'

'It's going,' Zukov told him. 'Be finished soon enough, then I can get back to doing something a bit more interesting than knocking on doors and being bored by old ladies.'

'Too good for door-to-door now, eh?' Donnelly asked. 'Just remember: occasionally it throws up something critical.'

'Yeah, well not so far it hasn't,' Zukov moaned. 'All we're getting is that people knew he existed, lived in a garage and was a druggie. That's about it. No one knows anything about the night he was murdered. No miracles happening here today.'

'Keep at it till you've spoken to everyone,' Donnelly ordered. 'The last person could be the most important. There was this one case where we kept calling at this flat, but no one was ever home. About a month later, the guy actually answered the door. Turned out he saw the whole murder from his bedroom window. Never bothered to contact us because he assumed we knew.'

'Really,' Zukov sounded bored and disinterested. There was a time not long ago when he'd have hung on Donnelly's every word, but now he smelled blood in the water and a possible vacancy for a soon-to-be detective sergeant. 'I want to get back in the action,' he continued. 'Stay a bit closer to the boss. Learn some stuff. Help him out. Know what I mean?'

'Aye,' Donnelly replied. 'The boss.'

'If this one goes down like the last one, I want to be right next to him, you know?' Zukov set his trap. 'Like you were. That's where I want to be.'

'Really?' Donnelly asked, his voice thick with suspicion and doubt.

'Fucking absolutely,' Zukov insisted. 'I want to be there at the death this time and next time. Just like you.'

'Aye,' Donnelly answered, taking a deep drag on his cigarette to try and control his pounding heart. 'Just like me.'

'You still suspended from carrying a firearm, by the way?' Zukov tormented him.

'I wasn't suspended,' Donnelly told him, sounding defensive. 'I handed my ticket in. Don't want to be in that position again.'

'Rather die, would you?' Zukov twisted the knife. 'Or let another copper get killed? Or let the boss be killed?'

'Son,' Donnelly replied, 'you don't know what you're talking about.'

'I know the boss needs people he can rely on.'

'You don't know anything about him,' Donnelly snapped. 'You may think you do, but trust me – you don't.'

'What's that supposed to mean?' Zukov asked, sensing Donnelly was holding back something important.

'Nothing. Forget it. Just get back to the door-to-door. Once you're done, I can give you something more *interesting* to do.'

Zukov looked him up and down. 'Whatever you say. You're the boss.'

'That's right,' Donnelly agreed. 'I am.'

He watched as Zukov wandered back into the stairwell, then flicked his cigarette away and jumped into his car. Pushing the back of his head as deep as he could into the headrest, he clung to the steering wheel, his knuckles white and his fingers turning bright pink where he was gripping it so tightly. He squeezed his eyes shut to try and keep the images and thoughts away, but it was futile. Suddenly he was back in the golf club car park with a hooded Jeremy Goldsboro raising his sawn-off shotgun towards Sean before being thrown against the side of his van by the bullets that burst from the barrel of Donnelly's pistol. He watched as for the thousandth time as The Jackdaw slid down the van's panel, leaving a thick smear of red. Then he sat slumped on the ground, the air from his last breath hissing through the holes in his chest.

Donnelly snapped his eyes open, but the images wouldn't go away: Goldsboro lying dead with Sean looking from the body to Donnelly and back again, calm and collected – like he knew it was going to happen. Like he planned everything exactly how it turned out. Like he'd done everything but pull the trigger himself.

'Corrigan,' Donnelly muttered, shaking his head. 'Fucking Corrigan.'

Sean strode along the narrow corridor at New Scotland Yard that led to the office of the SIU. He was pulling his coat off when he felt and heard his phone buzzing in one of his pockets. 'Shit,' he cursed and searched the tangle of material until he found it and checked the caller ID. It was Sergeant Roddis from the forensics team.

'Andy,' Sean answered with the sense of excitement that he always felt when Roddis called him unexpectedly. 'You got something?'

'Yes and no,' Roddis cryptically replied. 'The second victim – William Dalton: the lab have examined his clothes and found heavy traces of semen on his upper items – mainly his outer coat. First DNA examination suggests it's from the same suspect who left semen at the Tanya Richards crime scene.'

You needed the release – Sean immediately thought to himself. Just like you did at the first scene; you needed to release the power and the tension, but the victim was male, so you ejaculated over his body – his final humiliation.

'No great surprise,' Roddis continued. 'It was never very likely we were dealing with two different killers.'

'No,' Sean agreed. 'No, it wasn't.'

'And his DNA isn't on file,' Roddis reminded him, 'so it's not going to help us catch him, but it will obviously help us convict him when we do.'

'That's all well and good,' Sean replied, 'but I need to find him first.'

'I'll keep looking,' Roddis assured him.

'I know you will.'

As soon as he'd hung up, Sean headed for Sally's office, where she and Anna were sketching the offender profile for the killer on to a large whiteboard. He glanced at the scribbles written in red marker pen. 'You seen Dave?'

'No,' Sally answered. 'I haven't seen him all day.'

'Great,' he said sarcastically. 'We need an office meeting. I want to know where we are. Call everyone together,' he ordered, storming off to his own Perspex cubicle.

'OK,' Sally said, although he'd already left, and headed into the main office. 'All right, everyone,' she called out. 'Office meeting in a couple of minutes. Boss wants to know what progress you've all been making.' After a few nervous looks between the detectives present everyone began to gather around the boards, which were now covered with crime scene and other photographs, as well as dozens of facts that had been established and leads that needed to be chased down.

Having composed himself after his outburst, Sean strode into the main office, coming to a halt in front of the boards. 'All right,' he began. 'Listen up: I've just had a call from DS Roddis – the lab found semen on the clothing of the second victim. It looks like he ejaculated on him, but there's no other evidence of sexual assault. After initial examination, it would appear to be from the same man who left semen at the first scene. It'll take a few days before it's one hundred per cent confirmed, but it shores up what we already believed – i.e., we're dealing with the same suspect. DS Roddis was also able to confirm that the suspect's DNA is not on file.' There were a few murmurs of disquiet from the audience. 'So,' he told them, 'we'll have to solve this one the hard way. Nobody's going to be handing us a name and address for the suspect anytime soon, so we need to get on with it.

'Alan,' he turned towards DC Jesson. 'Any news on the CCTV?'

'TFL are examining both victims' Oyster cards,' he explained, 'so we should have their movements on the day they were killed and we can gather up the CCTV. We've had CCTV from Borough tube looked at from the night Dalton was killed, but all it shows is that, if he was being followed, he wasn't being followed closely.'

'You need to go back further,' Sean told him, remembering his visit to the Richards crime scene. 'There's a chance our man followed both victims for some time before he actually killed them. He may have been watching them.'

There were a few surprised looks and whispers.

'We need to go back at least ten days before the killing. And if that reveals nothing, we go back further.'

'That's a lot of CCTV to plough through,' Jesson pointed out.

'We have two victims,' Sean reminded him, 'and there'll be more if we don't find him, so I don't care how much footage there is, we need to do it. Concentrate on Tottenham Court Road and Borough stations for now. That should make it more manageable.'

'Why go back specifically ten days?' DC Maggie O'Neil asked.

'Because he's on a ten-day cycle, remember,' Sean reminded her. 'He probably concentrates entirely on one victim before moving on to the next. I could be wrong, but I don't think so.' He waited for any more questions – moving on when none came.

'OK,' he said, looking around to see if Donnelly had sneaked into the meeting, but he was nowhere to be seen. 'In the absence of DS Donnelly, is anyone here from the door-to-door team who can update us?' He was greeted with awkward silence until Sally spoke.

'They're all down at Mint Street,' she told him. 'I don't have any updates yet.'

'Fine,' Sean muttered, the irritation clear in his voice. 'Moving on: what about victim selection? Any ideas? Anyone?'

'Both young and vulnerable,' Sally offered.

'We know that,' Sean dismissed it, 'and that one was male, one was female and they both used class-A drugs, but *how* is he selecting them? What, if anything, ties them together?'

'What's to say he doesn't search the streets until he finds someone he's drawn to?' Sally asked.

'Nothing,' he admitted. 'But what if it's not as random as it first appears? What if there's more to his victim selection than just young and vulnerable?'

'We have nothing to suggest there is,' Sally reminded him.

'Not yet,' Sean told her, 'but if there is and we can find it, then we'll be a lot closer to finding him. I want you all to keep that in mind,' he ordered his team. 'If you get the slightest indication of a specific selection process, I need to know.' He was answered with lots of nodding heads.

'What about the killer?' Jesson asked. 'We know what sort of victims we're dealing with, but what about the killer? What sort of man are we looking for?'

'Anna?' Sean said, handing the question over to her.

'Well, he's clearly both psychopathic and sadistic, but he's also organized and confident, which suggests an older man – between thirty-five and fifty, and reasonably intelligent. I would anticipate he's been fairly successful in his life, although behavioural problems may have held him back, but he has no criminal record, so he's been able to control himself – at least until now.'

'He could be a failed dentist, then?' Sally asked. 'Hence the teeth.'

'I don't think so.' Anna frowned. 'When I say fairly successful, I mean he's probably qualified in a trade or perhaps a lower-level professional – all of which fits with him being married and likely with children, although I believe the marriage didn't work out.'

'Why?' Jesson asked.

'A psychopath is a very difficult person to live with,' she explained. 'Even one who lives an apparently normal life within the law. What we know of his movements – being out late at night, missing for hours on end hunting victims – wouldn't fit too well with married life or cohabiting with a partner. Whoever shared his life would be bound to ask questions – questions that would be difficult to answer. For what he's doing, it's better to live alone.

'And then there are his victims,' Anna continued, enjoying herself now, relaxed and lost in her impromptu lecture. 'Both young and, more importantly, white – which tells us he's almost certainly white himself. Serial killers tend to stay within their own ethnic group.'

'Why?' Sally asked. 'I mean, I know they do, but I've never understood why.'

'Because it makes it more personal,' Anna told her. 'Serial killers always want it to be as personal as they can make it. Our own race always feels that little bit more human to us than others. Remember, most serial killers are murdering strangers – so they'll do everything they can to make it feel more personal, starting with killing within their own ethnic group.

'They also like to feel as safe and comfortable as possible when stalking and killing their victims, which means they'll usually operate within a geographical area they know well.

If they're disturbed and have to run, they don't want to be in unfamiliar surroundings where there's a risk of becoming disorientated or lost. This one's almost certainly a Londoner, or someone who's lived here most of their adult life.'

'So we've got a middle-aged white male Londoner who's probably divorced, who's possibly anything from a carpenter to an office clerk,' Jesson sarcastically summarized. 'Not really a great help, is it?'

Sean noticed Anna visibly deflate and stepped in. 'Once we get close to him, it'll help,' he argued.

'*When* we get close,' Jesson emphasized.

'What about his sexuality?' Sally asked. 'He seems confused – a male and a female victim. We now know there was sexual activity at both scenes.'

'I don't agree,' Anna recovered. 'His sexual activity at the first scene was strongly heterosexual, but while it now appears he ejaculated over the male victim at the second scene, no clothes were removed and there is no evidence of sexual molestation.'

'Meaning?' Sally pressed.

'Meaning, his sexuality is important to him,' Anna explained. 'Very important. He sees himself as a red-blooded alpha male, and it's a self-image that everything else hinges around. He may actually be quite successful with women – initially, anyway – and the last thing he wants is to be mistaken for or accused of being homo or bisexual. Hence he doesn't interact with his male victim sexually.'

'But he did ejaculate over him,' Jesson reminded her. 'In my book, that's sexual activity. If his alpha-male image is so important to him, why do that and risk having people believe he's gay or bisexual?'

'Killing made him feel more alive than he'd ever felt in his life,' Sean tried to explain. 'So alive he would have felt like he was on fire. It was too much for him, so he needed a release. Ejaculating changed the chemical balance in his body long enough for him to calm down and regain his composure. He'd just committed murder. He needed to think.'

'If you say so, boss,' Jesson relented. He'd been working with Sean long enough to know there was a point at which it was better to accept what he said than try to argue.

'But none of this is telling us why he's killing,' Cahill pointed out.

'It's complicated,' Anna told her. 'He no doubt has a lot of issues in his life – probably a legacy of his childhood. Given what we know about him, he's likely very egotistical, so maybe his ego has been severely damaged at some point and he's looking to make himself feel in control again or—'

'Because it makes him feel a hundred times more special than he really is,' Sean interrupted Anna's diagnosis. 'He wants to be top of the food chain – something he can never be in his other life – and now he feels he is. Which is why he won't stop. He can't give up that feeling.'

He looked around at the quiet, concerned faces, picking DC Summers out of the crowd. 'Tony, I need you to go back over both victims' intelligence records. Dalton and Richards have criminal records going back several years. In isolation they haven't told us much, but we need to look at them together – see if there isn't a common denominator, an associate they share – a friend, a dealer, anything.

'Fiona,' he turned towards Cahill. 'We know he has no convictions in the UK, but maybe he's been indulging his unpleasant tastes somewhere else in the world. Liaise with the lab and have his DNA profile sent over to Interpol and the FBI – see if he's on someone else's files. Get his MO circulated too. It's distinctive enough that if they've come across it, they'll recognise it pretty quick.'

'What about the victims' phones?' DC Maggie O'Neil asked.

'They're at the technical lab being examined,' Sean told her. 'Nothing much so far, but as with everything else, if we don't find anything first time, we go back and dig deeper –

cross-referencing numbers and contacts to look for a common denominator.

'As yet,' he reminded them, 'we only have one suspect – Tanya Richards' pimp, Joey Mehmet. He's a long shot, but he needs to be found.'

'We're on it,' Sally assured him. 'He's circulated as wanted and we've made sure every intelligence office across the Met has his face taking pride of place on their bulletin boards.'

'Good,' Sean told her. 'As soon as we find him, I want to know. Anything else?' he asked the gathering. No one spoke. 'OK, well let's get on with it.'

He immediately headed back to his office, followed by Sally and Anna.

'We have a lot of information, but not much progress,' Sally complained.

'It's always like that at the beginning,' Sean reminded her. 'You know that.'

'I know,' she admitted. 'Could do with something a bit more solid though.'

'It'll come,' he assured her. 'Do we have the keys for Richards' home?'

'We should,' Sally replied. 'Tessa's taking care of all exhibits – but why do you want her flat keys?' Sally asked.

'Because I know how she died,' he answered. 'Now I need to see how she lived.'

David Langley sat at his desk, his digital camera connected to his work computer, the screen displaying a picture of the girl from the Roehampton estate immediately after she emerged from having degraded herself to feed her habit. He tapped his keyboard and scrolled through the pictures that had been snapped so close together that they almost looked like film. She was perfect – young and vulnerable, flawed but beautiful. His nostrils flared as he imagined what she smelt like: inexpensive soap mixed with clothes that needed cleaning, the reek of cigarettes and possibly alcohol. The memory of the smell of desperation made his entire body come alive. He felt the tightening in his groin and the beginnings of an erection that he ignored, telling himself it was merely a side effect of the power his body now possessed.

One particular photo came on to the screen that made him freeze, his finger poised over the clicker on his mouse. Instead of moving on, he enlarged the area of the frame showing the girl's throat – slim and elegant with pale thin skin. For a moment he thought he could almost see her carotid artery pulsing, thought he could feel her blood racing through his fingers as he tightened them around her neck. 'Only a few days now,' he whispered to himself. 'A few days more and you'll be mine.'

Suddenly his fantasizing was shattered as the assistant manager, Brian Houghton, burst in without knocking. 'Oi, oi,' Houghton smiled lasciviously, 'watching porn again. Eh?'

Calmly he clicked the mouse and made the photographs disappear. 'Do you want something?'

'It's my office as well,' Houghton reminded him, which drew a withering look from Langley. 'Anyway,' he moved on, 'thought you'd want to know that Jane's been looking for you.'

'Huntingdon?' Langley asked. 'She's been here?'

'No. She was on the blower, wondering where you were.'

'And what did you tell her?' he asked, the urgency thick in his voice.

'Calm down,' Houghton teased. 'I told her I was busy on the shop floor and that I'd seen you about, but didn't know where you were right that second. Why the panic?'

'Because she called me,' Langley told him, 'on my mobile. I told her I was in the stock room and away from my desk, which was why I wasn't answering my office phone.'

'Tricky bitch, eh?' Houghton smiled. 'Trying to catch one of us out. Or both of us.' Langley didn't respond – his mind racing with paranoid thoughts of what she might have discovered or suspected. 'Fit, though,' Houghton said in a hushed tone, as if she could hear him. 'I know what I'd like to do to her,' he smiled an ugly smile. 'I'd teach the bitch a lesson, I can promise you that. Bend her over your desk there and put her in her place, eh?'

The anger Langley felt towards Jane Huntingdon mingled with his contempt for Houghton like a chemical reaction. Rage began to surge through him, threatening to overwhelm him. Once he was with his little Roehampton girl, he'd be in complete control again, but putting up with the likes of Houghton and Huntingdon was becoming unbearable. He'd be doing the world a favour if he slit both their throats – just like his father had taught him to when he was a young boy and they'd hunted animals in the forest together, away from the mindless, squabbling chatter of his mother and sisters. Alone in the forest where they could be men, cooking whatever they'd managed to catch over an open fire while his father talked to him about the world they lived in – how it was a man's world, no matter what women like his mother tried to tell him; that when he grew older he should take whatever he wanted – including women. It was his father who'd taught him that he was different. That he was special. That he would do great things. He still missed him and wished the old man could see the great things that he'd done. Things a fool like Houghton could never understand.

'What would you know about teaching her a lesson?' he turned on Houghton – the need to be cruel too powerful to resist. 'Look at you. You really think she would ever want you?'

'Who said anything about her agreeing to it?' Houghton tried to bluff his way out of the awkwardness.

'You're talking about raping her?'

'No,' Houghton backed away. 'Course not. I was only— '

'Sounded like you want to rape her,' Langley continued. 'Force her to have sex with you.'

148

'Hey, look,' Houghton pleaded, 'it was a bit of banter, that's all.'

Langley smiled and took a few steps backwards. 'I'm just fucking with you,' he admitted, the burst of cruelty enough to satisfy his immediate need and restore his calm. 'You shouldn't take me so seriously.'

'Jesus!' Houghton breathed a sigh of relief. 'You had me going there for a minute.'

Langley smiled pleasantly. 'Well, you're right about one thing – she is most definitely fuckable.'

'Oh yeah,' Houghton grinned, his enthusiasm for puerile, sexual machismo having returned. 'You gonna have a crack at her then? Christmas party, eh? I've seen you – you're good with women. Reckon you've got a chance? Shagging the boss? Very nice.'

'I'm sure our paths will cross,' Langley told him as his hand covered the computer mouse and brought up the pictures of the Roehampton girl once more – his screen angled so Houghton couldn't see. 'And when they do, we'll see, won't we.'

Sean eased the key into the lock of the door that led to Tanya Richards' home – little more than a double room in a run-down Victorian house converted into as many bedsits as the landlord could get away with. He felt uncomfortable, like an intruder, and prayed that no one would see him enter her room. He'd climbed the stairs like a thief, listening for any sound of life that could send him fleeing from the building, but he'd made it to her front door without encountering anyone, although more than once he'd frozen on the stairs as raised voices or the sound of a television being turned up loud stopped him in his tracks. What type of people live here? he asked himself. Criminality leaked from every room. He turned the key and pushed the door, allowing it to fall open in its own time. The smells of Tanya Richards' life rushed at him: stale food, unwashed clothes, cigarettes, burnt crack cocaine, cheap booze and sex. It was a powerful, revolting and intoxicating mix that momentarily made him feel light-headed and nauseous. The original investigating team had left it relatively untouched and the windows closed. As much as he would have appreciated the fresh air, he was glad what remained of Tanya Richards had been sealed in the squalid room.

Once he'd adjusted to the smell, he stepped into the dimly lit interior – the only light coming from the rays of the weak winter sun that penetrated through the cheap net curtains – no doubt left closed by the North London MIT to keep journalists with cameras away. He tried the lights, but the electricity seemed to be out. He guessed it was on a room-by-room, pay-as-you-go meter system. No one would pay for a dead woman's electricity in this type of house. He closed the door behind him and walked across the room to the main windows, pulling the nets open wide to allow as much light in as possible. It improved things somewhat, but the room remained grey and depressing. His hand automatically went to his belt where his trusted Maglite waited, but he stopped himself. Somehow it was better like this – easier for him to be able to feel her, feel her desperation at where life had taken her, the trap it had led her into.

'Is that it?' he suddenly found himself speaking to the killer. 'Did you think you were killing them out of mercy – to end their painful lives?' He gave it some consideration for a few seconds. 'No. No, you're too cruel to show mercy. Taking their teeth and nails – there's no mercy in that.'

He began to walk around the cramped room, free to step wherever he wanted and touch anything – the forensic examination having been completed days earlier. He thought about the dozens of fingerprints that had been found in the room and the plentiful samples of DNA yielding semen. Some of the fingerprints and DNA had been matched to people with records, although none seemed to be likely suspects, but others belonged to people who weren't on record. People who were a mystery.

'Did you come here?' he asked. 'Did you come here with her? Did you spend time alone with her?'

He made a note to himself that all fingerprints and DNA from both scenes should be cross-referenced against those found in her bedsit. It ought to have been done as a matter of course, but with the change of investigating teams it was the sort of thing that could be overlooked.

'You would have liked to have been here with her before you killed her, wouldn't you?' he asked. 'It would have made it so much more special. Maybe even worth taking the risk of being seen with her, or her telling someone about you. Did you take the risk?' He stared at what was left of her bed – the mattress and covers long since removed to the lab. After a while he could see her sitting there, but he couldn't see the killer. 'No,' he concluded. 'You didn't come here. You're too careful. No matter how much you wanted it, you couldn't take the risk.'

He wandered over to the mantelpiece above the ancient electric bar fire and looked at the sad collection of photographs, all of which had Tanya Richards in them. Some were recent, selfies of Tanya alone, or with friends, but always her smile was dead. Others from when she was a child, when her smile was full of hope and dreams. 'What happened to bring you to this?' he asked. 'What went so badly wrong in your life?' He made a mental note to have her lifestyle research go much further back than usual – all the way to her childhood. Dalton's too. There could be something there to link them.

Without thinking, he found himself reaching out and taking hold of a picture of the victim as a little girl, dressed in a pink party dress. 'What drew him to you?' he whispered to the photograph. 'If you can help me find out, maybe I can trap him. I've done it before.' No answers came. 'Christ,' he complained, looking at the picture in his hand – suddenly feeling desperately sad and forlorn. He couldn't help but think of his own daughters and how many photographs exactly like the one he was holding they were in. What traps lay in wait for them in the future? The descent from happy childhood to being a young adult lost to the world could happen all too quickly, and as a cop he'd seen it played out more times than most people could imagine. He knew all too well that no one was immune.

As he replaced the photo on the mantelpiece and looked around the room it was as if he could feel Tanya Richards' desperate loneliness seeping into him, penetrating deep into his soul. Her unhappiness was almost overwhelming. He considered taking his time and going through her sparse cupboard and drawers. Not for anything critical – he knew the MIT would have found it if it was there to be found – but in the hope of understanding her life better. But as he looked around he realized it would be a waste of time. The room told him nothing about her – not the real Tanya Richards – not the little girl in the picture. It was as much an empty shell as her own dead body. He had to get out of the room before it crushed him.

He spun towards the door and fled from the room, sprinting down the stairs two at a time until he reached the front door – fumbling with the latch lock until he was able to yank the door open and escape into the relatively fresh air of Holloway.

Geoff Jackson grinned widely while shaking his head in disbelief when he saw Sean emerge from the run-down Victorian house where he knew the new killer's first victim had lived. When he got the tip-off from one of Sean's own that he'd be there, he was dubious at first, but his source had come up trumps. 'Well, well, well,' he said to himself as he lifted his camera to the small gap in his car window and held down the shutter to take a non-stop sequence of pictures. 'DI Corrigan, I presume.'

He watched Sean standing on the stairs, filling his lungs and then exhaling – as if he was recovering from a hard run.

'What you up to?' Jackson muttered under his breath. 'Running away from something, are we, Corrigan? Something got you spooked?'

Eventually, Sean skipped down the steps and walked the short distance to his unmarked car – looking up and down the street before climbing inside. Jackson reeled off another dozen shots as Sean disappeared from view. A few seconds later he watched Sean's car pull away and drive off down the street. Jackson lowered his camera and dropped it unceremoniously on the passenger seat as he sat scratching his chin – his mind racing with the possibilities of what Sean was doing at the house.

'This is an old crime scene, my friend,' he said. 'Nothing here for the cops any more, Corrigan, so what the hell you doing here? You keeping something to yourself? You'll talk to me, Corrigan,' he promised himself. 'One way or another, you'll talk to me.'

David Langley parked his car in a quiet side street off Putney Heath where he was sure there were no parking restrictions or CCTV and just enough cars so his own wouldn't stand out. He was some way from where he ultimately needed to be, but once the girl from Roehampton lay dead in a pool of her own blood, the police might well check a wide area for suspicious vehicles. Without CCTV or a parking ticket to guide them, it would be like he'd never been here.

He was wearing a pair of cold-weather waterproof running trousers, training shoes and the same hooded top he'd worn with the previous victims. The rain was pouring down in the freezing darkness outside his car, prompting him to pull a dark waterproof jacket over his torso before slipping his hands into thin, warm climbing gloves. After checking all around the car, using the mirrors to ensure he wasn't being watched, he pulled both hoods over his head and sprang out into the bitter night. Although it wasn't late, it was as dark as the foreboding woods he could see in the middle of the heath. He locked the car, threw his rucksack over his shoulder and began to jog through the streets – just another middle-aged man trying to stay in shape.

As he ran into Putney Heath heading towards Roehampton High Street, the traffic, both human and vehicular, grew heavier, but he barely drew a glance from drivers squinting to see through the rain and the darkness and pedestrians scuttling along the pavement, heads bowed. A few minutes of effortless running brought him to the same row of abandoned shops he'd followed her to the first time he'd seen her. He checked over his shoulder without breaking stride, then veered across the pavement and through the gap that led to the rear of the buildings. Once safely out of sight of the road, he surveyed his surroundings while he regained his breath and waited for his heart rate to return to normal – neither of which took long, his rigorous fitness programme serving him well. On his previous visit he'd spotted a dilapidated outhouse, little more than a shed, that offered a 180-degree field of vision over the old car park. He made his way there now and eased himself inside, using a couple of pieces of discarded hardboard to conceal himself. It was as he'd hoped: peering through the gap he could see pretty much everything that moved in the car park. Now all he had to do was wait and hope she would come tonight.

As he settled in, he was glad of the shelter the outhouse provided from the rain and wind outside, although the bitter cold soon began to penetrate his clothing, making him question his decision to begin his quest in the depths of winter. He reminded himself that, although it brought desperately cold weather, it also brought so many more hours of darkness, his greatest ally. Still, he began to wonder what it would be like to kill in the middle of a warm summer's night – the heat of the victim's blood almost unnoticeable on his already hot skin. Perhaps if he had the privacy, he could hunt in the nude – painting himself with their blood, waiting for it to dry on his skin, taut and cracked. He could remain sitting astride them, watching their dried blood falling like dust from his limbs and torso, untroubled by the cold. He could take as long as he wanted before washing the crimson powder from himself – the water turning it back into a liquid, only much thinner and faster-running than thick, oily blood – becoming less and less red the more he diluted it.

Suddenly his fantasy was disturbed when a hunched-over figure made their way into the car park, their hurried footsteps obliterated by the ceaseless rain that hammered down. He squinted to see better, praying it was the girl, the excitement rising in him though he had no intention of killing her – not tonight. But as the figure settled in the doorway at the rear of an abandoned shop he could see that it wasn't her. It was a male and judging by his clothes he was a teenager. He watched as the youth prepared his crack pipe, then the glow as a flame burst to life, followed by clouds of thick smoke billowing from his mouth and nostrils as he exhaled. A few seconds later, the smoker had finished; he slid down the wall into a crouching position, as good as trapping Langley in his lair. He could try and sneak past the semi-conscious youth, but he couldn't be sure how aware the junkie was. If he saw a dark figure emerging from the outhouse, he might talk to his friends – he might even get arrested for some petty crime and tell the police what he'd seen to try and help himself. Either way, Langley couldn't risk it. And there was still a chance she might come. So he settled in for the wait, using meditation techniques he'd taught himself to keep the worst of the cold at bay.

His meditation was disturbed by the entrance of a dark figure, sweeping the beam of a torch left to right and back again – searching every doorway and crevice. Langley froze rigid; instinctively he knew the hand carrying the torch belonged to a policeman – no doubt looking for an easy arrest to get himself out of the rain; some loser unlucky enough to be in possession of a class-A drug.

The cop came striding deeper into the car park, heavy steps splashing in the puddles. He was a big man – tall and lean. Powerful. If it came to a fight, the outcome would be unclear. Langley slid his hand into the rucksack on the floor by his side and gripped the handle of his knife; the soft rubber handle felt comforting and empowering. The policeman was now walking close to the walls of the abandoned buildings, heading straight towards the youth, who seemed unaware of the approaching danger until the beam of light from the torch was pointing straight at him.

From his vantage point, Langley watched as the disorientated youth struggled to get to his feet. The big cop seized him before he had a chance to flee, pinning him against the door and shining the torch directly into his face; helpless, the youth twisted and turned his head to protect his eyes from the glare. It was impossible to hear what was being said, the hammering rain drowned out all other sound. The policeman started searching through the surrendering youth's pockets and a troubling thought entered Langley's mind: What type of cop would be out in this weather looking for arrests? If he was looking to get out of the rain, surely there were easier ways to do it. It occurred to him that he might have underestimated the threat the policeman posed. If he arrested the youth, surely he would be calling for back-up and transport for his prisoner, which would mean more police – police with cars, flooding the car park with bright, white light. Suddenly his hidden lair felt like a trap as he tried to stay calm despite his rapidly increasing heart rate and tightening stomach.

If he left the outhouse, he would almost certainly be seen and the cop would be on to him. He could show himself and stand his ground – surprise the cop with his knife once he was close enough to slash him across his throat, sending him into shock as he finished him with a hack through his carotid artery. He was sure he was strong enough and fast enough to do it. But he hadn't planned on killing a policeman, hadn't considered the consequences. Hadn't fantasized about it for days before doing it. There would be almost no pleasure in it, although he would become instantly notorious. *Sebastian Gibran had killed a cop. He'd almost killed two.* He'd have to kill the youth as well. He couldn't afford to leave a witness.

As he started to slide the knife from his rucksack, the big policeman gave the youth a gentle shove, indicating with a wave of his hand that he was free to go. The boy needed no second invitation as he scurried away across the flooding, broken tarmac – slipping and falling as he ran, recovering his footing as he disappeared through the gap in the buildings and was gone.

Langley exhaled, careful to breathe through his nose so as not to create plumes of condensation that the policeman might see. As he felt the tension begin to leave his taut body, he inhaled deeply and began to slide the knife back into the rucksack. Surely now the cop would leave. There was nothing else for him here. But as he began to lower his torch he seemed to tense and look directly towards where Langley hid – cocking his head to one side, trying to detect the origins of a sound of interest. Langley held his breath as the policeman turned fully in his direction and began to walk slowly and purposefully towards him, the strong beam of light sweeping from side to side as he approached, illuminating every heavy raindrop that passed through it.

Slowly Langley extracted the knife from his rucksack. He was glad he'd bought one with a blackened blade that wouldn't reflect the light and betray him, glad that he'd worn dark clothing that also hid his face. He squinted his eyes to the thinnest of slits so he could see without the whites giving him away, and waited for the policeman to come closer – close enough for him to burst from his lair and strike him in the throat without the need for a single step. Holding his breath, he waited as the policeman came so close now that he could hear his footsteps in the water above the pounding rain, the torch beam passing back and forth over the entrance to the outhouse. Two more steps and he'd be close enough to kill.

Suddenly the radio attached to the policeman's shoulder gave a loud burst of static, sending Langley's heartbeat racing out of control, his eyes firing wide open as he prepared to attack. But the policeman had stopped in his tracks as he hunched the shoulder with the radio closer to his ear. Again Langley strained to listen and although he could hear the sound of a human voice coming from the radio he couldn't make out what was being said. He squeezed the handle of the knife tighter as he watched the policeman wrap a big hand around the radio and say something he couldn't understand, all the while pointing his torch in Langley's direction. The voice came from the radio again, prompting the policeman to start nodding as if he understood before replying. Maybe he'd been seen by someone else? Someone else who'd told the police. He braced himself to attack, but now the policeman straightened and seemed to relax, slowly turning away from the outhouse – his torch beam heading away now instead of relentlessly towards him. He appeared to take forever to drift from the car park – unaware that his life had been saved by that call on his radio.

Langley waited until the policeman was gone from sight before allowing himself a deep breath, the sudden intake of oxygen and relief making him feel dizzy. But he remained hidden for as long as his cramping, freezing limbs could stand, wary of a trap. Finally he stretched and uncoiled his body – shaking the blood back into his extremities – carefully pulling the rucksack on to his back as he climbed from his den and jogged away through the freezing rain in the direction of his car.

# 7

Sean pushed aside the latest stack of reports generated by the investigation, frustrated that he couldn't find anything in there to pique his interest. Muttering under his breath, he leaned back in his chair, racking his brains for some new proactive approach he could try that would open up a new line of enquiry. As he scanned the room for inspiration, his eyes alighted on his computer and it came to him: a search of the Met's crime reporting and recording system, CRIS. It was simple, unintuitive software and could only react specifically to whatever information the user was inputting, but nevertheless it could be a highly useful tool in skilled and creative hands. Just because the killer had never been convicted, it didn't mean he hadn't been reported for a crime, or arrested or charged and tried. He'd had the team searching for similar crimes to the murders – attempted murders and serious assaults where teeth and or fingernails had been targeted – but they'd drawn a blank. Now Sean wanted to widen the search.

He rested his fingers over the keyboard for a moment while he considered the parameters. Then his fingers sprang to life as he asked CRIS to search London-wide for assaults with a knife where the attacker had targeted the face or mouth. He knew his search would return details of pub fights, gang fights, even domestic assaults, but if the use of the knife was specific enough, it could have been the first sign of what was to come from a killer-in-waiting. There were more results than he'd hoped for, but fewer than he'd feared. Next, he narrowed the parameters for the suspect – specifying an age of between twenty-five and fifty-five. He agreed with Anna that the killer displayed the maturity and calmness of an older, more experienced man. At the same time he changed the suspect search details so CRIS would only return crimes with white suspects. The effect was to dramatically reduce the number of crimes CRIS found – easily few enough to check. As he began to read through the methods and details of the crimes he quickly discounted each one. Most involved slash wounds to the face; he was looking for stabbing in the mouth area. The few instances he did find involved stab wounds to other parts of the body too; it was soon clear those responsible hadn't been directly targeting the face and mouth, it was simply a case of collateral damage.

He leaned back in his chair, hands interlocked behind his head, until inspiration struck again. This time he kept the suspect details the same, but changed the point of attack to the hands and fingers – specifying the use of a knife or pliers. He pressed search. There were far fewer hits than before, but still enough to give him hope that he may yet find something. But again, once he started reading the details of the crimes he was disappointed. Most were minor injuries – slash wounds to the backs of people's hands, or defensive injuries, while others displayed all the hallmarks of criminal turf wars with fingers being severed as a punishment and a warning to others. He scratched his scalp in irritation, then ran a hand over his light brown hair to smooth it into place again and resumed staring at the screen while he waited for more ideas.

He was about to search CRIS for anything whatsoever related to teeth: theft of teeth, assaults involving teeth, threats mentioning teeth – anything that might throw up that diamond piece of information that would have the investigation suddenly spiralling towards a strong suspect and a swift conclusion, when a loud rapping on the doorframe to his office shattered his train of thought.

'What the fu—' was as far as he got before his brain registered it was Addis standing in the doorway. 'Sir,' he recovered as his eyes fell on the newspaper tucked under the assistant commissioner's arm. 'I was just checking CRIS to see if I could find anything in the past that could be down to our man.'

'Surely CRIS searches have been completed by now?' Addis replied as he entered the office and stood in front of Sean's desk.

'I was looking for something less obvious than the usual searches. Maybe a way in through the back door.'

'Any success?' Addis asked.

'No,' Sean told him bluntly. 'Nothing.'

'I see,' Addis replied, the disappointment in his voice was clear. 'Are there any positive developments? Anything at all?'

'We have a good idea of the sort of person we're looking for,' Sean tried to appease him.

'You mean the psychological profile?' Addis asked as if he'd already decided it was of no importance. 'Hardly going to provide us with the name and address of the suspect, is it?'

'I seem to remember it was your idea to have a psychiatrist on the team.'

'I merely provided you with a tool,' Addis recovered without missing a beat – a seasoned veteran when it came to thinking on his feet. 'It's up to you how you use her, but I don't expect miracles.'

Again Sean wondered whether Addis suspected that Anna had turned, but he couldn't see through his cold armour and gave up trying. 'We appear to be dealing with a stranger attack,' he explained. 'Those are always the most difficult cases to solve.'

'I appreciate that,' Addis assured him, although his tone

was anything but reassuring. 'What concerns me is the likelihood of another victim turning up. When the media start digging, are you sure you'll be able to say you did everything humanly possible to find him? Are you sure they won't identify mistakes made?'

'I'm doing everything I can,' Sean told him. 'If I've made a mistake, I won't try and hide it, but I have no match for the DNA, no previous cases involving that MO, and no associates that both victims had in common. If anyone wants to suggest some other line of enquiry I could be pursuing, I'm listening.'

'There must be something else you could be doing.'

'More media appeals.' Sean knew Addis could never resist an opportunity for media exposure – especially not with his eye on becoming Commissioner. 'Local media coverage hasn't turned up anything. We need to get on national TV and radio. Or rather, it would be best if *you* got on national TV. I'd prefer to keep a low profile.'

'I'll have Press Bureau arrange it,' snapped Addis. It struck Sean that he was less delighted than usual at the thought of being in the spotlight. The reason became apparent when he took the newspaper from under his arm, opened it at the centre pages and set it out on the desk in front of Sean. 'As you can see, there's something else we need to talk about.'

Sean looked down at that morning's edition of *The World*. It featured a large photograph of him standing on the steps outside the building where Tanya Richards had lived. 'Shit,' he cursed under his breath.

'Do you mind telling me why this journalist has such an unhealthy interest in you?' Addis asked. 'He appears determined to turn you into some sort of celebrity.'

'I have no idea,' Sean replied, shaking his head. 'I suppose he knows I run SIU investigations, so he assumes that if he follows me it'll lead him to a story eventually.'

'Clearly he's prepared to invest a lot of time in you,' Addis pointed out. 'Where was this photograph taken?'

'Outside Tanya Richards' place,' Sean sighed.

'What were you doing there?' Addis asked. 'That's not a crime scene.'

'Thought I might find something.'

'I see,' Addis said, giving him a knowing look. 'So he followed you there, or staked the place out knowing you might eventually turn up.'

'No.' Sean shook his head vigorously 'I wasn't followed. He couldn't have stuck with me through daytime London traffic.'

'Then what?' Addis asked.

Sean's mind was spinning. There was no way Jackson could have predicted that he would pay a visit to Tanya Richards' bedsit. As Addis pointed out, it wasn't a crime scene, there was no specific reason for him to go there, so it wouldn't have been worth staking it out on the off-chance that he might show up. In the event, Sean had made the decision to go there at the last minute, looking for any excuse to escape the claustrophobia of the Yard. Which meant there was only one way Jackson could have found out when he was going to be there. Someone must have told him. Someone from Sean's own team. But who knew he was going? He'd told Sally, but he trusted her with his life. The only other person who knew for sure was DC Tessa Carlisle, the exhibits officer who'd given him the keys. She was young, inexperienced and probably struggling financially, as were most young cops – all of which made her vulnerable to the sort of cash someone like Jackson would offer for seemingly harmless information. Then again, Sean could have been overheard, in which case anyone at the Yard could have tipped the journalist off.

At least now he knew there was a leak, although until he knew a lot more it would be best not to mention it to anyone. Keep his cards close to his chest until he had a chance to trap the mole in his team – if indeed there was one.

'I'll deal with Jackson,' he told Addis, 'although you have to give it to him – he's as resourceful as he is determined.'

163

'Sounds as though you admire him.'

'No,' Sean snapped. 'I respect him. If I'm going to *manage* him, then I need to respect him – and I do.'

'Fine,' Addis let it go. 'But bear in mind, this sort of publicity is not good for the image of the Metropolitan Police. When a newspaper like *The World* focuses its attention on an individual officer, it can only mean one thing: they're setting you up for a fall. The media's not interested in a hero cop catching the bad guy. When have you ever seen a positive story about an individual officer? People like Jackson only want the dirt – stories about corruption and police incompetence. Those are our enemies out there, Sean. You would do well to remember that.'

'I'm well aware of it,' he assured him. 'If I'd wanted people to treat me like a hero, I would have been a fireman.'

Addis grunted a low, short laugh. 'Good, but if you can't manage him, perhaps I know people who can.'

Sean had heard rumours that Addis had as many friends in low places as he did in high ones. As much as he considered Jackson to be an irritating rash he couldn't scratch, he wasn't ready to see Addis feed him to the unseen sharks. 'That won't be necessary,' he told him. 'I can handle Jackson. Maybe even use him to our benefit.'

'Maybe,' Addis replied, getting to his feet, 'but remember – if you're going to try and handle a snake, hold it by the neck. I'll get the media appeal organized. Keep me updated.' With that he spun on his heel and strode from the office, watched all the way by Sean. He was still watching the receding figure when the phone on his desk began to ring. He snatched it up to kill the shrill noise as much as to see who was calling. 'DI Corrigan.'

'Hello, sir,' replied the gentle but official-sounding voice. 'It's Sergeant Harding calling from custody at Islington. We have someone here who's apparently of interest to yourselves – a Joey Mehmet. He's circulated as wanted for questioning by the SIU.'

'He is,' Sean told him – a small flutter of excitement invading the pit of his stomach, although the lack of a surge of adrenalin told him he didn't believe Mehmet could be anything other than a useful witness. Either way, he still needed to be interviewed. 'Hold him there until I can get someone over to interview him.'

'No problem,' Harding answered. 'I'll let his brief know you're on your way.'

'Fine,' Sean replied and hung up as he got to his feet and knocked on the Perspex partition between his and Sally's office. She glanced up from her computer screen and he beckoned her to his room with a hand gesture. A few seconds later she stood in his doorway.

'Something up?' she asked.

'Joey Mehmet's been nicked,' he told her. 'He's in custody over in Islington, awaiting our attention. Grab hold of someone sensible and get over there and interview for us, will you?'

'You don't want to do it yourself?' she checked.

'No,' he answered bluntly. 'I've got too much other shit to sort out.'

'Then you don't consider him a decent suspect?'

'I'm not assuming anything,' he assured her. 'He needs to be interviewed. He may know something important. Something important about Tanya Richards we haven't heard yet.'

'OK,' Sally reluctantly agreed.

'Thanks,' Sean told her.

'What did Addis want?' she changed the subject.

'The usual,' he said. 'When will we arrest the suspect? Why haven't we already?'

'Not a patient man, our Mr Addis,' Sally replied.

'No, he's not, so the sooner you get Mehmet interviewed and I can give him a full update, the better.'

'Right-oh. I'll phone you when I'm finished.'

He waited until she'd returned to her own office before returning to the files and newspaper spread across his desk.

The door slammed shut behind Jackson, followed by the sound of heavy impenetrable locks being turned. Neither man spoke until the echoes subsided to nothing.

'You're early.' Gibran's face was as blank as his dead black eyes that still managed to shine with a raptor-like intelligence. Several years in Broadmoor, with constant counselling and medication hadn't remotely dulled his predatory presence. 'I wasn't expecting you for another week. Please – take a seat.'

Jackson cautiously did as he was told, placing his briefcase on the floor next to him – his eyes never leaving Gibran's tethered hands. 'Something came up,' he explained once he was safely in his seat.

'Oh?'

'I hope you don't mind me bringing things forward?' Jackson asked, ignoring Gibran's prompt. He wanted to buy himself some time to settle, to warm Gibran up before putting his ideas to him.

'Time,' Gibran answered, 'is of no relevance to me any more, Mr Jackson. Arrange your meetings whenever you wish.'

'Er, thank you,' Jackson replied, unsure what else to say.

'So what is it?' Gibran asked. 'What's brought you rushing back to Broadmoor?'

Clearly there would be no small talk with Gibran. Still Jackson played coy. 'Perhaps you already know?'

'Let's assume I don't,' Gibran hurried him.

'You've not heard there's a new serial killer in London?'

'I have access to a television and radio, Mr Jackson,' Gibran told him, 'and to the newspapers and even the internet to some degree – although I see little that interests me. Pointless people living pointless lives.'

Jackson was beginning to see up close how Gibran could kill so easily. To him, people were nothing. 'I thought this one

166

might interest you, though,' he persisted, hoping to goad Gibran into a reaction. 'DI Corrigan's in charge of finding him.'

Gibran brushed the name aside. 'I take it you're referring to the killings of a whore and a homeless man who was no doubt close to death anyway. Why would this be of interest to me?'

'I was hoping maybe you could give me some insight into what this killer is thinking?' Jackson appealed. 'Why he's doing it.'

'In other words, you think he and I must be alike,' Gibran said. 'If I can think like him then I must be like him – correct?'

'No,' Jackson tried to backtrack, but Gibran cut him off.

'And you thought that telling me DI Corrigan was in charge of finding him would somehow appeal to me, make me feel as if I had something in common with this killer?'

'No,' Jackson stumbled to recover. 'I thought it would be interesting to hear your opinion, that's all.'

'My opinion?' Gibran spat the words. 'My opinion is that whoever this killer is, he is of no consequence. He picks vulnerable, predictable victims – the sort of people a child could kill.'

'You did too.' Jackson pushed his luck, glancing at the restraints around Gibran's wrists. 'Occasionally you selected vulnerable victims.' His brow creased as he searched for the name in his memory. 'Heather Freeman,' he accused Gibran. 'She was what, fifteen? A homeless runaway. You cut her throat.'

'Now, now,' Gibran reminded him. 'I was interviewed about her, but never charged. Merely Corrigan trying to attribute cases he couldn't solve to me. As for *your* new killer, his work is of no consequence.'

'But yours was?' Jackson tried again.

'Be careful, Mr Jackson,' Gibran warned him. 'Trying to be too clever can be very dangerous – especially when you're close to me.'

Jackson swallowed hard before moving on. 'But I can quote you?' he asked. 'I can quote what you've said about him? That you think he's of no consequence?'

'Do whatever you want,' Gibran told him, looking bored. 'It means nothing to me.'

Jackson knew that Gibran's comments about the new killer would be enough to excite his editor and titillate the masses, but he wanted more. Having predicted Gibran's likely reaction, he'd brought something with him he hoped would elicit an even longer dialogue. He reached down into the briefcase at his side and produced that day's edition of *The World* from inside – spreading it open at the centre page. He saw Gibran's eyes look down at the photograph of Sean standing on the steps outside Tanya Richards' bedsit and for a second he thought he saw a murderous glint shining in them. Had Gibran's victims seen the same thing just before he killed them?

'You've already told me DI Corrigan's in charge of the investigation,' Gibran reminded him. 'Are you showing me his picture in the hope of eliciting a response?'

'No,' Jackson lied. 'I was just thinking that if this killer's as inconsequential as you say he is, then why have the Met got their best investigator trying to find him? Why not just leave it in the hands of the local Murder Team?'

'It can hardly be a surprise Corrigan's been given the job of finding him,' Gibran smiled. 'As insignificant as his killings may be, they are undoubtedly gruesome enough to warrant the attention of DI Corrigan. He does so like the *messy* ones.'

'You weren't his first, you know?' Jackson changed tack. 'His first serial killer . . . sorry – I mean *alleged* serial killer. I've been doing quite a lot of research about Corrigan – seems he's been involved in these types of investigations for longer than I thought – going all the way back to 1993 when he was barely out of uniform, yet somehow had a major role in capturing the Parkside Murderer and rapist. In 2000 he joined his first murder squad and caught Steven Millbank after he raped and murdered a woman in her own home. Six months later he was involved in the capture of Joseph Stubley after he killed several old women. Then there was Mao Ma, the Chinese serial killer, and Thomas Keller – not forgetting Jeremy Goldsboro, of course. I'm sure you recognize the names – given that most of them are locked in here with you. Do you ever discuss Corrigan with them? Ever talk about him?'

'No,' Gibran insisted. 'I hear the others do, but not me.'

'Even though he caught you too?' Jackson pushed.

'He didn't,' Gibran snarled. 'Someone else *caught* me. Someone I underestimated.'

'James Hellier,' Jackson said his name, despite fearing Gibran's reaction. 'The same man the police believe you were trying to frame for your *alleged* crimes.'

'If Hellier's as innocent as you believe,' Gibran argued, 'then why did he go missing after my arrest and why has he never been heard of since? Seems strange – don't you think?'

'Maybe he had other reasons to run,' Jackson answered, 'and yes, his role in identifying you is well documented, but Corrigan still worked out that you were the real killer.'

'Only because of Hellier's help,' Gibran insisted, 'although . . .'

'Although what?' Jackson seized on it.

'Corrigan does have certain . . . *gifts*. Gifts that are wasted on this man he's looking for now.'

'*Gifts*?' Jackson asked, feeling his heart quicken as he sensed Gibran was about to reveal something important.

'Certain *abilities*,' Gibran explained. 'Abilities that may have eventually led him to my door even without Hellier's help. Abilities I only realized he had when I sat across the interview table from him.'

'I don't understand,' Jackson admitted, shaking his head.

'You really don't know?' Gibran asked. 'You've been watching him for months, maybe even years – researching his background. You know everything there is to know about every major investigation he's ever been involved with, and yet you don't know him at all.'

'So tell me,' Jackson pleaded. 'What is it about Corrigan I don't know?'

'Think,' Gibran demanded. 'The Special Investigations Unit was set up so that the police could use his *talents* over and over again. When was the last time the Metropolitan Police set up an entire unit just to accommodate the abilities of a lowly detective inspector?'

'Because Corrigan's an exceptional detective,' Jackson tried to work it out. 'They want him where they can best use him – don't want to waste an asset.'

'No,' Gibran scolded him. 'You're missing the point. Asking the wrong questions.'

'Just tell me,' Jackson almost begged.

'What makes him an exceptional detective?' Gibran asked the questions he wanted Jackson to. 'What makes him so *special*?'

'I don't know,' Jackson struggled. 'He's insightful, he has a knack for predicting a killer's next move?'

'Close, Mr Jackson, but not close enough. He's more than just insightful. He can *think* like them. He can think like the killers he hunts. He doesn't merely predict their next move – he can see it.'

'What?' Jackson shook his head disbelievingly.

'He thinks like them,' Gibran repeated, 'and if he can think like them, then perhaps he *is* like them. My, my, imagine that – a natural-born killer hiding behind the disguise of being a policeman. But not just any policeman – a detective. A detective who hunts killers. Poacher turned gamekeeper, Mr Jackson. But how long before that particular leopard actually shows its spots? Unless of course it already has.'

'What do you mean?' Jackson asked, his head spinning.

'I read about the shooting of Jeremy Goldsboro,' Gibran told him. 'Because of my particular situation, I was able to obtain a few more details about the shooting than perhaps

170

even you could. You understand that if I were ever to be declared sane enough to be tried for my alleged crimes, part of my defence would be the credibility of DI Corrigan.'

'Because you always alleged he planted evidence in your case?' Jackson added.

'Exactly,' Gibran confirmed. 'Which means my legal team were able to access certain material relating to the Goldsboro shooting. To the untrained eye it would have meant little. Everything seemed in order. The killing was justified.'

'But?' Jackson encouraged him.

'He created the situation,' Gibran explained. 'It was quite the work of art. He even manipulated it so he wasn't the one who pulled the trigger. Very clever. If he'd shot the unfortunate Jeremy Goldsboro himself, then there would have been a lot more questions asked. Killing by proxy. The perfect murder.'

'Wait,' Jackson tried to slow him down. 'I covered that case. I don't see how he could have created the situation that meant Goldsboro had to be shot. The final confrontation all happened too fast.'

'Yet he had the presence of mind to tell DS Donnelly to book out a firearm. How could he possibly have known he would need a firearm if he didn't know what was going to happen?'

'Not that impossible,' Jackson argued. 'They knew The Jackdaw had access to a firearm.'

'Think,' Gibran ordered. 'Detectives don't walk around with guns any more. If they need to arrest an armed suspect they use SO19 or Armed Response Vehicles.'

'ARVs were there,' Jackson reminded him.

'As a decoy,' Gibran told him, 'sent to where Corrigan knew they would be useless. He planned it all. He planned it all because he had to know – he just had to know what it felt like to kill another human being. Donnelly pulled the trigger, but it was Corrigan's hand on the puppet strings.'

'You really believe that?' Jackson asked as he remembered

seeing Sean on TV shortly after the shooting – calm and composed, as if nothing had happened.

'I know a killer when I see one, Mr Jackson,' Gibran replied. 'I saw it as soon as I saw James Hellier and I see it when I see Detective Inspector Corrigan. Only question is, how long will killing by proxy satisfy his needs? How long before he needs to feel his own hands squeezing the life out of some doomed soul? He can't fight it forever.'

*Jesus Christ*, Jackson thought to himself. Too much of what Gibran said made sense. The forming of the SIU. Addis apparently feeding Corrigan every suspected serial killer investigation in London. The shooting of Jeremy Goldsboro. Even Corrigan's apparent ability to find killers more quickly than anyone else began to appear darker and more troubling than he'd previously suspected. Perhaps his journalistic instincts that Corrigan *was* the story had been right all along. Corrigan could predict *them*, could catch *them*, because he *was* one of *them*. 'Jesus,' Jackson whispered. 'I need to go,' he told Gibran, jumping to his feet.

'Of course you do,' Gibran smiled as he watched him. 'Of course you do.'


Sally and DC Maggie O'Neil sat across the desk from Joey Mehmet and his solicitor, Lucy Robinson, in an interview room at Islington Police Station. Robinson wore a smart but practical grey suit with a white blouse, her light brown hair cut short and practical. Sally guessed her to be in her mid-forties, but she looked fresh and attractive, her eyes awake and sparkling. Clearly she didn't spend much time trawling around London police stations in the dead of night representing low-level losers, which meant her firm of solicitors considered Mehmet to be worthy of the attention of one of their more valued employees. Sally couldn't help a pang of jealousy.

Mehmet, on the other hand, wore the look of desperation and fear that most in custody for serious crimes had, along with a white forensic suit, the clothes he'd been wearing having been seized for evidence. His face was gaunt and unattractive, his body and skin almost reptilian – wiry but strong. She could imagine him charming and seducing naive young girls into doing his bidding, just as she could imagine him beating the hell out of his more experienced, worldly-wise *employees*. She also knew Sean doubted he was the killer, otherwise he'd be here himself. But she needed to forget that now. He'd been wrong before. Maybe he was wrong again? Mehmet was a viable suspect for the murder of Tanya Richards and she'd treat him accordingly. Who knew what the interview might reveal? She pressed the red button on the dual tape recorder and filled the room with the shrill sound warning them that everything they were about to say would be recorded. When the unpleasant sound stopped, Sally began.

'This interview is being tape-recorded. The date is the thirteenth of January 2017 and the time is 3.45 p.m. This interview is being conducted in Islington Police Station. I am Detective Sergeant Sally Jones and the other officer present is . . .'

'DC Maggie O'Neil,' she introduced herself.

'We are interviewing – can you state your name for the tape, please?'

'Yeah,' Mehmet croaked, his throat strained through dehydration and talking too much as he pleaded his innocence to anyone who'd listen. 'I mean, Joey Mehmet.'

'Thank you,' Sally acknowledged, 'and also present is your solicitor . . .'

'Lucy Robinson,' the solicitor told them in a voice that was soft and feminine enough to surprise her, 'from Bishop and Bynum solicitors.'

'OK.' Sally nodded. 'Joey – before we begin, I need to remind you that you're still under caution, which means you don't have to say anything unless you wish to do so, but it may harm your defence if you fail to mention something when questioned that you later rely on in court. Anything you do say may be used as evidence against you. Do you understand?'

'I've fully explained the caution to Mr Mehmet,' Robinson answered for him. 'He understands it.'

'I need to hear it from Joey,' Sally reminded her.

'I understand,' Mehmet told her.

'And you have the right to free and independent legal advice,' Sally continued. 'This can either be on the phone or in person. You have your solicitor here anyway. If at any time you wish to speak to her in private, just let me know and I'll stop the interview. Is that clear?'

'Yeah,' Mehmet replied. 'I understand.'

'OK, good,' Sally drew a line under the introductory proceedings. 'Joey. Do you know why you're here?'

'No,' he answered, indignant and confused.

'You've been arrested on suspicion of having murdered Tanya Richards,' Sally explained.

'That's bullshit, man,' Mehmet answered, shaking his head. 'I didn't kill no one.'

'Is there any evidence to support Mr Mehmet's arrest?' Robinson intervened. 'If there is, then I haven't been shown it.'

'Joey was Tanya Richards' pimp,' Sally answered. 'He went missing immediately after she was killed and hasn't been seen since, despite half the Met looking for him.'

'Hardly evidence of murder,' Robinson argued, her expression displaying no emotion.

'Tanya worked the streets,' Sally explained. 'She was a prostitute and you were her pimp.' Mehmet shuffled in his chair but said nothing. 'That's right, isn't it, Joey?'

'I looked after her,' Mehmet insisted. 'If she had a customer who was giving her trouble, I'd take care of it, was all.'

'How very noble of you,' Sally told him, 'but the point is, when a prostitute is murdered and her *protector* goes missing, he's going to come under strong suspicion.'

'Is that the only evidence you have?' Robinson cut in. 'Surely you would have been better off interviewing Mr Mehmet as a possible witness – under caution, if need be.'

'This is a murder investigation,' Sally told her. 'Even with the slightest evidence against Joey it's only fair he's made aware he's a suspect and therefore afforded the full protection of his rights. If at some point in the future he is no longer a suspect, you will be informed and anything he says today will be transcribed into a witness statement that Joey can check and sign, but at the moment, Joey, you're not free to go and you will be interviewed as a suspect in the murder of Tanya Richards.'

'Whatever,' he agreed impatiently. 'Let's get on with it, yeah.'

'Joey Mehmet,' Sally continued. 'Did you kill Tanya Richards?'

'No,' he snapped back. 'Fuck no.'

'But you knew her?'

'I told you I did,' Mehmet answered.

'So tell us what your relationship with her was?' Sally asked.

'She . . . she was a friend,' Mehmet replied. 'I looked after her on the street, you know.'

'Like you said,' Sally reminded him. 'You were her *protector*.'

'Yeah,' he readily agreed. 'I was her protector.'

'And what did being her protector involve?' Sally asked.

'Is Mr Mehmet being interviewed on suspicion of being involved in the solicitation of women for prostitution, or the murder of Tanya Richards?' Robinson intervened.

'About her murder,' Sally told her. 'Their relationship is obviously relevant.'

'I don't mind answering,' Mehmet said, sounding desperate, as if only total cooperation would set him free. 'I want to answer.'

'I'm listening,' Sally encouraged him.

'I first saw her a couple of years ago, you know – wandering

175

around the West End begging and shit,' he explained. 'She was homeless, so I offered her something better – get her off the streets and that.'

Sally felt a slight spike of excitement at the mention of something both victims had had in common – *homeless in the West End*. 'Took her off the streets?' she questioned.

'Gave her somewhere to stay and that,' Mehmet explained.

'That was very generous of you,' Sally played along. 'And what did she give you in return?'

'Nothing.' Mehmet shrugged, looking embarrassed by his own feeble answer. 'We were just friends – boyfriend, girl-friend for a while, I suppose.'

'I see,' Sally said, knowing how it worked with people like Mehmet. First, they conned vulnerable girls into believing they cared for them – treating them well, like a proper girl-friend – then soon they put them to work, keeping them in line with a combination of emotional and financial dependence as well as threats of violence.

'It didn't last,' he continued, 'but she didn't have a job or nothing – nowhere else she could go, so I got her the bedsit – took care of her rent and that.'

'And in return she worked for you.' Sally was tiring of the game. 'She became a prostitute working the streets, most of what she was earning going back to you or her dealer – unless of course you were her dealer?'

'No,' Mehmet shook his head desperately. 'It wasn't like that.'

'You're in a lot of trouble,' Sally reminded him. 'Don't dance around the truth with me, Joey. You'll only dig your own grave.'

'You don't have to cooperate,' Robinson reminded him.

'No,' Mehmet told her. 'No. Listen – yeah she was a tom, but I didn't make her. I kept an eye out for her.'

'And for that she paid you.' It was a statement rather than a question.

'Yeah,' he admitted. 'Sometimes. When she actually had any cash.'

'Did that piss you off, Joey?' Sally jumped on it. 'That she didn't keep her money long enough to pay you.'

Mehmet grimaced like a trapped animal. 'No,' he pleaded.

'Really,' Sally nodded before moving on. 'So what do you mean, you *kept an eye out for her*?'

'Look,' he explained. 'Some of her customers could get a bit out of order or a bit weird – obsessive, y'know.'

'So?'

'So,' Mehmet continued, 'if someone was giving her a hard time I'd have a word with them and scare them off or get them to behave themselves.'

'And if they didn't take the warning?' Sally pressed.

'Nothing,' Mehmet squirmed in his seat – trapped under Sally's disbelieving stare. 'Look – maybe I'd rough 'em up a bit or threaten to show their wives photographs and shit, but only to get them to fuck off or behave themselves – that's all. Listen, if one of my girls ever got seriously hurt by someone I'd tell them to go to the Old Bill. I'm not stupid. Serious shit's for the police to sort out. Not me.'

'*Your girls*?' Sally smiled.

'Girlfriends,' Mehmet shrugged. 'Friends who are girls. You know.'

'Yes, Joey,' Sally replied. 'I know exactly what you mean.' She studied him intently before moving on. 'So – if someone was bothering Tanya Richards, she would have come to you?' Mehmet shrugged. 'Joey,' Sally poked him.

'Yeah,' he reluctantly admitted. 'Yeah.'

'And did she?' Sally laboured.

'Tanya could be hard work, you know,' Mehmet answered. 'She was always coming to me to sort shit out. This guy did this, this guy did that. This guy wants her to do this, this guy wants her to do that. There was always something with Tanya.'

'I'm not interested in the usual shit,' Sally told him. 'I'm looking for someone who stood out. Someone potentially dangerous. Someone who maybe even got your attention.'

Mehmet looked everywhere in the room except at Sally, as if he was afraid of taking the next truthful step that could embroil him deeper into the investigation and tarnish his image on the street. 'Maybe,' he finally conceded.

'Maybe?' Sally pushed him.

'About a week before, you know, she got killed,' he began. 'She came to me saying she was worried about a client who'd picked her up a couple of times.'

'Go on,' Sally hurried him, her own sense of excitement growing.

'Yeah,' Mehmet explained. 'She said the first time, he'd picked her up, but then didn't want to do nothing – just talk. Still paid her, though. It happens – lonely losers looking for someone to talk to. Only the second time he did have sex with her, but it was rough – rougher than usual. He almost strangled her to fucking death, man. I saw the bruises around her neck.'

'So what did you do?'

'I stayed close to her for a few nights,' he answered, 'waiting for him to turn up, but he never did – so I forgot about it.'

'Why didn't you go to the police?' Sally asked, 'or at least tell Tanya to?'

'Weren't like he beat the shit out of her,' Mehmet shrugged. 'Just got a bit carried away and he didn't come back, so I forgot about it.'

'But you said he almost strangled her to death and then she was killed only a few days later,' Sally reminded him through gritted teeth. 'Didn't you think that could be important?'

'Listen,' Mehmet pleaded. 'I thought you'd probably know all this already. Plus I knew once she was killed there'd be Old Bill all over the place, and me and the police don't get on, so I thought I'd keep my head down for a bit. Ain't no more to it than that. Look, she was an all right kid and I'm sorry she's dead, but it weren't me. It weren't me.'

'All right,' Sally sighed. 'Back to this customer who almost strangled her. What do you know about him?'

'Nothing,' Mehmet told her, his natural inclination not to answer when questioned by the police overtaking his desire to help.

'Come on,' Sally tried to help him help himself. 'You can do better than that. You went with her for a few nights to look out for him.'

'So?' he asked, looking confused.

'So she must have told you what he looked like,' Sally reminded him, 'so you'd recognize him if he turned up. Yes?'

'Yeah,' Mehmet shook his head as he remembered. 'Yeah. Right. She did tell me.'

'And what did she tell you?' Sally asked – her patience beginning to strain.

Mehmet's eyes looked up at the ceiling as he tried to recall. 'Said he was white – thirty, forty years old, I think. Shit, man,' he chastised himself, 'what else did she say?'

'Take your time,' Sally managed to say. 'Anything about his clothes?'

'Yeah. Yeah,' Mehmet's memory sprang to life. 'Said he always wore really dark clothing – like tracksuits and stuff and a hoodie – yeah a hoodie. I remember because she said he never took the hood off so she could never see his face properly, although she said he looked like he was probably a good-looking guy, you know.'

'Did she say if he had anything with him?' Sally probed.

'Yeah,' Mehmet almost shouted the answer. 'She said he always had a rucksack with him – that I should be looking for someone carrying a rucksack.'

'Thank you,' Sally told him before taking a moment to consider what she was being told. Instinctively she knew she'd discovered something important. A significant breakthrough.

'And strong,' Mehmet suddenly revealed without prompting. 'I remember she said he was really fucking strong, man. She said I should bring something with me – like a knife or a baseball bat or something. She said I might need it. I told her I didn't need anything, but she looked scared and she wouldn't stop going on about how I needed to bring something. Just made me think, you know, how he must have been really strong to freak her out like that.'

'And did you take anything?' Sally asked.

'You don't have to answer that,' Robinson interrupted.

'I'm not interested in charging Joey for possessing an offensive weapon,' Sally told her.

'Doesn't really matter now, does it?' Mehmet reminded them all. 'Whether I did or didn't, it's not going to help Tanya now.'

'No,' Sally solemnly agreed. 'No it's not.' There was a moment of silence before Sally continued. 'Most men looking for street prostitutes do it from a car,' she explained. 'Did she say anything about his car?'

'She said he had one,' Mehmet answered, 'but no more than that. They did it in his car, but Tanya wouldn't know one car from another anyway.'

'Hold on,' Sally said, something suddenly not making sense. 'If he was going to pull up in his car when she was working the streets, why would she describe him to you, but not his car?'

'Well, that's the weird thing,' Mehmet explained. 'She said he approached her on foot, but then took her to his car that was close by – in a side street or somewhere.'

'CCTV,' Sally accidentally said out loud as she realized what he was doing – parking his car away from the gaze of CCTV that covered almost every main street in London.

'Excuse me?' Mehmet asked.

'Nothing,' Sally lied.

'We done yet?' Mehmet asked. 'I don't know nothing more, I swear.'

'One last thing,' Sally told him. 'You knew Tanya well – socially and through business. Do you know if she used condoms?'

'Course she did, man,' Mehmet smiled. 'They ain't no use if they're pregnant or diseased.'

'You mean any *use* to you?' Sally accused him.

Mehmet's smile broadened as he held his hands wide apart. 'Now, now, officer. That ain't what I said.'

'I've got no more questions for now,' Sally told him. 'This interview will be transcribed into a witness statement. I'll contact your solicitor when it's ready to be checked and signed.'

'You mean I can go?' he asked excitedly.

'You can go, Joey,' Sally answered, 'but don't go far. We may need to speak again.' She leaned forward and rested her finger on the stop button. 'This interview is concluded.'

Sean rose towards the surface of Borough Underground station alone in the large lift. He was glad he was alone. Glad of the chance to imagine William Dalton standing in the same lift – tired after a day of begging, but excited about the crack cocaine he would soon be smoking and the effect it would have. Had he paced the lift in anticipation or had there been other passengers? Had his killer been in there with him – standing in the opposite corner, peering out from under his dark hooded top at his soon-to-be victim, imagining the exquisite, sadistic pleasure to come – rucksack on his back? *No*, he dismissed the possibility. Dalton lived a life on the street. His feral instincts to sense danger would have surely been singing if his killer had also been in the lift with him. He would have taken precautions to ensure the threat couldn't have followed him back to his makeshift home. But the killer knew he was heading for the garage, so if he hadn't followed him the same night he'd killed him, then he must have watched him. Studied him. Just like Sean was sure he'd watched and studied Tanya Richards. The lift reached the surface with a bump that knocked him from his daydreaming and the doors opened, allowing the freezing air from outside to flood in and swirl around him. The same freezing air that would have rushed at William Dalton the night he died.

Sean stepped into the ticket hall and walked to the only barrier that had a guard. He flashed his warrant card and the young white man in an oversized Underground staff uniform stood to attention as he opened the gate for him. 'I'm looking for Daniel Lincoln,' Sean told him.

'Over there,' the guard answered, pointing with his chin to another member of staff who was standing just inside the station entrance looking up and down Borough High Street.

'Thanks,' Sean replied and headed towards the tall, slim black man in his mid-thirties. 'Excuse me,' he got his attention and showed him his warrant card. 'Daniel Lincoln?'

'Who wants to know?' he asked.

'DI Corrigan,' Sean told him. 'Special Investigations Unit.'

'Oh yeah?' Lincoln said in his Southeast London accent. 'About the murder?'

'Yes,' Sean confirmed. 'Our enquiries say you were on duty the night it happened.'

'Yeah,' Lincoln agreed. 'I was here and I remember seeing him too.'

'Seeing who?' Sean asked.

'William,' he replied, sounding surprised that Sean had to ask.

'You knew him?'

'A little,' Lincoln told him. 'Most late shifts I'd see him. Not many people using this station that time of night, so I usually say hello to people I'm used to seeing. I could tell he was homeless – sleeping rough. I tried to help him a few times – told him where some shelters were that could get him a bed in the warm for a few nights, but he was never interested – said he was sleeping in an old garage which

182

weren't too bad. It's a shame, you know. He was an OK kid. Just took a wrong turn in life.'

Sean nodded in agreement while he also considered Lincoln for a few seconds. He'd met his type before – the accidental Samaritans who try to help everyone around them without even knowing they're doing it – never wanting praise or thanks. It was just in their nature. 'Can you remember anyone following him?' he asked. 'Or anyone who came out the lift at the same time and maybe headed in the same direction as William?'

'No,' Lincoln answered without hesitation. 'No way. Not that night.'

'How so sure?' Sean questioned.

'Because he was the only customer that came out of the lift,' Lincoln explained. 'Just like you tonight. It's unusual for here. Even this late. I was going to say something to him about it, but he seemed in a hurry. Figured he'd scored some drugs.'

'Possibly,' Sean admitted. 'What about the days or nights before the last time you saw him? Did anyone look like they might be following him?'

'The nights before?' Lincoln shook his head while smiling. 'Don't see how I'd know he was being followed.'

'Someone maybe caught your attention,' Sean suggested. 'Someone who looked out of place or suspicious.'

Lincoln's smile broadened. 'Inspector. This is the Borough. That time of night round here, most people look suspicious.'

Sean thought about the killer, remembering everything he thought he knew about him. 'Someone carrying a rucksack or backpack,' he told Lincoln. 'Probably wearing dark clothes – possibly sports gear and a hoodie. The hood would have been up and pulled tight over his face so he couldn't be seen properly.'

'Plenty people coming through here wear hoodies,' Lincoln shrugged.

'But it was late,' Sean argued, trying to trigger Lincoln's

hidden memories. 'There wouldn't have been many people around and they would have been close to William, in front or behind him. They would have been in a rush to get through the barrier and make it outside.' He could see Lincoln's mind straining, but he needed more prompting. 'Try and remember where you were when William came through. Try and see the people around him.'

'Yeah,' he suddenly said. 'I was right by the barriers – in case anyone's ticket didn't work.'

'And you saw William?' Sean encouraged him.

'Yeah,' Lincoln continued. 'I said "You OK?" and he said he was and then . . . wait. I see him now – another guy – another guy went through the barrier, with his hoodie pulled tight and a bag – he was carrying a backpack.'

'You sure?' Sean asked, his heart pounding.

'I'm sure,' Lincoln insisted. 'I remember him now. I couldn't see his face or almost none of it, but I saw enough to know he was white. That's all.'

'When?' Sean demanded.

'A few nights ago,' Lincoln answered.

'When exactly?' Sean pressed.

'I can't be sure,' Lincoln shook his head. 'Three . . . four nights ago. I'd have to check my shifts and stuff.'

'OK,' Sean relented. 'We'll need a statement from you and a photo-kit ident.'

'Sure,' Lincoln shrugged.

'And the CCTV for the last week,' he continued.

'You'll need to ask BTP for CCTV footage,' Lincoln reminded him.

'Fine,' Sean answered, distracted by his phone ringing somewhere inside his coat. Finally, he found it and snatched it from an inside pocket. The caller ID told him it was Sally. He slid a finger across the screen and pressed it hard against his ear. 'Sally.'

'Mehmet's a blow out as far as being a suspect,' she told

184

him without bothering with pleasantries, 'but he was worth talking to.' She paused, listening to Sean's silent anticipation. 'I think he's given us a description of our suspect.'

'White,' Sean stole her thunder, 'between thirty and forty. Wears dark clothing, possibly sports gear and always a hoodie. And a rucksack. He always has a rucksack with him.'

'OK,' Sally sighed. 'How did you know?'

'Guard at Borough tube station,' he revealed. 'He saw Dalton being followed by our suspect three, four nights ago. You?'

'Mehmet said Tanya Richards was having trouble with a punter who was getting way too rough,' she explained. 'A customer she'd met more than once – up until he almost strangled her. Mehmet said he'd trailed Tanya for a couple of nights, so he could warn the guy off, but he never showed again. A few days later she was dead.'

'So if he's our man,' Sean replied, 'he made contact with her before he killed her. Proper contact. He didn't just follow her – which means he may have made contact with Dalton too.'

'If it's true,' Sally said, 'then he's taking enormous risks. Why would he do that?'

'I don't know,' Sean told her, although his mind was spinning with reasons why. He remembered Anna's words about serial killers wanting it to be as personal as they could possibly make it. *He wanted to kill, but he wanted to know them first.* 'We need to get hold of Dalton's friends and associates. See if anyone can recall someone new coming into his life shortly before he was killed. Anyone at all.' He took a long breath of the cold London air tainted with vehicle fumes. 'Meet me back at the Yard. We need something ready for the rest of the team by morning.'

'Everything all right?' asked Lincoln, watching as he put his phone back in his pocket.

'Sorry?' Sean asked, drifting back to the present. 'I mean yes. Everything's fine. I need to go now, but thanks for all your help. We'll be in touch.'

# 8

Witney Dennis wandered into the kitchen of the small flat just as her mother was struggling to find enough food to prepare for her siblings from a different, but also absent father. While her mother was distracted, she quickly looked inside her purse but found nothing more than a few coins. Maybe her mum had some more cash hidden somewhere for emergencies or because she was fed up with what little cash she had going missing from her purse. She decided to try her luck.

'Mum,' she asked, trying to sound as pleasant and innocent as possible, but her mum couldn't hear her over the din of the younger children impatient for food. 'Mum,' she called a bit louder, causing her mum to round on her with a look of frustration and anger spread across her face.

'What d'you want, Witney?' she snapped. 'Can't you see I'm busy?'

'I need to borrow some money. You got any?'

'What the fuck does it look like?' her mother replied. 'I ain't even got money for food for the kids.'

'Ain't you got something put away?' Witney pushed. 'Even a fiver.'

'No,' her mum almost shouted. 'What you want it for anyway? Drugs?'

'I don't do that any more,' she lied.

'You expect me to believe that?' her mother asked. 'Don't expect me to help you kill yourself.'

'I just want to go out with me mates for a bit,' she lied again. 'I can't stand being stuck in here all the time.'

'You could help out a bit more is what you could do,' her mum told her. 'Or get a job and pay for all the food and clothes you get through.'

'I don't need a lecture, I just need some cash. I'll pay you back.'

'I ain't got it,' her mum barked at her, 'and if I did I wouldn't give it to you.'

'Fine,' she shouted back. 'I'll get it somewhere else.' She spun away from her mum and moved fast to the front door and out into the freezing night wearing only a light tracksuit – the sound of her mum calling after her still audible as she sprinted down the communal stairway and out into the open space at the foot of the tower block.

She kept walking until she reached the playground, where despite the freezing cold and the lateness of the hour, there was the usual huddle of teenagers with hoods pulled up over baseball caps – peering out from barely visible faces like a pack of wary hyenas. She reached the outer rim of the pack before being stopped by two of the gang.

'It's all right,' the leader told his subordinates. 'It's only Witney.' The two guards let her pass. 'What d'you want?'

'The usual,' she told him – constantly looking around for risks, of which there were plenty.

'Got the money?' he asked with a condescending grin on his face.

'No,' she admitted.

'Then fuck off,' he dismissed her.

'Wait,' she pleaded as the two bodyguards moved towards her. 'I thought . . . I thought . . . maybe I could do what I did last time again. You know.'

'Did ya?' the leader sneered, looking her up and down as he considered her offer. 'I tell you what,' he told her. 'You do us all and I'll give you what you want.'

'What?' she asked disbelievingly, suddenly feeling the bitter cold cutting through her meagre clothing.

'You heard me,' the leader smiled – looking around at the gang of a dozen youths. 'You do us all and I'll give you what you want.'

'No,' she argued. 'Just you. I ain't doing no one else.'

'Then you ain't getting nothing,' he insisted.

'Yeah,' one of the gang joined in. 'Come on, you slag. Suck us off.'

The rest of the gang joined in now – insulting her and jostling her – grabbing at her intimate places as she backed away. 'Leave me alone,' she screamed at the top of her voice, stunning the youths long enough for her to break from the crowd and run towards the safety of the well-lit multi-lane road that separated the estate from Putney Heath. Their laughter and insults chased her all the way as she ran across the dual carriageway, dodging the few cars that were using it at such a late hour – the headlights reflected in her scared eyes.

Once she reached the safety of the pavement on the other side she slowed to a walk and looked back at the estate – the lights of thousands of windows sparkling in the distance like a metropolitan island stranded off the coast of London. She turned her back on the sight and walked to the local convenience store – the type you found in all poor areas of London – the type that never seemed to close. She'd been there hundreds of times. As she pushed the door open the shop was filled with the shrill sound of an alarm warning the shop attendant someone had entered. It made the same awful sound as it swung shut behind her. A glimmer of optimism sparked inside her as she recognized the young Asian man standing behind the counter. She approached him smiling as pleasantly as she could.

'Hi,' he greeted her in his Sri Lankan accent.

'Hi,' she replied.

'What would you like?' he asked.

'Twenty Benson and Hedges please,' she answered.

'You over eighteen?' he questioned her.

'Yeah,' she lied, 'but they're not for me anyway. They're for my mum.'

The shopkeeper shrugged and retrieved a packet from the blacked-out locked cabinet behind him. 'Eleven pounds please,' he told her while holding on to the pack.

Witney made a show of checking each and every pocket of her outfit before faking disappointment. 'Shit,' she cursed. 'I forgot the money. My mum's gonna go mad. Can I pay you tomorrow?'

'I can't do that,' the shopkeeper told her. 'I need payment first.'

'But it's freezing out there,' she pleaded. 'If I don't go home with the fags, my mum'll make me come all the way back. I'll pay you tomorrow. I promise.'

'I can't do it,' he stood firm with a smile.

'Fuck you then,' she insulted him, knowing he wasn't going to give in. 'Bloody Paki,' she called back as she headed for the exit, but as she reached the door it was pushed open by someone else, filling the shop with the same shrill sound and making her spin to confront whoever was in her way before she realized she was closer than she'd expected to be – her face only inches away from his chest. She took a step back to better see the human obstacle. He wore a tracksuit, the ubiquitous clothing of choice on the estate, but his was more for function than style – expensive and weather-proof – like the clothes she'd seen people wearing on the television in programmes about exploration in places she'd never heard of. He looked strong. Not the strength that came from the sort of bulk that dominated the estate – born of cheap fast food and even cheaper booze, but a toned power, tailored into a lean physique. She chose to edge around him before yanking the door open and walking quickly on to the street outside. She was still within earshot of the shop when she heard the sound of the door alarm shrieking. If it was the hooded man leaving the shop then surely he hadn't had time to buy anything. She picked up her pace as she looked over her shoulder, expecting to see the dark figure hurrying along the pavement after her, but she saw nothing. She turned and headed for home and another fight with her mum until a hand falling on her shoulder made her gasp with fright and stagger slightly. The hooded man gently steadied her with two strong hands then released her.

'What do you want?' she demanded, fighting the fear that was wrapping itself around and constricting her.

'You look cold,' he told her in a deep, almost machine-like voice. 'My car is not far away. It's warm and comfortable.'

'For what?' she snapped, her courage returning.

'I heard you in the shop,' he told her. 'You wanted cigarettes.'

'So?' she asked.

'But you didn't have any money,' he continued.

'I have the money,' she lied. 'I just forgot it.'

He ignored her, slipping a hand into his tracksuit top and pulling out five new-looking ten-pound notes. He saw her eyes grow large as she locked on to the cash. 'Fifty pounds,' he told her. 'It's yours if you want it.'

'You're going to *give* me fifty pounds?' she asked suspiciously.

'Like I said,' he reminded her, 'my car is warm and dry.'

She understood what he meant. 'I don't do that sort of thing,' she insisted.

'Yes, you do,' he told her.

'What?' she asked, her eyes squinting in confusion. 'How do you know what I do?'

'I don't want much,' he ignored her. 'I'm not after full sex. Just some relief.'

190

Again she looked at the cash in his hand. 'I can't do this.'

'You'll do it for drugs, but not for cash?' he asked.

'How do you . . .'

'Fifty pounds,' he said again, only now he reached out and took her hand, lifting it from her side and placing the money in her palm. 'More if it's good.'

She looked into what was little more than a silhouette of his face, but it was enough to give the impression that behind the hood he was handsome. For a second she wondered why he would hide his features if they were as pleasant as she suspected, but the feel of the cash, warm and dry in her hand, distracted her. 'Why me?' she asked, on the verge of surrendering.

'I've seen you before,' he admitted. 'You're pretty.'

'But you're not from round here,' she shook her head. 'How could you have seen me?'

'Enough talking for now,' he told her in the same emotionless tone. 'It's this way to my car.' He released her arm and began to walk away, then turned to look at her. She glanced at the money in her palm, rolled it into a tight wad and slid it inside her top, walking silently after the stranger through the near-deserted streets. Within a few minutes they reached his car, parked on a quiet side street. There was no one else about. He unlocked the car and opened the passenger door for her. Not something she was used to, but she recognized the cue and slipped inside the warm interior of the car. He closed the door and walked around the front of the vehicle watched every step of the way by Witney until he too was sitting inside. 'It's cold tonight,' he said as he pushed the keys into the ignition and half turned it so the electrics and heaters burst into action, but the engine remained lifeless. 'You should wear warmer clothes.'

'So what you want me to do?' she asked, keen to get it over with and be on her way. 'D'you want me to just use my hand?'

'No,' he answered in his usual monotone. 'More.'

'I understand,' she replied and moved a hand quickly to his groin as she lowered her face towards his lap, feeling his fully formed erection. 'You weren't lying,' she said as she pulled him free from his tracksuit bottoms. 'You really do need some relief.' She felt his hand gently rest on the back of her head and guide her towards him until he was deep inside her mouth – holding her until she thought she might choke. When he finally released her, she pulled away for a second then once more took him in her mouth, moving up and down, feeling him twitching with the pain of absolute pleasure.

After little more than a minute she felt him climax into her mouth. She tried to pull away, but he pushed down on her head, keeping her in his lap – making her swallow and gag at the same time. When he released her this time, she tucked his shrinking penis back inside his tracksuit and sat upright, wiping her lips with the back of her hand.

'OK?' was all she asked.

'OK,' he confirmed.

'I have to go,' she told him as she reached for the door handle, but he grabbed her by the arm before she could escape.

'Wait,' he insisted.

'I've done what you asked,' she reminded him. 'I have to go.'

'It's just . . . I thought maybe we could make this a regular thing – for a while. You'll be well paid. You'll have your own money to spend how you want.'

'Regular thing?' she checked – her mind thinking of the things she could do with the cash. 'I'm not sure.'

'Do you know the car park behind the closed-down shops opposite your estate?' he asked.

'Yeah,' she answered, wondering how he knew such a place.

'Meet me there in two nights' time,' he told her. 'Same time. Don't tell anyone and come alone. If I see you with anyone I'll drive away and there'll be no more money. If you're not here, I'll know you're not interested. Understand?'

She looked long and hard into his barely visible face, although she could see the brightness of his eyes sparkling in the darkness. 'Yeah,' she answered. 'I understand.'

# 9

Sean was back in his office, searching the Home Office Large Major Enquiry System, known as HOLMES. Everything from door-to-door forms to witness statements was entered into the system, giving anyone trained to use it an instant overview of the investigation. Reccurring names would be identified and highlighted, preventing suspects from being overlooked or potential key witnesses or information being missed. It was clear to Sean that most of their enquiries so far had concentrated on the days of the killings and a couple of days prior to that, but now he knew that the killer almost certainly made contact with his first victim earlier, they needed to go further back. Unless he could find a way of somehow cutting through to the killer – of knowing his mind so well he could see his mistakes, maybe even before he made them, then they could be facing a lengthy and difficult investigation. The spark of a dangerous idea ignited in his head only to be extinguished by the ringing of his desk phone. He snatched the phone up. 'DI Corrigan.'

'It's Chris Lewis here,' the voice told him. 'From the technical lab.'

'I'm listening,' Sean cut to the chase.

'You submitted two phones, as part of a murder enquiry.'

'That's right. One from each of our victims.'

'Well, we've had a chance to examine them both fully now,' Lewis continued, 'and apart from the occasional tele-sales or PPI-type calls, both phones have only one private number in common.'

Sean felt himself go rigid. It had to be him. It had to be the killer communicating with them. He wanted to know them before killing them. 'Go on.'

'Both phones received and made calls to the same private number,' Lewis repeated, 'although there were significantly more calls made to the phone belonging to William Dalton than there were to the one found on Tanya Williams. There are texts too—'

'Jesus,' Sean accidentally interrupted. 'What do the texts say?'

'All pretty mundane: Can we meet? When? Where? I'll call, etc. Nothing conversational. Some of the calls lasted several minutes though.'

'Do you have the number?' he asked.

'Of course,' Lewis replied. 'Would it be easier if I emailed it across to you?'

'Yes. You have my address?'

'I've got it here,' Lewis told him.

'Do you have a name?' he asked before Lewis could hang-up, his heart now in his mouth. Was it really going to be that easy?

'Afraid not.' Lewis sounded disappointed. 'It's an O2 pay-as-you-go. No subscriber.'

'Did he use a credit card to top-up?' Sean asked, more in desperation than hope.

'No. He used the top-up voucher system. You buy the voucher then enter the code into the phone, so O2 should be able to say where they were bought from easily enough. Most stores have CCTV.'

New hope raised his mood. 'Thanks,' he told Lewis, 'and I need that email immediately.'

As soon as he'd hung up, Sean logged into his email

account, impatiently drumming his fingers on his desk until at last the email from Lewis popped up in his inbox. He clicked to open it and quickly scanned the list of calls made to each phone from the pay-as-you-go number. The calls to Tanya Williams' phone had only started about a week before she was murdered and had abruptly stopped after her death. 'You knew she was dead,' he whispered to himself, 'so there was no need to call her again. You knew she was dead because *you* killed her.' He checked the calls to Dalton's phone and found the calls to his phone had started several days before he was killed, but had stopped just as abruptly after his death. 'Jesus,' he mouthed in disbelief, then sprang from his chair and headed into Sally's office, arriving at the same time as Sally herself, shrugging off her winter clothes as she went.

'Tech lab's been on the phone,' he told her. 'Both victims received calls from the same private phone.'

'Please tell me you're not joking,' she replied, stone-faced.

'I'm not,' he assured her. 'The killer was in contact with both our victims *before* murdering them.' He saw the confusion in her face, then continued: 'Texts and calls. The texts give details of when and where he met them.'

'So they had a shared contact,' Sally repeated, trying to slow him down, make sure she had it straight.

'Whoever was calling them,' Sean explained, 'the calls started a few days ahead of each murder and, more importantly, stopped as soon as the victims were dead.'

'Then they knew they were dead,' Sally said what they were both thinking.

'And we're not just talking about one phone here,' Sean stressed. 'We're talking about two. If calls had stopped that abruptly to one phone after death it would look bad enough, but to two phones – to two separate murder victims? It has to be the killer.'

'Why?' Sally asked. 'Why take the chance of associating with his victims?'

'Because it's what he needs. It's all part of it for him. Finding them, following them and then making contact. It's the way it has to be. It's how he makes the killing . . . *personal*.'

'I don't suppose we have a name and address to go with the phone number?' she asked.

'No. Whoever he is, he's not that stupid. In fact, he's anything but. The calls were made from a pay-as-you-go mobile on the O2 network, but he did top it up using the voucher system, so he had to go into a shop or shops to buy them. We need to find out everything there is to know about that phone.'

'If he still has it,' Sally pointed out.

'He kept it after the first murder, didn't he?' Sean reminded her.

'Could he have used a credit or debit card?' she asked.

'Possibly,' Sean answered, 'but I doubt it. He's too careful. Using vouchers says he was probably paying by cash.'

'O2 will want a production order,' Sally told him.

'Then get one,' Sean demanded. 'Let's find out if he's still using it and what shops he bought the vouchers in. I want that CCTV, OK? We need to double our efforts, especially with the CCTV from the Borough Undergound. We need to go back further. A week. Ten days maybe. If he's been in contact with them, God knows how long he's been following them for. Same with friends and associates. We need to ask them about the victims' movements over a much longer period than the few days leading up to the killing. We need to find out if they told anyone about someone new coming into their lives.'

'Find the hooded man.'

'That's right.' Sean nodded. 'Find the hooded man. All right, let's bring the rest of the team up to speed.'

Back in his own office, the desk phone started to ring. Sean dived in to answer it.

'Mr Corrigan,' Roddis replied in his usual manner of avoiding ranks. 'I have an update on forensics for you.'

'I'm listening.'

'Firstly, it's almost certain that both victims were killed by the same weapon,' he explained. 'The length, depth and wound shapes match, although it's always difficult to be one hundred per cent certain from an evidence point of view with wounds – especially if we only have lacerations and no actual stab wounds. But everything points to it being the same weapon. Also, we've completed our tests on the semen found on Dalton's outer clothing and the semen found on the first victim and the DNA is a match – it's the same man,' Roddis confirmed. 'Why he chose to ejaculate on the second victim's clothes is more your field of expertise, I believe.'

'Anything else?' Sean ignored the comment.

'Not at the moment. When I have more, I'll let you know.'

'Fine,' Sean told him and hung up. He was about to head into the main office to brief the team when DC Jesson burst into his office looking agitated.

'Guv'nor,' Jesson stuttered.

'What is it, Alan?'

'There's some guy on the phone,' Jesson told him. 'He says he's the killer, boss.'

'What?' Sean checked he wasn't hearing things as he rose to his feet and banged on the Perspex partition to get Sally's attention. 'You sure he's not a crank?'

'He knows about the fingernails,' Jesson answered. 'It was one of the first things he said.'

'Christ. Put him through to my phone,' Sean ordered.

As Jesson ran back to his desk, Sean spotted Anna entering the main office. He waved her over and signalled for Sally to join them.

'Problem?' Sally asked.

'Alan's got someone on the phone claiming to be our man,' he told them, speaking as fast as he could, pacing the space in front of his desk waiting for the phone to ring.

'Another sick idiot?' Sally suggested.

'Maybe,' he replied, 'but this one knows about the finger-nails.' The phone started to ring. Sean reached for it cautiously – as if he was about to pick up a snake.

'Careful,' Sally warned him. 'Could be a journalist. They have their sources.'

Sean knew it all too well and gave a single nod before lifting the phone to his face while pressing the speaker button so they could all hear. 'DI Corrigan. Who am I speaking to?'

'Tut, tut,' the flat, accentless, almost mechanical-sounding voice answered. Instinctively Sean knew it wasn't the killer's real voice. 'What do you expect – that I'll give you my name and address? You'll have to work harder than that to find me, Inspector.'

'How do I know you're not just wasting my time?' Sean asked, trying to be deliberately provocative. If it was the real killer he wanted to immediately rattle his cage. He wanted to see how he'd react. Wanted to test his self-control. 'How do I know you're not just some pervert who gets turned on by claiming someone else's crimes?'

'You know I'm not,' the voice answered calmly.

'What?' Sean pushed him. 'Because you know about the fingernails?'

'Information you withheld from the media,' the voice reminded him. 'For the very purpose of filtering out the fools.'

Sean glanced at Anna to gauge her early impressions. She shrugged, but her expression told him she at least was taking the caller seriously. 'How do I know you're not a journalist?'

'Because as well you know,' the voice told him, 'not even the media know about the nails.'

'Maybe not from me,' he argued, 'but they have other sources.'

'You mean other *police* sources?' the voice answered. 'Is your ship a leaky one, Detective?'

'I need to be sure,' Sean ignored the question. 'As it happens

I've only recently found out something myself that no one other than the man responsible for the deaths of Tanya Richards and William Dalton could know.'

'Go on,' the voice encouraged him.

'After murdering William Dalton, the killer did something to the body. Something intimate. If you can tell me what it was, we can talk – otherwise, I hang up right now.' There was a long silence, but Sean held his nerve, despite Sally frantically spinning her finger to encourage him to keep talking.

'Discovered that, did you?' the voice finally responded. 'I suppose it was only a matter of time.'

Sean could detect a slight change in the tone. A degree of embarrassment. 'You need to tell me exactly what it was,' he insisted, 'or this conversation is over.'

'I . . .' the voice tried, but stalled. 'I . . . I masturbated over his body. His fully clothed body.'

'Are you a homosexual?' Sean deliberately tried to anger him. Anna glared at him.

'You know I'm not,' the voice answered. 'If you're trying to make me angry, you're wasting your time.'

'I'm not trying to make you angry,' he lied. 'And you still haven't told me why you masturbated over the body of a dead man.'

'I think you know why,' the voice told him.

'No,' Sean lied. 'No I don't, so why don't you tell me.'

'We'll get nowhere if we can't be honest with each other, Inspector,' the voice insisted. 'But if you want to play games, so be it. It was nothing more than a release. When you take a life you also take that person's power. It can be almost overwhelming. You feel like you're going to explode as the energy surges through your body. Ejaculating over him freed some of the power. Calmed me. As I grow, I'll learn. Learn to control the power without the need for such things.'

'Sounds like a load of shit to me,' Sean continued to provoke him. 'I think you masturbated over him because

200

you're some sort of pervert and killing him turned you on. Maybe it's the only way you can get it up.'

'Don't make yourself sound like a fool,' the voice refused to take the bait. 'You're anything but a fool, which is why right now you're thinking about having this call traced. But you needn't waste your time. I never registered this phone in any name, let alone my own, and once this conversation is finished it'll be resting in some very deep water.'

'Is this the same phone you used to call your victims on?' Sean asked, hoping to unsettle him. He was met with only silence. 'That's right – I know you called them. I know you made contact with them before you killed them.'

'It doesn't matter what you know. What matters is this will only stop when I decide it is time and when that time comes you have my word that I'll walk into Scotland Yard and surrender myself to you and no one else but you.'

'*This*?' Sean used the killer's own word. 'What exactly is *this*?'

'My pre-defined path,' came the answer. 'What I was born to do.'

'*Born to do*?' Sean again used the killer's words. 'What sort of sick fantasy world are you living in?'

'Oh it's not fantasy. It's very much reality, as well you know. I'm familiar with your work, Inspector. You already know exactly what I was *born to do*.'

'No,' Sean told him. 'No I don't. So why don't you enlighten me?'

'Very well,' the voice calmly agreed. 'They started when I was very young, but it was in my early teenage years when I began to understand them.'

'What started?' Sean interrupted, memories of his own troubled teenage years flashing in his mind.

'The dreams,' the voice told him excitedly. 'The thoughts that filled my mind day and night.'

'What thoughts?' Sean asked, his intention to provoke the killer forgotten. He wanted to hear about these dreams. Were they the same as his own?

'Wonderful thoughts,' the voice answered. 'Thoughts that came to me when I least expected them, filling my mind. There was no explaining why they were there or where they came from. I tried to ignore them – to occupy myself with anything I could so my mind would always be too busy for the thoughts to come, but nothing worked. They wouldn't be ignored. They grew more and more vivid until I realized they were nothing to be afraid of. I wasn't a monster. It was simply my nature and I saw the beauty of that. The power. I was born for a true purpose, not merely to exist like so many of you, and I embraced my task. My future. My path. I can never go back to being just another sheep in the flock. If only you had tasted what I have tasted.'

Anna moved close to Sean and took hold of the hand that held the phone. Her mere touch was enough to make him freeze. She leaned in close to his ear and whispered. 'I need to speak to him. Tell him I want to speak to him.'

Sean nodded in agreement. 'Listen,' he told the voice. 'There's someone else here. Someone who'd like to talk to you.'

'I should imagine there're quite a few people there,' the voice replied.

'No,' Sean corrected him. 'Actually, there's only myself and one of my sergeants, and a psychiatrist who helps us with people like you.'

'What are their names?' he demanded.

'I can't tell you that,' Sean explained.

'I should know their names, Inspector,' the voice insisted. 'Very rude of you not to introduce us properly. Perhaps I should go now?'

'Why do you need to know their names?'

'Goodbye, Inspector.'

Sean immediately looked at Sally and Anna who nodded almost simultaneously. 'Wait,' Sean told him. 'DS Sally Jones and Dr Ravenni-Ceron.'

202

'Ah yes,' the voice said. 'Dr Ravenni-Ceron. Your resident psychiatrist – there to solve the case for you.'

'She helps with profiling,' Sean divulged as little as he thought he could get away with. 'It can be useful.'

'Helped you catch Thomas Keller, didn't she?' he taunted. 'Not to mention The Jackdaw.'

'She helped,' was all Sean would say, 'and now she wants to speak to you.'

'Why?' the voice questioned. 'Does she think she can get inside my head? Does she really think she's capable of understanding what I'm doing?'

'I just want to talk,' Anna joined in, her voice picked up by the speaker-phone. 'If that's all right with you?'

There was a long silence, followed by: 'Ask your questions, Doctor.'

'These visions,' Anna began. 'When did you first start having them?'

'I can't say for sure,' he answered. 'Nine or ten.'

'Were you afraid – when they first started?'

'No,' he told her firmly. 'Confused. I didn't understand why I had been *chosen*.'

'And you said you tried to keep your mind occupied to stop the thoughts coming?'

'Mind and body,' he explained. 'But they came anyway.'

'Did they disturb you? Were you afraid of what you might be?'

'Maybe,' he replied tentatively, 'but soon I accepted it and I was glad. I was going to be the wolf or the tiger – not the goat or pig.'

'Did the images grow stronger as you grew older?'

'Stronger,' he agreed, 'and more beautiful.'

'Did you talk to anyone about it?'

'No. How could anyone possibly understand what was happening to me?'

'Listen to me,' Anna told him. 'I think you're suffering from what's known as Intrusive Thoughts Syndrome.' They all waited for a response from the other end of the phone, but none came. 'It's a condition known to psychiatry,' Anna explained. 'Ordinary people suffer from it.' Again they waited for a reply that didn't come. 'These . . . images invade the mind. No one really knows why. They can be very frightening, but it doesn't mean you're going to do or want to do the things you see. I can only try to imagine how troubling and disturbing it is to have thoughts like that playing in your mind.'

'They are neither troubling or disturbing,' he spoke at last. 'They're wonderful and beautiful.'

'You said you used to try to keep so busy that the thoughts couldn't come?' Anna persisted. 'That's a classic reaction to intrusive thoughts. Some people take it to such extremes that they develop OCD. You need help. I can help you.'

Once again the room was filled with a heavy silence until he spoke. 'But I don't want your help,' he told her. 'The thoughts guide me. Guide me to achieve the great things I'm doing. Now I have the strength to turn dreams into reality. Why would I want to stop that?'

'You need help,' Anna pleaded.

'No,' he said firmly. 'It's . . . it's too late for that. I have begun the long walk along the path to greatness. Do you think me such a coward that I would turn back now?'

'I know you're not a coward,' Anna told him, 'but I do think you're ill.'

'You understand nothing,' he dismissed her coldly. 'But perhaps you do – Inspector?'

'You're sick,' Sean took over. 'I know that much.'

'Don't—' the voice snapped. 'Don't dismiss this with your pointless talk of illness and syndromes. You more than all others know what I am, if not who I am. If you insist on continuing with this foolish game I shall do exactly as Sebastian Gibran and so many others have done and when you catch me I shall declare myself insane and use your own words to prove it, even if it's not true. But if you admit you understand

'. . . if you, Detective Inspector Corrigan, admit you understand, then I promise you, when *this* is all over, I'll turn myself in and plead guilty to everything. That's what you want, isn't it?'

'I know you make contact before you kill them,' Sean tried to wrest control of the conversation back. 'Not just on the phone, but in person. You meet them. Try to get to know them. Why?'

The voice sighed long and hard. 'Maybe even you don't understand. It's for them. I do it for them.'

'What do you mean, you do it for them?' Sean asked.

'So they can feel my presence for a few days. So they can feel my power for a while and bask in the warmth of it. I give them a better life for a few days, then I take their life. None of us gets to meet our maker, Inspector, but at least they have a chance to meet the bringer of their end.'

'Is that what you think you are?' Sean pushed. 'Death? Do you think you're some sort of god?'

'No,' he replied quickly, 'but perhaps godlike. Compared to everyone else living their pointless little lives, never achieving anything, yes, godlike.'

'It wasn't very godlike when you almost strangled Tanya Richards in your car.' Sean reminded him. 'We know a lot more than you think. It's only a matter of time before I find you.'

'I showed her mercy,' the voice ignored him. 'I spared her life. Was that not godlike?'

'Only for a few days,' Sean argued. 'Then you raped and murdered her. There's nothing godlike about that.'

'I didn't rape her.'

'So she was already dead?' Sean seized on it.

'It was merely a release – as it was with the other.'

'You had sex with her dead body,' Sean spelt it out. 'I have to agree with Dr Ceron – you're sick and need help. Hand yourself in and I'll make sure you get it.'

'Tell me,' the voice ignored him, 'have you seen today's copy of *The World*?'

205

'Not something I read very often,' Sean answered.

'Sebastian Gibran has been talking about me,' he revealed, 'to *that* journalist.'

'Jackson,' Sean muttered under his breath.

'I have to admit, I'm disappointed,' the voice continued. 'I thought Gibran would understand what I was trying to achieve. Its importance. But instead he appears to be lost in his own vanity and jealousy. I sense his fear – fear that soon I will be more revered than he ever was. Soon it'll be me they write books and make films about. Not him. And when *this* is all over, I won't hide behind a mask of insanity like him. I'm proud of what I'm achieving. What would be the point in denying it? It is something to be celebrated, not to run from. I thought he was so much more, but now I know he's just a coward. My father always told me to be the best at whatever you do. I don't intend to live under anyone else's light.'

'Is that what this is about?' Sean asked. 'Who can be the most revered? Who can be the most infamous? So you can become some sort of celebrity?'

'I expected more from you, Inspector.'

'I'm happy to disappoint you.'

There was a long silence before the voice spoke again: 'Do you really think you're clever enough to find me?'

'I've caught others like you.'

'Not like me, Inspector,' he insisted. 'You see, you've already missed the trick. I'm right here under your very nose. I have been for weeks and yet you don't see me. You can't possibly imagine where this started and where it will end.'

'What do you mean?' Sean demanded, but the voice ignored him.

'Goodbye, Inspector. Perhaps I'll call again sometime.' The line went dead.

Sean immediately turned to Sally. 'Get hold of technical and get some trace equipment set up here in my office.' Sally nodded. He turned to Anna. 'Any thoughts?'

'From what he said, it definitely sounds as if he's been suffering from intrusive thoughts from a young age,' she explained. 'He has all the symptoms.'

'Intrusive thoughts?' Sally asked. 'What is that?'

'Exactly what it sounds like,' Anna answered. 'Thoughts that invade a person's mind, thoughts they would rather not have.'

'Like what?'

'Like seeing yourself committing murder or acts of paedophilia, for example.'

'So they're mentally ill?' Sally continued. 'They see themselves doing terrible things and then they act on them?'

'Not necessarily,' Anna insisted. 'Many sufferers are normal people who for some unexplained reason have incredibly ugly, terrifying thoughts. They start to believe that perhaps they are murderers-in-waiting or paedophiles.'

'But they're not?' Sally checked.

'No, they're not,' Anna told her, 'which is why many develop OCD as a result of their efforts to counter the thoughts, to keep their minds so busy that the intrusive thoughts can't invade their minds. Ultimately, it doesn't work. They need proper psychological help, but many people are afraid to seek help. They're scared that if they tell anyone, the police or their employers or their families may find out. I treated a teacher who suffered from such thoughts. He saw himself committing acts of paedophilia that sickened and terrified him, but he was desperately afraid his employers would find out and sack him to protect the children. If that happened, he'd never get another job in teaching again.'

'So they have these . . . terrible images,' Sean joined in, 'but they have no intention of ever carrying them out?'

'That's correct,' Anna told him. 'They hate the thoughts. They're tormented – haunted by them.'

'But this one has acted on them,' he reminded her. 'So maybe you're wrong about him? Maybe he's something else?'

'I don't think so,' she argued. 'From everything he says,

it sounds like classic Intrusive Thoughts Syndrome. The only difference being, he's embraced them and is now acting them out.'

'You ever seen that happen?' Sally asked.

'No,' Anna answered. 'Never.'

'What does that mean?' Sean demanded.

'It means he's a very dangerous psychological combination,' she explained. 'A psychopathic personality with OCD tendencies brought on intrusive thoughts. He likes what he's doing, and clearly has no intention of stopping – or at least not until he decides to.'

'All that talk about "when *this* is all over, I'll turn myself in" – what was that about?' Sally asked.

'Power,' Sean answered. 'He wants to believe only he has the power to end it. Doesn't want to admit that we'll be the ones to end it.'

Anna agreed: 'It's very apparent that he craves power as well as notoriety, hence his reference to newspaper articles about himself and his interest, possibly his obsession, with Sebastian Gibran. It sounded as though he saw Gibran as a role model, until he started talking to the press.'

'What do you suppose he meant by "I'm right here under your very nose . . . yet you don't see me?' Sally asked.

'I don't know,' Sean admitted. 'Could be a reference to the fact he's been meeting with his victims out in the open. Get hold of a copy of today's *World*,' he ordered Sally. 'I need to know what Gibran's been saying about our boy.'

'Doesn't sound like he's been too complimentary,' Sally answered.

'No,' Sean agreed. 'No, it doesn't, which is likely to stir him up and make him even more dangerous.'

'So?' Sally asked. 'If Gibran's article is full of less than flattering comments, what do we do about it?'

'Jackson,' he spat the name. 'We speak to Jackson.'

\* \* \*

Witney Dennis lay on her unclean bed in the small bedroom she shared with her younger sister, counting how much of the fifty pounds she'd earned was still left. After more drugs and some cigarettes, there wasn't much. She began to think about the strange man – her need to have more cash overwhelming her initial nervousness about seeing him again. Now she was hoping he would be where and when he said he would. She didn't like what she had to do to earn the money, but she'd done worse for less and at least he was clean – unlike some of the hooded teenagers she'd had to do favours for in the past. And his car was quite nice too. Maybe it would become a regular thing, she thought. She could do with the money. Maybe it would turn into something more, she fantasized and he'd take her away from the estate and give her the sort of nice things she'd never had. She knew she could keep him happy. She knew how to keep men happy.

It bothered her that she had no real idea what he looked like, but from what little she could see, he seemed quite handsome. She told herself that there was nothing to be afraid of; after all, if he'd wanted to do her harm, he could have done it when she was alone with him in his car. He could have done anything he liked – she wasn't strong enough to have fought him off and there had been no one else around to help. But he hadn't hurt her. OK, he got a bit rough when he'd pushed her head down and almost made her choke, but it wasn't like that had never happened to her before. She could handle it. For that sort of regular cash, she could handle quite a lot.

Sean walked into the Dog and Duck pub in Bateman Street, Soho, and scanned the clientele for Jackson. He found him quickly enough, sitting in a big brown chair huddled over a table enjoying his lunch and a beer while flicking through the pages of a rival newspaper. Sean slid into the chair opposite and waited for Jackson to notice him, but Jackson carried on reading as if he wasn't there. Until he finally spoke without looking up:

'DI Corrigan. Late as usual.'

'Jackson,' Sean replied.

'So why d'you want to meet?' Jackson asked, meeting Sean's eyes at last. 'Changed your mind about doing the interviews? Finally seen sense?'

'You can shove your interviews where the sun don't shine,' Sean told him. 'It's never going to happen.'

'Shame,' Jackson shrugged, returning to his newspaper. 'Could have earned us both a lot of money. And don't try and tell me you don't need it. Never met a cop yet who wasn't skint. So, why are you here?'

'To warn you about these interviews with Gibran,' Sean answered. 'You've no idea how dangerous and manipulative he is. You need to stay away from him.'

'This is the same speech you gave me about The Jackdaw,' Jackson reminded him, 'but that turned out pretty well for me. It was the story of the year. I won a prize for it and the paperback sales did all right too. Wouldn't have happened if I'd listened to you.'

'It's not all about money and prizes, Jackson,' Sean warned him. 'You think Gibran cares about that? He just wants to use you.'

'Use me for what?' Jackson smiled. 'He's locked up in Broadmoor. What can he possibly do to me?'

'You've got him talking about the new case,' Sean snarled. 'Got him talking about another killer, and you're printing every word he says. Every insult.'

'So?'

'You don't think the man I'm hunting might get pissed off about those insults?' Sean questioned. 'Might go looking for payback?'

'You're saying he might come after me?' Jackson grinned. 'That's not going to happen.'

'Gibran is as clever as he is vicious. For all you know, he could be putting this killer on you. I imagine Gibran would take great pleasure in reading about your unpleasant demise in your own newspaper. For him, it would be the next best thing to killing you himself.'

'Killing by proxy, eh?' Jackson kept smiling. 'I don't think so.'

'Then maybe you're trying to provoke the killer into contacting you,' Sean guessed, 'so you can repeat what you did with Jeremy Goldsboro.'

'Not a bad idea,' Jackson goaded. 'Now why didn't I think of that?'

'Forget it, Jackson,' Sean told him. 'This one won't be contacting you. He despises you.'

'And how would you know that?' Jackson seized on it. 'Unless he's contacted you.'

'You don't know what you're talking about.'

'Come on,' Jackson grinned. 'What did he say? Did he tell you why he's killing them?'

'I'm not in contact with the suspect,' Sean lied.

'Has he seen my piece in the paper?' Jackson asked eagerly. 'Is that why you're here – because he said something about coming after me?'

'No,' Sean insisted. 'Look, Jackson, you might think you understand people like Gibran and this new one, but you don't. Not really. Not like I do. I read your interview with Gibran and I know it will have pissed off this new one. Why wouldn't he come after you? You think you're something special? Not to him, you're not. He'd kill you and not lose a minute's sleep over it. I don't like you, Jackson, but I have no desire to see you lying in a pool of your own blood with your throat cut. The last thing I need is another victim.'

'I appreciate your concern,' Jackson sarcastically replied, 'but you don't have to worry about me. I can look after myself.'

'Don't be a fool,' Sean warned him.

'Well then, let's work together,' Jackson changed tack. 'Work together to trap him. We could use Gibran without him knowing he's being used. Get him to provoke the killer into doing something – to walk into a baited trap where you'll be waiting.'

'You're out of your fucking mind,' Sean tried to kill the idea at birth. 'Gibran will see it coming a mile away.'

'Not necessarily,' Jackson argued. 'We could use Gibran to get the killer to go after a specific target. Goad him into it, to the point where he couldn't resist the challenge.'

'A specific target?' Sean shook his head. 'You want to try and get him to go after a member of the public? Are you insane?'

'Not a member of the public,' Jackson spoke quickly. 'You could use an undercover cop as the bait. You've done it before – to catch Mao Ma. Remember?'

'That was different,' Sean answered. 'Ma had a specific type. I just put someone who fit the profile on the street and waited for him to take the bait. I didn't use a killer locked up in fucking Broadmoor to talk a killer at large into going after someone. It can't be done.'

'What about if I were the target? You say he despises me – we could make use of that. Tell me what buttons to press on Gibran and I'll do it. I'll get Gibran to provoke him into coming after me. I trust you. I know you won't let anything happen to me.'

Sean took too long to say no as Jackson's idea spun in his head. 'I can't,' he said, without conviction.

'Come on,' Jackson sensed the chink in his armour. 'How else you going to catch him?'

'Forget it, Jackson. It ain't going to happen.'

'All I ask for is exclusive access to the arrest,' he pleaded, 'and an interview with yourself.'

'Not happening,' Sean told him as he got to his feet.

'OK,' Jackson backtracked hurriedly. 'No interview – just the arrest.'

'Goodbye, Jackson.'

'It'll be my arse in the sling,' Jackson kept trying. 'I'll sign any legal waiver you want.' Sean merely shook his head and tried to walk away, but Jackson grabbed him by the arm. 'Think about it,' he insisted.

Sean pulled his arm free and headed for the door, but Jackson's idea had sparked something in his mind – the idea of provoking the killer into walking into a trap. Only he didn't need Jackson and Gibran to pull the strings of the killer – not now he'd established direct contact with him. He was sure the killer would call again and when he did, he'd be ready. Ready to entice him into his web where eventually they'd meet. Just the two of them. Alone.

David Langley wrapped a towel around his waist and headed for the fridge. He'd had a long, hard work out followed by a cold shower and his muscled physique was tensed and toned as he poured himself a tall gin and tonic. He took a sip, savouring the flavour, then reached into the freezer and removed a transparent bag and a plastic box. He placed the items on the table next to his drink and sat in front of them. First he emptied the bag, the photographs spilling on to the table like a deck of cards. He separated them into three neat piles: Tanya Richards, William Dalton and the girl whose name he didn't know yet. Next, he took the two bags from the plastic container, one marked with a 1 and the other with a 2. He emptied the contents of bag 1 on to the table next to the pictures of Tanya Richards – each tooth and fingernail making a distinct sound as it landed on the wooden table. He arranged them to his satisfaction, then repeated the procedure with bag 2, careful to make sure the contents stayed close to the photographs of William Dalton. He picked up two of Tanya

Richards' teeth and dropped them into the palm of his hand, making a closed fist around them until he could feel them digging into his skin. The article in *The World* had infuriated him and the conversation with Corrigan, far from assuaging his anger, had only made things worse. In the end he'd had to resort to a workout, shower, and now this, to restore his equilibrium.

He unclenched his fist and stared at the teeth as they rolled from his hand back on to the table, allowing his eyes to drift from his trophies to the photographs of the girl from Roehampton, still full of life, warm and breathing – for a little while longer, at least. He lifted one of the photographs and raised it to his face, inhaling deeply. It was as if she was standing next to him, her scent filling his head – cheap body-wash mingled with cigarettes, the reek of chip-fat coming off her clothes. He imagined her pink-and-grey tracksuit hanging on a clothes rack in the warmth of her kitchen, soaking up the odours of whatever was cooking. He remembered her taking him in her mouth and how his hands had hovered above her head, ready to strangle the life from her, and how he'd been strong enough to resist – to save it for another, better time.

He closed his eyes to relish the moment, but became aware of his own arousal – much to his disappointment. His work was too important to be reduced to mere sexual fantasy. He needed to rise above such petty human emotions. When it was all over, the world needed to marvel at him. A sexually motivated killer was a thing of scorn, to be labelled as yet another sick pervert and dismissed. He aspired to be an enigma, a riddle that would keep them occupied for years, arguing about what made him kill. He would be the ultimate bogeyman, the subject of books and films and documentaries, talked about in the street, in pubs and cafés, at dinner parties and academic conferences for years to come. The demonic god who had walked amongst mere men, exercising his right to take life whenever he wished. Prison was inevitable, but even there he would rule by absolute fear – a merciless tyrant whose legacy would never die. And if they kept him locked in solitary confinement, he would still have his memories. Those could never be imprisoned; all he'd have to do was close his eyes and he could relive every beautiful, sweet moment as the blood poured from their slit throats over his hands and through his fingers like liquid red silk.

Keeping his eyes closed, he focused on his breathing, taking deep, long breaths that relaxed his body and allowed his mind to curb his physical reactions. Images of drawing his knife across her slender throat filled his consciousness, but his body was under control now, his erection falling away as the power of his mind overwhelmed his body. 'Yes,' he whispered to himself as the images grew ever more vivid, while his reaction to them grew ever more spiritual and less physical. At last he was gaining mastery of the great power that surged inside him.

Suddenly his eyes fired open and stared at the photograph that was only inches from his face – the girl from Roehampton more alive now than she had been in the flesh, that night in his car – a deserving patch of material to be woven into the tapestry of his greatness. 'Soon,' he whispered to her soothingly. 'Soon.'

Sean's intention had been to drive straight home, but as he passed through Southeast London he found himself drawn to St Thomas Moore Catholic Church in Dulwich, where he knew, despite the lateness of the hour, he'd find the door unlocked and Father Alex Jones somewhere inside, ready to help, talk with or simply listen to anyone in need.

Sean parked in the quiet street outside the church and made his way through the front gate. When he reached the door, he rested his hand on the handle, fearing it might be locked he gently turned it – prickles of relief running across his body as he discovered it was open. He pushed the heavy door aside and entered the church, lit only by the dim orange glow from the bulbs of fake candles scattered randomly about the interior. Health and Safety comes to us all, he thought to himself. Even God. As he walked deeper inside he made no attempt to subdue the sound of his footsteps. He was in no mood to have to deal with a startled stranger, no matter why they were there, but most of all he wanted to alert Father Jones to his presence. He needed to talk in total confidence and over the last few years the priest had become his counsellor and sounding board.

As he wandered through the church the tall, athletic priest stepped from the darkness – his long black hair hanging around his dog collar. Even in the dim light, or perhaps because of it, Sean could see the sparkle in his bright blue eyes. Jones was in his late thirties, but to Sean he still looked too young to be a priest.

'Detective Inspector Corrigan,' the priest smiled, using Sean's professional title for the first time. 'Your usual time of day for a visit, I see.'

'It's difficult during the day,' Sean reminded him. 'Work.'

'And you like the peace and quiet of night. The privacy.' Sean merely shrugged. 'Anyway,' Jones continued, moving closer to him. 'What can I do for you, Sean? Problems?'

'Am I that transparent?'

'It's gone eleven o'clock, and you're here in an empty church, talking to me. That would imply problems.'

'Can't be an empty church if we're in it,' Sean couldn't stop himself saying.

'Always so precise,' Jones smiled. 'Now – what's on your mind?'

'I've got a new case.'

'Ah,' Jones sighed. 'Another troubled soul for you to find.'

'Not sure about that,' Sean admitted. 'I sense no mental illness in this one. Only evil. He likes what he does.'

'You probably don't expect to hear this from a priest, but I'm not so sure that *evil* actually exists – or at least not in the spiritual or mythological sense: the Devil guiding the hands of his disciples. Don't get me wrong, I've seen many evil acts and the results of them, but the people committing them aren't evil so much as lost in a moment of madness or reacting to a lifetime of bad breaks. You could say that even God commits acts of evil sometimes – disease, famine, earthquakes – but you wouldn't say God was evil.'

'No,' Sean agreed. 'Just merciless.'

'I don't know about that,' Jones shrugged, 'but I sense you have a dilemma. It's what usually brings you here.'

'A dilemma,' Sean frowned, 'or an idea.'

'About what?' Jones asked.

'About how to catch him.'

'Surely there can be no dilemma there?' the priest queried. 'If you have an idea of how you can catch him, you should try it.'

'It's not that easy,' Sean told him.

'Oh? Why?'

'Because it would involve goading him into trying to commit a crime,' Sean admitted. 'Possibly into committing a murder.'

'An agent provocateur,' Jones replied, surprising Sean with his knowledge. 'Provoke him into committing a crime he wouldn't otherwise have committed. Wouldn't that render your evidence worthless?'

'You seem to know a lot about it,' Sean told him, 'for a priest.'

'You'll find I've taken an interest in a great many things since I met you,' Jones answered.

'So it would appear,' Sean replied. 'But to answer your question: no – it wouldn't make any evidence worthless. He could try to use it as mitigation, but it wouldn't be difficult for me to prove he would have killed or tried to kill anyway, so it was justified and right to trap him.'

'Trap him?' Jones' eyes shone with curiosity. 'So you mean to provoke him into going after someone in particular?'

'Yes,' Sean admitted coldly.

'Who has he killed?' the priest asked.

'A prostitute and a young homeless man.'

'Ah,' Jones nodded. 'I've heard about this one on the news, but I don't see how you could provoke him to go after someone in particular. Sadly there are all too many possible victims for him to choose from.'

'True. But in this instance, *I* would choose his next victim.'

'And how would you do that?' Jones asked.

'I'm talking to him,' Sean admitted. 'He called me. We spoke.'

'I still don't see how you could provoke him into going after one particular person. Surely, for it to work, the victim would have to be known to both you and the killer? You'd have to both know who you were talking about.'

'Maybe there is someone,' Sean told him.

'Really?' Jones asked. 'Who?'

'I don't know . . .' he shied away from revealing the thoughts flickering in his mind. Small flames of a dangerous plan to trap the killer. 'Not yet.'

'You're a good detective, Sean,' the priest assured him. 'You'll think of a way to find him.'

'But will I be in time to stop him killing again?'

'Well,' the priest answered, 'let us pray you will be.'

'I think I'll need more than prayers,' Sean replied. 'I need him to make a mistake.'

# 10

Only a few members of the team were at their desks when
Sean entered the main office next morning. Tired and down-
beat after hours of trying unsuccessfully to formulate a plan
to trap the killer, he made straight for his own office where
he found two engineers from technical support, installing
phone listening and tracing equipment.

'All done,' the lead engineer announced. 'If your target
calls, hit this button and it'll start recording and trying
to triangulate his location. It's good stuff, this gear,' he
added, 'but it needs time. Try and keep him talking. The
job sheet says your suspect's using a pay-as-you-go
phone?'

'He was the last time he called,' Sean told him.

'All this will be for nothing if he keeps using them and
junking them,' the technician warned. 'Even if we locate his
phone, chances are he'll have abandoned it – or chucked it
in the Thames.'

'I'm aware of that,' Sean replied, irritated.

'Recorded conversation's difficult too,' the technician
continued, sounding like a car mechanic explaining the need
for expensive repairs. 'Had a few cases lately where the
recordings were ruled inadmissible. Suspect hasn't been

cautioned, see, and the tapes were declared to be interviews, therefore *technically* he should have been.'

'Then I'll caution him,' Sean told him.

'Make sure you do,' the technician insisted, 'or you won't be able to use them as evidence.'

'You finished?' he snapped.

'Yeah,' the technician replied cheerfully. 'If you need us, page us.' He pointed to an old-fashioned device clipped to his belt. 'We're only a couple of floors away – we can be here in minutes. And don't forget to press the start button.'

As soon as they'd gone, he headed to Sally's office.

'All done?' Sally asked as he entered.

'Sorry?' he asked, distracted by the sight of Anna sitting in the visitor's chair.

'The phone-tap,' Sally reminded him.

'Yeah,' he remembered. 'It's all set.' He quickly turned to Anna. 'I need to know if you think our man could be pushed into going after a specific target?' he asked. 'If we're clever enough and subtle enough, could we goad him into going after a target of our choice?'

'Possibly,' Anna answered. 'But I don't think we know enough about him to steer him towards a specific target. We don't yet know how he selects his victims. It appears to be very random, which makes it difficult to judge what psychological buttons to push.'

'But we do know,' Sean argued. 'We know he's egotistical, driven by a need to become infamous. We could use that.'

Anna shook her head. 'That's not enough for me to devise a psychological map to manipulate him.'

'But it's possible?' Sean persisted. 'If we can get him to tell us more about himself, keep him talking, we could do it?'

'How are we going to do that?' Sally joined in, uneasy about what she was hearing. 'We don't even know if he's going to call again.'

'He'll call,' Sean assured her. 'I know he will.'

'The more information we have, the better our chances of designing a trap,' Anna admitted. 'But if, as I suspect, his method of victim selection is non-specific, it's hard to see how we could use it effectively.'

'By selecting a victim for him,' Sean explained, 'and then encouraging him to go after them. Make it so his ego won't be able to resist. Dangle the promise of guaranteed infamy.'

'What?' Sally looked at him, aghast. 'Who do you have in mind?'

'I don't know yet.' Again he shied away from disclosing what he had in mind. He was spared further questions by the arrival of Addis in the main office. 'Heads up – trouble heading this way,' he warned.

A few seconds later, Addis sauntered into Sally's office.

'Sean,' Addis greeted him. 'DS Jones. Anna.' No one returned the greeting. 'Just dropped in to tell you I'll be doing the media appeal later. I'll need the photo-fits and any other relevant information on the hurry-up. It may be our best chance yet of catching him.'

'I'll see you have everything you need,' Sean assured him.

'Any progress in the investigation?' Addis added.

'Nothing in particular,' Sean shrugged.

'Very well,' Addis said, with barely concealed frustration. 'Send what I need up to my office as soon as you have it.' Then, spinning on his heels in true Addis style, he made his exit.

'What was that all about?' Sally asked once he'd gone.

'Just letting us know he's watching us,' Sean told her. 'But don't worry about Addis. Let's just find this bastard and find him quickly.'

David Langley was almost half an hour late arriving for work and found his boss, Jane Huntingdon, already in his office sitting at his desk waiting for him – her fingers typing on his keyboard. His heart stopped for a second as he thought of his browsing history, until he remembered it was all on his private account and Huntingdon would be using her company password to gain access. But still the sight of her at his computer made him feel sick with anxiety. If she'd discovered something, he'd have to kill her there and then and worry about hiding his crime after.

'Can I help you with something?' he asked.

'Where the hell have you been, David?' She kept her eyes fixed on the monitor, her tone completely neutral. 'You're supposed to start work at eight, not eight thirty.'

'Traffic was bad,' he answered, mimicking her tone.

'Traffic?' she queried. 'You could walk to work from where you live. Or have you moved and not bothered to tell HR?'

'No . . .' He imagined himself crushing her slim neck with one hand while the other cut her throat. 'Still at the same place, but sometimes I drive.'

'Well you shouldn't. Not if it's going to make you late. Christ, David—' Finally she looked up at him, allowing some emotion into her voice. 'People at head office have their doubts about whether it's worth keeping this store open at all. Sales are falling and rent is going up. The store is at risk. Your job is at risk. If it wasn't for me fighting your corner, you'd be gone. Now is not the time to be seen to be running a sloppy ship.'

'Maybe if I had a bit more support from head office things would be better,' he argued, picturing her blood running over his fingers and down his forearm.

'Head office has got nothing to do with it,' she insisted. 'You spend too much time sitting in this office doing God knows what, instead of being out on the shop floor, selling – unless of course it's someone you'd like to shag. It's not good enough, David. Things have to improve or you're history.'

'All because my face doesn't fit,' he accused. His anger was rising dangerously now. If she knew who he really was, she wouldn't dare speak to him like this. If she only knew how close she was to having the life torn from her. How easily he could crush her throat . . .

'Don't be so immature,' she told him. 'Any problems you have with head office are all of your own creation. Now grow up and get on with your job before you lose it.' She got to her feet and snatched her briefcase from his desk. He stood to one side to let her storm out of the office, but instead she came to a halt centimetres away from him. He could smell her perfume and skin cream. He breathed it in deeply so he could hold her scent in his lungs for as long as possible. 'Remember what I said,' she warned him. 'This is your last chance.' A second later she was gone.

He moved slowly across the office and sat in his desk chair; only then did he allow himself to breathe out. The room was still heavy with her scent. He closed his eyes to better see his knife sliding across her throat, her hands grasping at the open wound in a futile attempt to stop the blood flowing from her body, her eyes wide open with terror as her pupils dilated to their full circumference before freezing in the stare of the dying as he severed her carotid artery, the blood spraying wildly from the cut in the side of her neck. But as her life slipped away, her face slowly began to change to that of the girl from Roehampton. The rage that Huntingdon had triggered in him now transferred to the girl. For a moment he opened his eyes before slowly closing them again, seeing the image of his victim pinned to the floor, her desperate struggling becoming little more than helpless twitching until there was nothing. She gave one last tiny gasp and her hands fell away limply to her side.

'Soon,' he promised her. 'Soon.'


It was mid-morning by the time Donnelly appeared, heading for the office he shared with Sally, but Sean intercepted him.

'Dave, a word please – my office.'

Donnelly looked at him, making no move to follow as Sean walked back inside his office. Sean turned and stared back at him, waiting for Donnelly to enter before committing the very unusual act of closing the door – something half the main office noticed, prompting many a raised eyebrow and hushed comments.

'Something wrong?' Donnelly asked, tossing his coat over a chair and sitting in another without being asked.

'No,' Sean lied, hoping he could find out what he wanted to know as gently as possible. 'Just need an update on the door-to-door.'

'Door-to-door's fine,' Donnelly answered flippantly.

'Can you give me a little more?' Sean asked, fighting his rising irritation.

'Such as?' Donnelly replied.

'Such as,' Sean kept going, 'have you found any witnesses? Anybody see anything? Hear anything?'

'Not as far as I know,' was Donnelly's disinterested reply.

'Not as far as you know?' Sean repeated. 'You have been checking on it, right? You are in charge of the door-to-door, yes?'

'I know what my responsibilities are,' Donnelly responded through gritted teeth.

'Then why can't you give me an update?'

'I just did.'

'That wasn't an update.'

'Why don't you get off my back,' Donnelly snapped.

'I will,' Sean assured him, 'just as soon as you start doing your job.'

'What do you know about my job?' Donnelly sprang to his feet. 'What do you know about being a detective? A real detective? This isn't a job to you. It's some sort of obsession. How you . . . how you get your fix of whatever it is you need.'

'I don't know what you're talking about,' Sean lied, 'but I know you haven't been doing your job properly for months.'

'Oh aye,' Donnelly replied, 'and whose fault is that, eh?

Do you not think I'm aware that I've barely been coping? And why do you think that is?'

'I don't know,' Sean answered, calming down as Donnelly started to confess his problems. 'You won't tell me.'

'It's because of you,' Donnelly accused him. 'You made me like this.'

'What?' Sean asked, falling back into his chair.

'You did this to me – when you set me up to do your dirty work for you.'

'What are you talking about?'

'Jeremy Goldsboro,' Donnelly answered. 'You set me up. You knew I was going to have to kill him. You set it all up exactly the way you wanted it, so Goldsboro would end up dead. You would have pulled the trigger yourself, only you're not an authorized shot, are you? So you needed me to get the gun. To pull the trigger. You as good as murdered him and you used me to do it.' Donnelly, too, slumped back in his chair and both men fell silent, unable to look at each other for what felt an age.

'Is that what you really believe?' Sean asked when he felt able to speak again. 'That I *used* you to kill Goldsboro?'

'Didn't you?' Donnelly asked, before relenting: 'I don't know. Maybe.'

'No,' Sean promised him. 'Nothing was planned. Things unfolded so quickly. I had no idea Goldsboro was The Jackdaw until we confronted him. I couldn't have. No one could.'

'You always seem to be able to see it long before anyone else.'

'I saw it,' Sean admitted, 'but I saw it too late.' He could see that Donnelly was unconvinced. 'Look, Dave – I would give anything for it to have been me that pulled the trigger instead of you. Hell of a thing to take a man's life, no matter who it is or what he's done.'

'Aye,' Donnelly agreed. Sean had never seen him so vulnerable. 'Aye, it is.'

'Dave,' Sean said gently. 'Even a fool like me can recognize

225

when someone needs help as badly as you do. You're a good detective. Good enough to convince the psychologists the police made you see that you're fine, but you're not. See someone independent. Speak to someone . . . I could ask Anna.'

'No,' Donnelly snapped. 'No one connected with the Job.'

'OK,' Sean agreed, 'but you'll see someone?'

'I'll speak with my GP,' Donnelly promised him. 'Maybe she knows someone.'

'Good,' Sean relaxed slightly. 'You need to take any time off, say the word. There's no need for anyone else to know what's happening.'

'OK,' Donnelly replied, getting to his feet. 'If I need it, I will.'

'Good,' Sean told him, although he knew it would take time for Donnelly to truly move on. 'We should have discussed this a long time ago.'

'Aye,' Donnelly agreed. 'I'd better get back to work.'

'OK,' Sean said. 'Remember – this conversation never happened.'

Donnelly nodded that he understood and walked slowly towards the door, pausing to compose himself before yanking it open and bouncing into the main office in his usual manner as if nothing had happened. Sean knew it was an act, but at least Donnelly was trying. He could only hope it was his first step towards something like recovery. He needed Donnelly like a fast car needed brakes and he knew it. Without him, tangled wreckage was never too far away.

Zukov and Sally had walked half the length of Oxford Street looking for a young man that other associates of William Dalton had said was the closest thing he had to a real friend. They'd checked in every unused doorway, under every large piece of flattened-out cardboard and in every sleeping bag, as well as accosting every beggar in their search for the mysterious friend, until they found him sitting outside Pret a Manger opposite Marble Arch – his identity betrayed by his distinctive long blond hair and even more defining red-dyed beard.

'You must be the man we've been looking for,' Zukov told him as he hovered over him, his warrant card open in his hand. 'Jonnie Freyland, I presume.'

'Who wants to know?'

'You blind?' Zukov shook his warrant card to make it even more obvious. 'Police. Been looking for you for a few days now.'

'Why?'

'Seriously?' Zukov answered, already fed up.

'We're investigating the death of William Dalton,' O'Neil took over. 'Lot of people are telling us you were his friend.'

'His death?' Freyland questioned. 'Don't you mean his murder?'

'Whatever,' Sally said. 'You were his friend, right?'

'Yeah,' Freyland reluctantly admitted. 'As much as anyone can be a friend in this fucked-up world.'

'His best friend?' Sally continued.

'We spent a lot of time together,' was as much as he would commit to. 'We were about the same age. Ended up homeless in the West End about the same time too. Better not to be alone around here. Safer if there are two of you.'

'I'm sure it is,' Sally agreed.

'He didn't deserve to die like that,' Freyland said. 'Will was all right. Just couldn't handle the shit that's life. Then the devil took him,' he virtually whispered. 'That's what everyone's saying – that it's not a man, it's a devil. A devil come to London to prey on the weak and vulnerable. People like us, because no one cares about us. No one will try to stop him. We're sacrifices so all these people living their *normal* lives will be safe.'

'You don't want to listen to that shit,' Zukov interrupted. 'It's definitely a man we're looking for.'

'And we do care,' Sally added. 'That's why we're here talking to you. That's why we've been looking for you for days.'

'I've been keeping my head down,' Freyland explained. 'It's not good around here to be seen talking with the police.'

'This is different,' Sally insisted. 'Everyone wants to find who did this to Will. No one's going to give you a hard time for speaking with us.'

'Maybe.' Freyland didn't sound too convinced.

'Listen,' Sally told him. 'We think that whoever killed him may have made contact with him some days before he attacked him. Can you think of anyone William met recently? Someone who suddenly came into his life? May have seemed like a perfectly normal person. May have offered to help him, but almost certainly someone new.'

Freyland suddenly looked even more edgy and afraid, looking all about him as if he could be attacked from any direction at any time. 'Look,' he told them, 'I didn't know anything about that. I thought it was a stranger. A madman. If I'd known about what you just said, I would have told you, you know. I would have said something sooner.'

'Don't worry about that,' Sally reassured him. 'Just tell us what you know.'

'Yeah,' Freyland agreed, rocking backwards and forwards with nervous energy. 'Yeah.'

'So, what do you want to tell us?' Sally urged, sensing he could change his mind at any minute.

'OK. Yeah,' Freyland continued to battle with himself, then suddenly stopped rocking and started making sense. 'Few days before he got killed, I was sitting with Will outside M&S, hoping someone would give us something to eat, when this guy comes and sits down with us, starts talking to Will. Just small talk and shit, but it was strange because he weren't homeless – you could tell. He was clean and smelt of warm showers and body wash and his clothes were expensive training gear stuff and he had a hoodie he kept up all the time, but it was cold, so I didn't think too much of it. You get strangers, now and then, come sit with you, but usually they want to lecture you, or save you or pay for sex, but he didn't. He talked about how cold it was and how most people were arseholes for walking right past us without even seeing us. Then he gave Will twenty quid and said he'd see him around. Then he just fucked off.'

'Just like that?' Zukov asked.

'Yeah.'

'Did he say who he was?' Sally jumped in.

'No,' Freyland shook his head.

'He must have talked about himself?' Zukov prompted. 'Must have said something personal?'

'No,' he insisted.

'A stranger sits next to you,' Zukov persisted, 'and starts chatting about this, that and the other and you don't ask him anything about himself? That doesn't sound right.'

'That's not how it works out here,' Freyland explained. 'Someone you don't know starts talking to you, you let them. You never know where it's gonna go – whether they're gonna give you some food or money or a bed for the night. You don't scare them off with questions. And this time Will got lucky. We got twenty quid out of it.'

'*We*?' Zukov asked.

'He gave me half,' Freyland answered. 'Like I said – Will was all right.'

'Can you tell us what he looked like?' Sally tried to get things back on track.

'I don't know,' Freyland struggled. 'Like I said, he wore expensive sports gear – all blacks and greys and a hoodie.'

'You already told us that,' Zukov complained. 'Fuck me, this is hard work.'

'What about his face?' Sally ignored him. 'Can you tell me anything about his face? Like, what colour was he?'

'He was white,' Freyland answered, sounding relieved to have a simple question to answer.

'How old?' Sally patiently asked.

'Hard to say,' Freyland shook his head. 'He had his hood pulled up tight across his face the whole time, but somewhere between thirty and forty, maybe.'

'What about the rest of him?' Sally tried to keep him going. 'Do you remember anything about the rest of him? Just picture him in your mind and tell me what you see.'

'Yeah,' Freyland agreed. 'Yeah, sure. OK . . . he was tallish, maybe six foot, and slim – or more like an athlete. He looked strong.'

'How could you tell?' Sally checked.

'The shape of him.' Freyland frowned, trying to picture him. 'His clothes fitted tight. You could see he was in fucking good shape, know what I mean. Reckon his chest was twice the size of his waist. Looked like he could fuck up most people if he wanted to.'

'Can you tell me anything about his face?' Sally asked.

'Looked like he was maybe decent looking,' Freyland answered, pulling a face of uncertainty. 'Hard to say with that hood, man.'

'His accent?' Sally tried. 'Where was he from?'

'He didn't have an accent. Maybe a bit of London, but his voice was plain – you know, flat.'

'Clean-shaven? Beard?' Sally asked.

'Clean-shaven.'

'His clothes?' Sally continued. 'What make were they?'

'Can't remember,' he replied, shaking his head again. 'North Face, maybe. Something like that. Not Nike or anything. Real outdoor gear, you know.'

'Sure,' Sally nodded. 'And did you see him again?'

'Not properly,' Freyland insisted, 'but Will did.'

'You know that?' Zukov asked.

'Yeah, sure,' he shrugged. 'Will told me he had. After the first time, Will said he'd bumped into him in Oxford Street again. Said he'd taken him for a meal in Burger King.'

'Which one?' Sally checked.

'The one in Tottenham Court Road,' Freyland clarified, then, sounding less sure, added: 'I think so, anyway. And then I saw them together, sitting in Oxford Street, must have been a couple of days later, but when I walked towards them the guy got up and walked off. I asked Will what that was all about, but he said he didn't know. The guy just saw me and took off.'

'Did you get a better look at him that time?' Sally asked.

'No,' Freyland shook his head. 'He still had his hood pulled up tight.'

'OK,' Sally said, feeling he was running out of useful information. 'Is there anything else you can tell us about this man?'

'Not really.' Freyland shrugged again. 'Except Will thought he'd got lucky, you know. Thought he'd found a bit of an easy touch. Someone who was good for a bit of cash and food when he needed it and didn't seem to be after anything in return. Didn't even hassle him for sex. That's sometimes all the good Samaritan types are really after.'

'I'm sure,' Sally replied. 'Well, look, thanks for your time. If we need to get hold of you, how do we do that? You got a mobile?'

'Nah,' he laughed. 'Ain't got no one I wanna call. Ain't no one I want to call me. I got better things to spend my cash on. But you'll find me if you need to. I'll always be around here somewhere.'

'OK, well, thanks again.' Sally was turning to leave when Freyland stopped her.

'Don't you want to know his name?'

'His name?' Zukov repeated. 'You said you didn't know his name.'

'No,' Freyland corrected him. 'I said he didn't tell *me* his name, but he did tell Will.'

'Don't play silly games with me,' Zukov warned him.

'Marcus,' he quickly told them before Zukov could say anything else. 'Will told me he called himself Marcus.'

'Any surname?' Sally asked in hope more than expectation.

'No,' he shook his head. 'Just Marcus.'

'Thank you,' Sally told him. 'Be careful out here, yeah?'

'I will,' Freyland promised. 'I know the devil's out there now, but he won't get me. I'm too smart.'

'Of course you are,' Sally assured him. 'Of course you are.'

Sean was going stir-crazy trapped in his office drowning under an avalanche of paperwork and unanswered emails. He felt an overwhelming urge to be out and about doing something to make him feel as if he was moving forward instead of stagnating in bureaucracy. He stared at the phone that the technical boys had rigged with tracing and recording devices willing a call to come through, but it was the standard phone on his desk that started to ring. 'Shit,' he cursed and grabbed the handset. 'DI Corrigan.'

'Guv'nor,' Jesson got straight to the point. 'The pay-as-you-go was bought in the O2 store in Oxford Street. Whoever bought it loaded it up with eighty pounds of vouchers and paid cash for everything. He hasn't topped it up since the original purchase and the phone's still well in credit. He doesn't use it often, boss. The store's checking their CCTV as we speak. Should get some nice footage of him.'

'Good work,' Sean told him. 'Anything else?'

'Not yet,' Jesson replied. 'I'll call you as soon as I have more.'

'Good,' Sean told him and hung up. Almost before his hand had left the set it rang again.

'Boss, it's Paulo,' Zukov told him.

'What's happening?'

'Sally and me found Jonnie Freyland,' he announced triumphantly.

'Who?' Sean asked – the name familiar, but its relevance distant.

'William Dalton's best buddy,' Zukov enlightened him.

'He tell you anything?' Sean hurried him.

'Oh yeah,' Zukov replied. 'It appears Dalton made a new friend a few days before he was killed. White male, thirty to forty years old, athletic, wearing outdoor sports clothing with the hood permanently covering his face.'

'Jesus,' Sean said, nodding his head in approval. Now we're beginning to get somewhere, he thought to himself. 'How was contact made?'

'He approached the victim in the street,' Zukov explained. 'Freyland says they saw each other at least three times. Sometimes he gave him money, sometimes he gave him food. I'll get the CCTV checked at all known locations. Oxford Street is covered in it.'

'He's clearly not camera shy, our man,' Sean added.

'Does he not think we'll check CCTV?' Zukov asked.

'He knows we will – he just doesn't care. For whatever reason, he's confident he won't be recognized.'

'The hood?' Zukov suggested.

'The hood hides his features,' Sean explained, 'but someone could still recognize his style of dress or the way he moves – unless he changes that too. Did you get anything else?'

'I got a first name,' Zukov gleefully played his trump card. 'Marcus. Freyland said that Dalton called him Marcus.'

'Probably not his real name,' Sean deflated him slightly, 'but it might mean something. OK. Good work, Paulo. Come see me when you get back to the Yard.'

'Marcus,' Sean said quietly to himself as he replaced the receiver. 'Why Marcus?' He tapped in his password on the police computer, opened an internet browser and entered the name into the search bar. Within seconds he had a page full of results; he selected the link for *The meaning of the name 'Marcus'* and quietly read the definition to himself: 'Marcus, from the Latin, meaning to harvest – derived from Mars – the god of war.' Sean leaned back in his chair to consider this. 'To harvest,' he repeated. 'That's what you do, isn't it? You harvest the lives of others. You chose that name deliberately because of what it meant.' The sudden appearance of DC Cahill in his doorway tore him away from his thoughts.

'Boss,' she called to him.

'What is it?' he asked, noting the urgency in her voice.

'I think it's him again. Came through on my number.'

'Put him through to the reserved number,' he ordered, spinning to hammer on the partition between his and Donnelly's office – summoning Dave and Anna with an urgent beckoning with his arm. 'Then get back in here. I may need you.' Cahill nodded and disappeared into the main office as the others entered Sean's.

'Him?' Donnelly asked, looking at the rigged-up phone instead of Sean.

'We think so.' He took a few deep breaths to compose himself, but still he jumped a little when it started to ring. He pressed the switch to activate the trace and record, then picked up the receiver and, speaking as matter-of-factly as he could, answered: 'DI Corrigan.'

'Hello . . . again,' the voice said, speaking in the same toneless robotic style as last time. Sean couldn't detect the use of any sort of voice-altering equipment – more a deliberate effort by the speaker to physically change the sound of his voice.

'Who is this?' Sean asked, just to settle himself.

'You know who this is.'

'Perhaps,' Sean stalled, aware the technical equipment needed time.

'Not like you to engage in such puerile conversation,' the voice replied cheerfully. 'I assume it's for the benefit of whatever recording equipment you're using – or, more importantly, tracing equipment. I wouldn't waste your time, if I were you. I'll be gone before you know where I am and this phone will be destroyed. I won't be using it again. Phones are so cheap these days – don't you think?'

'Why are you calling?' Sean lost patience.

'To talk.' The playful tone had vanished.

'About what?' Sean asked.

'Anything,' he replied. 'Everything.'

'Why me then?'

'Because you understand,' the voice told him. 'Because I know you understand.'

'Understand what?'

'Me,' the voice answered. 'What I'm trying to achieve.'

'No,' Sean lied. 'No, I don't, but I want to.'

'Don't underestimate me,' the voice warned, 'or yourself. You know exactly why I'm doing it.'

'I'm a detective,' Sean pointed out. 'You're a murderer. How could I know why you're doing what you do unless you tell me?'

'Because you know how it makes me feel,' he insisted. 'You can *imagine* how it makes me feel. You can imagine their warm blood on your cold hands, can't you? As if you were killing them yourself.'

'You don't know anything about me,' Sean snapped, feeling the prickly heat from the looks of the others.

'Not true, Sean,' the voice used his Christian name for the first time. 'I've been watching you for a very long time. I know so very much about you.'

'You know about cases and investigations,' Sean argued, 'but you don't know anything about *me*. You don't know how I live.'

'You live in torment,' the voice told him, 'because you're just like me and the others you caught, but you won't admit it, even to yourself.'

'This is getting us nowhere,' Sean tried to move on, nodding at Cahill, who'd slipped back into the crowded office.

'You caught them because you could feel their desires and fears,' the voice told him. 'Their hatred and jealousies, and eventually it led you straight to them.'

'I followed the evidence,' Sean lied.

'No,' the voice insisted. 'Those investigations were going nowhere until sudden breakthroughs – breakthroughs that can't be explained, but always you were there at the sudden, bitter end. Always you.'

'That's the nature of investigations,' Sean tried to dismiss it. 'Everything seems impossible, then something breaks and suddenly it all makes sense.'

'No,' the voice chastised him. 'Stop denying yourself. You're not like all those other dim fools, lacking imagination or purpose. You understand the beauty in what we do.'

'There's no *beauty* in what you do,' Sean told him. 'You need help. You're unwell. I have Dr Ravenni-Ceron here with me again. I want you to speak with her.'

'I didn't call to talk to her,' the voice replied.

'Do it for me,' Sean said, as he watched the two Technical Support staff quietly enter the office, index fingers pressed to their lips as they fell on to the equipment like vultures on a corpse.

'This is Dr Ravenni-Ceron,' Anna jumped in.

'Hello, Doctor,' the voice replied politely. 'Come to look inside my mind? I'm afraid you might not like what you find.'

'I was wondering if you'd thought more about what we discussed last time we spoke?' she asked. 'About the intrusive thoughts I believe you may be experiencing?'

'I know all about intrusive thoughts,' he assured her, 'but the things I see inside my head are so much more than mere *intrusions*. They are the guiding light that shows me the way – shows me the way to the truth of what I am and what I must do. They show me how to achieve my great purpose.'

'What great purpose?' Anna asked. 'What is your great purpose?'

'Why don't you ask DI Corrigan?' the voice answered. 'I'm sure he could tell you.'

'Don't *you* want to tell me?' Anna cajoled him. 'Are you afraid?'

'I have no fear,' he told her coldly. 'I am beyond fear.'

'Then what is your great purpose?' Anna repeated.

There was a long silence. Everyone in the room seemed to be holding their breath, waiting for the voice to speak again. 'I want the world to know my name. I want others like me to revere me and everyone else to fear me. I want to be the ghost story parents tell their children. I want people to be afraid to say my name louder than a whisper for fear that its mere mention could conjure me there to reap their souls.'

Sean was distracted from the words by the sight of one of the tech guys writing something on a piece of paper and giving him the thumbs-up sign. He beckoned for the paper as the voice continued his monologue.

'My great purpose is to leave a legacy that no one will ever forget.'

Sean snatched the paper and headed for the door, mouthing to Anna: 'keep him talking'. Cahill and Donnelly were right on his heels, but only when he was sure he couldn't be heard by the caller did Sean speak. 'We got a trace on his phone,' he told them excitedly. 'He's calling from The Terrace in Barnes. It runs along the riverfront.'

'He's going to chuck the phone in the river,' Donnelly guessed. 'As soon as he's done, he's going to chuck it.'

'Get hold of Central Control,' Sean ordered, 'and tell them what's happening. I want every car and cop to hit that area and find him. Any white male they see between thirty and fifty I want stopped and checked. And get the helicopter up and the dog units there.'

'On it,' Donnelly told him, and headed for the nearest phone.

Sean turned to brief Cahill: 'Barnes is in Wandsworth Borough. Get hold of their local control and see if they have any CCTV covering The Terrace. If they do, can they patch in live to it. Let's see if we can get eyes on our man. I better get back in there.'

When Sean returned to his office, the voice was still droning on:

'. . . and when I'm finished you'll all understand and you'll never forget what you have witnessed.'

'Marcus,' Sean dropped the name in for the first time. 'That is your name, isn't it? Marcus?'

'It's the name I use,' he freely admitted, 'or used. I suppose I'll have to think of something else now.'

'Marcus,' Sean explained, 'from the Latin meaning the harvester. You chose it deliberately because of its meaning, didn't you? Because you *harvest* the lives of your victims.'

'You see,' the voice replied, 'you do understand me. Think like me. Who else would have thought to research the meaning of such a benign name?'

'Most,' Sean told him.

'I don't think so.'

'Tell me about Sebastian Gibran,' Sean changed the subject. 'You seem obsessed with him.'

'Hardly obsessed,' the voice answered casually, 'but yes, he interests me. After all, not many people get away with murder, let alone a series of murders, and you and I both know Gibran must have left untold dead in his wake that can never be attributed to him – and he'll never confess. He's worthy of my interest, don't you think?'

'No,' Sean answered. 'I don't think your interest in him is anything other than a petty jealousy for his notoriety. You want the same infamy he has.'

'No, no, no,' the voice laughed softly. 'I want far *more* infamy than even Gibran. His achievements will pale into insignificance compared to mine. Do you really expect me to be jealous of a man who never wanted to reveal himself to the world and make mere men marvel and tremble at the splendour of what he was?'

'But Gibran is mortal,' Sean told him. 'In fact, he's less than that. He's insane – and so are you.'

'Goodbye, Sean,' the voice told him unexpectedly, and hung up.

'Shit,' he cursed.

'I don't think that was very smart, Sean,' Anna argued. 'You called him insane.'

'Well, he is, isn't he? I couldn't listen to any more of his self-important crazy shit.'

'I thought we were supposed to be establishing trust with him,' she reminded him. 'Building a relationship that could possibly lead to him handing himself in.'

'Oh, he'll hand himself in all right,' Sean told her. 'When he's ready. He couldn't bear to miss out on all the celebrity. The *glory*. Only he won't get the chance to surrender, because I'm going to find him first.'

'I thought you wanted me to keep him talking?'

'We have a trace. The area's being flooded. I didn't need him on the phone any more. He's trapped himself.'

Cahill burst into the office before Anna could reply. 'No CCTV covering The Terrace,' she announced. 'We're blind. No description of the suspect.'

'Fuck,' Sean cursed. 'Where's Dave?'

'Still on the phone to Central,' Cahill told him.

Sean strode into the main office and joined Donnelly, who was standing by a desk with a phone pressed to his ear. 'What's happening?'

'Wandsworth, Richmond and Hammersmith boroughs are all diverting as many units as they can into Barnes, but they want a description of the suspect.'

'Male, white, thirty to fifty.'

'They have that,' Donnelly explained, 'but they need more. What about CCTV?'

Sean shook his head. 'We blew out on CCTV.'

'They can't stop every white man they see,' Donnelly told him. 'It's not possible.'

'Damn it,' Sean hammered the desk with the side of his

fist. 'He's right there. He's right there. What about India 99?'

'They're refuelling,' Donnelly answered. 'They'll be up in the air in a few minutes.'

'Jesus Christ – by the time they get there, it'll be too late. What about the dog units?'

'On their way.' Donnelly broke off to listen to whoever was at the other end of the line, then covered the mouthpiece and turned back to Sean. 'They want to know what to do.'

'Tell them to concentrate on males in tracksuits, outdoor gear – anyone with a hooded top or carrying a backpack. They should stop and search as many white males as they can and verify their details. Tell them we want details of everyone stopped. If someone's not quite right, arrest them, bring them in to Wandsworth and hold them until we can take a look for ourselves.'

'That could be a lot of people,' Donnelly warned him.

'Jesus Christ. We're after a serial killer,' Sean vented. 'Just do it.'

'OK,' Donnelly shrugged.

'I'll be in my office,' Sean told him before striding back to his office. Anna was sitting alone, waiting for him. 'Where are the guys from technical?' he asked.

'Gone. Said they'll be back soon.'

'Fine,' he shrugged as he paced his office like a caged animal.

'Do they have him?' she asked. 'Did they get there in time?'

'Still looking.'

'Sean, we need to talk.'

'Not now. I'm a little busy.'

'It's about this case,' she insisted.

'What?' he snapped. 'What about the case?'

'Your interaction with the suspect. What happened there? You're supposed to keep it neutral. Keep him talking and listen to what he has to say. Tell him you understand and offer help – you know the drill. So why are you being confrontational with him?'

'Because he's a murdering prick who thinks he's something special,' Sean snapped. 'I was sick of listening to his crap.'

'And talking about Gibran,' Anna continued. 'Are you sure that's wise? The last thing we want to do is over-stimulate him . . . unless that was your intention all along.'

'I'm trying to stop him,' Sean insisted.

'By making him angry? By goading him into trying to . . . outdo Gibran?'

'I needed him unsettled, off-guard, so I could work him out. If I'd kept it neutral, stuck to protocol, all we'd have to go on is whatever spiel he'd rehearsed, all that crap about his "great purpose" – the things he wanted us to know, not the things I need to know if I'm going to find him.'

'Are you sure you don't already know?' she pressed him. 'Are you sure you're not trying to make him do something specific?'

'Like what?' he asked, feigning puzzlement.

'I don't know,' she replied, 'but I know you. I know how you work these cases. You're like a chess player. You make a move that makes no sense until four or five moves later – then it all becomes clear.'

Before Sean could answer Donnelly came barrelling into the office. 'The units in Barnes have found the phone,' he informed them. 'He could have tossed it into the Thames, but the son of a bitch left it for us – on the wall overlooking the river.'

'Then he's there somewhere,' Sean insisted.

'They've done a heap of stop-and-searches,' Donnelly explained, 'but everyone checks out. They can't arrest them all.'

'Tell them to keep looking.'

'OK,' Donnelly sighed, 'but they can't keep this going

forever. Once their emergency calls start backing up, we'll lose them.'

'Then tell them to keep looking until that happens,' Sean demanded, 'and make sure they photograph everyone stopped and their ID.'

'I'll do my best,' Donnelly agreed.

'And get a dog unit to the phone,' Sean added. 'Maybe it can pick up his scent and chase the bastard down.'

'Will do,' Donnelly assured him and headed back into the main office.

'Christ,' Sean complained. 'He's right there. I can feel him. He's playing with us. Hiding somewhere, watching us running around like headless chickens.'

'I wouldn't hold out too much hope,' cautioned Anna. 'It must be like looking for a needle in a haystack. He could be using a motorbike, a normal bike, or jumped on a bus or—'

'I know, I know. He's smart. A thinker. He didn't call us on impulse, he planned it – chose an area with no CCTV, where there'd be plenty of white males fitting the profile so he'd blend in, and went there with his escape route worked out in advance. But still I can feel him. Watching us. Learning.' He broke off, stuck his head out the door and shouted to Donnelly who was back on the phone.: 'Anything from the dog unit?'

Donnelly shook his head and covered the mouthpiece of the phone he was still on. 'No, boss. Dog handler reckons the phone's been sprayed with something – probably ammonia. A dog's no use.'

'This just keeps getting better,' he moaned as he walked back into his office and slumped into his chair. 'Damn him. Why's he playing games? Why is he playing games with me?'

'With *you*,' Anna suddenly had an epiphany. 'This is becoming about *you*, isn't it? He calls to speak to you.'

'He's insane,' Sean reminded her. 'He doesn't know what he's doing.'

242

'This is becoming about you and him, isn't it?' she accused him. 'And you know it. You're deliberately trying to make him angry with you. You're trying to put yourself next to him. Just the two of you. What the hell is it with you, Sean? Why do you have to put yourself in harm's way all the time? Why do you need to be alone with them?'

'I don't,' he tried to calm her down. 'You're overreacting.'

'No, Sean,' she told him. 'No, I'm not. And I won't help you get yourself killed. If you want to make him come after you, you'll have to do it without me.'

'Anna,' he tried to stop her as she walked out of the room and crossed the main office without speaking or stopping and disappeared through the door. 'Shit,' he cursed and slumped deeper into his chair. 'Shit.'


Geoff Jackson entered the Cahoots bar and restaurant just off Carnaby Street and scanned the crowd for his long-term girlfriend, Denise Adams. He found her easily enough, a mass of blond hair piled up on top of her head, wearing a figure-hugging blue dress that showed off her tall, slim body. At thirty-four she was sixteen years younger than Jackson, but their relationship seemed to thrive regardless, as neither longed for a quieter life. Jackson had tried that and had an ex-wife and two children to show for it, but it was no more in his nature to settle down than it was to stop taking risks others would balk at.

He squeezed almost unnoticed through the mass of bodies crowding the bar area until he reached their table for two. She smiled when she saw him as he bent down and kissed her on her lips.

'How you doing, beautiful?' he asked.

'OK,' she answered, sounding a little down.

'What's the matter?'

'That audition I told you about,' she answered, referring to her latest attempt to launch her acting career and escape the need to work as a waitress. 'I didn't get the part.'

'Why not?'

'Too old.' She shook her head in mock disbelief.

'Too old? That's crazy. You're only thirty-four – and you don't even look that.'

'Yeah, well,' she argued, 'try telling that to the casting director.'

'Screw him. What does he know?'

'Her,' Denise corrected him.

'Oh well, there you go then. She's obviously jealous.'

'Maybe,' she shrugged and sipped her white wine.

'There'll be other parts,' he assured her. 'You're good. You're really good. Eventually you'll get what you deserve.'

The waiter appeared, hovering next to them.

'Can I get you a drink, guys?' he asked too familiarly.

'Sure.' Jackson glanced up at him. 'I'll have a very large Jack Daniels and a glass of champagne for the lady.'

'No problem,' the waiter replied and spun away.

'Champagne?' she questioned. 'We celebrating something?'

'Yeah,' he smiled. 'We're celebrating you.'

'You're mad,' she smiled.

'A bit,' he admitted, 'but I don't want you worrying about bringing more money in. I've got enough for us both. And if this latest thing pays off, there'll be more soon enough.'

'You mean this thing that's got you going backwards and forwards to Broadmarsh?'

'Broadmoor,' he corrected her.

'Wherever.' She rolled her pretty blue eyes. 'The place where you interview murderers and lunatics.'

'Technically, they're lunatics who are murderers,' he grinned.

'You need to be careful,' she warned him. 'Those people are dangerous. I don't like you meeting them.'

'I'll be fine,' he waved her concern away. 'All the interviews take place under secure conditions.'

'What about when they get out?' she asked. 'What's to stop them coming after you?'

'It's not *them*. I'm only interviewing one person there.'

'Yeah,' she pulled a concerned face. 'Sebastian Gibran. About the worst one you could have chosen.'

'Which is exactly why I *did* choose him,' he told her proudly. 'But don't worry about Gibran. He's not interested in me. I'm just the guy who tells the story.'

'Yeah, well you said some pretty bad things about him in that book you wrote,' she reminded him. 'What was it you called him? Evil. A madman. A natural-born killer.'

'None of which would bother him,' he assured her. 'To Gibran, those are compliments.'

The waiter reappeared with their drinks, temporarily postponing their conversation. 'The champagne for you,' he said, handing her a flute glass of bubbles, 'and the Jack Daniels for you,' he added, placing the heavy glass on the table in front of Jackson. He also placed a small metal bucket of ice in the centre of the table. 'There's ice if you need it,' he added, before disappearing back into the crowd.

Jackson dropped two ice cubes into his drink and lifted it close to his lips. 'Cheers,' he toasted her and took a decent swig and exhaled in pleasure.

'Geoff, I'm serious,' she returned to her concerns. 'What if he does want revenge for the things you said? What if he gets someone on the outside to come after you? Some of these serial killers have fans, don't they? What if one of his fans is as mad as he is? What if he persuades one of them to come after you?'

'Not going to happen,' Jackson smiled. 'Besides, if some deranged fan was going to come after me, they would have done it by now, wouldn't they? But I haven't had so much as a nasty letter or email. No one cares what I say about Gibran. Least of all Gibran himself.'

'What about this new killer?' she persisted. 'All the things Gibran's been saying about him – that he's nothing and irrelevant . . . I know about these things, Geoff. I read your books.

This new one won't like it, and if he can't get to Gibran maybe he'll decide to take it out on you.'

Jackson took another slug of bourbon. 'Look, far as Gibran and this other killer are concerned, I'm just a reporter. They read my words, but they don't see me. Even if this new one is reading *The World*, he'll be hearing Gibran's voice – not mine.'

'I don't know, Geoff,' she shook her head and sipped her champagne. 'Can't you just report their crimes? Stop the interviews – keep them at a distance.'

'Any fool could do that. The interviews are where the money is – and my inside information gives me the edge. Keeps me on top.'

'It worries me though, love,' she insisted. 'It really worries me. And what about this DI Corrigan character? I saw you put his photograph in your paper again.' Jackson couldn't resist a wry smile. 'Seriously, Geoff, he doesn't look like the sort of man you should be pissing off.'

'DI Corrigan and I are old friends,' he lied. 'Trust me – he loves the publicity. Might even give me an interview one of these days: how he catches the killers. How he sees into their minds.'

'Really?' she replied – her tone making it clear she didn't believe a word of it. 'Somehow I don't see that ever happening.'

'Ye of little faith,' he smiled.

'Be careful, Geoff,' she warned him. 'If you insist on pissing off these insane killers, then it's probably not a good idea to piss off the police too.'

'Don't worry,' he told her, his smile growing ever wider. 'I have them all exactly where I want them.'

'I hope so, Geoff. For your sake – I really hope so.'

Sean arrived home earlier than usual. He'd hardly seen his kids in days and was determined to spend at least a few minutes with them before Kate ushered them off to bed. Once through the front door he completed his usual ritual of emptying his pockets on to the hallway table and throwing his coat and jacket over the overloaded coat stand. The warmth and glow of the house felt pleasant and welcoming after the harsh barren lights of the Yard and freezing cold of the streets outside. Downstairs was still, but he could hear the commotion of bath-time spilling from upstairs and quickly bounced up the steps and into the small crowded bathroom. His two daughters saw him before Kate did.

'Daddy,' Amanda, his seven-year-old, cried out and stood up in the bath covered in bubbles.

'Hi, Dad,' Louise, his nine-year-old, acknowledged him in an enthusiastic, but more grown-up manner as she sat on a small stool wrapped in a towel looking warm and damp.

'Hello, princesses,' he beamed, grabbing Amanda despite the bubbles and kissing her forehead. Once released, she threw herself back into the water, splashing everyone else in the room as Sean spun towards Louise, cupped her face in his hands and kissed her on the forehead too.

'You got away early then?' Kate asked, reminding him that she was there.

'Yeah,' he answered and kissed her softly on the lips. 'Can't promise I won't get a phone call though.'

'I know the score by now, Sean,' she reminded him.

He grabbed a towel from the rack and stood in front of the bath. 'Come on, munchkin,' he told Amanda. 'Let's get you out.' Amanda stood immediately and jumped from the bath into the waiting towel with a shriek of joy that only the very young ever feel in such small moments of pleasure. 'What did you do at school today?' he asked.

'I got a merit in art,' she told him proudly, 'and made friends with a new girl.'

'Oh yeah,' he chatted, on autopilot. 'And what's her name?'

'Jemma,' she smiled.

'Well she sounds very nice,' he replied, looking over his shoulder at Louise.

'And what about you, Looby-Loo?'

'All right, I suppose,' she answered, sounding far older than her years.

'Only all right?' he asked.

'Wednesdays are the worst,' she complained. 'We have Spanish and maths.'

'Yikes,' he played along. 'Spanish and maths. Sounds like a day from hell.'

'It is,' she agreed, rolling her eyes to the heavens for emphasis.

He looked up at Kate, who was standing watching the scene in silence. 'Why don't you go downstairs and chill out?' he suggested. 'I'll put the kids to bed.'

'By chill out, you mean tidy up and make dinner?' she answered confrontationally.

'Whatever,' he turned away from her, concentrating on drying Amanda's hair. When he looked back, Kate was gone. 'Come on, you two – time for pyjamas and bed.' Neither argued as they sprinted along the short hallway to their bedroom and wriggled into the pyjamas then dived into their beds, giggling uncontrollably. 'OK,' he pleaded with them. 'Settle down now and I'll read you a story. What book are you reading at the moment?'

'We don't want a book,' Louise insisted.

'Oh,' he asked, puzzled. 'Then what do you want?'

'We want you to tell us about the bad man you're trying to catch,' Louise explained.

'Yeah,' Amanda joined in. 'We want to hear about the madman.'

'Really?' he recovered. 'And what do you know about it?'

'Mummy said you were always home late because you had to catch a very bad man,' Amanda explained.

'She said he was very dangerous,' Louise added, sounding more serious.

He decided a degree of honesty was the best policy. 'OK

. . .' he gathered his thoughts. 'Yes – I am trying to find a very bad man.'

'Is he dangerous?' Louise asked immediately.

'He is,' he admitted, 'but not to you or me or Mummy.'

'What's he done?' Amanda interrupted.

'He's killed some people,' Louise answered for him.

'He has,' Sean confirmed.

'Why?' Amanda demanded.

'Well . . .' he thought about his answer, 'because he's sick.'

'But you're a policeman,' Louise argued, 'not a doctor.'

'The police have to catch him first,' he told her, 'and then he can be treated – looked after by the doctors, somewhere safe where he can't hurt anyone else.'

'Why's he hurting people because he's sick?' Louise asked.

'It just . . . it just happens sometimes,' was the best he could do.

'Why's it always you that has to catch them, Daddy?' Amanda wanted to know.

'It's not,' he smiled. 'Plenty of other cops do the same thing.'

'That's not what Mummy says,' Louise frowned.

'Oh.' He nodded, forewarned that all may not be well with Kate. 'Did she now?'

'Yes,' the girls answered together, restoring the smile to his face briefly.

'Is the bad man going to try and hurt you, Daddy?' Amanda asked.

'No,' he answered too quickly, shaking his head. 'No. He's not interested in me. Probably doesn't even know I exist,' he lied. 'I just happen to be the detective leading the case. I'm nothing to him and he's nothing to me. He's only a job.'

'I don't think Mummy thinks it's only a job,' Louise told him. 'She looks scared – like she did when you were looking for that Jackdaw man. The police killed him, didn't they, Daddy?'

He drew in a deep breath through his nose. 'Yes,' he admitted. 'Yes we did. We had no choice.'

'Why?' Louise asked.

'Because he was about to hurt someone really badly,' he answered.

'Who?' Amanda asked.

'Oh, another man,' he tried to end their interest.

'Why?' Louise quizzed him.

'Well,' he stalled, 'I guess he saw the other man as his enemy.'

'Was he?' Louise continued.

'Yes,' he told her. 'Yes I suppose he was. Now go to sleep. School in the morning.'

'Why does Mummy look scared again, Daddy?' Louise ambushed him with one last question.

'She's just tired,' was the best he could do. 'She'll be fine, now goodnight.' He kissed them both on the forehead and walked from the room listening to their sleepy night-time farewells.

Downstairs in the kitchen, Kate was busy making dinner. 'You OK?' he asked. 'Can I help?'

'I'm fine,' she answered without stopping or looking at him. 'Steak and salad all right?'

'Yeah. Great. Better than another sandwich from the canteen.' She didn't respond. 'The kids told me something's bothering you. The new case.'

She stopped what she was doing and turned to face him. 'Someone at work showed me a copy of *The World* today. It was from a couple of days ago, but they'd kindly kept it for me. They thought I'd be interested in seeing the pictures of you on the centre pages – alongside an article about Sebastian Gibran.'

'Oh,' he said, cringing inside. 'That.'

'No doubt you thought you'd got away with it,' she accused him, 'seeing as it was a few days ago.'

'I didn't want you to worry,' he explained.

'But when I find out from somebody else, I *do* worry,' she told him, 'because I know you're trying to keep it from me, which makes me think it *is* something worth worrying about.'

'OK,' he put his hands up. 'If it happens again, I'll tell you.'

'*If* it happens again?'

'Look, I'll speak to the journalist – warn him off.'

'It's that Jackson,' she said, shaking her head. 'Why the hell is he so interested in you?'

'He's not. It's the cases the SIU get he's interested in. His job is to report on the more sensational crimes, which means our paths are bound to cross. He knows Gibran was one of my old cases, so he used my photograph. End of story.'

'Your face was in the paper though,' she complained. 'For God's sake, Sean – you used to work undercover.'

'I haven't done any UC work for years,' he reminded her. 'And all the cases I was involved with have long since been through the courts.'

'But what if they want you to work undercover again?'

'They won't,' he assured her. 'They can't. Not now I've been in the newspapers and on TV. It won't happen.'

'Can you promise me all this isn't putting you or me or, God forbid, the children at risk?'

'I promise.' He stepped forward, wrapped his arms around her and squeezed tightly. 'I'll speak to Jackson, see if I can appeal to his better side.' He let go of her, hoping she would be ready to move on, but she wasn't.

'Tell me about this new one,' she demanded. 'Is he dangerous?'

'Of course he is,' he answered flippantly – instantly regretting it.

'I mean to you,' she clarified, 'or us?'

'No,' he replied, sounding as serious as he could. 'The girls asked me the same question and I'll give you the same answer

251

I gave them. He's not interested in me. As far as I'm concerned, he's just someone I need to find and stop, that's all.'

'They're never "just someone" to you, Sean,' she reminded him. Neither spoke for a few seconds. 'The paper said he pulls their teeth out.'

'He does – amongst other things.'

'Jesus Christ,' she said, turning her back on him while she reached for her glass of warm white wine. 'The people you have to share your world with.' She took a swig, pulled a face of distaste and turned back to face him. 'Why do I get the feeling you're not telling me everything?'

'I can't. There are some details we're deliberately holding back. If I tell you, you might accidentally tell someone at work and that could be bad for the investigation.'

'That's not what I meant,' she told him. 'What I want to know is, is there something between you and him that you're not telling me? If there is and I find out from someone else or read about it in the papers. I'm . . . I'm not going to be very happy at all, Sean.'

He considered the risks for a few seconds, decided they were too considerable. 'OK,' he confessed. 'He contacted me. We're talking.'

'Talking?' she asked, shaking her head. 'What are you – old school friends?'

'We're not friends at all,' he told her. 'He enjoys playing games. Makes him feel like he's in control.'

'Sounds like he is,' she snapped.

'Hardly,' he dismissed it. 'We're taping his conversations and tracking his phone. Talking with him is our best hope of catching him quickly, so I'll keep talking.'

'Why is it always you?' she demanded. 'Why can't someone else do it? What about Sally, or that psychologist woman?'

'Anna,' he reminded her, although he suspected she hadn't forgotten the name.

'Yeah,' she said, hand on her hip. 'Her.'

'Because he wanted to speak to me.'

'Why you?'

'It's something to do with my connection to Gibran,' he answered before throwing his arms open. 'Maybe. I don't really know. He's fucking insane. How am I supposed to know what's going through his mind?'

'Did he threaten you?' she asked him directly. 'Has he threatened you?'

'No,' he assured her. 'He's never said anything threatening to me. If anything, he's been complimentary. Respectful.'

'Great,' she laughed sarcastically. 'Now he's a fan.'

'Doesn't matter what he is,' he told her. 'He's not a threat.'

'You don't know that though, do you?' she challenged him. 'Not for sure. You can't be absolutely certain, can you?'

'I'm certain,' he told her, despite the doubts creeping into his own mind. 'He's not interested in me.'

'You'd better be right, Sean,' she warned him, 'because I'm not ready to watch you lying in a hospital bed again, and nor are the girls. They were younger then. They didn't understand, but if it were to happen now . . .'

'It won't,' he promised. 'I'll find him, then let others take him out.'

'Don't get drawn in, Sean,' she told him. 'Don't use up another life. Do what you have to do, but keep your distance.'

'I will,' he gave his assurance, but his stomach was twisting inside at what he was saying. He could no more keep his distance than the man he hunted could stop killing. Their natures were beyond changing. 'I will.'

Witney Dennis was in her small shared bedroom getting ready under the light of the uncovered bulb that hung from the ceiling. Sheets pinned over the windows acted as curtains to keep watchers in the other tower blocks at bay as she pulled on her best tracksuit and checked herself in the frameless full-length mirror her mother had found in a junk shop. The reflection was imperfect due to the deteriorating silver leaf, but she was happy with what she saw. She hoped the man she was going to meet would like what he saw too. After one last check of her make-up she left the room and headed down the short corridor to the kitchen that always smelt of cheap meals and grease.

'I'm going out for a bit,' she told her mum, who was busy with her unruly younger siblings.

'Oh yeah,' her mum looked her up and down with obvious disgust on her face. 'Where you going then?'

'To meet someone.'

'New boyfriend, is it?'

'None of your business,' Witney told her.

'It is while you live in my house,' her mum tried to impose some discipline.

'It's a flat, not a house,' Witney smiled unpleasantly, 'and it's not yours – it's the council's and you never pay your rent.'

'You cheeky bitch,' her mum's parenting skills degenerated to their normal level.

'I'll see you later.' Witney turned her back on her and hurried from the overheated, cramped flat and into the freezing night – walking at her usual fast pace, checking over her shoulder every few seconds in case her mum had pursued her. She called for the lift, keeping a wary eye on the walkway, relieved to step inside the small metal box that reeked of urine, where she hammered the button for the ground floor until the door slid shut – beginning her descent to street level. As soon as the lift jerked to a halt and the doors grated open she headed out across the estate, head bowed to avoid catching the eye of anyone who might know her. She didn't want to be stopped and she didn't want to talk. She just wanted to get to where they'd arranged to meet.

As she left the boundaries of the estate and crossed the main road, her pace slowed and she began to have second thoughts. What if he wanted to have full sex with her? She'd never done that before. Oral sex had often been a means-to-and-end – a virtual currency accepted by most men on the estate, but fucking someone for money made her a prostitute. No matter how she tried to spin it to herself, she was possibly about to become a whore. But if it was only with this one man and he looked after her and paid her well, then perhaps it was more like a relationship, she told herself. Didn't most men give their girlfriends money and nice things?

Before she knew it, she'd reached the car park at the back of the abandoned shops, as they'd arranged – her heart sinking, despite her concerns, when she couldn't see his car. 'Fuck,' she cursed as freezing rain like ice bullets began to fall from the sky. 'Where are you?' She turned through three hundred and eighty degrees, hoping to spot his car but seeing nothing beyond the driving rain shining in the street lights – rain that stung the skin on her face and made short work of her clothing. 'Fuck,' she cursed again as it dawned on her she had no choice but to head home, cashless, to her mum's wrath and a future of giving teenage drug dealers oral sex to feed her crack habit.

She'd no sooner taken a step towards the exit when she saw, or perhaps sensed movement coming from the shadow of the outhouse that once served as a storage room for the shops. She tried to rub the freezing darts from her eyes as the dark, hooded figure moved slowly, but relentlessly towards her, seemingly oblivious to the rain and the cold, until he was close enough for her to realize that it was *him*, despite the fact his hood was pulled as tightly around his face as before. There was something about the way he moved that was unmistakable.

'You came,' she said when he was only inches away from her, but he didn't answer – just a faceless, silent figure standing still and stiff in front of her. 'I thought maybe you'd changed your mind,' she told him, but he wouldn't answer. 'Where's your car?' she persisted. 'It's fucking freezing out here.'

'I'm going to make you special,' a voice she hardly recognized told her from the darkness of the hood. 'I'm going to make you famous. No one will ever forget your name.'

'You what?' she answered in confusion – survival instincts beginning to flush her body with chemicals. She took a step backwards, but he was too quick – his hand flashing towards her face – something heavy and solid connecting with her temple, making her legs buckle as she fell to the floor on her hands and knees, feeling as if she was about to throw up. She managed to look up, her head tilted to one side, and saw him standing over her, looking at her like a conquering gladiator as he casually tossed the small iron bar on to the rain-soaked ground before lowering the zip of his waterproof top. She watched as he slipped his hand inside and pulled out an evil-looking combat knife that he held out in front of him – the raindrops splashing off the blade and reflecting in the street light. She tried to pull away as he reached down and grabbed the ponytail on top of her hair, jerking her backwards so her throat stretched out as she stared up at him – wild and terrified.

He gently placed the cutting edge of the knife across her throat, then suddenly let go of her hair and grabbed her around the throat instead, squeezing hard enough to make her gasp for breath as she clawed at his hand and face. She felt the punch before she saw it – a fierce blow to her nose, causing an explosion of deep red blood as she momentarily slumped with shock and pain. He took advantage of the few seconds of stillness he needed to pull her tracksuit bottoms and knickers to her knees with the hand that still held the knife – its blade catching her bare thighs numerous times, leaving small, bloody cuts.

'No,' she managed to beg, but her pleas for mercy were wasted as he thrust the knife deep into her shoulder and let go of it. Her mouth gaped open in surprise and horror while he used his free hand to release himself from his trousers and force himself inside of her. His grip tightened around her throat – her own hands ineffectively pawing at his face, growing weaker and weaker until slowly her hands fell away and lay limp at her side. She felt her life ebbing away as he reached climax without making a sound. He remained inside her as he twisted and pulled the knife free, releasing his grip around her throat, allowing her to cough and gag back to life. Her eyes flickered fully open and she glared at the knife being held in front of her. 'Please,' she whispered.

He drew the knife long and deep across her throat, exposing tendons and her trachea – her blood flowing like an oil slick from the wound, but she was too weak to raise her hands to try and stem the flow – too resigned to death. 'You'll never grow old,' he told her, 'and you'll never be forgotten. Time to die.' He grabbed her hair and pulled her head off the ground, placed the blade against the side of her neck and drew it powerfully through her soft, white, bloodstained skin – the wound immediately opening like it was giving birth to the blood that seemed to take a few seconds before spraying into the rain – soon turning into a flow, carrying her life with it. As her blood pressure dropped and her heart stopped beating, the flow dwindled to little more than a trickle. Not once did his eyes leave hers as she slipped into the darkness while he remained inside her – one blood-soaked hand clamped around her throat as he looked down on the scene of beauty he had created, feeling more god-like than ever.

He could have stayed like that for hours, but as he calmed he realized he was out in the open. Exposed. Quickly he released himself from inside her and pulled his tracksuit bottoms back up. Adjusting his position, he now sat astride her and opened her mouth wide. He was pleased to see her teeth were in good condition – her body was too young to have been badly damaged by her lifestyle. Without hesitation, he went to work with the tip of the knife, cutting deep into her gums to loosen some of her teeth before he removed the backpack taking two plastic freezer bags and a pair of pliers from inside. One by one he gripped the teeth he wanted – twisting and pulling until they tore free – pieces of bloody flesh clinging to the roots as he dropped them into one of the bags. It was hard work, but he was strong, determined and gaining in experience. When he had all that he needed he turned his attention to her fingernails. As usual, he intended to take them all and knew from the others that they were far easier to extract than the teeth – especially if they were quite long, as the girl's were. He packed everything away in the backpack, except the pliers and the empty plastic bag, then lifted her small right hand, pinched the end of the nail on her little finger in the pliers and with one hard tug pulled it free and dropped it into the bag. A small piece of bloodied flesh clung to the end. He moved from finger to finger, repeating the process until he'd collected every nail, then dropped her right hand and lifted her left, repeating the process. He held the bag up to the sky to examine its contents in the streetlight, placed it in the backpack and stood over his victim, looking down at what he'd created. Her tracksuit bottoms and knickers were down around her knees, her legs spread, her arms lying almost straight by her sides. For a second he considered pulling her tracksuit up, but decided the aesthetics of her lying semi-naked on the dark grey ground in the rain that mixed with her blood were perfect. Covering her up would be a sign of weakness, of mercy or shame. He felt none of those things. He pulled the bag on to his back, took one last look at the girl from Roehampton, and then jogged away into the dark, rainy night.

# 11

The hooded man circled around to the back of Sean's house and quietly climbed over the fence, moving fast and smooth across the garden until he came to the back door. He tried the handle, but found it locked. He was strong enough to force the door, but in the middle of the night the noise was bound to be heard. He needed to find another way. The two smaller windows above the larger kitchen windows caught his attention. He couldn't see any security locks. Maybe because Sean was a policeman he felt invulnerable or maybe he considered the latches to be sufficient security and the windows too small, but he knew his knife would make short work of them and that he would be able to slide his supple body through the gap.

He pulled himself on to the window ledge and once he was sure of his balance he took the knife from inside his top and forced it into the gap, seesawing the blade until its tip reached the latch. Gently and patiently, millimetre by milli-metre he rotated the latch until it was completely out of its circular housing. He took a deep breath and pulled the knife back through the gap. The window was open just enough for him to catch the bottom edge and lift it completely open with his fingers – the warm air that smelt of Sean's family rushing at him from inside. He froze without breathing for a long time while he listened and watched for any sign of life stirring within the house. Once he was sure he had not been heard, he heaved his head, arms and shoulders up and through the small space, tipping his lower body into a forty-five degree downwards angle to slide inside, landing neatly next to the sink on the kitchen worktop – crouching and ready to strike – his knife at the ready.

Again he paused, listening and smelling the air, before climbing down. Without making a sound, he walked across the neat kitchen out into the hallway – listening to the night-time sounds of the house – tiny ticks and creaks that only someone like himself would notice. The staircase stretched out in front of him, leading the way to where the family slept – all on the same floor, which presented a dilemma. Should he kill Sean first and eliminate any danger, then go to the children, or was it worth the risk so Sean could see what he'd done before he put him out of his misery? He decided he couldn't give up the chance of seeing the horror on his face – the realization that he'd been wrong – that he was much, much more than just another madman. The children had to be killed first.

He began to make his way up the stairs – one careful step at a time, feeling for squeaky floorboards before he committed his full weight – adjusting his position as and when he found one, until he reached the first-floor hallway. The door of one bedroom was slightly ajar and in darkness. The menacing Corrigan was no doubt asleep in the room, lying next to his wife. The other room's door was open wider. *The children's room*. From within came a soft red light that drew him towards it like a tiger to a tethered goat until he reached the door and slowly pushed it open to reveal the two small sleeping figures. They were almost fully hidden under their duvets, but he could clearly see their delicate young throats waiting for him. He looked down at the knife in his hand and stepped into the room, moving like a dancer until he stood between their beds – the blade moving relentlessly towards the younger girl's neck when she suddenly stirred – her eyes flickering open, then her lips.

'Daddy,' she asked sleepily.

'No,' the cold voice from the blackness inside the hood told her. 'Not Daddy. Hell.'

As the knife flashed towards her throat, Sean woke up with a jolt, gasping for breath and trying to get his bearings – stuck in both the world of nightmares and the real. It took him a few seconds to realize it was his mobile ringing that had woken him and although he knew he'd been dreaming he had to fight the urge to run to his daughters' bedroom. 'Shit,' he cursed and checked the luminous display of his alarm clock. It was four fifteen in the morning. It could only be work and unless he was very lucky it could only be bad news. 'Shit,' he cursed again as he snatched the phone from his bedside table and answered it, still half asleep. 'DI Corrigan.'

'DI Jamie Coles speaking,' the grim, accentless voice informed him. 'Wandsworth CID. I have a suspicious death you may be interested in.'

'I'm listening,' Sean told him as he stood and walked to his daughters' bedroom – his heart pounding despite knowing it had to have been a nightmare.

'Teenage girl,' Coles began, 'from the Roehampton Estate. Her throat and side of her neck have been cut and there's a stab wound to her shoulder. Probably bled to death. Her lower clothing's been pulled down and, judging by her body position, she's been sexually assaulted. If that wasn't enough, some of her teeth have been hacked out and her fingernails are missing. We've tented the body, but the weather's shit and I can't cover half of Roehampton.'

'I understand.' Sean looked into the bedroom and saw his daughters sleeping peacefully. His heart rate beginning to

261

slow. 'Text me your exact location to this phone. I'm on my way.'

'I'll be waiting,' Coles replied and hung up.

Sean's hand holding the phone fell to his side as he continued to watch his daughters sleeping peacefully – the very thought of losing one of them had left him racked with pain. But tonight someone else had lost their daughter, in the most terrible way imaginable. Too slow, he told himself. I was too slow and now someone else is dead. 'Christ,' he whispered and headed towards the bathroom.

Less than an hour later he pulled up outside the taped-off crime scene. The magnetic blue light attached to the roof of his car had cleared what little traffic there'd been and helped speed him to Roehampton and the dead girl. There were several uniformed vehicles parked at the scene, all unusually with their blue lights still spinning and he noticed more uniformed cops guarding the scene than he was used to seeing. Murder scenes tended to be deathly quiet for the first few hours, at least until the investigating detectives had had a chance to see the place exactly how the killer had left it – haunting and eerie. Then it needed to be photographed and videoed before forensic examiners took over, turning it into something more like the scenes people were used to seeing on their TVs. He approached two uniformed officers standing on the edge of the scene, with a tall slim man in a raincoat sheltering from the persistent rain under a black umbrella.

'DI Coles?' Sean asked, pulling his warrant card from his coat pocket. 'DI Corrigan. SIU.'

'Sorry about dragging you out of your bed,' Coles apologized without confirming who he was, 'but I thought you'd better take a look.' He lifted the tape to allow Sean to duck under before doing the same while still managing to stay under his umbrella. 'Bloody filthy night,' Coles complained as they walked towards the small tent in the middle of the disused car park.

Sean wasn't listening to his small talk. He was taking in all he could about the scene – the closed-down shops, the broken windows, abandoned outhouses and rubbish-strewn doorways. 'Sorry,' he said, when he realized Coles was speaking to him. 'I couldn't hear – the rain.'

'I was saying it would happen on a filthy night like this,' Coles repeated. 'Evidence doesn't like being rained on.'

'No,' Sean agreed as they drew closer to the tent and the horror it hid. 'How long was she exposed to the weather?'

'Hard to say,' Coles answered, 'but I'd guess a couple of hours at least. Local crack-head called Martin Connor found her when he came to get high. We're lucky he bothered to report it. Probably because he knew her. Fortunately the tent was still in the car park at Wandsworth. It was due to go back to Lambeth today, but looks like they'll have to wait a while longer now.' They reached the tent. 'Shall we?' Coles asked and pulled one of the front flaps open so they could both step inside out of the rain and into the last moments of her life, forever now frozen in death. 'Connor says her name's Witney Dennis,' Coles told him mournfully. 'She lived on the estate over the road there. Next of kin haven't been told yet.'

Sean took out his Maglite and shone it down on her life-less body. The corpse had already taken on the waxy yellow look of the dead, although her cold wet skin glistened arti-ficially in the beam of his light. The rain had washed away much of the blood and he could see the terrible wounds to her neck and throat as well as the stab wound to her shoulder. Her tracksuit bottoms and knickers were around her knees, exposing her pubic hair. Sean moved the torch light on to her face and guessed she was about sixteen or seventeen, before moving it back to the stab wound. 'Why would he do that?' he asked out loud.

'Why would he do any of it?' Coles replied.

'Because it's what he lives for,' Sean told him.

'If you say so,' Coles shrugged, his eyes on Sean and not the body.

'But this isn't part of his ritual,' he continued.

'Ritual?' Coles asked. 'You mean his MO?'

'To him it's the same thing,' Sean explained, 'but this isn't . . .' He crouched down close to the dead girl, his eyes fixed on the wound to her shoulder. 'Why stab her here?'

'You tell me. These sort of nutters are your speciality.'

Sean looked from the wound to her lower clothing and back again – disjointed pictures flashing in no particular order or sense in his mind. He knew himself well enough to not try and force it. He'd learnt to allow himself to see what others couldn't, trusting that eventually the random images would play like a scene from silent film in his head. 'He raped her or he had sex with her after she was dead,' he said to himself.

'Nice,' Coles said, mistakenly thinking he was speaking to him.

'With the other female victim he almost certainly sexually abused her after she was dead.' The image of Tanya Richards jumped into his head. 'The only wounds she had were to her neck and throat. Wounds that killed her. There were no signs that she tried to defend herself because . . . because she was already dead. She couldn't defend herself. She was no threat.'

'You all right?' Coles asked, realizing that Sean had gone into a different world.

Sean didn't hear him as again he shone his torch on her lower clothing. Then he set it down on the floor, pulled out a pair of latex gloves and started pulling them on.

'What you doing?' Coles asked. 'Forensics are going to be seriously pissed off if you start touching things.'

'I've got to check something,' Sean insisted, lifting her hand by the wrist as he recovered the torch and held the light close to her fingertips. The rain had cleaned her fingers of any obvious signs of skin or blood, but he could see tell-tale traces. He quickly swapped hands and found the same on the fingertips of her other hand – barely visible, but he was sure of what he was seeing.

'You see something?' Coles asked.

'Blood,' Sean told him.

'He pulled her fingernails out,' Coles unnecessarily reminded him.

'With the other victims, the only blood we found belonged to them. They didn't scratch him.'

'Hard to be sure, when he takes their nails,' Coles argued.

'If they'd scratched him, we'd have found his DNA,' Sean insisted.

Coles wasn't convinced. 'Not if the weather was like this.'

'I wonder if she scratched him,' Sean continued. 'Tried to fight him off. Tried to stop him.'

'I'm sure she did,' said Coles, not registering the significance.

'It would mean she was alive when he raped her.'

'You don't know that,' Coles argued. 'She could have tried to fight him off when he first attacked her, then—'

'No.' Sean pointed to the wound on the side of her head – an area of her hair matted with dried blood despite the best efforts of the rain. 'They don't see him coming. He takes them out with a blow to the head. Before they fully come to again, he cuts their throats, lets them bleed for a while and then cuts through the carotid artery.' Images of the other victims clutching at their own throats and necks played in his mind. 'They couldn't defend themselves or hurt him because they were using their hands to stop the blood from the wounds. That's how he had control. But not here.'

'So what happened?' Coles asked, enthralled as a child wanting to know what happened next in a scary fairy-tale.

'He hit her,' Sean explained to himself as much as Coles, 'and she fell. He planned to kill her just like the others . . .

265

so he must have had his knife in his hand, but something made him change his mind.'

'What?' Coles interrupted again. 'Why did he change his mind?'

'I don't know why,' Sean admitted, 'but I think she was alive when he raped her. For some reason he wanted her to be alive when he raped her. If I'm right, it's a significant change. He wants us to believe he's more than just a sexually motivated killer, but at the end of the day that's exactly what he is – so he kneels between her legs – one hand around her throat and the other holding the knife.' As if suddenly remembering something, he shone the torch on the inside of the girl's exposed thighs. The rain had cleaned away the blood, but clearly visible were numerous small scratches and nicks. 'You see?' he asked excitedly. 'He was holding the knife when he pulled her clothes down, which means she was almost certainly alive, otherwise he could have put the knife down. He wasn't used to it. Hadn't done it before. That's how she got the cuts on her thighs.'

He was moving too fast for Coles. 'You sure?' he asked.

'As sure as I can be,' Sean snapped, irritated by the interruption. 'Looks like she became aware of what was happening and fought back. She scratched him.' The images suddenly stuttered to a halt while his imagination caught up. After a few seconds the scene started to play again. 'He was angry and frustrated. He needed her compliance, but he couldn't control her with only one hand around her throat – he needed to free a hand if he was going to enter her, but . . . but he needed to keep the knife close so . . . so he kept hold of it. But why stab her in the shoulder?'

'To make her more compliant?' Coles suggested.

'As much as anything,' Sean answered before quickly changing the subject as he was rushed by more thoughts. 'Was she searched?'

'Only for ID,' Coles told him.

'Did you find any?' Sean asked.

'A fake driving licence,' Coles replied, 'but it's in the same name Connor gave us – Witney Dennis. Her details match up with our intelligence records, but the age is out by a couple of years. Probably used it to buy fags and booze.'

Sean wasn't interested in her fake ID. 'Did you find anything else?'

'Some cash,' he shrugged. 'Twenty, fifteen pounds – something like that.'

'Any drugs?' Sean asked, remembering the rubbish-strewn doorways outside the tent and the fact Coles had told him her body had been found by a local crack-head.

'No,' Coles shook his head.

'Was she a user?' Sean persisted.

'Intelligence says she was,' Cole said matter-of-factly, unable to see the relevance. 'What's your point?'

'Ever known a drug addict to have cash in their pocket?'

'Maybe she came here to meet her dealer?' Coles suggested. 'But died before that happened?'

'Possible, but I don't think so,' Sean told him. 'However, her killer may have pretended to be a dealer and arranged to meet her here. Either that or he lured her here by promising her cash.'

'Lured her here?' Coles questioned. 'Then he would have had to have been in contact with her.'

Sean ignored him as his mind continued to consider her last few minutes alive. 'Look at where she was killed,' he insisted. 'It's been raining all night. If she got here first, she would have been sheltering in a doorway. If he was here first and she didn't know him, she'd have run back out into the street. So she must have been expecting to meet him, because when she saw him she walked out into the middle of the car park.'

'Maybe he chased her down?' Coles played devil's advocate.

'And dragged her into the centre – out into the open?'

Sean dismissed the possibility. 'If she'd run from a doorway heading to the street, he would have caught her by the building line. He could have pulled her into a doorway out of sight and out of the rain. But he didn't do that, because she went to him willingly.'

'Is that his MO then?' Coles asked. 'He gets to know them before he murders them?'

'Something like that,' Sean answered. 'You know this area better than me. Any council CCTV? Any chance of witnesses?'

'No CCTV,' Coles told him. 'Cameras don't last long around here. Most get smashed. Some get stolen. As for witnesses – good luck. She was a local girl, so that might help, but people around here don't like talking to the police. It appears your suspect chose the place as carefully as he chose the victim.'

'He likes to plan,' Sean admitted, standing up, the pain and stiffness in his knees after crouching making him unsteady on his feet. 'I need to keep this quiet for as long as possible. Even if it's only a few hours.'

'We already have a cover story up and running,' Cole told him. 'As far as the few locals who've asked are concerned, it's an unexploded Second World War bomb under here, not the body of a teenager. Should persuade people to keep their distance for a while.'

'Good,' Sean nodded. 'Thanks.' He pushed his way through the tent flap and back into the freezing rain outside, closely followed by Coles. 'Keep it wrapped up as tightly as you can,' he ordered. 'My people will be here soon to take over. No-one to be allowed in until they get here, OK.'

'OK,' Coles agreed, struggling to open his umbrella. 'No problem.'

'You've done a good job,' Sean thanked him as the two men shook hands.

'Pleasure,' Coles replied. 'Hope it helps you catch the bastard.'

'It will.'

As Sean made his way back to his car, his mind spinning, his body aching and feeling sick to his stomach – images of the dead girl from Roehampton burned themselves into his memory alongside the others. Faces that would be with him until he joined them in the land of the dead. 'You'll tell me why you're doing this,' he whispered into the rain. 'One way or the other, you'll tell me why you're doing this.'

David Langley stepped out of the hot shower and dabbed himself partially dry before wrapping the towel around his waist and walking to the kitchen, guided by a trail of candles. All other lights in the flat had been turned off so he could better appreciate the flickering shadows on the walls. The bright light from bulbs and spotlights would have been inappropriate for the occasion. With his TV and radio off and the rest of the world asleep, he could hear the candle-flames burning – the only sound that he would tolerate when enjoying what were always the most special hours for him – those first few hours after a kill, when he'd made it home safely with his prizes and fresh memories, the smell of his victim still filling his nose and mouth. Few people on the planet were privileged to indulge in an extraordinary experience such as this; conscious of that, he savoured it to the full. Memories of the kill mixed with older memories of sitting by a fire in the forest with his father, calm and relaxed after a day of hunting and killing whatever animals they could track – their hands stained with blood, the pelts drying in the warmth close by.

He considered how truly different he was from the mass of humanity – just as his father said he would be. Few people could appreciate what it felt like, the sense of peace, the sense of his own power. He longed to be able to speak about how he felt in that very moment, but it would have to be someone who understood, one of the few, the chosen. Someone like

Gibran or perhaps Sean. He considered calling him, but decided he was unlikely to be in his office at this hour. Assuming the body had been discovered, he was probably at the crime scene at this moment.

At the thought of the girl's body, lying in the middle of the car park, his eyes were instinctively drawn to his backpack sitting unopened on the kitchen table. He went to it now, sliding it towards him and unzipping it slowly, his hand sliding inside and removing the two plastic bags. Placing them reverently on the table, he pushed the backpack aside and sat down. Drawing in a deep breath, he lifted a plastic bag in each hand and examined the bloody contents – each tooth and nail helping him to relive the moment he'd ripped them from the girl's body. His breathing quickened as his thoughts travelled back further, to when he was inside her while the blood – her life – drained from her body. If only he had someone *special* to share it all with. Someone who could appreciate what he was.

Again his mind drifted to Sean as he imagined him at the crime scene, walking around the girl's body. Crouching next to her to examine her wounds – trying to get inside his skin, feel as he had felt, see what he had seen. That was how Corrigan worked, he'd decided. He was different to other detectives. He didn't wait for forensic reports to tell him what happened or clumsily try to imagine how the killer had killed – he imagined how *he* would have killed, what would have made it special for *him*. Clearly it enabled him to paint a vivid picture of how it happened, using his experience of other scenes and other killers to fill in the gaps. That had to be how he did it, how he caught killers like Gibran and Thomas Keller as quickly as he did. Now he'd be doing the same thing, trying to catch him. But this time it wouldn't work – not quickly enough, anyway. Langley would achieve all he wanted to achieve and then hand himself in so the whole world could learn about him and all the wonderful things he'd done. Corrigan would never be able to claim his scalp.

Corrigan and Gibran, he thought to himself. Two names forever linked. One still free to hunt while the other rotted in Broadmoor. Even so, he craved Gibran's approval. His recognition. Maybe now, after his latest creation, Gibran would give him the respect he was due and realize that it was only a matter of time before he had to relinquish his crown.

Sharp pains in the palm of his hands distracted him from his dreaming as he realized he was in danger of crushing the plastic bags containing the girl from Roehampton's fingernails and teeth. He snapped his hands open and let the bags fall to the table. 'Soon everyone will know my name,' he hissed into the semi-darkness – his words making the flames of the candles on the table bend away from him as if they were trying to escape their wick tethers. Once his plan was revealed to the world, both Corrigan and Gibran would have to acknowledge their inferiority and kneel before him.

'Sleep now,' he told himself, leaning forward and blowing out the candles.

# 12

Sean had gone straight from the scene to his office, where he'd waited for an hour before scrambling Sally and Donnelly, trying to allow them as much sleep as he could, knowing it was going to be a very long day. An hour later, he called Anna and the rest of the team. Now he sat in his office drinking black coffee while he prepared to brief everyone. Sally was buzzing around the main office, clearing room on the whiteboards for more photographs, while Donnelly sat in his office looking lost in his own thoughts.

As soon as he spotted Anna coming through the door, Sean jumped to his feet and headed into the main office, popping his head into Donnelly's office en route.

'I'm about to brief the team,' he said. When Donnelly continued to sit, dazed, at his desk, Sean asked, 'You all right?'

'Yeah.' Donnelly ran a hand through his unkempt hair. 'Wee bit tired is all.'

'You want to sit this one out?'

'No,' Donnelly replied, getting to his feet. 'I'm fine.'

'If you're sure . . .' Sean called over his shoulder, striding towards the whiteboards where Sally had pinned photographs of the victim taken on Sean's smartphone and printed on A4 paper. The professional copies would arrive later, showing the true horror of the scene in all their detailed garishness. 'OK, everybody,' he called out. 'Listen up.' He waited for the room to quieten and the detectives to move closer. 'As you all know by now, we have another victim.' He pointed to the pictures of the girl from Roehampton. 'Witney Dennis. Sixteen years old, lived on the Roehampton Estate, about two hundred metres from where she was found by a local crack-head in a raely used car park behind some closed down shops. The victim was also known to use crack when she had the cash. Other than that we know she was unemployed, a petty thief – shoplifting mostly – and Wandsworth Borough Intelligence Unit say she was probably an occasional sex worker.

'She died pretty much the same way as the others,' he explained. 'Hit on the head, knife wounds to her throat and the side of her neck. Probable cause of death was blood loss, but we'll have to wait for Dr Canning to confirm it. Several of her teeth and all of her fingernails have been removed, so we're sure it's our man . . . But be aware, there are some significant changes to his method this time around.' The team waited in silence for him to explain. 'Firstly, I'm sure he raped her while she was very much alive. There are numerous cuts to her upper legs. These pictures aren't great, but you can make them out here, here, here' – he indicated each wound on the photograph of her thighs. 'I don't think these were deliberate. They're consistent with the sort of injuries you'd expect if he was holding the knife while tugging at her clothing prior to the rape. And that tells us she must have been alive, trying to fight him off. It's possible she scratched him, but with her nails missing, it's hard to say for sure. We'll have to wait for forensics to see if they can find traces of his blood and DNA on her fingertips.'

'Could that be why he takes the nails?' Jesson asked. 'To stop us getting his DNA?'

'No,' Sean dismissed it. 'He's left his semen at each scene, so he's not concerned about removing traces of his DNA. The nails are trophies.' Jesson nodded his agreement. 'And then there's this,' Sean continued, pointing to the stab wound in her shoulder. 'She was trying to fight him off so he stabbed her here, in the shoulder, to make her comply and—' He was about to share his theory that it wasn't just about compliance, but decided against it. He didn't want them wondering how he could even consider such a thing.

'Also,' he changed tack, 'judging by the location and the time she was attacked, it appears she must have gone there to meet him. That she knew him and knew he'd be there at that time. That they'd arranged it. If he'd ambushed her, it would have happened under cover of the buildings, but she was killed in the middle of the car park, which suggests she walked out to meet him there and was then taken by surprise. As with his previous victims, he'd selected her in advance and made contact with her. But this time around he eliminated the need to spend hours following her by arranging to meet her at a specific place and time.'

'I didn't think this type of killer liked to change their method,' Sally said. 'At all.'

'They will do,' Anna joined in. 'As their confidence grows and as they learn from experience, they can adjust their methods – fine-tune them. It's possible that's what he's doing.'

'This will be the method he uses in future,' Sean insisted. 'It appeals to his nature. It's efficient and effective, while allowing him to make the killings feel personal – and that's important to him.' He registered the nods and shrugs amongst his audience.

'OK. Moving on. We know he's used public transport in the past, particularly with William Dalton, but Roehampton's a public transport wasteland – nearest tube is Southfields and the nearest over-ground station is Barnes, and they're both a good hike from where she was killed. My gut feeling is he wouldn't want to be hanging around waiting for a night bus, giving other passengers a chance to study him, maybe notice blood on his clothing. He'd want to know he could get away quickly, unobserved, so his best bet would be some form of private transport, a car or bike—'

'Or he lived close by,' Sally suggested. 'Maybe he knew the victim for a lot longer than the other two. Maybe he planned on making her one of his victims a long time ago, but he's smart enough not to kill on his own doorstep first, so he made her victim number three and not number one, to throw us off the scent.'

'We can't rule it out,' Sean admitted. 'Her associates, friends and family need to be checked out thoroughly in case Sally's right. We also need to check all vehicles in the vicinity of the scene, any bikes chained to lampposts. The car park itself isn't covered, but perhaps he was captured by CCTV on his way to or from the scene. Check for witnesses too: maybe someone saw him running or walking through a nearby street. That time of night, in that weather, he might have stuck in someone's memory. We'll need to check all buses in and out of the area before and after she was killed—' There were audible groans at the size of the task. 'I know,' he sympathized. 'I know, but it needs to be done. Check each bus's CCTV, what Oyster cards or credit cards were used by passengers, and track them all down in case they remember seeing our man.' The moaning grew louder. 'Hey,' Sean snapped. 'A young girl is dead because we didn't catch this bastard soon enough, so let's not moan about the size of the task in hand. Let's just do our jobs properly.' The moans changed to nods of agreement. 'Good,' he acknowledged the change in attitude. 'Alan,' Sean turned to Jesson. 'How we getting on with the pay-as-you-go enquiries?'

'Definitely bought in the O2 mobile shop in Oxford Street,' Jesson reported, 'and we now have CCTV of the suspect.' He dashed their raised hopes by adding, 'But again he has his hood pulled almost completely over his face. The cameras caught a glimpse of his mouth and nose, but nothing that's going to identify him. The member of staff that sold it to him got a better look at his face than the cameras did and has agreed to help with a photofit, but I'm not expecting much.'

'Still,' Sean reminded them, 'it could be the best image of him we have so far. What about CCTV from the Borough tube?'

'We have CCTV of the victim leaving the station the night he was killed,' Sally took over, 'but he wasn't followed. However, three days earlier he was followed by a man we believe to be the suspect, wearing a hooded top and carrying a backpack. There are no decent shots of his face and he wasn't using an Oyster card. Instead he used a one-day travel card bought at four twenty in the afternoon at Charing Cross Underground station. The suspect paid in cash and once again CCTV shows him wearing his hooded top and carrying the bag.'

'Careful son of a bitch,' muttered Donnelly, with a hint of admiration.

'Anything else from the victims' Oyster cards?' Sean asked.

'TFL have examined their travel patterns based on Oyster card usage,' Jesson explained. 'There's nothing that stands out – nothing to show their movements showed any regular pattern. From a travel perspective, their paths didn't cross.'

'We need to find something else then,' Sean moved on. 'What about their friends, associates, doctors, social workers – anything?'

'So far we're coming up blank,' Sally answered. 'We'll keep looking.'

'Dave,' he turned to Donnelly. 'Anything from the door-to-door?'

'Nothing we can use. They lived their lives like ghosts, drifting around barely noticed. People knew of them, but not much more. Probably why the killer chose them.'

'Probably,' Sean agreed. 'OK. That's it for now. See Sally

and Dave for your assignments.' The gathering broke up with no one directing questions his way so he returned to his office and sank heavily into his chair. Almost immediately the phone rang. He snatched up the handset. 'Corrigan.'

'Ah, Mr Corrigan,' Roddis began. 'Just to let you know we're all set at the scene, although I dread to think how much we lost to the rain before the tent arrived.'

'Too much,' Sean answered.

'The good news is, the unexploded bomb story is holding. The bad news is, we're going to be here a while and I doubt it'll last much longer.'

'Do what you can. Have the victim sent to Dr Canning at Guy's when you're done.'

He hung up just as Addis appeared in his doorway.

'Another damn murder,' Addis growled, marching into the office and standing in front of Sean's desk. 'Three now. This is modern London, for God's sake, not the Victorian era. You can't move without being filmed by CCTV, so how is he literally getting away with murder? Christ. Media will have a field day when they find out. It seems to me that this entire investigation has been lagging from the start.'

'Stranger attacks are extremely difficult,' Sean reminded him. 'However, we do now have a description of him and the name he's using.'

'I've seen the investigation progress reports,' Addis corrected him. 'You have a partial description and a made-up first name. Hardly fills me with confidence that you're about to find him. And these phone calls he's been making to you – why haven't we been able to trace him yet or talk him into walking into some sort of trap?'

'Because we have no one to use as bait,' Sean argued.

'Then we need to find someone,' Addis insisted. 'Get something organized and authorized – a properly run undercover operation. We need to do something, Sean. He's got to be caught before three turns into four.'

'He's making mistakes, soon he'll make one that will lead us right to him.'

'I don't see him making many mistakes,' Addis argued, 'and *soon* isn't soon enough.' He wagged his index finger at him. 'Find him, Sean or I'll give the case to somebody who can.' He spun on his polished heels and marched from the office before Sean could reply.

'Shit,' Sean cursed quietly. Addis's loss of patience was a problem. He was just about to curse again when a thought blossomed in his mind. If Addis was putting him under pressure, it was because someone higher up the food chain was putting Addis under pressure. And pressure made people more willing to take risks. If he played his cards right, it could all be used to his advantage.

Geoff Jackson was sound asleep next to his girlfriend when the shrill tones of his mobile phone cut into his dreams. It took a while for him to be anything like awake. He was tired and hungover from his night out with Denise and a few drinks always made her frisky so he'd had precious little sleep. His hand padded around the bedside table until it found his phone. 'Bloody hell,' he complained as he squinted to check the caller ID, but it showed no number. 'Hello,' he answered it anyway, trying to sound more awake than he was.

'Don't say my name,' the voice he immediately recognized insisted. 'Whatever you do, don't say my name.'

'OK,' Jackson replied, becoming more alert by the second as he searched for his cigarettes.

'I have some information for you,' DCI Ryan Ramsay told him. 'Something no one else has.'

'I'm listening,' Jackson encouraged him, lighting the cigarette.

'There's been another murder.'

'This is London – there's always "been another murder",' Jackson replied flippantly.

'Yeah, but this is another by the person you're interested in,' Ramsay told him.

'You sure?' Jackson checked.

'I wouldn't be bothering you if I wasn't.'

'What makes you so sure it's our guy?'

'Same method,' Ramsay answered without emotion. 'Blow to the head, throat cut and his special calling card – her teeth were pulled out.'

'Jesus,' Jackson paused for a second to consider the victim's ordeal. 'When did this happen?'

'Last night,' Ramsay told him. 'Body was found about one in the morning.'

'That's hours ago,' Jackson puzzled. 'It should be all over the news by now.'

'They've put a cover story in place,' Ramsay explained. 'An unexploded Second World War bomb.'

'Clever,' Jackson nodded and exhaled thick white smoke. 'Where?'

'Roehampton. The victim was a local girl, so I hear. About sixteen or seventeen.'

'Christ,' Jackson shook his head. 'What a piece of work. Anything else?'

'Yeah,' Ramsay told him. 'I got something for you not many cops know, but you have to be careful with this information. As soon as you use it, Corrigan will suspect a leak in his team and I don't want any of this leading back to my door.'

'It won't,' he promised. 'I'll make sure there's distance between you and the information.'

'You'd better,' Ramsay warned.

'So tell me what it is,' Jackson lost patience.

There was a pause, then Ramsay spoke: 'He doesn't just take their teeth. He takes their fingernails too. All of them.'

Jackson swung his legs over the side of his bed and sat upright – the cigarette hanging limply from his lips. 'What?'

'You heard me. He takes their fingernails. Pulls them out, we suspect, with pliers.'

'Is he worried he may have been scratched, his DNA will be trapped underneath them?' Jackson asked.

'Corrigan doesn't think so. He reckons they're trophies. This one likes his trophies.'

'Are they alive when he takes them?' Jackson pressed, looking for details he could shock his readers with.

'No,' Ramsay told him. 'Or at least, if they are they're only barely alive.'

'Anything else?' he asked.

'My source tells me Corrigan and the suspect are talking.'

'To each other?'

'Yeah,' Ramsay confirmed. 'The suspect's been calling him.'

'I bloody knew it! What they been saying to each other?'

'That I don't know,' Ramsay admitted. 'My source either doesn't know or won't say.'

'Your *source*,' Jackson seized on it. 'And who exactly is your source?'

'I never reveal my sources,' Ramsay insisted, 'but this one's reliable. I'm not lifting this stuff from police computers and intelligence records; I have someone inside the SIU. Someone close to Corrigan.'

'And you trust them?'

'Do you trust yours?' Ramsay threw it back at him.

'Only as far as I can throw them,' he answered without smiling.

'Anything I give you is one hundred per cent reliable,' Ramsay assured him. 'Just so long as I can rely on you to keep to our deal. I've no intention of struggling to get by on a police pension.'

'The job's yours,' Jackson promised. 'Assistant crime editor for *The World* – Britain's biggest-selling newspaper. But don't worry – you won't be tied to a desk. We'll have someone else actually doing the writing, someone with a bit of editorial experience. It's your contacts we need *you* for.'

'Fine. Just make sure you stick to your promise,' Ramsay warned him. 'Oh and there's one more thing – the killer's told Corrigan his name. Marcus. He calls himself Marcus.'

'Marcus,' Jackson repeated. 'So he's not anonymous. Sounds like it's getting personal between him and Corrigan.'

'It's always personal with Corrigan,' Ramsay reminded him, then immediately hung up, leaving Jackson staring into space, lost in thought – phone in one hand and his cigarette smouldering in the other.

'Everything all right?' he heard Denise ask sleepily.

'Yeah,' he answered over his shoulder. 'Everything's fine. I just need to go see an old friend of mine.'

# 13

David Langley was back at work feeling relaxed and happy – the euphoria from the night before washing away the tiredness he should have felt. Rarely had he felt so energized – energy that he hadn't wasted. Suspecting he was soon to receive another surprise visit from his area manager, he'd rearranged the store to look better than it had for years. He'd even sorted out his small office so it looked organized and ready for business. As soon as any customers walked through the doors he was next to them, smiling and offering his assistance. He'd already taken a deposit on a sleigh-bed and some bedside tables. Sure enough, shortly after ten, he saw Jane Huntingdon enter through the front doors and come to an immediate standstill as she looked around the transformed store. Langley wandered over to her with a smile fixed on his face.

'Good morning,' he greeted her warmly. 'See anything you like?'

'Did you do this?' she asked suspiciously.

'Thought the whole place could do with a revamp,' he replied. 'Made a few beds up and created a number of spaces to help people see how our furniture could work in their homes. It was all a bit too random before.'

'It's . . .' she struggled to comprehend the change in the

store and Langley. 'It's great. A huge improvement. You have a good eye for this sort of thing. Makes me wonder why you've kept it to yourself for so long?'

'I used to do it a lot,' he lied, 'but I suppose I lost interest, to be honest. Getting passed over for the area manager's job knocked me a bit. I guess I've been sulking, but I thought about what you said and decided to sort myself out. I like this job and I want to keep it. Not just that – I want to be the best I can at it.'

'Wow,' she shook her head and smiled. 'That's some change in attitude and a very welcome one. Congratulations.'

'No need for congratulations,' he told her, his eyes suddenly attracted by the sight of the pulse flickering in her carotid artery. He saw his knife sliding through her slender neck, severing the artery, allowing the bright red blood to spray into the air under the pressure of a beating heart – the blood seeping through his fingers as he held her throat. 'Just doing my job.'

'I look forward to telling Head Office how well you're doing,' she promised.

'This is only the beginning,' he assured her as he imagined pinning her to the floor, holding the knife in front of her terrified face before forcing her mouth open and stabbing the blade deep into her gums – using his weight and strength to lever out her teeth.

'Good,' she smiled, 'but remember, any major changes have to be approved by me first.'

'Of course,' he agreed, certain that one day his fantasy would become reality. In the meantime, he would smile and grovel and appease as much as was necessary. It was of no importance. All that mattered now was his *work*. Killing her would be the sweetest yet. The most *personal*.

'Well,' she shrugged, 'there's nothing else for me to see here. Keep up the good work.'

'You can be sure I will,' he called after her as she passed through the front door. Raising his upturned hands in front of his face and staring at them as if he could see her blood drying on them. 'You can be sure I will.'

'You all right?' Brian Houghton appeared by his side. 'That bitch giving you a hard time again?'

'I'm going out for a few hours,' he ignored him contemptuously. 'Cover for me.' He walked out into the street without so much as a glance at Houghton.

Sean felt the eyes of the locals on him and Sally as they walked across the Roehampton Estate. Clearly, everyone knew who they were – the occasional shout of *CID* echoing off the buildings as younger children circled them at a distance on bikes – tiny sentries sent to watch and track them, to make sure the entire estate knew where they were at all times. Sean felt like a snake being hounded by meerkats. They'd parked their car at the scene, where it would be safer, and had a quick discussion with Roddis before walking the most likely route taken by the victim from her flat to the place where she was killed. They walked in silence, Sean trying to imagine the young girl walking the same route but in the opposite direction; wondering what she'd felt like, making this journey alone in the dark and the freezing rain. Was she afraid? Excited? Had he promised her something she couldn't resist?

Sally left him to it, speaking only once, to let him know they'd reached the block they were looking for. The lift carried them to the eighth floor and the front door of the flat that had been Witney's home. Sean took a deep breath and knocked. They heard movement inside and saw the shape of someone approaching through the frosted glass. A few seconds later the door was opened by DC Tony Summers, who'd been assigned as family liaison by Sean – his first duty having been to tell the victim's mother that they believed her daughter had been killed.

'Boss, Sal,' Summers greeted them.

'Everything all right?' Sal checked. Summers shrugged.

'How is she?' Sean asked quietly.

'In shock, I think,' Summers answered, 'but coping. The other kids have gone to stay with their aunt on the other side of the estate. People round here don't move far,' he added in a whisper.

'Where's the mum?' Sean asked.

'In the kitchen,' Summers told them, stepping aside to let them enter. 'This way.' He walked along the short, narrow hallway until they reached a room cluttered with furniture with drying clothes seemingly hanging everywhere. The air was thick with the smell of chip fat. Rowena Dennis sat at the table, which was littered with the detritus of breakfast. She was holding a mug in both hands and had clearly been crying, although she wasn't now. She looked small, too thin and a lot older than her thirty-nine years. The white singlet she wore showed off her tattoos, which looked garish on her thin, pale skin. Her dirty blond hair was pulled back in a long tight ponytail. A cigarette was jammed between her index and middle finger, making it look as if it was somehow protruding from the mug.

'Mrs Dennis,' Summers gently spoke to her, but she seemed to be in a deep trance. 'Mrs Dennis,' he repeated, louder this time, and she looked up at them, confusion etched on to her face. 'This is DI Corrigan, the officer I was telling you about,' Summers explained. 'He'll be in charge of the investigation.'

'DS Sally Jones,' Sally did her own introduction. 'I'll be part of the team trying to find whoever did this.'

'You don't know for sure it's her though, do you?' Mrs Dennis suddenly said. 'Because you said I might have to formally identify the body. You wouldn't have said that if you knew it was her for sure.'

'That's true to an extent,' Sean told her, 'but we have found some things that make us as sure as we can be at this stage that the person we found is Witney.' He noticed her slump further into her chair. 'I don't want you to get your hopes up.'

'No,' she replied wearily. 'I don't suppose you do.'

'I'm afraid I need to ask you some questions,' Sean moved on. 'I know it's difficult and you haven't had much time to . . . to . . .'

'To mourn,' Sally helped him out.

'But these questions can't wait,' he insisted. 'Do you think you could answer some questions, Mrs Dennis?' She nodded in tentative agreement. 'What happened last night?' he asked. 'With Witney?'

She took a short, sharp drag on her cigarette and talked quietly while she exhaled. 'She come in here about ten o'clock or something, same as she always does, pissed off and full of cheek. We had words and she ran out. She weren't dressed for the weather neither. I tried to stop her, but she wouldn't listen. I never saw her again.'

'Do you know why she went out?' Sean asked.

'I assumed to meet up with some friends,' she answered, 'or to get drugs if she had any money, which I doubt. Bloody drugs. She was a good girl until she got caught up in all that. Them bastards down there in the playground. They got her into it. They get everyone into it.'

'Did she mention going to meet anyone specific?' Sean pressed.

'No,' she replied. 'She didn't say no names. She didn't say anything.'

'Had she met anyone new lately?' he continued. 'Did she mention anyone new?'

'No,' she answered and took another quick drag. 'She never talked about her friends.'

'Did she have a boyfriend?' Sean persevered.

'Not that I know of,' she told him.

'Did she talk about meeting a man?' he kept trying. 'Possibly within the last few days or couple of weeks?'

'I told you,' she shook her head, 'she didn't tell me nothing. I'd ask sometimes, but she'd get pissed off and start shouting and calling me an interfering bitch, so I stopped asking.'

Sean gave it a few seconds, then asked, 'Does the name Marcus mean anything to you? Did she ever mention that name?'

'No,' she told him, shaking her head vigorously. 'Look, Witney was a stranger to me. I don't know anything about her life. Before she got into drugs she used to hang around a lot with her best friend Tasmin Durrant. Maybe she still did. You should ask her. I seen her about the estate. You should find her easy enough.'

'OK,' Sean relented. 'Thank you.' He gave her a little time before moving on to his next request. 'Mrs Dennis,' he asked.

'Ugh?' she grunted in reply as she slipped back into her protective trance.

'Is it all right if I take a look in Witney's bedroom?' he asked. 'She may have hidden something that's important.'

'The only thing that was important to Witney was drugs,' she coldly stated, but the tears welling up in her eyes were the same tears as those of any parent who'd lost a child – no matter what the child may have become.

'Straight down the hallway, boss,' Summers told him. 'Last room on the left.'

Sean nodded and headed off alone. Fifteen steps later he was standing outside the girl's bedroom door. He tentatively rested his hand on the handle and slowly pushed the door open as if he half expected someone to be waiting inside to meet him – the girl, dead and mutilated, pale bluish skin, sitting on her bed, ready to watch him as he searched through her personal things, just watching, never speaking. But the room was empty. He exhaled long and hard and stepped inside.

The small room had two single beds squeezed into it, both covered with tacky-looking clothes, as was most of the floor, although there were a few genuine designer items hanging on wire coat hangers in the small wardrobe, the doors of which hung wide open. The windowsill too was used as a makeshift storage facility and was covered in the detritus of a disorganized teenage girl, as was the only set of drawers in the room, made of unpainted wood. He imagined Witney walking in and out of the room, restlessly sleeping on the bed occasionally, but it would have offered her no sanctuary or peace, shared as it was with a younger sister and devoid of any comforts or the usual teenage luxuries such as a TV or games console. This was a place to dress and to sleep and little else.

'Why did he select you?' he whispered. 'What was it about you that made him choose you?' He began to wander around the room, searching with his eyes, moving the odd item of clothing with a foot, not sure of what he expected to find. 'I know you'd met him,' he continued, 'before he . . . but when and where and how? How did he enter your life?' He stopped for a minute and listened to make sure he could still hear voices coming from the kitchen, which would mean he wasn't about to be interrupted. Once he was sure, he pulled an ever-present pair of latex gloves from his pocket, slipped them on and tentatively searched through the drawers of the cupboard, feeling uncomfortable and slightly embarrassed at the intrusion.

He wasn't surprised to find several homemade crack pipes hidden under some clothes and thought about bagging them as evidence, but decided against it. If it came to it at trial, they would never try to pretend the victim had been an angel. He closed the drawer and opened the next; this one was even more disorganized than the first – an unholy mixture of under-wear, cheap jewellery, stickers, cards, lighters and dozens of other random items, as if she'd emptied her pockets straight into it every day. He fished around the junk carefully until he was sure he hadn't missed anything, then moved on to the final drawer, his hands recoiling in surprise at what he found: dozens of loose photographs of a girl he assumed to be the victim in various stages of her life – sometimes alone and sometimes with friends and family, smiling and happy when she was younger, looking sad and withdrawn as she grew older.

He felt he could have stuck a pin in the timeline of her life at the exact point when drugs had become a part of it, but seeing her as a young child, particularly when she was a similar age to his own daughters, stung him deeply. He wondered if the killer would still have taken her life if he could have seen these pictures first. Some strange feeling told him that he probably wouldn't have. He checked the backs of the more recent photographs for anything that could have been written by the man he hunted, but found nothing. Unable to stand the pain of looking at the photographs any longer, he slid the drawer shut and moved on to the wardrobe. The few prize items hanging inside didn't take long to search and he found only empty pockets. Nothing looked brand new – nothing still had any tags on, which meant they almost certainly hadn't come from the killer. But the idea of him baiting his trap with presents or cash felt right. He took a couple of steps back from the wardrobe, taking a last glance at the sad-looking clothes hanging inside before he turned to face the beds.

One of the beds was littered with soft toys and a few dolls that identified it as Witney's sister's bed. He decided to search that one first to eliminate it from his mind so he could fully concentrate on the last thing in the room and his best hope of finding something important. It only took a few minutes to search everything in, on and under the bed. He even checked the soft toys for split seams and the dolls for loose limbs – signs that things may have been hidden inside – but he found nothing.

With a sigh he stood up straight and turned towards the victim's bed. A few short steps and he was hovering over the thin mattress on its cheap wooden frame, covered with a duvet and sheets that clearly hadn't been cleaned in some time. On top of that lay the pile of clothes – some clean, some not. One by one he lifted the items of clothing, searched them and, having found nothing, set them carefully aside to be replaced once he'd finished. After all were checked with a negative result, he moved on to the duvet, carefully patting it down with his gloved hands, checking every centimetre, every corner and seam, until he was satisfied nothing was hidden inside. He dropped it on the floor and lifted the pillow, gently pulling it from its case and checking both, but again found nothing. Next he pulled the fitted sheet away from the mattress, recoiling slightly from the smell of stale sweat as he checked it for incisions she may have made to create a most effective hiding place, but there were none.

His disappointment was short-lived. When he turned the mattress over, he found a five-pound note and a ten-pound note lying together on the bed frame, pressed flat by the weight of the mattress. For a moment he didn't breathe or move as he stared at the two notes. *The killer had given William Dalton cash. Had he done the same with Witney?* He was sure he had. After lowering the mattress to the ground, he pulled out his phone and took several pictures of the notes in situ before pinching the ten-pound note by a corner and lifting it close to his face. It was old, which was unfortunate. It had probably been in circulation for some time, which meant the killer almost certainly hadn't recently drawn it from a bank account, but he'd check it anyway. He pulled out a small plastic evidence bag and dropped the note inside – sealed it and slid it into his coat pocket. Next he lifted the five-pound note in the same way and again examined it, discovering that it too looked old. He placed it in another plastic evidence bag and sealed it. When he was done he removed the first bag from his pocket and held it out in front of him together with the second one. He was certain that both would have the killer's DNA and finger-prints on them. It wouldn't help them catch him, but at least the evidence was stacking up to ensure a conviction.

He'd dealt with plenty of drug users in his time and knew that it was rare to find one with cash unless they were on their way to meet their dealer. Witney had gone out without the cash, so it was possible she'd already had her fill of drugs for the day and still had cash left over, or she'd believed whoever she was meeting would be giving her more. Given what he'd learnt about the killer's 'generosity' to Dalton, Sean suspected Witney had cash left over and expected more.

He took one last look around her bedroom then headed back to the kitchen where Mrs Dennis was still sitting at the table clutching her mug and smoking another cigarette. Sally had moved closer and was trying to comfort her. Summers was leaning on the sink with his arms folded; he stood up straight when Sean marched back into the room holding the evidence bags. He set them on the table in front of Mrs Dennis.

'I found these,' he told her gently, 'hidden under Witney's mattress.'

'What?' she asked, shaking her head in disbelief.

'Would that be something she did often?' he asked. 'Ever?'

'If it was, she didn't tell me,' she answered, looking confused.

'Do you know where this money could have come from?'

'Not from me,' she assured him.

'Could she have taken it without you noticing?'

'Trust me – I'd have noticed fifteen pounds,' she told him. 'Sometimes that's all I have to feed them for a week.'

Sean noticed how she said *them* and not *us*. What food she could afford she was giving to her children to the detriment of herself. 'Where did Witney get her money from?'

'She got some benefit money,' she explained. 'I make her give me a bit of it to help out, but she ain't had none in about ten days. Anything she did have would have been well gone by now.'

'So you don't think this is benefit money?' Sean asked.

'No,' she said, wiping away fresh tears with the back of her hand. 'She gets her money on Thursday and it's gone by Saturday. Silly little . . .' Unable to finish her sentence, she pushed the cigarette between her lips to try and hide her fragility.

'OK.' Sean had no more questions for her; he was sure

now that the money had come from Witney's killer. How little had she sold her life for, he wondered. 'We'll leave you with DC Summers. Is there anyone coming to stay with you?' he checked. 'Friends? Family?'

'No,' she answered, exhaling smoke. 'Not yet. I want to be on my own for a while.'

Sean thought he understood. 'OK. We'll be in touch about identification of the body. Probably a good idea to have someone come with you – if you can think of anyone.'

'I understand,' she managed to say.

'I'm sorry,' he told her awkwardly.

Sally stood, ready to escape the oppressive atmosphere of sadness. 'I'm very sorry too,' she added her condolences. 'And thank you for all your help. You've been really strong. I'll stay in touch. See how you're doing.'

'Thank you,' was all Mrs Dennis could say as Sean and Sally both nodded to Summers and headed for the front door. They waited until they were in the privacy of the lift before speaking.

'Well?' Sally asked.

'Well what?' he replied.

'You know what I mean,' she told him.

'What?' he shrugged. 'You expect me to suddenly know everything about her because I looked in her bedroom?'

'You found the money, didn't you?' Sally reminded him.

'And so would you have,' he argued.

'Maybe,' she admitted. Nothing more was said until the lift bounced to a halt on the ground floor and they were once more walking through the estate – the meerkats on bikes instantly whistling warnings to each other and everyone else on the estate that the police were on the move. 'You must have learnt something?' Sally started at him again. 'You were in there long enough.'

'I didn't find anything.'

'Except the money,' she said.

'Except the money.'

'Don't hold out on me Sean,' she warned him. 'Don't try and do this alone.'

'What do you want me to say?' he asked as they kept walking. 'That I found out her life was shit. Barely worth living. That she was a crack-head. That she was so desperate she was prepared to leave her home in the freezing night to meet a virtual stranger in the hope he'd give her some cash.'

'So you did learn something,' Sally told him. 'That she already knew him and that he'd given her the money.'

'I thought I'd said that,' he argued.

'No,' she corrected him. 'You said you'd found some cash and the mother couldn't explain where it came from. You didn't say you were sure it came from the suspect.'

'I thought it was obvious – we saw how he used cash as the bait to lure Richards and Dalton. Probably why he chooses the desperate. The prospect of easy money is hard to resist.'

'No doubt,' Sally agreed. 'So what now?'

'Here,' he told her, digging the evidence bags from his inside coat pocket and handing them to her. 'Get these to the lab. Have them checked for DNA and fingerprints. They'll find dozens, including our man's. It won't help us find him, but it's good evidence of his method and premeditation. Make a note of the serial numbers first and get them over to the Serious Fraud Squad in the City. They have contacts at the banks. I want to know the history of these notes. Where were they first drawn out of the banking system and from what account. They're old notes, so it'll probably be a waste of time, but don't tell them that. Hopefully they'll be falling over themselves to be involved in a murder case. Got to be better than crunching numbers all day.'

'Fine,' she agreed, slipping the evidence bags into her pocket. 'You want to drive or do you want me to?'

'You drive,' he told her, 'and drop me at East Putney tube station.'

'You not coming back to the Yard then?'

'No,' he replied.

'Anything interesting?'

'Said I'd meet Anna for a catch-up,' he admitted.

'You couldn't do that back at the Yard?'

'She had to meet someone over in Chiswick,' he explained. 'Besides, the Yard has too many eyes and ears.'

'You have something private to discuss with her?'

'Yes,' he answered as he stopped walking. 'There are some things going on that even you don't know about or need to know about – for your own protection as much as anything else. You're just going to have to trust me.'

'OK,' she agreed after a brief pause. 'Be careful though. She likes you, you know.'

'I know,' he said, and started walking again, afraid that she was going to keep questioning him about his feelings towards Anna, 'but nothing's happened and nothing will. We're both grown-ups.'

'That's what worries me,' Sally said under her breath.

'What was that?' Sean asked.

'Nothing. Just talking to myself.'

Geoff Jackson was back at his office sitting with his feet on his desk, chewing a pencil, cursing the building-wide smoking ban while he mulled over the morning's events. The beginnings of his story about the latest murder was on his computer screen, but he'd lost interest in it for now. He knew that no matter what the newspaper did, by the time tomorrow's edition hit the streets it would no longer be news that the killer had claimed another victim. He needed to concentrate on the story behind the news and come up with some new angle or an exclusive.

A voice over his shoulder snapped him from his thoughts.

'Jesus, Geoff! You look like shit. Must have been a big night.'

He turned to see the smiling face of Sue Dempsey. She

pointed at the article on his screen. 'You going to have this ready any time today?'

He shrugged. 'Piece will write itself,' he assured her.

'Ah,' she nodded knowingly. 'Got something else in mind, have you?'

'It was something Gibran said,' he dived straight in. 'He reckons the reason Corrigan has such a high success rate for catching killers is because he thinks like them . . . and if he can think like them – perhaps he is one.'

'So you're saying a DI in the Met is a killer?' she asked disbelievingly.

'Well, no,' he tried to explain, 'but perhaps he has the mindset of a killer, but somehow suppresses it or maybe doesn't even know what he is.'

'Are you mad, Geoff?' she warned him. 'You can't accuse a serving police officer of being some sort of psychopath-in-waiting without any proof. We'll be crucified.'

'I know. I know,' he agreed, 'but if there is something in it, what a story it would make: the Met's top detective is as dangerous as the killers he hunts. It doesn't get any better.'

'You don't have enough to run a story like that,' she insisted.

'Not yet I don't,' he admitted, 'but it's a start. I just need to work on it.'

'And how you going to do that?'

'Go back to Gibran. Find out everything he knows about Corrigan.'

'Still won't be enough. Gibran has no credibility – especially when it comes to Corrigan. It'll just look like he's trying to get back at the man who caught him. You need something else. Someone independent who can corroborate what Gibran's saying.'

'I know,' he told her, drumming his fingers on his desk. 'Perhaps there is someone.'

'Go on.' Her scepticism was giving way to anticipation.

'This new one,' he said, pointing at his computer screen. 'I have reliable information that he's talking to Corrigan.'

'How reliable?' she checked.

'Very reliable,' he assured her.

'A cop?'

'I can't tell you that,' he insisted.

'Technically, I'm supposed to know who all your sources are,' she reminded him. 'For your protection as much as theirs.'

'Rules are for the obedience of fools and—'

'—the guidance of the wise,' she finished it for him.

'Exactly,' he grinned.

'So Corrigan's talking to this new killer?' she got back to the point. 'It's interesting, but it doesn't help your story.'

'But ask yourself this,' he told her. 'Why would this new one be so interested in speaking to Corrigan? Could it be that he wants someone to talk to who understands him? Understands him because they're like-minded. Add that to what Gibran's saying and we've got something, surely?'

'Not enough,' she dismissed it. 'Get your source to give us the official line from the Met on Corrigan, or something in his file they don't want us to see. Then you'll have something. Maybe he failed a psych test at some point in his career. If he's a wolf in sheep's clothing, like you say he is, then maybe he tried to join the firearms branch. No better way of killing someone legally than that. Maybe they saw something in his psychological make-up they didn't like.'

'Maybe,' he shrugged, not enamoured at the idea of asking Ramsay to go digging through personnel files.

'In the meantime,' she told him, 'try and get your source to give us more information about this latest murder. That's what'll sell copies.'

For a second he thought about telling her the killer was taking their fingernails as well as teeth, but he knew the police needed it as a filtering tool and decided neither she nor the great British public needed to know. 'Sure,' he answered.

'I need it for tomorrow's edition,' she told him and wandered off looking for more of her charges to chase up.

Jackson leaned in close to his screen – as if he was face-to-face with the killer. 'What's really going on?' he whispered. 'What's really going on between you and DI Corrigan? What the hell are you saying to each other?' His phone beeped and buzzed as it received a text message. He snatched it up and read the screen. It simply said – *Your visit to Broadmoor this afternoon has been approved.* 'Excellent,' he whispered. 'If you won't tell me what this is all about,' he told the screen, 'then perhaps Gibran will.'

Sean entered Patisserie Valerie in Chiswick High Street and looked around for Anna, relieved to see she'd already arrived. The place was crammed with forty-something well-heeled local mums in tracksuits or skinny jeans. It was the sort of place Kate liked to drag him into while he'd rather have been somewhere quieter. He gave Anna a half-hearted wave and ordered an Americano before making his way over to her.

'You OK?' he greeted her.

'I'm fine. How's your day been?'

'Same as always,' he shrugged, taking a sip of his drink and grimacing at the taste. 'You wanted to meet,' he reminded her.

'I thought we should catch up,' she told him.

'My office not good enough?' he joked, echoing Sally's words earlier.

'I thought we should meet away from the Yard.'

'Something wrong?' He tensed. 'Does Addis suspect—'

'No,' she shook her head. 'Addis is difficult to read, but I think everything is all right.'

'You think?' Sean raised an eyebrow.

'I'm more concerned about the way you've been trying to avoid me.'

'I haven't,' he answered, not sure if he was lying or not.

'It feels that way,' she told him. 'I was wondering if everything was all right with you. Are you feeling OK?'

'You asking me as a psychiatrist or as a friend?'

'A friend,' she assured him. 'Is everything all right at home? Kate? The girls?'

'It's never easy with a new case like this one,' he reminded her. 'I don't get to see them much. It puts extra pressure on Kate, and the kids miss me. Puts a strain on things.'

'Of course. But things are OK there?'

'We'll be fine,' he answered evasively, keen to move on.

'And you and me?' she asked. 'Will things be fine between you and me?'

'Things are fine between you and me,' he told her, 'and I haven't been avoiding you. Just our paths haven't crossed as much lately.'

'Our arrangement aside,' she continued, 'do you still want me around? Is it causing you problems, me working on the case?'

'No,' he assured her. 'I want you with us. You can help.'

'Only if you let me,' she reminded him.

'I thought I was,' he argued.

'What about work?' she asked. 'Everything OK there?'

'OK,' he smiled. 'Now I know you're trying to get inside my head. Does Sally have something to do with this?'

'She expressed a concern that you're trying to do too much yourself,' she explained. 'Cutting her out.'

'There are issues with the team,' he confessed. 'I need to be a bit more careful with information and ideas.'

'You think Sally could be talking to someone you don't want her talking to?'

'No,' he said unconvincingly, 'but she might unwittingly say something to someone who is?'

'Like who?'

'I don't know,' he admitted. 'Not yet.'

'You sure you're not just being paranoid?' she asked. 'Sally tells me that you were like a different person when you were helping other units out, but as soon as you got this new case you reverted to the old Sean – withdrawn, reckless sometimes, irritable.'

'I'm fine. It's good to have a proper case to investigate at long last,' he tried to reassure her.

'Back on the edge again,' she said.

'I'm better on the edge,' he admitted.

'And a case like this keeps you on the edge?'

He nodded. 'It's where I need to be – if I'm going to catch this lunatic.'

'I can understand that,' she told him, 'but there's something I've noticed about your behaviour on a case that sets you apart from the other cops on your team.'

'Oh,' he replied and sipped his coffee – hiding behind his cup. 'And what would that be?'

'The others enjoy the chase, but what they live for is the result – catching the bad guy and seeing him locked up. That's their pay-off.'

'And me?' he asked warily.

'You live for the chase. You're only truly alive when you're chasing someone like Gibran or Keller or this new one. When you catch them, it's almost as if you're disappointed. Like you didn't want it to end.'

'Maybe,' he admitted. 'Maybe not.'

'Question is, why?' She stared hard into his eyes.

'I suppose I'm just a bit different.'

'Yes,' she agreed. 'Yes, you are.' They were both silent for a while until Anna spoke again. 'How are things between you and Dave? I couldn't help but notice things seemed a bit strained.'

Sean took a deep breath. 'We had some issues,' he explained, 'but everything's all right now. We talked it through.'

'Such as?' she kept going.

'Jesus,' he laughed. 'You're nosey, ain't you.'

'Comes with the territory,' she smiled.

He shook his head and again looked serious. 'Dave blamed me for the Goldsboro shooting,' he told her. 'He got it stuck in his mind that I deliberately created the circumstances whereby he had to shoot him. He thought I'd set the whole thing up – that I wanted Goldsboro dead.'

'And did you?' she asked matter-of-factly.

There was a long pause before he answered. 'I don't know. Sometimes I think maybe I could have done things differently, then other times I think there's no way I could have foreseen what was going to happen. I'm not sorry for what happened,' he explained. 'I'm just sorry it was Dave who had to pull the trigger.'

'Would you rather it had been you?'

'Yes,' he told her coldly.

'Why?' she sounded concerned.

'Because I could have handled it better.'

'In what way?'

'It wouldn't have affected me as much,' he explained. 'I would have been better able to accept it and move on.'

'Better able than Dave, or better able than most people?'

'Now I know you're messing with my head,' he told her, but he gave her an answer anyway: 'Most people, I suppose.'

'Do you know why that is?' she asked.

'No.'

'Do you think it could be because you value human life less than most?'

'I value life,' he assured her. 'But if I'd had to take a life in the circumstances Dave did, I would, and I wouldn't lose sleep over it.'

'Would you have any remorse?'

'No,' he answered with a shrug. 'Not if it had been necessary to save a life.'

'Even when they've acted to save a life,' she said, 'people often feel traumatized and remorseful about killing another human being.'

'Some people. But not all,' he argued.

'No,' she agreed. 'Not all.'

'Well then, I guess I'm one of the few who wouldn't,' he told her.

'Maybe,' she conceded, 'but I don't suppose you'll know for sure until it happens to you.'

'Trust me,' he insisted, 'if I'm ever in that position, I won't hesitate to do what I have to do – and I'll deal with the consequences.'

'I know you will,' she assured him. 'Let's just hope you're never in that position.'

'Absolutely,' he replied unconvincingly. 'But, like I said, better me than someone else.'

'Maybe, but don't' go looking for it, Sean,' she appealed to him. 'Please don't go looking for it.'

'I won't,' he said, again unsure whether he was telling the truth. 'You have my word.'


Zukov and Maggie O'Neil approached the group of youths hanging around the playground in the centre of the Roehampton Estate, half expecting them to make a run for it as they drew closer, but they held their ground – their contemptuous looks making it clear that they abandoned their turf for no one.

'That her?' O'Neil asked.

Zukov glanced down at the photograph supplied by the Wandsworth Borough Intelligence Unit based at Earlsfield Police Station and nodded. 'I think so,' was as sure as he could be until they got closer.

'They don't look very friendly,' O'Neil tried to joke.

'Leave them to me,' Zukov told her. 'I know how to handle these little bastards.'

'Just remember we're after witnesses,' she reminded him. 'Not suspects.'

'Yeah,' he replied unconvincingly. 'Sure we are.'

They walked straight up to the group, who stared at them silently. Zukov took another look at the photograph and then at one of the only two girls present. She was strikingly similar to the victim in stature and dress, although her hair was brown, not blond. He pulled out his warrant card and held it out for the girl to see. 'Police,' he said. 'You Tasmin Durrant?'

'Maybe,' she shrugged and lit the cigarette clamped between her fingers with a plastic lighter.

'Photograph says definitely,' Zukov said, showing her the photograph in his hand.

'What you doing here anyway?' the apparent leader of the group spoke up from inside his hooded top. 'Police got no business here.'

'Wrong,' O'Neil told him. 'We're investigating a very serious incident and we need to speak to Tasmin. Alone.'

'So you,' Zukov said, pointing at Tasmin, 'stay here. The rest of you can fuck off.'

'You can't tell us what to do,' the leader insisted, getting to his feet.

'Wrong,' Zukov told him, confident and aggressive. 'Want me to have a van full of the Territorial Support Group here in a couple of minutes – turn you all over and see what they can find? Play terrible rough, them TSG boys.' The leader looked nervously around the group. Their expressions told Zukov that they'd encountered the TSG in the past and didn't like it. The leader jutted his chin towards the others as they began to slowly drift away. 'No,' Zukov nodded. 'Didn't think so.'

O'Neil spotted Tasmin trying to slip away with them. 'Not you, Tasmin,' she stopped her. We need to talk.'

Realizing her escape attempt had failed, the girl rolled her eyes and folded her arms. 'I ain't done nothing wrong,' she complained. 'Why you giving me a hard time?'

'You're not in trouble,' O'Neil assured her as she moved closer to the girl. 'You eighteen, Tasmin?'

'Yeah,' she answered, sounding bored. 'Couple of weeks ago.'

'Listen,' O'Neil told her, 'we've got some really bad news for you. Would you like to have your mum here or someone else?'

'What bad news?' she asked, her eyes squinting with suspicion.

'We could go to your mum's house?' O'Neil offered again.

'No,' Tasmin insisted. 'Just tell me what it is.'

'We were speaking with Witney Dennis's mum,' Zukov told her. 'She reckons you were good friends with her.'

'Used to be,' she shrugged. 'I still see her around. We talk a bit, I suppose.'

'I'm really sorry,' O'Neil told her, 'but there's something you need to know. I'm afraid Witney's been killed. She was murdered.'

'Oh my God,' Tasmin exclaimed, staggering backwards a few steps until her hand found the chain of a swing. She allowed her legs to give way until she was sitting on the wooden seat – the whole thing squeaking and rattling under her weight. 'Oh my God,' she repeated slowly, her hand over her mouth. 'That's what them police is doing down the road, isn't it? That's what all that taped off bit's for? And that tent I seen – that's not for no old bomb, is it? That's Witney under there.'

'Yes,' O'Neil told her. 'The old bomb's a cover story we're using to keep things from the media, until we can get a few important things done for her. It won't last forever, but I need you to keep it quiet until then – for Witney's sake.' Tasmin nodded in agreement as she wiped the tears from her cheeks. 'I need to ask you some questions,' O'Neil explained. 'Whenever you're ready. Take your time.'

'I'm fine,' she said, then shook her head and cursed. 'Fuck!

This place' – she looked up at the tower blocks – 'people like Witney don't have a chance round here. They can't handle it. It wears them down. She wasn't *mean* enough to survive this place. She was nice. That's what Witney was – she was nice. That's why I liked her. But then she got into drugs – to help her cope with living round here. It fucked her up. She was always running round after money for drugs. Borrow it, steal it – she didn't care, so long as she got it. Once the drugs took hold, she was lost, just like the rest of us here. Lost and forgotten.'

'What can you tell us about her lifestyle?' Zukov asked. 'Where'd she get her money from? Did she have a boyfriend? Anything that might help us.'

'She didn't have no boyfriend I knew of,' Tasmin told them. 'Money. Like I said – she stole it or borrowed it.'

'Did she ever earn any as a prostitute?' Zukov asked bluntly.

'Listen,' she said, looking embarrassed, 'I heard she did *things* for drugs, but only when she was skint. She never worked the streets or nothing. Never did it for money.'

'She ever put a bit aside?' Zukov ploughed on. 'Keep a bit of cash for a rainy day?'

'Witney?' she laughed through her tears. 'You're joking, ain't you? As soon as she had it, she spent it. They all do – the crack-heads.'

'So if she had, say, fifteen, twenty quid on her,' Zukov asked, 'what would you say about that.'

'If it was a day or two after she got her benefits, then maybe,' Tasmin explained, 'but any other time? No way. As soon as she nicked it or borrowed it, she spent it. If she had money on her she was on her way to her dealer.'

'No,' Zukov told her. 'Not this time.'

'What?' she asked in confusion.

'Doesn't matter,' he told her. 'That's all we need for now. I'll arrange for someone to take a statement from you. You've been a lot of help.'

'Funny, isn't it,' she said as they were about to walk away. 'When she was alive no one ever helped her. Like she didn't really matter. Like she didn't really exist. But now she's dead, everyone will want to know about her. That's the way it is round here. You ain't nothing till you're dead.'

Zukov and O'Neil looked at each uncomfortably for a second. 'Go home,' O'Neil told her. 'Out of the cold.'

'No,' she replied, staring up at the tower blocks. 'Think I'll stay here for a bit.'

'Suit yourself,' Zukov shrugged and started to walk away. O'Neil took a last long, forlorn look at Tasmin, trying to think of something to say before she too turned and walked away.

Sean walked into his office back at the Yard, already emptying his pockets and pulling his coat off. Sally was sitting at his desk, monitoring the phone rigged by technical in case the killer called again. 'Anything?' Sean asked, as he watched Anna walk into the office next door.

'No,' Sally replied. 'All quiet.'

'Too busy enjoying his memories to call . . .' Sean commented, more to himself than to her.

'Sorry?'

'Never mind,' Sean told her, slumping in his chair.

'All right if I go now?'

'Yeah. Sure,' Sean agreed, staring at the phone as Sally got to her feet. 'Why don't you ring me, you son of a bitch?' he whispered to the phone. 'Don't you want to talk about last night – all the *fun* you had?' Donnelly knocked on his door-frame and brought him back to the world. 'Dave?'

'Thought you'd want to know, I've got a team down on the Roehampton Estate doing door-to-door,' he informed him. 'Not much yet, but a couple of people said they saw her walking across the estate last night, heading in the direction of what's now the scene.'

'I guess that's the end of the cover story,' Sean moaned.

'Press will be all over it soon enough. Thanks anyway.' Donnelly nodded, but got no further than a couple of steps when the phone began to ring – shrill and piercing in the confines of the small office. He immediately turned and moved quickly back into the office. Sean was banging on the partition, summoning Sally and Anna to join them. Sean scrambled past his desk, pressing the buttons to activate the trace and recording devices before snatching up the handset. 'Hello.'

'Sean,' the voice answered, sounding cheerful. 'Is that you?'

'This is DI Corrigan,' he confirmed.

'And you know who this is?' the voice asked.

'Of course,' he told him.

'Have you had time to activate whatever it is you are using to trace my calls?' he asked. 'I can give you more time if you need it, although I shouldn't talk for so long this time. Last time I cut things a little too close for comfort. My, my. There were so many policemen looking for me, I almost don't know how I slipped away.'

'What do you want?' Sean demanded. 'You planning on giving yourself in?'

'I wanted to see whether you now understand the importance of what I am doing? What I'm trying to achieve?'

'No,' Sean insisted. 'No, I don't, but if you hand yourself in, we can talk about it. You can explain it to me.'

'Oh, I think you're lying to me, Sean,' he accused him. 'I think you understand exactly what I'm doing. I think you can almost feel what it was like killing her, can't you? When you looked at her dead body lying on the floor, did you imagine your hands around her neck?'

'How do you know I saw her?' Sean asked.

'Because it's what you do,' he answered. 'You always like to see them in situ, don't you, Sean? It's what helps you catch them – the killers. Killers like me. As I told you last time we spoke, I know your work, Sean.'

'And I know you're sick,' he told him with a trace of contempt. 'Give yourself up before anyone else gets hurt and I'll make sure you get help.'

'I neither want or need help,' he snapped. 'It's the rest of the world that needs help, Sean. Not me.'

'What's that supposed to mean?' he asked – anything to keep him talking. The man from Technical Support hurried in and began trying to trace the caller's location.

'Maybe now Sebastian Gibran will take notice too,' he said, ignoring Sean's question. 'Appreciate my work. Maybe even respect me. Fear me.'

'I don't think so. I don't think Gibran understands the concept of fear. Sociopaths rarely do.'

'We'll see,' he replied.

'What is it with you and Gibran, anyway?' Sean asked. 'You seem obsessed. Is that what this is all about: fame? You trying to become more infamous than him?'

'In a way,' he openly admitted. 'I want to be remembered. I want my work to be remembered and revered – particularly by my own kind.'

'You mean people like Gibran?' Sean asked.

'Of course,' he answered. 'Those of us who were selected to rise above the pointlessness of human existence. Those of us chosen for greater things.'

'Why do you need to know them before you kill them?' Sean asked. The phone was silent for a few seconds while the killer thought.

'You're full of surprises,' he eventually answered.

'We know a lot more than you think we do,' Sean tried to put him under pressure.

'I doubt that,' he laughed, 'but to answer your question, why do I need to know them first – because it brings so much more intensity to the experience. They're no longer mere strangers I've picked on the street. I know them. I've watched them living their lives. Spoken to them and touched them.

Even been intimate with them. Anyone can kill a stranger. It's like putting a dog down. But killing someone you know – now that's an altogether different experience. It's almost as if they're willing to die for my work. To sacrifice themselves for the greater good – for something that truly matters, when their lives don't. All this information and you still can't catch me. Tut, tut, Sean. Not doing very well, are you?'

'You need to hand yourself in,' Sean repeated, 'before anyone else gets hurt.'

'Oh, you'll have to do better than that if you want to stop me. I have no intention of handing myself in until my work is complete.'

'And when will your work be complete?'

'Goodbye, Sean,' the voice told him. 'Mustn't stay on the phone too long.'

The line went dead.

'Fuck!' Sean turned to the man from technical. 'Did you get it?'

'Got close,' he answered, 'but not close enough. He's somewhere within a mile radius of Oxford Circus.'

'Him and about half a million other people,' Donnelly sighed.

'Son of a bitch! Dave, get the locals to the area will you – same drill as last time. They won't find him, but we'll be expected to look anyway.'

'Consider it done,' Donnelly assured him, and bounced off into his own office.

Sean turned to Anna. 'Any thoughts?'

'Well,' she began, pacing the small room. 'He won't stop. Even if he wanted to, I doubt he could now. He's got something I call quest syndrome. He believes what he's doing is more important than anything. Even himself. He'll try to finish it at all costs.

'He certainly has an ego too,' she continued. 'This need for infamy and recognition is a strong theme with him, but if he has an ego then he probably has a reason to. It wouldn't surprise me if he was quite successful. Also, he can be quite charming and he's clearly manipulative, as well as being physically strong. From what we know from witnesses and CCTV, it appears he's probably an attractive man, so it's possible he's not unsuccessful with women, although I suspect his relationships fail.'

'Why?' Sally asked.

'Because he's extremely controlling,' Anna explained, 'and possibly violent – violent sexual behaviour that has satisfied him until now. Now he wants more. He may have been reported for domestic violence of both a physical and sexual nature, but not necessarily convicted. As you know better than me, a lot of victims of domestic violence shy away from following their allegations all the way through to court once they're out of the abusive relationship and safe, but it might be a way of identifying him.'

'There'll be hundreds – thousands of possible suspects if we try to identify him through domestic violence,' Sally reminded them.

'Not if you look for *extreme* sexual violence,' Anna told them. 'Look for allegations of wives and girlfriends being raped or seriously sexually assaulted.'

'There'll still be too many,' Sally insisted.

'Not if we eliminate the usual,' Sean spoke up. 'We're not looking for drunken thugs coming home and abusing their wives or girlfriends – we're looking for something that stands out. Our man's most likely a professional – the clean-cut fitness-freak type. This is something that's in his DNA – not something fuelled by booze or drugs. It's worth checking.'

'And given his manipulative nature,' Anna added, 'it's possible he didn't *attack* women he was in a relationship with. Instead he may have coerced them into doing his bidding. Convinced them his violent sexual behaviour was merely erotic and exciting, which would have worked for a while,

309

but eventually they would have realized what was happening and left him or tried to leave him, which is where the police may have become involved.'

'Could he still be in a relationship with someone he's abusing?' Sally asked. 'Someone who's too afraid to leave him?'

'It's possible,' Anna admitted, 'but this new level he's gone to – I can't help but feel he'd want to be on his own, to live out his fantasies undisturbed.'

'He's on his own,' Sean agreed. 'He needs the privacy.'

'But what he needs even more than privacy,' Anna continued, 'is recognition and respect. That need seems to be his primary motivator. It comes across very clearly in everything he says.'

'He's said, more than once, that when it's all over he'll hand himself in,' Sally reminded them. 'Do you think he will?'

'If it ever gets to the point where killing no longer excites him, then yes, he may do,' Anna explained. 'How else is he going to let the world know who and what he is? The circus that would follow – the court case, media coverage – it would all be very appealing to him.'

'Then let's offer it to him,' Sally suggested. 'Next time he calls, we tell him we'll give him more exposure in the media than he could dream of, so long as he hands himself in.'

'We'd be wasting our time,' Sean dismissed it. 'We can't control the media and he knows it. Doesn't matter when or if he surrenders himself, he'll get all the media coverage he could dream of anyway. We need something else.'

'Like what?' Sally asked.

'He craves respect from Gibran and others like him,' Sean explained. 'Sees himself as some sort of top dog.'

'So maybe we can use that to trap him,' Sally suggested.

'Maybe,' he agreed, hoping she would say the name on his mind before he had to. 'But who?'

'We don't know nearly enough about him to set a trap,'

Anna cut them off. 'It would be far too dangerous to try it without a better understanding of his state of mind.'

'Anyone got a better idea?' he asked impatiently. 'He's going to kill again, people. We need to try something different, even if it is dangerous.'

'Let's face it, we're wasting our time,' Sally told him. 'Addis won't sanction a sting operation unless it can be guaranteed to work. He won't risk his career. It's not going to happen. We should look into this domestic violence angle Anna talked about. It might give us some names to check out.'

'Fine,' Sean reluctantly agreed, 'why don't you get on with that. Everyone else should get back to checking CCTV and door-to-door and every other thing that needs to be done, because you can be sure he's out there right now, looking for his next victim. He's going to keep killing until it no longer thrills him. He's making us look like fools.'

'He has the advantage at the moment,' Sally told him, 'but that won't last. It never does. There's no need for us to do anything risky. We're closing in on him, even though it may not feel like it. You know that.'

'I hope you're right,' Sean told her, 'because this one's only going to get worse. What we've seen so far – it's only the beginning.' His mobile started ringing. He checked the caller ID and saw it was Kate. For a second he considered not answering it, but the need to hear her voice and connect with something other than questioning detectives made up his mind. 'I need to take this,' he told Sally, who took the hint and left, followed by Anna.

'Kate,' he began. 'Everything all right?'

'There doesn't have to be anything wrong for me to call you, does there?' she asked.

'No.'

'You sound tense,' she told him. 'Are *you* all right?'

'Work,' was all he said.

'People daring to disagree with you?' she joked.

311

'Something like that,' he smiled for the first time in a long time.

'Try to understand not everyone can keep up with you,' she reminded him. 'Not everyone knows you like I do.'

'No,' he agreed. 'No, they don't.'

'Are you really all right?' she asked again. 'You've been so distant lately. Even more distant than usual when you have a case like this. Is there something you need to tell me?'

'No,' he insisted, his skin burning with guilty heat as he thought about the brief moment he'd spent with Anna years before. 'Just this case,' he lied. 'It's difficult. Can't seem to get a break.'

'OK,' she backed off. 'If you're sure.'

'I'm sure.'

'I'm here for you when you need me.'

'I know.'

'I'd better go,' she said, a hint of regret in her voice. 'It's getting busy here.'

'OK. Don't wait up.'

'I'll stay up as long as I can,' she insisted. 'Bye.'

'Bye,' he answered and held the phone to his ear, listening to the connection going dead before dropping the phone on to his desk. 'Christ,' he whispered, more aware now than ever that he was flirting with losing everything that was precious to him because of his obsession with finding and stopping the madmen.

The heavy door slammed shut, once again locking him in an interview room in Broadmoor with Sebastian Gibran, but Jackson recovered his composure quickly.

'Thanks for seeing me at such short notice,' he began.

'We seem to be seeing quite a lot of each other,' Gibran replied, smiling – his straight white teeth gleaming, his eyes a deep, piercing blue that sparkled with intelligence and intent. Jackson knew that, if he was free of his restraints, Gibran was capable of killing him before the guards could get the door open – just for fun. 'I assume this is about the latest killing?'

'You know about it?' Jackson asked.

'I heard about it not much more than an hour ago,' Gibran explained. 'Unfortunately, the details were scant.'

'A teenage girl,' Jackson added, feeling uneasy and tainted to be discussing such a thing with the likes of Gibran. But the story was too good to walk away from. 'Killed in the same way as the others.'

'And how were they killed?' Gibran asked.

'You know how they were killed,' Jackson told him. 'You don't need me to repeat it.'

'Getting squeamish on me, Jackson?' Gibran toyed with him. 'Very well – how do you know it's the same killer? It could be a devoted disciple.'

'No,' he insisted. 'There's information the police withheld – to eliminate cranks claiming responsibility – information that a copycat wouldn't know. Something he does to the bodies that was also done to the latest victim. It's the same killer.'

'But you haven't seen the body yourself,' Gibran deduced, 'so you must be getting information from somewhere else?' Jackson said nothing. 'Someone who knows about the investigation. A detective.'

'I can't share that information with you,' he told him, 'but my source is reliable.'

'Then the man you're interested in has killed three people,' Gibran said, 'that you know of. He's running very hot, our friend, and he'll need to kill again soon. But no matter how many he kills, he'll never achieve anything truly memorable. He's not doing anything that hasn't been done before, merely repeating the same pattern. There's no development – no progression. A true artist grows with his work, becomes more expressive, but this is no artist. This is a one-trick-pony. I find him tiresome. He won't be remembered for long.'

'Not like you,' Jackson appealed to Gibran's vanity. 'Everyone remembers you.'

Gibran smiled. 'They remember me for the crimes I'm accused of, but never convicted of,' he reminded Jackson. 'But you see, this rather boring fellow aspires to be a creature like the one the public imagine Sebastian Gibran to be, but he hasn't a hope.'

'Why?' Jackson asked.

'Because the type of person people want to believe I am, is born to do the things I'm accused of,' he explained. 'It's in their nature – from birth. Gods amongst men. They don't seek fame or notoriety – what do they care what the little people think of them? It's irrelevant. They know what it is they must do, and doing that is enough. Enough to make their lives *extraordinary*. I wonder how many of these gods are out there – walking amongst you – killing with impunity.'

'They get caught,' Jackson argued. his eyes wide with wonder and fear. 'Like you did.'

'Allegedly,' Gibran reminded him. 'But what if they kept it simple, covering their tracks by varying their method, their prey. A vagrant here, a prostitute there. Strangle one – stab the other. Who would ever know?'

'Is that what you did?' Jackson couldn't help asking. 'Until you became more . . . elaborate.'

'What I did is no longer important,' he smiled pleasantly.

'But you said this new one can never be like you,' he scrambled. 'I mean, like the person people believe you are. What do you mean by that?'

'I mean he wasn't born to do what he does,' Gibran explained. 'It's clearly not his birthright. This one's made, like all those other sad fools locked up in here or some other prison. Somebody somewhere *made* him the way he is now. His father. His mother. An abusive uncle, perhaps, but someone *made* him. He's nothing more than a product.'

'Are you not worried that what you say about him will

314

make him angry?' Jackson asked. 'Are you not concerned that in some way you may be driving him to kill even more people?'

'If it concerns you,' Gibran smiled, 'you don't have to print what I'm telling you, Mr Jackson. Besides, why should I care? I am insane, after all.'

Jackson paused, but more questions jumped into his mind and spurred him on. 'Aren't you afraid he might come after you?'

'That would be difficult,' Gibran answered casually, 'with me tucked up in here and him out there having all the fun. But who knows – one day we may share a space, and then let us see what happens.'

'Given the chance,' Jackson stayed with it, 'do you think he'd try to kill you?'

'Almost certainly,' Gibran told him, as if it were obvious.

'Why?'

'Because he's a collector.'

'A collector?' Jackson asked. 'Of what?'

'Souls,' Gibran answered in a hissing tone. 'He collects souls. Look beyond the physical trophies he takes. They are merely trinkets to remind him of all the fun he's had. It's their souls he's really interested in. It's their souls he wants.'

'So he wants your soul?'

'Oh very much, I should imagine.' Gibran smiled, his eyes burning with excitement. 'More than anyone else's in the whole world.'

'Why?' Jackson asked again.

'Because he believes that if he killed me, he wouldn't just be taking my soul, he'd be taking the souls of everyone I ever killed.'

'You mean, allegedly killed?' Jackson reminded him.

'Exactly.' Gibran smiled – suddenly calm again – like a warm blue sky after a passing storm. 'I would be quite a prize.'

'Yes,' Jackson agreed. 'I'm sure you would.'

\* \* \*

315

It was late as Sean pulled up outside St Thomas Moore Catholic Church. He knew he should have gone straight home and grabbed some rest, but Kate would be asleep and he needed to talk to someone he could trust. Father Alex Jones had very much become that person to him. A confidant and a friend. As usual he found both the gates and the church doors open, despite the lateness of the hour. He moved into the quiet peace of the interior of the building – warm in winter and cool in summer. For a moment he envied the calmness of the priest's life, until he reminded himself of all the burdens people unloaded on to his shoulders. He may not have seen all the terrible things Sean had seen, but he certainly heard about them, and usually from the horse's mouth.

Sean wandered about the church for a few minutes, deliberately clicking his heels on the hard floor to let the priest know he was there. In his typical, almost supernatural way, Father Jones suddenly appeared, drifting from a shadowy corner in his black clothes and white collar.

'Good evening,' the priest welcomed him. 'I had a feeling it would be you.'

Sean returned the greeting. 'Tell me, do you ever wear anything other than . . .?' He held out a hand as he looked the priest up and down.

'Well, I am a man of the cloth,' he replied with a smile, 'but I have been known to dress down when I'm out running or playing sport. Now,' he got to the point. 'What's troubling you?'

Sean slumped on one of the benches. 'I wasn't fast enough,' he confessed. 'Someone else has been killed. A teenage girl.'

'I see,' the priest said, moving closer. 'I'm very sorry to hear that.'

'So was I,' Sean told him.

'And now you bear the burden of another person losing their life,' the priest sympathized.

'That,' Sean agreed, 'and the burden of finding him before he kills again.'

'I'll pray that you can,' the priest promised, 'but you shouldn't blame yourself for not being able to save the girl.'

'Who should I blame then?'

'The man who killed her,' the priest answered bluntly. Sean said nothing as he stared at the floor. 'This is not the first killer you've had to catch. Try to think of all the lives you've saved by catching these men. People who don't even know their lives have been saved – because of you.'

'That's a bit too abstract for me, Alex,' Sean told him, looking up from the floor. 'My boss, the public, they're not interested in victims that never became victims. They only care about those who did.'

'You're probably right,' the priest agreed, 'but maybe you should think about it from time to time.'

'Maybe.'

'So what's happening with this man you need to find?' the priest asked. 'Would you like to talk about him?'

'He's a mean, vicious bastard, I can tell you that. And he likes to talk.'

'Talk?' the priest asked. 'Who to?'

'To me,' he told him.

'Oh,' the priest sounded surprised. 'Do you know why?'

'He's obsessed with Sebastian Gibran,' Sean revealed.

'A murderer who you caught,' the priest said. 'You've spoken about him before. I can understand how another killer could be obsessed with someone with Gibran's notoriety.'

'He seems hell-bent on getting his respect,' Sean explained.

'How would he know if he'd succeeded?'

'Ever read *The World?*'

'No,' he laughed. 'Not on my preferred reading list, I'm afraid.'

'There's a journalist who's been visiting Gibran in prison – asking him what he thinks about the man I'm after. So far,

317

Gibran's dismissed him as being irrelevant. He's been rather insulting about him.'

'That won't please him,' the priest said.

'No,' Sean agreed. 'Probably not, but it's a way for him to communicate with Gibran, or at least it's a way for Gibran to communicate with him. To let him know what he thinks of his most recent crime.'

'You think he's trying to impress Gibran?' the priest asked.

'Yes,' Sean told him. 'But Gibran isn't impressed.'

The priest remained silent, sensing there was more Sean wanted to say.

'There was another reason this man wanted to talk to me,' Sean confessed, looking uneasy.

'Which was?'

'He said . . . he said he thought I could understand what he was doing,' he explained. 'That I would understand *why* he was doing it.'

'Well,' the priest surmised, 'it's not surprising that he'd expect that from you. He knows you're a very experienced murder detective, after all.'

'That's not what he meant,' Sean elaborated. 'He said I could feel what he had felt. When I was at the crime scene – I could feel how it had felt to kill her.'

'I see,' the priest replied. 'And is he right?'

'No,' Sean answered, then immediately changed his mind. 'Maybe. I don't know.'

'You're unsure?'

'I see things,' he told him. 'I *feel* things – at crime scenes, when I'm alone with the victims. It's like a movie playing in my head, only I can feel it too.'

'Is it a spiritual experience?' the priest asked. 'A connection with the victim?'

'No,' he shook his head. 'The connection is with the *killer* – not the victim.'

'You see things through the killer's eyes,' the priest looked for a logical explanation. 'An uncomfortable experience, I'm sure, but understandable, given your profession.'

'No,' Sean told him. 'I *become* them. When I'm at the crime scene I *am* them. I can feel everything, from their sense of power to their sense of shame.'

'And it helps you find them?' the priest searched for something.

'Yes. Yes it does. It helps me predict them. Second-guess them. Once I know what motivates them – what they're looking for – what they *desire* – I can use it against them.'

'Then perhaps it's a gift,' the priest suggested, 'given to you by things we don't understand?'

'A gift,' Sean smiled ironically. 'Feels more like a curse.'

'Some gifts do feel that way,' the priest assured him as he looked up at Christ crucified on the cross. 'The point is, no matter how disturbing these feelings are, you use them for good. To save lives.'

'It's how I exorcise my demons,' Sean explained, 'stop myself from having dark thoughts.'

'And do you have dark thoughts?'

'No,' he shook his head. 'Not when I'm awake, anyway. When I'm asleep the bad dreams come.'

'Bad dreams?'

'I see the victims,' he admitted. 'Sometimes they talk to me.'

'What do they say?'

'They ask me why I didn't save them,' he answered without emotion as he got to his feet.

'And what do you tell them?'

'It's late,' Sean said. 'I need to go home.'

'Of course,' the priest replied.

'Another time.' Sean was already heading for the door.

'Another time,' the priest agreed, but Sean stopped after a few steps and turned back to face him.

'These killers I chase,' he told him, 'most were abused themselves when they were children. It's why they do what they do as adults. It's why they *think* the way they do. Goodnight, Father.' He turned to walk away, but the priest's words stopped him.

'So what was it with you?' he asked. 'When you were a child.'

Sean looked him up and down for a few seconds before answering. 'My father.'

'I see,' the priest nodded. 'Was it just violence or was it something else?'

'Something else,' Sean found himself admitting, 'although there was plenty of violence too.'

'How old were you?'

'It started young,' Sean told him, aware that he was telling the priest more than he'd ever told anyone but Kate. Not even Anna knew. 'I can't remember exactly how young, but young. He used to take me to his bedroom. The bedroom he shared with my mother. She knew what was happening, but she was too scared to stop it. He could be a dangerous man. She was as much a victim as me. While he was . . . while he was doing *things,* I could hear my brothers and sisters laughing and talking downstairs, but I could never hear my mother. I've since learnt she used to lock herself in the toilet downstairs and cry until it was over. He used to go straight out to the pub to get drunk, and I remember she used to just hold me. Hold me and cry.'

'I suppose he was drinking to help deal with the shame,' the priest offered a spiritual reconciliation with his father. 'Perhaps he was a weak man with his own unfortunate cross to bear.'

'Maybe,' Sean replied, but his voice was thick with the hate he still felt for his father. A hate that he believed would never fade.

'Where is he now?' the priest asked.

'Dead,' Sean spat. 'He died a drunk. None of the family went to his funeral.'

'I see,' was all the priest said as Sean turned and walked towards the exit. Again he stopped and turned to face the priest.

'A part of me wishes he was still alive,' Sean called back to him.

'Oh?' the priest asked. 'Why's that?'

'So I could kill him,' Sean said, and with that he walked out of the church.

Outside the freezing air hit him, revitalizing him for a second until it combined with his exhaustion and made him desperate to be somewhere warm where he could find rest. He began to trudge towards his car, but even in his beaten state his cop instinct alerted him to something that didn't look right – a car parked at the side of the road about thirty metres away, at a slight angle, like it was ready for a quick getaway. Its lights were on and its engine running. Sean's tired eyes squinted into the darkness until he could make out the shape of someone's head and shoulders leaning out of the window, pointing something black in his direction. He realized it was a camera – and that could mean only one thing. 'Jackson,' he said through gritted teeth as he broke into a run, his tiredness forgotten now.

Instantly the figure disappeared inside and the car pulled away, its tyres squealing, trying to find purchase, then the car lurched forward. 'Police,' he shouted after it. 'Stop!' But the car accelerated away. 'Jackson, you son of a bitch,' he yelled. 'Stop the car,' but it was too far away now, and his aching lungs told him it was a lost cause. With the last of his breath, he repeated the make, model and registration number of the car to ensure it was burnt into his memory, then jotted it down in the CID notebook he carried in his pocket: *Red Vauxhall Vectra, index no. AF16NDX*. He slid the notebook back into his coat and headed towards his own car. 'Jackson,' he hissed under his breath. 'Fucking Jackson.'

# 14

Sean stormed across the main office to his own room and immediately started ransacking his drawers like a man possessed. Donnelly saw the commotion, pushed himself out of his chair and casually made his way to Sean's doorway.

'Everything all right?' he asked.

'Jackson!' Sean spat the name out.

'Oh.' Donnelly stepped further into the office. 'What's our friendly neighbourhood journalist gone and done now?'

'Son of a bitch followed me home, or had one of his team follow me. Snapped some photographs of me when I— when I stopped off last night. Bastard's gone too far.'

'Following a cop home,' Donnelly winced, 'not good. Breaks all the rules of engagement.' His eyes returned to Sean's hands, still frantically searching in his drawer. 'Looking for something?'

'Jackson's card,' he answered. 'It's in here somewhere.'

'His number not in your phone?'

'You think I'd violate my phone with his number?'

'Clearly not,' Donnelly said, as Sean's hand appeared with a business card pinched in his fingertips.

'Time to deal with this prick once and for all,' Sean muttered as he punched the numbers into his desk phone, pushed the speaker button and stood hunched over it waiting for an answer, looking like a cat waiting to pounce on a mouse. After an age the phone was answered by a sleepy-sounding Jackson.

'Hello,' he said. 'Who is this?'

'Jackson,' Sean barked at him. 'What the hell do you think you're doing?'

'Ah,' he instantly became more alert. 'DI Corrigan. To what do I owe the pleasure? Changed your mind about doing the interview? You won't regret it.'

'Who the hell do you think you are, following me?' Sean launched into him. 'Next time I see you anywhere near me, I swear I'll arrest you and lock you up for—'

'Wait,' Jackson told him. 'What the hell are you talking about?'

'You know what I'm talking about,' Sean insisted. 'You or someone working for you followed me and took my photograph.'

'Oh,' Jackson seemed to relax. 'That. Look, I didn't follow you – there was no need, I knew you'd turn up eventually. But that was days ago. You only just found out?'

'What do you mean, days ago?' Sean asked, exasperated. 'I'm talking about last night. I saw you.'

'Last night?' Jackson sounded genuinely confused. 'I didn't follow you last night. I didn't follow you *ever*. Like I said, I knew it was only a matter of time before you'd turn up at Tanya Richards' address, so I waited for you. No big deal. It made a nice little side piece, was all. *Lead detective visits crime scene* – you know the score.'

'Are you sure?' Sean asked, his mind now on fire with unpleasant possibilities. 'You didn't follow me or have me followed last night?'

'No,' Jackson laughed nervously. 'Why would I follow you home? I know where the line's drawn with cops' personal lives, Corrigan.'

'Then if it wasn't you, who the . . .' He fell silent as the realization sank in.

'Jesus Christ,' Jackson said before Sean could hang up. 'It was him, wasn't it? He's not just talking to you – he's following you as well.'

'My mistake.' Sean slammed the phone down.

'How does he know you've been talking to him?' Donnelly asked.

'What?' Sean snapped – his mind still trying to comprehend the fact he'd only been metres away from the man he was hunting and had let him slip away.

'Jackson,' Donnelly clarified. 'How does he know you're speaking with the suspect?'

'Fuck knows.' He pushed the problem of a potential leak on his team to the back of his mind. 'It's not important right now.' He paused, staring at the phone, collecting his thoughts before looking up at Donnelly. 'Son of a bitch followed me,' he said. 'Bastard might know where I live. If Kate finds out, I'm dead – especially after last time. Shit.'

'Did you get all the way home?' Donnelly asked, trying to be logical and calm.

'No,' Sean answered, sounding relieved.

'Then there's no reason to assume he knows where you live,' he tried to reassure him.

'But it might not have been the first time he's followed me,' Sean pointed out.

'Just think about it,' Donnelly slowed things down. 'He's obsessed with Gibran, not you. If he'd followed you before, he'd have told you, gloated over it. You said he took photographs of you?'

'I think so,' Sean answered.

'Aye,' Donnelly assured him. 'To *show* you. To show you how clever he is. Think about everything we know about him. He wouldn't have been able to resist showing you the photographs. This has to be the first time he's followed you.'

'Maybe,' he replied. He could see the logic in it. 'But what better way to impress Gibran than to come after me – or my family.'

'OK,' Donnelly nodded. 'What d'you want to do?'

'Kate's at work today . . .' Sean thought out loud. 'And the kids are at school. Shit!' he cursed and shook his head, thinking of the conversation he'd have to have with Kate the next time he saw her. 'Get close protection teams on them, but tell them to be discreet. Keep as much distance as they can without compromising their safety. Shit,' he cursed again.

'You don't think we should tell them?' Donnelly checked.

'Tell them what?' he raised his voice. 'That I've put them in harm's way *again*. Fuck.'

'Stated case, boss,' Donnelly reminded them. 'R v Brindle. We have a duty to tell someone if there's a credible threat to their—'

'I know the fucking law,' Sean cut him off. 'Jesus Christ, Dave. She's *my* wife. They're *my* children. No one says anything to them until I've spoken with them.'

'It's your call,' Donnelly told him.

'Yes it is,' Sean ended it. 'You still PNC authorized?'

'Of course,' Donnelly shrugged. 'Why?'

'Because I took the index number,' Sean revealed. 'If he's half as smart as I think he is, the car would have been stolen or false-plated, but we need to check.'

'You never know your luck,' Donnelly replied, already placing himself in front of the nearest computer screen to begin logging on to the Police National Computer. 'What's the number?' he asked, as soon as he was in.

'Alpha, foxtrot, one, six, November, Delta, X-ray,' Sean read from his CID notebook. 'Should come back to a red Vauxhall Vectra.'

Donnelly typed fast and within seconds he had the result. 'Aye,' he said, sounding almost surprised. 'It does come back to a red Vauxhall Vectra – not reported stolen either. No interest reports. The current keeper is shown as John Redmayne – home address in Battersea.'

'Put that name in,' Sean told him. 'Don't worry about a date of birth.'

'It's a fairly unusual name,' Donnelly said as he typed. Sure enough, the list of possible matches was short. 'One here born Brixton. The others are a bit further afield.'

'What's the form for the one from Brixton?' Sean asked, excitement stirring in his stomach. If Redmayne had previous convictions, he couldn't be their man else they'd have his DNA and fingerprints, but just maybe something would show in his history that would make him a viable suspect.

'Not much,' Donnelly answered. 'No insurance convictions, just a caution for common assault that's well and truly expired. Nothing we'd still have his DNA or prints for.'

'So we can't rule him out then?' Sean pointed out.

'No,' Donnelly agreed. 'We can't.'

Sean suddenly sprang into action, grabbing his coat from its hook and filling his pockets with everything he'd need.

'Going somewhere?' Donnelly asked.

'Yeah,' Sean answered, 'and you are too.'

'Don't tell me,' Donnelly replied, getting to his feet. 'Battersea?'

David Langley sat in his office reading that morning's edition of *The World*. He'd turned straight to the centre pages hoping his latest act had spurred the journalist on to visit Gibran to seek his opinion. He wasn't disappointed, but once he started reading his optimism and excitement faded fast, replaced first with a sense of disillusion and then fury. How dare he dismiss his importance? How dare he lie to the world and tell everyone he was created by an abusive childhood and not born a man-god? His parents loved him, in their own separate ways. He was born in his newfound greatness – not created by human failings. He scrunched the pages of the newspaper into a ball then frantically ripped it to pieces and stuffed it into his wastepaper basket. If it hadn't been for the smoke alarm, he would have set it on fire and watched Gibran burn.

He turned his back on the overflowing bin and logged on to the internet, searching and finding articles and pictures of Gibran. He needed to see his tormentor, although what he really wanted was to stand in front of him and slice open his throat. He pictured himself, lifting Gibran with one arm, his fingers wrapped around his neck, holding him high, watching his kicking legs growing weaker and weaker as the blood seeped through his fingers and flowed down his arm and across his body. Once he was sure Gibran was dead, he threw him to the floor as if he was nothing. Never again would he mock his importance. His teeth and nails would make a fine addition to his collection.

Thoughts of killing Gibran finally brought him the calm he needed to think clearly. It was obvious to him now that Gibran felt safe locked in his brick and steel cage, but even the mighty Gibran couldn't possibly imagine the plan that he'd set in motion. A plan that would see him reach inside and pluck the bastard creature from his sanctuary. If he could do that, the world would never forget his name. His eyes darted from side to side as he imagined executing his plan – how, when and where. His fingers danced on the keyboard and the pictures of Gibran were replaced by the mandatory list of internet sites all professionals felt they needed to belong to – Facebook, LinkedIn, Twitter, Instagram. She was on them all – small neat pictures of a smiling and undeniably beautiful woman attached to each profile.

'Yes,' he whispered, reaching out to touch the images on the screen – her radiance making her all the more perfect. He leaned back, smiling. 'Once I have her, you'll give me what I want, won't you, Sean? You'll have no choice. Then the world will see my genius.'

\* \* \*

Sean and Donnelly pulled up opposite the small terraced house in Battersea. The red Vectra was parked outside.

'Looks like our man's home,' Donnelly said, nodding towards the car.

'Yeah,' Sean answered distractedly as he studied the neat, well maintained, but sterile-looking house with its clean white walls and freshly painted grey front door, white blinds in the windows instead of curtains. The small front garden had been turned into a parking space. Could this be a place where a monster lived? Yes, he decided as he imagined the killer arriving home late and stepping from the car wearing his hood, clutching the rucksack that contained his precious trophies. He saw him putting the key in the lock and opening the door before disappearing inside to examine his haul – the outside world oblivious to the horrors he was responsible for.

'What do you think?' Donnelly asked.

'I can't tell anything from out here,' he lied.

'I thought maybe . . .' Donnelly began, then stopped himself. 'Perhaps we should get some back-up, now we know he's home?'

Sean shook his head. 'Let's take a look at him first. Then, if we like him for it, we'll say nothing, make our excuses and leave, and put a surveillance team on him until we work out our next move.'

'OK,' Donnelly reluctantly agreed. 'You're the boss.'

'It'll be fine,' Sean assured him, climbing out of the car.

'Here we go again,' Donnelly sighed, trying to gear himself up as he too left the warmth of the car and followed Sean across the road between passing vehicles. Once they were both standing by the front door, Sean rang the doorbell and they took a step back while they waited for it to be answered. A minute later the door was opened by a tall athletic man in his early forties, his short, neat blond hair matching his overall clean-cut appearance. He looked uneasily from Sean to Donnelly, but there was no flicker of real concern or fear. Sean felt he was either ice cool or they had the wrong man.

'Hi,' he greeted them in a deep, accentless voice. 'Can I help you with something?'

'Police,' Donnelly told him, holding up his warrant card and hoping for an immediate reaction. 'DS Donnelly from the Metropolitan Police Special Investigations Unit.'

Sean casually held up his own ID. 'DI Corrigan – from the same.'

'Is there a problem?' the man asked.

'We need to speak with a John Redmayne,' Donnelly answered.

'You're speaking to him,' Redmayne confirmed, looking more worried.

'Can we talk inside?' Sean asked quietly. He needed to see how Redmayne lived behind closed doors.

'Yeah, sure,' Redmayne replied with a shrug and stepped aside to allow them to enter, closing the door behind them once they were inside. 'Come through to the kitchen,' he said cheerfully, leading the way. Sean and Donnelly glanced at each other before following. If he was the man they were looking for, the last place they wanted to be in was his kitchen with the knives and boiling water, but they didn't want to spook him by ordering him around in his own home.

On the way to the kitchen, Sean took in everything from the polished wooden floorboards under his feet to the framed paintings of flowers and landscapes on the hallway walls – none of which seemed to fit the man he was looking for, although the lack of photographs of a family kept him interested. The kitchen had the same show-home feel to it – every surface clean and sparkling, the only scent that of disinfectant. At least now there were some signs of a normal life – snaps of Redmayne on holiday, some alone, some in the company of two attractive children about the same age as Sean's own, although there were no pictures of anyone who could be their mother. Sean made the immediate judgement that he was divorced, probably against his wishes, and that he'd tried to completely eradicate her from his life. He had his reasons to be bitter, but were they enough to make him kill?

'Are you going to tell me what this is about?' Redmayne asked.

'It's about your car,' Donnelly told him. 'The red Vectra parked outside.'

'What about it?' Redmayne's expression was one of genuine confusion. 'I've had it for years – bought it from a main Vauxhall dealer. You're not going to tell me after all this time that it's stolen, are you?'

'No,' Donnelly assured him, 'but I am going to ask where it was yesterday – about eleven in the evening to midnight?'

'Well, it doesn't really matter what time you're interested in because I didn't use it at all yesterday. In fact, I rarely ever use it during the week. I walk down to Clapham Junction and get the train to work. I was actually thinking of selling it.'

'But your car was seen late last night in Dulwich,' Donnelly tried to pressurize him.

'My car?' Redmayne stared at him in disbelief.

'Yes,' Donnelly confirmed. 'By a police officer.'

'And what was my car doing in Dulwich?' Redmayne asked, amused.

The playful reaction didn't fit with the man Sean was hunting. The man he was after was ambitious, restless and remorseless. When they'd spoken on the phone he'd been smug and condescending. He'd feigned amusement but seemed incapable of the genuine thing.

'Whoever was driving the vehicle was interfering in a police investigation,' Donnelly told him. 'A murder investigation.'

'Wait!' Redmayne held his hands up, his face suddenly deadly serious. 'This is all beginning to sound very heavy. Should I have my solicitor here?'

'Only if there's something you don't want us to know,' Donnelly replied. 'Is there?'

'You don't need a solicitor,' Sean intervened, tiring of the jousting. He could sense no menace or malice in Redmayne. If this was the man he sought, he'd want to show his power – test Sean in some way. The man he hunted would stand his ground and look him hard in the eyes – challenge him to make his move. But Redmayne was playing harmless games – enjoying the attention of the police safe in the knowledge that he'd done nothing wrong and probably never would. 'There's just a few things we need to clear up.'

'Like what?' Redmayne shrugged.

'Has your car been in any garages lately?' Sean asked. 'Within the last two or three months?'

'No,' Redmayne answered, 'unless petrol stations count?'

'No,' Sean told him. 'I'm only interested in the garages for repairs.'

'That's definitely a no then,' he confirmed.

'Anyone been paying attention to your car that you noticed?' Sean continued.

'No,' Redmayne laughed. 'It's a Vauxhall Vectra.'

'Ever get the feeling someone was following you?'

'No,' he shook his head, 'and like I said, I hardly ever use it.'

'Have the number plates ever been tampered with or stolen?' Sean asked.

'No,' Redmayne assured him. 'Look, nothing has happened to me or the car, so why don't you tell me what this is all about?'

'Someone we'd very much like to speak to has been using your registration number on their car,' Sean explained.

'Somebody who killed someone, right?' Redmayne asked.

'Maybe,' Sean admitted. 'We won't know until we speak to him. In the meantime,' he told him, pulling a business card from his wallet, 'if you think of anything, give me a call. And remember, this is an ongoing investigation, so we'd appreciate it if you didn't tell anyone about what we've discussed.'

'Of course,' Redmayne agreed, although Sean knew he was lying.

'Thanks for your time,' Sean told him and headed for the front door.

'Aye,' Donnelly said, sounding less than happy. 'Thanks for your time.'

As soon as they were back in the safety of their own car, he demanded an explanation from Sean. 'Jesus. Why so soft on him? You got something in mind?'

'No,' Sean waved it away. 'It's not him.'

'You sure?' Donnelly asked, unconvinced. 'He felt like a wrong 'un to me.'

'He's a bit of a prick,' Sean dismissed him. 'Probably why his wife left him. But he's not our man.'

'How d'you know his wife left him?' Donnelly asked, bemused.

'Did you see any pictures of her?'

'No. I was too busy questioning him.'

'Take it from me then: there weren't any. See the state of the house? Bet he's never even cooked in there. No wonder she left.'

'You make him sound like a decent suspect,' Donnelly argued. 'Not someone we should dismiss.'

'Forget him,' Sean insisted, bored of justifying himself. 'He's not our man, but at least we know what he drives now. It's something.'

'Unless he stole a car,' Donnelly argued, 'and false-plated it. Or maybe he wanted you to see him – have us all chasing after red Vectra owners when he actually drives something completely different?'

Sean shook his head. 'There's no evidence he has any skills as a thief. Stealing a car's not easy any more. He'd have to know what he was doing, which means a professional criminal – and as we both know, a criminal like that would have convictions, but our man doesn't. He's not going to risk driving around in a stolen car. This is too important to him for that. He likes his comfort zones, things that are familiar to him – like his own car. Best guess is, he kept his eyes open until he saw a red Vectra of a similar age to his own and simply made a note of the registration and made plates using Redmayne's number. He's probably changed the plates back by now.'

'So what next?' Donnelly asked. 'Find every red Vectra owner in London?'

'Yes,' Sean told him, starting the car. 'That's exactly what we do – until I can think of something better.'

Geoff Jackson was standing at the water dispenser in his office talking intensely to a couple of colleagues when another reporter shouted across to get his attention.

'Oi, Geoff. I got someone on my line says he needs to speak with you,' the reporter yelled. 'He says you'll really want to take this call.'

'That's what they all say,' Jackson muttered under his breath. 'Fine. Put him through to my extension,' he yelled. The reporter nodded and transferred the call. 'I'll catch you later,' Jackson told his colleagues and headed quickly back to his ringing phone. He snatched the handset up and stood straight, half expecting to be hanging the phone up as soon as the caller spoke. 'Geoff Jackson speaking.'

'Mr Jackson,' the human, but slightly robotic voice replied, setting Jackson's instincts on fire. 'Chief crime editor for *The World*, no less.'

'Who is this?' he asked, lowering himself into his chair.

'You know who this is,' the voice told him. 'I dare say you've been expecting this call.'

'How do I know it's *you*?' Jackson asked in little more than a whisper.

333

'I take their fingernails as well as their teeth,' the voice told him. 'Did you know that, Mr Jackson?'

Jackson took a few seconds to compose himself. 'Yes,' he answered. 'Yes, I did.'

'Then you are one of the few,' the voice replied, 'and you now know for sure who you're talking to.'

'What do you want?'

'Simple,' the voice answered. 'I want to know why you printed those lies about me. I want to know why you think it is acceptable to write such garbage.'

'Please,' Jackson faltered slightly. 'I'm a journalist. It's my job to report what he says, whether I believe it or not. It wouldn't be ethical for me to change his words.'

'Ethical,' the voice spat the word. 'What do you know about *ethical*? You print every word that fool Gibran says, yet you all but totally ignore my extraordinary work. In what way is that *ethical*? You're supposed to be a crime journalist, yet you fail to understand what I'm trying to achieve.'

'Then tell me,' Jackson pleaded.

'More than anyone else has ever done, Mr Jackson,' the voice told him. 'More than Gibran could ever dream of. And unlike him, I won't be afraid to revel in my achievements. I won't hide like a coward behind a mask of insanity, afraid to admit what I've done and what I am.'

'What are you?' Jackson asked, wide-eyed.

There was a few seconds' silence. 'Soon, Mr Jackson,' the voice answered, having regained its composure. 'Soon, you and the whole world will know the answer to that question. In the meantime, I'm planning a surprise. Maybe we can meet, before too long. Goodbye, Mr Jackson.'

'Wait,' Jackson pleaded, but the caller had hung up. 'Shit.' What now? he thought to himself. Dig himself in deeper with another dangerous and unpredictable killer or tell the police everything and keep his distance this time? He thought of his pretty girlfriend, his nice flat in Soho and the books he had yet to write. A second later he found himself reaching for the phone.

Sean and Donnelly approached the morgue at Guy's Hospital, neither of them under any illusion as to the unpleasantness of the task ahead. Sean suddenly became concerned for Donnelly, remembering it would be the first time he'd seen a dead body since he'd shot and killed Jeremy Goldsboro.

'You all right with this?' he asked.

'Aye,' Donnelly answered without conviction. 'I'll be fine.'

'You sure?' Sean checked. 'I can do it on my own if you prefer.'

'I'm good,' Donnelly tried to assure him. 'Step by step, right? If I walk out, you'll know why.'

'Of course,' Sean told him. 'Everything else OK?'

'It'll take time,' Donnelly shrugged. 'Been off the drink for a couple of days at least.'

'Good,' Sean replied. 'Good.'

They reached the entrance to the morgue and entered to find Dr Canning standing next to the pathologist's stainless steel examination table, upon which Witney Dennis' tiny body lay. A pristine green sheet covered her from the waist down, but her upper body remained exposed – her skin, pale in life, had long since taken on the strange hue of the dead. Her wounds were clearly visible, even from a distance and somehow more repelling and grotesque now they had been cleaned, her blood no longer able to flow or leak from the crude openings in her skin and muscle. Instead it had pooled in the lower regions of her body, turning the skin wine-red.

Canning heard the approaching footsteps and looked up from his table of instruments. 'Gentlemen,' he acknowledged them as they drew closer. 'Sergeant Donnelly – long time no see.'

'Aye,' Donnelly shrugged. 'I've been otherwise engaged.'

'I'm sure you have,' Canning replied. He looked down at

335

the body of Witney Dennis. 'How unfortunate that these should be the circumstances of our reunion.'

'Always likely, I'm afraid,' Donnelly told him. 'Given our chosen professions.'

'Indeed,' Canning smiled for a second then looked deadly serious again. 'You saw the body in situ?' he asked Sean, who nodded. 'Any thoughts?'

'Plenty,' he admitted, 'but no answers. I can tell you he's getting increasingly confident and sadistic, and he's got a real taste for it now. It's only going to get worse.'

'Well he certainly appears confident,' Canning agreed. 'We know his pattern is to incapacitate them with a blow to the head before carrying out the other acts.' He pointed to the wound on the front of her head. 'Judging by the shape and position of this wound, it appears it was a frontal attack. It's possible that he came from behind her, that she sensed him and spun around, but when people turn to face a threat they almost always raise their hands in self-defence, whereas she appears to have been caught completely by surprise.'

'She was expecting him,' Sean explained. 'She went to meet him. She had no reason to believe she was going to be attacked.'

'Makes sense,' Canning nodded. 'There are no obvious defence marks on her hands or arms, and unfortunately her fingernails have been removed, so if she did scratch the suspect and trap some of his skin under them, it's been lost. There is of course blood, but whether it's the suspect's as well as hers, we won't know until the swabs I've taken are examined by the lab. The blow to the head,' he continued relentlessly, 'was almost certainly not sufficient to kill her, maybe not even enough to knock her unconscious, although I won't know for sure until I examine the brain. There are no signs of haemorrhaging in her eyes, ears or nose.'

'Perhaps he's losing his touch?' Donnelly suggested. 'He certainly took his first two victims down with one blow.'

'He didn't want her unconscious,' Sean insisted.

'How can you be sure?' Canning asked.

'Because if he did,' he explained, as if it should have been obvious to them, 'he would have hit her again, but we only have one head wound. He wanted her disorientated, but conscious.'

Canning and Donnelly glanced at each other before the pathologist continued: 'The first wound to her throat is a deep right-to-left laceration that cut through her trachea. The injury that killed her was this one' – he pointed to the gaping cut to the side of her neck – 'a knife wound that severed the carotid artery, causing her to bleed to death. The injuries are consistent with those inflicted on the previous two victims. What interests me are the wounds we haven't seen on the other two – starting with this,' he told them, allowing his hand to drift over the wound in her shoulder. 'This is not like anything we've seen him do before.'

'He did it to stop her struggling,' Sean explained, revealing thoughts that had been developing in his mind since he'd first seen the victim's body. 'He was trying to rape her, but she fought back. First he tried to subdue her by punching her in the face,' he told them, nodding towards her injured nose, 'but she kept struggling, so he stabbed her in the shoulder. He stabbed her in the shoulder because he didn't want to kill her and . . .'

'And what?' Canning encouraged.

'And it was a convenient place to keep his knife while he raped her,' Sean answered.

'A convenient place?' Canning asked, shaking his head in disbelief.

'The cuts on her thighs,' Sean replied, his eyes falling on the green sheet over her lower body. 'They happened because he was still holding the knife as he was pulling her clothing down. The blade kept catching her skin and it was awkward. It was hard, pulling at her clothes with the knife in his hand, so he buried it in her shoulder, freeing his hands but keeping the knife close. The shock alone would have taken the fight out of her.'

'There are definitely signs of recent sexual activity,' Canning explained. 'I found what I believe to be semen in her upper and lower vagina, so if she was sexually assaulted, you believe she was alive when it occurred?'

'Yes,' Sean admitted. 'It's the picture her injuries paint.'

Canning carefully folded the sheet down to reveal her lower body and the cuts to her thighs. 'Yes,' he agreed after a few seconds. 'I think you're probably right.' There was a silence between them for a few seconds as each, in their own way, tried to comprehend the horror of what she'd been through in her last moments. 'And as if all that wasn't enough,' he concluded, 'she's had five teeth crudely removed with a bladed instrument – most likely the knife – and a tool such as a pair of pliers. As previously mentioned, all her fingernails have been traumatically removed, again most likely with a pair of pliers.'

'Poor wee cow,' Donnelly sympathized.

'Quite,' Canning agreed.

Sean said nothing.

'What's this bastard all about?' Donnelly asked. 'What the hell makes a man do this to a wee thing like her?'

'Power,' Sean answered. 'Power and recognition. Killing makes him feel powerful, but it's the after effects he's most interested in. He wants fame. He wants the world to know what he's done. He killed her in the middle of a car park. He could have dragged her a few feet into the privacy of a doorway, but he felt so untouchable he killed her right where she stood, out in the open, and left her there for us to find. He wants us to know he's not afraid of being caught.'

'Maybe he's just out of control?' Donnelly argued. 'Killed her in the open because he couldn't hold himself back any longer?'

'No,' Sean disagreed. 'He's never out of control, except maybe for the sexual element to his attacks. Maybe that's something we can use against him.' His phone ringing in his pocket pulled his wandering mind back to the present as he checked the caller ID before answering it. 'Sally.'

'Sean,' she replied, sounding troubled. 'Have you seen today's copy of *The World*? It's like Gibran's daring our man to kill again. Goading him. Telling him he needs to do better. And Jackson's printed it all. We need to stop him.'

'It's in hand,' he assured her.

'What do you mean, "in hand"?'

'I mean I've spoken with him,' he admitted. 'He called me when I was on my way to Guy's – wants to meet. Says he's got something I need to hear.'

'You're not actually going to meet him, are you?' she asked, incredulous. 'You can't trust him.'

'I thought you said I needed to stop him,' he reminded her.

'Yes,' she agreed, 'but not by meeting him, not by walking into a set-up. I meant, ask Addis to use his contacts to put pressure on him – get him to back down.'

'No,' Sean told her. 'I need to have it out with him. Besides, he sounded . . . worried. Maybe he's getting cold feet.'

'I doubt it.'

'Well, I guess I'll find out,' he replied. 'Anything else happening?'

'Nothing ground-breaking,' she admitted. 'You?'

'A few things from the preliminary post-mortem,' he explained. 'I'll tell you all about it when I get back.'

'Fine,' she answered, 'and be careful with Jackson.'

'I will,' he promised, and hung up.

'Problem?' Donnelly asked.

'No.' He turned to Canning, 'We have to go. Anything of interest turns up, you'll call me directly, yes?'

'Of course,' Canning agreed. 'Sergeant,' he nodded to Donnelly.

'Doctor,' Donnelly nodded back.

Canning watched the two detectives, physical opposites, walk from his morgue lost in thought. 'Good luck, gentlemen,' he found himself whispering. 'Good luck.'

Anna studied the man sitting opposite her in her consulting room in Swiss Cottage: handsome, athletic, she guessed him to be in his early forties with troubled eyes that never smiled even when the rest of his face did. It was the sixth time she'd seen him over the last few weeks, but still she felt they were making no progress – as if the man was hiding something, never telling her the complete truth about himself. It wasn't unusual, particularly with male patients. Some took a lot longer than others to truly open up, but she wouldn't rush him. Right now, she was glad of any excuse to take a break from the increasingly oppressive investigation – and Sean.

'So, David,' she asked. 'How have you been?'

'Fine,' he told her with a faint smile.

'And what does fine mean for you?' she encouraged.

'Fine means fine,' Langley insisted, the smile slipping from his lips.

'Have the suicidal thoughts returned?' she checked.

He shook his head. 'Suicidal thoughts? I fear my GP may have overstated things.'

'Oh?' she questioned. 'When you first came to see me on an urgent referral, you told me you'd had them.'

'Not exactly,' he argued. 'I'd thought about what it would be like to kill myself, the effect it would have on others – my children mostly – but I never seriously considered it. Never planned how it could be done. Isn't that how you know someone is serious about taking their own life – when they actually start planning how to do it?'

'Perhaps,' she played along. 'But your GP must have thought it was something you were serious about or he wouldn't have urgently referred you to me.'

340

'He didn't refer me to you,' Langley corrected her with a wry smile. 'He merely gave me a list of private psychiatrists and *I* selected you myself.'

'I see,' she replied, squirming in her seat, not for the first time feeling somewhat uncomfortable in her new client's company. 'Any particular reason?'

'You had an interesting name,' he answered, showing her his straight white teeth, 'and you came with excellent recommendations.'

'Recommendations?' she asked.

'The internet,' he explained. 'You'd be amazed what you can find out about a person.'

'No,' she assured him. 'No I would not.'

'For example, I discovered that you occasionally help the police,' he told her, 'with *murder* investigations.'

'Oh,' was all she could reply as she swallowed dryly.

'Yes,' he continued. 'I was . . . thinking about you and thought that if you're going to be fumbling around inside my head, perhaps I should know a bit more about you than patient recommendations. You've worked on some interesting cases.'

'I was only a consultant. And I'm afraid I can't discuss those cases.'

'Of course,' he pretended to understand, before continuing in the same vein: 'Are you helping the police with any investigations at the moment?'

'I'm not at liberty to say,' she insisted, shifting in her chair.

'I thought perhaps you were helping them catch this lunatic who's running around killing homeless people?'

'They weren't all home—' She stopped herself, realizing she'd slipped up.

'So you do know something about it?' he seized on it.

'Only what I've seen in the papers,' she lied. 'I believe only one victim was homeless.'

341

'Perhaps,' he smiled, 'although none sound like a great loss to humanity. I only hope the killer turns out to be a lot more interesting than the people he's killed. Anyway,' he quickly moved on. 'I'm not really interested in such things. Although this DI Corrigan looks like an intriguing fellow. Very serious-looking. You must know him well?'

'Not really,' she lied again. 'As I said, I'm only a consultant.'

'But you've worked with him on several cases,' he reminded her. 'Surely you got to know him?'

'Why don't we talk about you?' she insisted. 'That's why you're here.'

'Indeed,' he agreed.

'Tell me about your relationship with your ex-wife and children.'

Langley leaned back in his chair. 'My wife and children? Let me tell you about my wife and children . . .'


Sean and Donnelly entered the café in Wapping, a basic establishment built under a converted railway arch, serving endless varieties of a full English breakfast. They saw Jackson sitting at a table, head buried in his phone, fork in the other hand brandishing a piece of bacon. They picked their way through the tables and sat – Sean opposite, while Donnelly sat intimidatingly next to him. No one spoke for a few seconds until Jackson lowered his phone and looked from Sean to Donnelly and back again.

'Before you think about trying anything silly,' he warned them, 'I'm amongst friends in here.'

'We know,' Donnelly told him, staring down the other customers who were curious enough to look over at their table.

'Been a long time since we last met,' Jackson reminded them.

'Not long enough,' Donnelly said.

'Not since The Jackdaw investigation,' Jackson nodded.

342

'That one didn't end too well, I seem to remember.' He turned to Donnelly. 'What was it like – killing a man?'

'You son of a bitch!' Donnelly cursed between gritted teeth and tried to get to his feet but Sean's hand on his shoulder held him down.

Sean glanced around and realized everyone in the café was now looking at them.

'I told you I was amongst friends,' Jackson reminded them.

'What do you want, Jackson?' Sean demanded. 'Why the meeting? You better not be wasting my time.'

'We're both interested in the same thing,' Jackson told them. 'We both want to see this killer caught.'

'Really?' Sean said disbelievingly, pulling that day's edition of *The World* from his coat pocket and dropping it on the table in front of Jackson. 'Doesn't look like it to me. Looks like you're goading him into committing more murders by printing these interviews with Gibran.'

'It's a story and I'm a journalist,' he shrugged. 'People like to hear what someone like Gibran thinks. Gives them a bit of a thrill. But if you think I don't want to see him caught, you know nothing about me.'

'Save the sermon, Jackson,' Donnelly told him. 'You make a living out of other people's misery.'

'Don't you?' he snapped back.

'Enough of this shit,' Sean intervened. 'You didn't want to meet just to talk about Gibran – something else has happened, so why don't you tell us what it is?'

'OK,' he climbed down. 'I got a phone call.'

'Who from?' Sean asked.

'The killer.'

'How do you know it was genuine?' Sean pressed.

'Because he knew things,' he explained. 'Things not released to the press.'

'What things?' Sean demanded, his stomach tightening.

'Things like he takes their fingernails as well as their teeth.'

343

Sean's worst fears were confirmed: Jackson had a source very close to the investigation.

'How do you know that's true?' he asked. 'He may just be making it up.'

'Maybe,' Jackson played along, 'but the looks on your faces tell me he didn't. It's true, isn't it – he takes their fingernails too?'

'I swear, Jackson,' Sean warned him, 'if you breathe or print a word of this, I'll bury you.'

'I knew it was true,' he smiled, 'but you have my word I won't tell anyone.'

'When did he contact you?' Sean demanded.

'Just this morning,' Jackson answered.

'If I find out you've been holding back—'

'I haven't,' Jackson insisted. 'As soon as I finished talking to him, I called you.'

'Why?' Sean asked. 'Why're you telling us this? Why didn't you just keep it to yourself – keep talking to him and run the story like you did with Goldsboro?'

'I have my reasons.'

'You're scared,' Donnelly smiled. 'I can smell your fear.'

'I'm not scared,' Jackson insisted, sounding unsure of himself.

'Then you're a fool,' Sean told him. 'This is no Jeremy Goldsboro we're dealing with here. Goldsboro had an agenda. He needed the media. If you meet this one, he'll kill you. I promise you. This one's out to shock, not rally people to his cause.'

'Fancy that, do you, Jackson?' Donnelly asked, moving closer to the journalist. 'Having your throat cut and your teeth pulled out?'

'No,' Jackson regained his composure. 'That's why I called you. I'm trying to work with you here.'

'Tell me everything you know,' Sean cut to the chase.

'He's a cold, intimidating bastard, I'll tell you that,' Jackson began, 'and he's obsessed with Gibran.'

'Tell us something we don't know,' Donnelly cut in.

'It's like Gibran is the itch he can't scratch.'

'Probably because you keep printing what Gibran's saying about him,' Sean reminded him.

'It's as if he sees Gibran as some sort of king,' Jackson explained, 'and he wants to depose him – take his crown.'

'Bullshit,' Donnelly laughed, but Sean stayed silent. Jackson had come to the same conclusion he had and with nowhere near as much information. He may not like him, but he had to admire him.

'And how's he planning on doing that?' Sean asked.

'He didn't say. But he said that soon the whole world will know what he is and that he's planning some sort of surprise. Do you think he could be trying to get to Gibran?'

'No chance,' Donnelly dismissed it. 'Gibran's safely locked up in Broadmoor. He can't get to him.'

'Don't assume anything,' Sean warned them.

'You mean, he could be a guard at Broadmoor?' Jackson asked, his eyes wide with the possibility. 'Or a nurse or doctor – someone with access?'

'Worth checking,' Donnelly reluctantly agreed.

'Everything's worth checking,' Sean agreed. It hadn't occurred to him to take a look at Broadmoor staff; his grudging respect for Jackson continued to grow. 'What else did he tell you?'

'Nothing that made sense,' Jackson assured them. 'Nothing we can use.'

'*We*?' Donnelly asked.

'Of course,' Jackson shrugged. 'He calls me, sends me anything, I'll let you know. Maybe there's something you want me to ask Gibran about him? A killer's perspective. Unless, that is, you already have one.'

'And in return?' Sean ignored his last comment, although he knew it was aimed at him.

'You let me cover the investigation,' Jackson answered,

345

'from close up. The scenes, should there be any more, the arrest, interview – the whole thing. It would be good press for you guys. We stand a better chance of tripping him up if we work together – share information.'

'No,' Sean told him flatly, getting to his feet. 'I can't do that.'

'Come on,' Jackson pleaded, his arms stretched out wide. 'You're joking, right?'

'Sorry, Jackson,' Donnelly patted him on the back as he too got to his feet. 'Better luck next time.'

'Corrigan,' Jackson called out as Sean pulled the café door open, 'you know I'm right. We stand a better chance of catching him together.'

Sean turned to face him, his hand resting on the door handle. 'I'll think about it,' he called back. 'He contacts you again, call me immediately.'

Anna entered the underground car park beneath her office building in Swiss Cottage and headed towards her car in the dim light. The car park was quiet, most of the places were reserved for residents and business owners. There were a few spaces for visitors, but only those who had appointments. She had her car keys already in her hand when she reached her car, which was when she noticed a red car parked too close to her driver's side, preventing her from being able to open her door enough to allow her to slip inside.

'For God's sake,' she complained, gesticulating at the offending car. 'What inconsiderate fool would park like that?' She scoured the dark corners of the car park for signs of life, hoping the owner of the offending car would suddenly materialize. Seeing no one, she walked around to the passenger's side, intending to climb in and slide across into the driver's seat, but as she came around the back of her car a dark figure wearing a hooded top and sunglasses stepped from behind a wide supporting pillar and blocked her path. For a second she thought she recognized the man, but it was impossible to see his features buried in the darkness of his hood. Her heart began to pound with fear as she realized who it was standing in front of her. 'Who are you?' she asked as she began to walk backwards away from danger. 'What do you want?'

'You know who I am,' he told her in the same fake, gravelly voice he used on the telephone. 'What do I want? I want you, Anna.'

She tried to turn and run, but the man was fast and strong. He covered the distance between them quickly, his right fist coming from nowhere and crashing into her jaw. She dropped to the floor unconscious.

Langley stood looking down on her for a few seconds before he kicked her in the stomach, almost as a reflex action. She groaned, but remained motionless. He took a quick look around to ensure they were still alone, then bent over her, sliding his hands under her armpits and dragging her to the rear of his car, which he'd parked deliberately close to hers. He popped the boot and grabbed a roll of thick silver insulating tape from inside, tore a strip off and covered her mouth with it. Moving with speed and agility, he used the same roll of tape to secure her wrists behind her back and to tie her ankles together. Confident she couldn't escape, he lifted her off the floor and laid her as gently as he could inside the boot, which he'd layered with blankets, keen that she should stay unconscious for as long as possible. If she started thrashing around, the padding in the boot would deaden the noise, but it was better she remained motionless. He tore off a final strip of tape and used it to cover her eyes, then carefully closed the boot and pressed it shut with a quiet click. Calmly he climbed into the driver's seat and reversed from the parking space. Seconds later he eased into the busy traffic outside and headed west – just another commuter trying to get home.

*   *   *

Sean and Donnelly arrived back at the Yard and went straight to Donnelly's office. Sally was waiting for them.

'You boys have been busy,' she greeted them. 'Find anything?'

'Let's just say it's been an eventful day so far,' Donnelly replied, slumping into his chair.

'Care to share?' she asked.

'The car lead was a blow-out,' he explained, 'although we're pretty sure our man drives a red Vauxhall Vectra – assuming, that is, he didn't steal one. No number plate.'

'Where did this information come from?' she asked, her hand on her hip.

Sean and Donnelly looked at each other. Donnelly answered: 'We think our man followed the boss home last night. Took photographs of him. He was driving a red Vectra. Boss took the index number. We checked it out, but it came to nothing. Looks like our man used false plates and attached them to his own car – hence we're pretty sure he drives a red Vectra.'

'Wait a minute,' Sally backed up. 'What the hell do you mean, Sean was followed by someone who could be the suspect?'

'At first I thought it was Jackson,' Sean explained, 'but it wasn't. Using false plates, who else could it have been?'

'Another journalist?' Sally suggested. 'Someone with a grudge against you?'

'Well, that narrows it down,' Donnelly joked.

'No,' Sean insisted. 'It was him. I know it was him. He likes to play games. Likes to be in control.'

'This is bad, Sean,' Sally said, pacing around the office.

'That's not all the good news,' Donnelly continued. 'We paid a visit to Jackson.'

'And?'

'The killer has contacted him,' Sean told her.

'Great,' Sally rolled her eyes. 'That's all we need. Is he planning on interviewing him like he did Jeremy Goldsboro?'

'No,' Sean answered. 'He says not.'

'And you believe him?'

'Yes.'

'Why?' Sally pressed.

'Because he was scared. Jackson knows that if he met him, it would be the last thing he ever did. Any publicity Jackson could give him, he'd get tenfold by killing him – and Jackson knows it.'

'Not to mention he's been writing things in his rag of a newspaper our man's not exactly pleased about,' Donnelly added.

'And he's agreed to tell us if he contacts him again,' Sean added. 'He wants to cooperate.'

'Oh yeah,' Sally scoffed at the idea. 'In exchange for what?'

'Access to the investigation,' Sean told her.

'You didn't agree to that, did you?'

'No,' Sean assured her. 'Not yet.'

'Not yet?' Sally's brown eyes burrowed into Sean's.

'What else have we got?' Sean argued. 'We have a possible make and model of car he drives, a vague description and a made-up first name. It's nothing.'

'And he uses public transport and he likes to make contact with his victims before he kills them,' Sally reminded him.

'It's nothing,' Sean insisted. 'He's outsmarting us every time, and he's getting bolder and bolder. More people are going to die unless we try something different. We're out of time and we have no choice.'

'So what are you suggesting?' Sally asked.

'We use Jackson's interviews with Gibran to goad him into a trap,' Sean said, speaking quickly so he couldn't be interrupted. 'Work with Jackson and figure out what we can print that'll make him do what we want him to do for a change, instead of him always being one step ahead.'

'You're talking about using someone as bait in a trap again,' Sally pointed out.

'We need to do something,' Sean answered.

'But who could we use other than Sebastian Gibran?' she continued. 'Because we can't use him.'

'Me,' Sean told her, finally revealing what he'd been considering for days without telling anyone. 'Provoke him into coming after me.'

'Have you gone mad?' Sally asked, shaking her head in disbelief. 'No way.'

'We could make it work,' he insisted. 'We could cover it. I've done decoy work before. It's not that difficult.'

'Absolutely no way,' Sally refused again.

'We have no choice,' he pleaded. 'Has anyone seen Anna?' he asked.

'She said something about having to go and see a client,' Sally told him, frustrated at his attempt to change the subject, 'but I know Anna would tell you it's way too dangerous.'

'I'm talking about a planned operation,' he explained. 'We'd be working with SO10 and SO19. We'd have complete control over the situation.'

'It's still too dangerous, Sean. This one's clever. Really clever. The likelihood is he'll smell a trap and change the circumstances to favour himself, and that's when I worry about you. If things start to go off-plan you won't just pull the plug on the operation, Sean, you'll go after him – alone if you have to. When you get close to these people you become reckless. You're like a greyhound who sees a hare. You have to chase it. It's in your nature. You can't help yourself. Find another way to catch him, Sean. For the sake of everyone around you.'

He gave a long mournful sigh. 'Fine,' he said. 'I'll think of something else.'

'Good,' she told him with relief. 'It's the right thing to do.'

'Well, if you'll excuse me, it appears I have much to do.'

She rested a hand on his forearm. 'You don't have to try

and do everything alone,' she told him gently. 'You have good people around you. Use them.'

'I will,' he said as she removed her hand. 'I better get on.'

Sean headed straight back into his own office and closed the door. He looked out into the main office as covertly as he could to make sure neither Sally nor Donnelly were paying him any special attention and was relieved to see them both busy chatting to other team members. He sat at his desk and took his mobile from his pocket, spinning his chair around so he had his back to the world beyond. He was about to call Kate when he suddenly changed his mind and threw the phone back on to the desk. 'Shit,' he cursed to himself as he looked at the reflection of himself in the Perspex window. 'Shit.'

David Langley drove his Vectra along a bumpy dirt track through the forest that he'd known since he was a boy. People sometimes skirted around the edges of the forest, but it was a dark and threatening place that few dared to enter. The lack of any nearby pubs or cafés kept the casual walkers away, leaving him alone as master of the woods. Eventually he turned off the track and drove between the trees, occasionally catching sight of the tyre tracks from his previous trips, although the fallen leaves had all but completely concealed them. Slowly he drove deeper into the forest until he came to a small clearing where an old caravan that nature had almost completely disguised waited for him. It had been here since he was a child – brought to the forest by his father, as a special place where they could go to escape his mother and sisters. A place where they could be men.

He allowed the car to roll to a halt right outside the caravan as memories of those special trips with his father cascaded through his mind. He could see his father's face and hear his voice as clearly as if he was there with him now.

'Don't ever let a woman tell you what to do, son,' his

father would tell him in his thick London accent. 'Men rule this world. Women are just here to do our bidding and make us happy. If you're with a woman, she does what you tell her to – that's what they really want and you take them when you want them. Don't be putting up with that *not tonight* shit, and don't be too gentle. That's not what they want. Be good and rough. Slap them round a bit, if that's what it takes. You want to fuck them up the arse, fuck them up the arse. Don't fucking ask.

'All that shit most men put up with makes me sick,' he would explain – his young son listening to every word of his hero, the keen student taking it all in. 'Men like me need more and you're my son, which means you're going to need more too. Let them boring fuckers live their boring fucking lives, but not us, son. We're different. We live by different rules. We take what we want when we want it. Anything we want.'

He still missed his father. When he was only sixteen he left their family home with no explanation offered, although he knew it must have been something his mother had done. She'd betrayed him somehow, just like his father had warned him all women eventually would. He saw him occasionally, although less and less. For a while they carried on coming to the caravan, until his father completely disappeared. He died penniless when Langley was only eighteen. He went to the funeral somewhere in North London on a rainy Wednesday afternoon in February. There were less than a dozen people there and no one cried. He lived at home for another year, barely speaking to his mother or sisters until he finally left home, getting a job and renting a tiny one-bedroom studio flat in Merton, but the words of his father always stayed with him – guiding his life to where he was now. On the cusp of greatness.

He snapped himself from his daydream and leapt out of the car, checking the surrounding forest to ensure he was alone. All he could see were the tall thin trees swaying gently in the breeze and all he could hear was the creaking of wood and the occasional squawk of a crow. Satisfied, he walked to the caravan and used a shiny key to unlock the new padlock that secured the door. He pulled the door open and peered into the small space where everything was just as he'd left it. There were few creature comforts inside – a sleeping place for one, with a mattress and pillow laid on top, in addition to another thin mattress on the floor. There was a tiny gas cooker, a small fridge as well as a sink and a built-in ward-robe. A foldaway table attached to the wall and a horseshoe-shaped bench completed the furnishings. Thanks to the use of tanks and batteries, the place had running water, gas and power. Satisfied, he made his way to the back of his car, taking a deep breath before popping open the boot.

Anna immediately began to struggle once she felt the light and air from outside invade the darkness of her metal prison, but the insulating tape around her ankles held her legs together, while more of the same tape wrapped her wrists together behind her back. Her mouth and eyes were also covered with the thick, wide tape, turning her pleas into desperate mumbles. Her chin was beginning to turn black and purple from where he'd punched her and knocked her unconscious. When he grabbed her under her armpits, her struggles grew even more frantic, but he was still able to drag her up and out of the boot and let her fall to the leaf-covered ground. He was tempted to kick her – payback for all the times she had spoken to him like a naughty child. It's what his father would have done to teach her a lesson. But he was afraid once he started he wouldn't be able to stop, and he needed her alive – for now. So instead he grabbed her under her arms again and dragged her backwards towards the caravan, her head thrashing from side to side and her heels trying to gain purchase on the loose ground as she fought for her life, no matter how futile her efforts might be.

Strong as he was, it was an effort dragging her up the few steps into the caravan and he was relieved to be able to throw her on to the mattress. He stood watching her writhe as he recovered his breath – wiping the sweat from his top lip, enjoying every second of her helplessness and vulnerability. After a minute or two he returned to the car and grabbed his backpack from the passenger seat, then headed back to the caravan where he opened the bag and took out his knife and mobile phone, setting them down on the bed next to his hostage. For a second he considered taking the tape off her eyes and showing her the knife, but decided she was already terrified enough. Instead, he leaned over her and ripped the tape off her mouth. She immediately cried out in pain, gasping for breath, before trying to regain some degree of composure. After a couple of minutes, her panting calmed down enough for her to be able to talk, although her words still trembled.

'David,' she stuttered. 'Are you there? Answer me.' He didn't like the fight in her words and his anger flared. He grabbed her by the back of her hair and twisted her face towards him. With his other hand he took his knife and pressed the blade into the soft skin of her cheek until it drew a small amount of blood, taking away her breath and fight. He pushed her back down into the mattress and picked up the pay-as-you-go mobile phone, pointed it at his victim and pressed record without speaking to her. 'Why are you doing this?' she struggled to speak. 'Talk to me. I can help you.' He grabbed her around the throat and squeezed hard enough for her to feel his power before releasing her again. 'Talk to me,' she pleaded – her tears threatening to loosen the tape around her eyes. 'Please talk to me. Tell me what you want.' She struggled to calm down before speaking again. 'I won't tell anyone,' she said. 'If you just let me go, I won't tell anyone. I promise. I swear. Please, let me go. You need help. I can get you that help. The police need never know.'

He'd seen enough. He stopped the recording and delved in his backpack until he found the roll of insulating tape. He tore off a strip about eight inches long – the sound of it ripping made Anna wince and writhe until he grabbed her by the hair again and slapped the tape roughly over her mouth, then smoothed it into a neat seal. Next, he lifted a long piece of metal chain from the floor that he'd brought to the caravan previously, and wrapped it around her already taped wrists. When he was done, he dragged her backwards and forced her into a sitting position that allowed him to chain her to the cooker – securing her with a heavy padlock. He pulled at the chain to make sure it was secure, then wrapped a powerful hand around her throat and squeezed until she couldn't breathe. When she began to turn purple, her eyes bulging, he released his grip, allowing her to fall to the floor on her side, coughing behind the tape. He stared at her for a few seconds, feeling no pity or regret, only a mild sense of amusement at the sight of the self-important psychiatrist who'd thought she could help the police catch him, now lying on the floor of his old caravan in the middle of nowhere – her life completely in his hands. Quickly he packed his things into the backpack and jumped out of the caravan. He took one last look at his moaning victim before he slammed the door shut and locked it with the padlock. Seconds later he was back in his car heading through the trees towards the dirt road and his destiny.

Sean sat in his office looking over old information reports as well as new ones, praying that something would jump out from the pages or the computer screen that would clear the endless fog, but nothing glinted in amongst the dull files. He knew he now had the green light to try something more radical, but to do so would risk alienating Sally, Anna and probably the rest of his team, not to mention what Kate would do if she ever found out. He sighed deeply as he looked up just in time to see Zukov walking past his office. 'Paulo,' he called out, getting to his feet and stretching.

Zukov stopped and walked backwards a few steps until he was level with Sean's open door. 'Yes, boss?'

'How you getting on with the suspect's car?' Sean asked.

'Working our way through them, boss. But there are thousands of the things across London. Only thing worse would have been if he'd driven a Prius.'

'I appreciate that,' Sean let his impatience show in his voice.

'We've got all the local CID offices checking Vectras in their boroughs,' Zukov explained, 'but it's going to take them a long time to check them all, and even when they do – what they supposed to be looking for?'

'Something obvious, I guess,' Sean answered. 'Tell them to be discreet. Have them look through the windows when the owners aren't around. If they see a backpack or hooded top or anything that piques their interest, I want to know.'

'Yes, boss,' he replied.

Sean immediately switched his attention to DC Cahill as she walked within range. 'Fiona,' he stopped her.

'Boss?'

'How we getting on with the CCTV enquiries?'

'We're getting there, but there's a hell of a lot of it. We've got footage from Oxford Street, several different tube stations, the underground system, phone shops, and now we're seizing CCTV from buses in and out of Roehampton. There are plenty of images of who we think is our suspect, but nothing you can identify him from. We'll keep going, but it's—'

'Going to take time,' he finished for her. 'What about enhancement?'

'We've done it on some of the images,' she answered, 'but quality's not really the issue – concealment is. He's always hooded and looking away from the cameras. He's careful. Really careful.'

'OK,' he gave in with a shake of his head. 'Just keep trying.'

He slumped back into his chair and started biting the rough skin around his thumbnail. He needed something more and he needed it immediately. He wondered what the man he hunted was thinking right now. No doubt he was feeling clever and superior – always one step ahead.

'What am I missing?' Sean whispered. 'You're violent, but cold – never in a rage – and there's a sexual motivation to your crimes, even if you don't want to admit it to yourself. You take trophies so you can relive everything. But above all it's recognition you want. You want people to believe you're something special. Your crimes aren't really progressing and you're obsessed with Sebastian Gibran, but he only ever mocks your insignificance. And you like it to feel personal, so you meet them before you kill them. Or are you just showing off? . . . Recognition and infamy. Recognition. Infamy. You want to feel powerful and you want recognition, but so far you haven't been getting the attention you feel you deserve. That must piss you off. Make you angry. And we're all expecting you to do the same again, because that's what you do, but it's not going to make the world take notice for long. You're not doing anything new. It's not going to help you eclipse Gibran. You need to do something else – and you know it, don't you? The things you've said to me and the things you've said to Jackson all point to you planning something. Something that's never been done before – something no one can predict.' He leaned back in his chair with his hands behind his head. 'What are you up to, my friend?' he asked the empty room. 'What the hell are you planning?'

Sebastian Gibran sat in the common room of his wing at Broadmoor Hospital watching an animated film – specifically chosen and vetted by the staff to ensure it contained no sex or violence. Gibran tried his best to enjoy the film, concentrating on the beauty of the animation – the vivid colours and some of the incidental music score appealed to him. Many of his fellow viewers had been sent to Broadmoor indefinitely for unspeakable crimes that rivalled his own, but unlike him they were unarguably insane. The other inmates knew Gibran was something completely different, revering and fearing him because of it. Their insanity had given them the ability to sense when a dangerous animal was about to strike and, with Gibran, they sensed it all the time.

His trance-like state was disturbed as he became aware of the fidgeting of another inmate sitting close behind him. It wasn't much, but the slightest disturbance of the normal drug-induced calm could spell danger – even for Gibran. He looked over his shoulder and saw one of Broadmoor's most hated inmates staring straight at him.

Albert Cramer was a sweetshop owner who killed two little girls, a five-year-old and a six-year-old, within weeks of each other. When Greater Manchester Police caught up with him, they searched his flat above the shop and found blood inside a suitcase that he later admitted he'd used to transport their bodies to where he'd dumped them.

'Do you mind,' Gibran warned him quietly. 'You're spoiling the film.'

'I'm not saying anything,' Cramer whispered back, glancing over at the two burly male nurses keeping watch over the patients.

'You're looking at me.' Gibran smiled dangerously. 'I find it . . . distracting.'

'I was wondering if it's true,' Cramer asked.

'What are you talking about, Cramer?' Gibran demanded.

'That you've been talking to some journalist about this new one,' Cramer elaborated.

'New what?' Gibran snapped at him in a whisper – pretending he had no idea what he was talking about.

'The new killer out there,' Cramer answered, glancing at

the window to the world beyond. 'Rumour is, you've been telling this journalist what you think of him.'

'I have no interest in talking to anyone about some petty murderer,' Gibran lied, confident neither Cramer nor any other Broadmoor resident would have been allowed access to his articles in *The World*.

'Perhaps you should have,' Cramer told him. 'I heard something about him on the radio. It said he cuts their throats and pulls their teeth out. The whole of London's afraid.'

'I doubt that,' Gibran laughed. 'He kills prostitutes and drug addicts, so unless you're one of those there really isn't much to fear – is there?'

Cramer looked crestfallen, but quickly recovered his nerve. 'At least everyone knows he's out there,' he replied. 'They know he exists. He doesn't hide his killings – he marks them. Unlike some.'

'Then he's a fool,' Gibran insisted. 'Just like you.'

'You have to admire him though,' Cramer argued. 'To have the guts to let everyone know he exists, like that. Even the police. Sounds like a very dangerous man. Maybe one day he'll end up in here and then we'll see if you're really as *bad* as you want everyone to think you are.'

Gibran was aware that many of the other inmates were now listening in to what Cramer was saying – like wild dogs looking for signs of weakness in the pack leader before they dare mount a serious challenge, but he'd never felt fear in his entire life and he felt none now. A dozen ways to kill at least two or maybe three of them before the guards could restrain him flashed in his mind. He leaned closer to Cramer. 'Maybe one day he will be locked in here with me,' he whispered, 'and then, if it amuses me, I'll gut him like a rabbit, but I'll be careful to keep him alive so I can feed him his own testicles and watch him choke. Then perhaps I'll skin him, although for something like that I'll need to practise. I wonder – would anyone care to volunteer?' The other inmates leaned away, like wheat bending in the breeze. Cramer looked around frantically for a way to escape – his eyes wide with fear and his face deathly pale, but he needn't have worried – Gibran had no interest in killing him – not today. 'I thought not,' Gibran told them and turned back to watch the animated film. Within a few seconds he was again lost in the colour and music, but in a dark chamber of his mind he was already planning how best to dispose of the irritating Albert Cramer.

By the time Sean arrived home it was late and most of the on-street parking had gone. Eventually he found a space some distance from his house. Walking back along the frozen street he passed an unmarked car with two bored-looking plain-clothes officers inside. He assumed these were the guards for Kate and his girls he'd asked Donnelly to sort out and nodded to them. He only hoped that Kate hadn't noticed she was being followed. By the time he reached the front door he had his keys in his hand and let himself in as quietly as possible, but was surprised and a little disappointed to see the kitchen light still on. As usual when he arrived home late he was in no mood to talk and if Kate had stayed up it meant she had bad news or wanted to talk to him about something he invariably didn't want to speak about. He locked the front door, emptied his pockets on the hall table and then made his way tentatively to the kitchen where he found her with a glass of red wine – typing away on her laptop.

'You're up late,' he greeted her and headed to the fridge for a beer.

'Lots of work to catch up on,' she replied frostily without looking at him, which always meant he was in trouble. 'I didn't finish my shift until late and then the kids were a nightmare, so now I'm having to catch up on paperwork. You're back late,' she added, 'but I suppose I should just expect that.'

'What do you want me to do?' he shrugged as he pulled a beer from the fridge and went in search of a bottle opener.

'The girls miss seeing you,' she told him. 'I miss seeing you. Can't you come home in time to see them just once in a while? Is that too much?'

'I've got a violent murderer who's already killed at least three people. It's a little difficult for me to *slip away*. I'll make it up to you once I've found him.'

'And how long will that be?'

'Not long,' he shrugged again and opened his bottle.

'I don't know, Sean,' she sighed. 'Sometimes I think you're actually happy you've got this new case. That this is what you've been waiting for.'

'It's better than being a gofer for the Flying Squad or SO13,' he admitted. 'It's my responsibility. If it goes well, it's because of me. If it doesn't – also down to me.'

'You like it because it keeps you on that tightrope you like to walk,' Kate insisted. 'Admit it, Sean – being here with me and the girls bores you. You want to be out there chasing these madmen – not at home with us.'

'That's not true,' he tried to convince her. 'It's just when a case like this comes up it takes priority – at least until I find him. People will die if I don't find him.'

'So what about me and the children?' she demanded. 'We just get pushed to one side while you run around London chasing this lunatic?'

'It's not a game, Kate,' he told her.

'And nor is our family,' she snapped back.

They both fell silent. After a while, Sean decided he might as well tell her everything. 'There's something you need to know,' he admitted.

'What?'

'You should go away for a few days,' he told her. 'You and the girls. Go and stay with your mum.'

'What are you talking about?'

'Only for a few days,' he explained, 'or until—' He managed to stop himself saying more.

'Until what? Until you find him? It's the middle of the girls' school term. Why the hell would I take them to my mother's?'

He took a deep breath and swig of beer before answering. 'I was followed,' he revealed.

'Followed? By who?'

'At first I thought it was the journalist,' he answered, 'but it wasn't. It was him.'

'How can you be sure?'

'The car he was using had false plates,' he explained, 'but I'm sure it was him.'

'So he knows where we live?'

'I don't think so,' he tried to calm her fear.

'He didn't follow you home?'

'No,' he assured her, before making things worse. 'Not that night.'

'Not that night?' she raised her voice as she stood up. 'What does that mean?'

'I mean if he followed me that night,' he tried to explain, 'then I have to assume he may have followed me home some other time.'

'Oh Jesus, I don't believe this,' Kate said, resting her hand on her forehead, trying to think rationally. 'Have we got protection?' she asked.

'Yes,' he admitted sheepishly. 'They're watching the house now and they've been watching your work and—' he stopped himself again.

'And?' she demanded.

'They've been watching the kids,' he winced.

'The kids,' she repeated, nodding her head in sarcastic appreciation. 'So now our kids are in danger.'

'I didn't say that,' he argued. 'It's just a precaution.'

'Once again your work has followed you home,' she told

him, throwing her arms in the air. 'First that madman everyone called The Jackdaw and now this.'

'Goldsboro never followed me,' he pointed out. 'He just mentioned me in one of his videos.'

'And then a few days later tried to kill you,' she reminded him. 'What is the matter with you, Sean? Why are these weirdos so drawn to you? And why is this journalist so obsessed with you? What is it about you that they see? Why always you, Sean? Why always you?'

'I don't know,' he shrugged.

'You're going to put yourself in harm's way again,' she warned him. 'I know you are.'

'I'm not,' he lied. 'I'll get us close and then SO19 or TSG will take him down.'

'You know that's not true,' she accused him. 'You won't be able to resist the chance to be face to face with him – a little one on one.'

'Not this time,' he tried to persuade her.

'I don't believe you, Sean,' she told him, shaking her head, 'and I won't watch you go through it all again. I'm not going to sit next to your hospital bed wondering if you're going to be OK, just so you can get well and go out and do it all over again. And the kids and I aren't going anywhere. This is our home and they need to go to school and I need to go to work. We need to live like normal people and no madman is going to chase us out of our lives. You can get rid of your guard dogs too.'

'That's not a good idea,' he argued.

'I won't live like this,' she warned him, 'and neither will the children. You need to sort it out,' she told him calmly. 'We're your family and we're not going to run off and hide, leaving you to deal with this alone. You need us and we need you.'

'I know,' he agreed, her strength and determination reminding him why he loved and needed her, despite his confusion about Anna. 'I'm just not sure I can do my job properly if I'm worrying about you and the kids all the time.'

'Well you'll have to deal with it, Sean, because we're not going anywhere,' she insisted. 'We get through this together.'

'OK,' he told her, doubts swimming in his head about them staying, but relief too. Whatever his feelings for Anna, Kate and his girls were the rock he was anchored to. If he broke the chain he could only imagine how far he could drift from safety. He was already on the edge at work.

'Right now we both need some sleep,' she told him.

'You go,' he answered. 'I'll be up in a minute.'

'OK,' she said, knowing he needed time to unwind before he could sleep. 'But don't be long.'

'I won't,' he assured her, although he didn't really know how long he'd be.

She turned away from him and walked from the room, leaving him alone in the silence. He took his beer to the table and slumped on to a kitchen chair. As he rolled his head to relieve the stress his eyes caught sight of a framed photograph on the windowsill. He stretched out and took hold of it – placing it on the table in front of him. It was of Kate and his girls on some day trip he'd missed – as usual. They looked happy – a happy unit of three. He suddenly realized that his office had become more like a home to him and his team more like his family. He was becoming an intruder who sneaked into the house when everyone else was asleep, to eat, sleep and wash, but his emotional ties had drifted elsewhere. His life was increasingly elsewhere. The madmen were ruining his family and he'd been complicit. 'Shit,' he cursed quietly. 'Shit.'

# 15

After snatching a few hours of restless sleep, Sean was back in his office feeling exhausted. He looked at the framed picture of Kate and his children on his desk, which immediately reminded him of the previous night – sitting at his kitchen table with the terrible feeling that he was drifting away from them. Images of Anna suddenly popped into his mind and made him doubt his future even more. The appearance of Maggie O'Neil at his door broke him free of his tortured thoughts.

'What is it, Maggie?' he asked.

'Someone on the phone saying he's the killer,' she said. 'Says he knows about the fingernails being taken. He wants to speak to you.'

'Put him through to the reserved number,' Sean told her. 'If it's him, I'll recognize his voice and let technical know he's back on the phone.' Maggie nodded and ran back to her desk. A few seconds later the phone started ringing in his office. He took a few seconds to make sure he was ready before activating the trace equipment and lifting the handset. 'DI Corrigan.'

'Sean,' the voice replied cheerfully. 'It's me, but you already knew that.'

'You're early today,' Sean replied, trying to drag the conversation out to give technical as good a chance as possible to get a fix on his location. 'Couldn't sleep?'

'Small talk, Sean?' he asked. 'I thought we were beyond that.'

'We are,' Sean agreed. 'So why don't you tell me what you want?'

'I have something for you,' he told him – a worrying hint of excitement in his voice.

'OK. Why don't you deliver it in person?'

'I don't think that's a good idea,' the voice laughed softly.

'You want to leave it somewhere for me?' Sean suggested. 'Have it delivered.'

'It's a short film I made,' he answered. 'If you have a smartphone I can send it to you.'

Sean looked at his own mobile sitting on his desk, but knew using his personal phone wasn't an option. Suddenly he remembered he had a police-issue smartphone somewhere in his desk he kept for covert use that he hadn't used in months. 'I can give you a number to send it to,' Sean told him as he searched through his desk drawers.

'I'm waiting,' the voice replied. 'What's the matter? Don't you know your own number?'

'It's a new phone,' Sean lied. 'I switched supplier so now I have a new number.' He found the phone hiding under some envelopes and instantly switched it on, praying it still had some power. He was in luck. It had less than 10 per cent, but it was enough. He went to contacts and found the phone's number. 'I have the number,' he told him. 'Do you want me to read it out?'

'No,' the voice replied. 'I assume you're tracing this call so the number I'm calling on is no doubt displayed.'

Sean looked at the display panel of the phone. It showed the mobile number the killer was calling from. 'It is,' he admitted.

'Send me a text,' he explained. 'Then I'll have your number.'

'Fine,' Sean agreed, pressing the *text message* icon, entering the killer's number into the address bar and pressing the send arrow.

'Good,' he answered. 'My turn.' Sean waited for a second until the mobile chimed that it had received a text. 'Did you get it?' he asked.

'Yes,' Sean confirmed.

'And the attachment?'

'Yes.'

'Then open it,' he demanded.

Sean's heart was beating hard and his mouth was dry at the thought of what could be in the attachment. He touched the screen and saw that it was a video. He held his breath and tapped play. It only lasted a few seconds and wasn't the best quality. He guessed it had been filmed on a phone and it appeared to have been badly edited in places, but still it clearly showed him what the killer wanted him to see – Anna, bound and gagged and lying on the floor of a room somewhere. Despite the poor quality of the footage, he could see her terror. It felt as if he was being tricked into watching a scene from one of his own nightmares. It was all his mind could do to accept the reality of what his eyes were seeing.

'Can you see?' the voice asked, excited.

'Yes,' Sean answered, struggling to overcome the nausea that threatened to overwhelm him. 'I can see.'

'Good, good.'

'If you touch her, I swear I'll—'

'Don't get so emotional. She's only an irrelevant pawn in a higher game.'

'Just don't hurt her,' Sean interrupted, knowing his temper would snap if he were forced to listen to another rambling monologue on the killer's grandiose delusions.

'Hurt her?' the voice sounded insulted. 'I've no intention

of hurting her, Sean. She means nothing to me. Nothing at all. Although, clearly she means much to you.'

'Why are you doing this to her if she means nothing?'

'To bring about a great coming together,' the voice answered. 'A meeting of like-minded men. A meeting which only one of us will walk away from.'

'You need to tell me exactly what you want,' Sean demanded. 'You need to be very clear about what you want. Do you understand?'

'I understand perfectly,' the voice answered. 'I want Sebastian Gibran.'

Sean felt his stomach drop and his chest tighten to the point where he could hardly breathe. He felt completely outmanoeuvred and out-thought. With Gibran locked in Broadmoor, he'd never considered the killer would demand that Gibran be *given* to him. If the killer was going to come after anyone, he'd been sure it would be himself. Now he had to re-think everything if he was to catch the killer and have any chance of seeing Anna alive again. 'You want Sebastian Gibran?' he checked.

'Why so surprised?' he asked. 'Surely you understand there can only be one of us. The world simply isn't big enough for two. Gibran will understand, even if you don't.'

'I can't just hand him over to you,' Sean told him. 'He's a psychiatric patient receiving treatment in Broadmoor. What you're asking for is impossible.'

'What he is, is a cop-killer,' he argued, 'whereas Anna is a completely innocent. A cop-killer for an innocent woman. No one will blame you.'

'Listen,' Sean pleaded with him. 'It's impossible.'

'But the public will demand it,' he insisted.

'The public?' Sean asked. 'What have the public got to do with it?'

'Because they're going to know,' he answered. 'They're going to know everything.'

'How?' Sean demanded.

'I've told your journalist friend Jackson what I want,' he explained, 'and we both know he won't be able to resist printing it. There's no way he'd pass on a story like this, and once he splashes it all over *The World*, the public will demand you give Gibran to me. A sociopathic killer to save an innocent young woman. You'll have no choice. And remember – I'll be checking the newspaper every day, so if you try any tricks I'll know about it because you're going to keep Jackson informed of your every move. If you don't, she dies.'

'You're asking the impossible,' Sean tried to reason with him.

'Then find a way to make it possible,' the voice demanded, 'or you'll never see Anna again and her innocent blood will be on your hands, Sean.'

'Wait,' he tried to stop him hanging up, but it was too late. 'Shit,' he cursed. 'Do you have him?' he asked the technician who'd come to trace the call.

'Somewhere in the West End,' he answered. 'That's all I can say.'

'Great,' he replied, 'Jesus Christ, not Anna,' he begged. But it was too late to stop the unthinkable from happening. It already had. He shook his head to clear his thoughts. If he was going to save her, he would need to think straight and do what he did best. He immediately grabbed his phone and called Anna's number, hoping that by some miracle she would answer, but she didn't. Next, he frantically searched his drawer for Jackson's business card. As soon as he found it, he punched the numbers into his desktop phone – complaining with each unanswered ringing tone. 'For Christ's sake, answer your damn phone.' A few seconds later a familiar voice answered.

'Hello.'

'Jackson,' Sean said through gritted teeth.

'DI Corrigan, what took you so long?'

'What the hell's going on?' Sean demanded.

'He called me, told me not to call you – that you'd be calling me soon as he'd finished speaking to you. Likes to pull the strings, this one.'

'What did he tell you?'

'Told me he'd taken Dr Ravenni-Ceron. He sent me a particularly unpleasant video to prove it. He also said that if you don't hand Sebastian Gibran to him, he's going to kill her. And if you don't provide me with regular updates, or if I don't print those updates, he'll kill her anyway. He also said that if I don't continue to see Gibran and print what he has to say about all this, again, he's going to kill her. Or if he thinks I'm not being truthful—'

'He'll kill her,' Sean finished for him. 'Shit.'

'What do you want me to do?' Jackson surprised him with his cooperative tone.

'You'll have to play along with it for now,' he told him. 'Until I can come up with some ideas.'

'You could always be seen to be doing what he wants,' Jackson suggested. 'Take Gibran out of Broadmoor. Arrange to hand him over in some forest somewhere and take out the killer when he comes for his prize.'

'No,' Sean dismissed the idea. 'He's careful. He likes to be in control. He'd never agree to meet in a location chosen by us. And even if we did get lucky, what about Anna? We may not find her until it's too late. I also have to consider the possibility that he's working with Gibran – that they've found a way to communicate and this whole thing's an elaborate charade to get him out in the open away from his guards so he can make a break for it.'

'An escape attempt?' Jackson asked.

'Gibran's clever enough,' Sean told him, 'and he has enough fans out there. Maybe one has been talked into helping him.'

'Maybe,' Jackson agreed, before remembering something important. 'By the way – there's something else he wants me to do.'

'What?'

'He told me I have to tell Gibran everything,' he explained, 'and write about his reaction in the paper.'

'Christ,' Sean sighed. 'You'd better do it. We've got no choice. But don't print anything until you've run it by me first – and don't give me the usual shit about journalistic material.'

'Fine,' he agreed. 'But what're you going to do, Corrigan?'

'I'll think of something,' he answered and hung up just as Sally and Donnelly walked into the main office. He waved to catch their attention.

'Problem?' Donnelly asked as he entered Sean's room, tugging his coat off.

'Yeah,' Sean told them as he connected the covert phone into his own laptop. 'Our man's been in contact again. He's taken Anna.'

'What?' Sally asked – the blood draining from her face. 'What do you mean he's taken Anna?'

'Abducted her,' he told them brutally.

'How?' Sally asked, feeling dizzy with disbelief.

'I don't know yet,' he admitted, 'but he wanted me to see this.' He pressed play on the phone and spun the laptop around so they could all watch it on a larger screen. 'He says if we don't give him Sebastian Gibran, he'll kill her.'

Sally moved closer to the screen to better see her friend and counsellor. 'Does he really believe we're going to hand Gibran over to be killed?'

'We don't know he intends to kill him,' Sean pointed out, 'but, regardless, it doesn't matter what he believes, it's what he wants that matters.'

'This is not good,' Donnelly said. 'My God, Anna.'

'It gets worse,' Sean explained. 'He's also told Jackson what he wants. We're supposed to brief Jackson on our progress or he'll kill her anyway.'

'Jesus Christ,' Sally moaned. 'Anna should have been protected. We should have been protecting her.'

'Now is not the time to beat ourselves up over what we should have done,' Sean argued. 'No one saw this coming. There was nothing to suggest he would go after her. Nothing.'

'So what do we do?' Donnelly asked.

'We go along with what he says,' Sean told them. 'Agree to his demands.'

'You'll never get authority to swap Gibran for Anna,' Sally argued. 'It's impossible.'

'I didn't say we'd hand Gibran over. I said we go along with it: agree to his demands and look to be cooperating. Buy some time until we can work out how to use it to our advantage and trap this bastard and find Anna.'

'Trap?' Sally questioned, shaking her head. 'He's too smart to be trapped – always ahead of the game. If we try and trap him it could cost Anna her life. Are you prepared to take that chance?'

'We have no choice,' he insisted. 'He has Anna and we all know he'll kill her if we don't do as he says.'

'He'll probably kill her anyway,' Donnelly mournfully said what they were all thinking.

'Maybe,' Sean agreed, 'but we can't think about that. We need to get things started. We need to make him believe we're willing to hand Gibran over so we can draw him into the open, and we need to find out how he took her and where from.' He tapped the phone's screen and played the footage again. 'We know he took her yesterday, right. She was here yesterday morning, so where did she go after that?'

'She said she had to see a client,' Sally remembered. 'She left mid-afternoon.'

'To go to her office?' Sean asked.

'She didn't say,' Sally answered.

'We need to know her movements,' he insisted. 'Did she head to her office, and if so did she make it there? He probably took her from the London area, it's where he knows best. And he put this thing together quickly. Really quickly.'

'You don't think he planned it?' Donnelly asked.

'I don't know. He would have had to spend time researching her – planning how to take her with minimum risk to himself.'

'But he didn't have time,' Sally argued. 'He likes to take a week between victims, but Witney Dennis was only a couple of nights ago. This is not his usual pattern.'

'So maybe he already knew her,' Donnelly suggested. 'Knew her movements and how he could take her.'

'Could be,' Sean nodded, 'and look,' he pointed to the screen. 'It's been edited. There are sections where she's talking that he's edited. She must have been saying something he didn't want us to hear – like where they are or . . . his name.'

'So he does know her,' Sally concluded.

'Has to,' Sean agreed. 'So we need to find out what links them. It's the best chance we've had so far of identifying him, and we need to work out how to trap him. Either way, Addis has to be told. I'll need to put him in the picture and get this thing with Gibran authorized.'

'Think he'll go for it?' she asked.

'He'll have to. He was the one who had Anna attached to the investigation in the first place. He'll agree to anything if it gives us a chance of finding her.' He stopped for a second as he again looked at the screen. 'Where is she anyway?' he asked himself more than Sally. The quality was poor, but as he squinted at the screen he began to notice things for the first time. 'There's something wrong about this place.'

'It's a very small room,' Sally agreed. 'Maybe a house that's been converted into small bedsits,' she offered.

'Maybe,' he said, though it didn't strike him as likely. 'Look at the furniture. The bed is narrower than the average single bed and it looks like it's built on top of something. And here –' he pointed to the horseshoe-shaped bench. 'That's a kitchen bench, but's where's the table? He's either moved it out of the way or it's a foldaway. What type of room has foldaway tables and beds built into the walls?'

'Never go caravanning when you were a kid?' Sally asked, looking closer at the screen.

'No,' he replied.

'It's a caravan,' she told him, 'or a mobile home or maybe even a boat or barge, but it's definitely something like that.'

'OK,' Sean nodded. 'I want every caravan site, canal mooring and boatyard in and around London searched. We'll have to look beyond the Met, so get something out to the surrounding forces too.'

'I'll get on it,' she assured him.

'And get hold of Broadmoor,' he added.

'Why?'

'Tell them to pull Gibran from the general population,' he told her. 'I want him held in isolation until I figure out our next move.'

'They'll probably want a court order,' Sally argued.

'Not if it's for his own protection,' he answered. 'If they think he's at risk, they'll do as they're told. While that's being arranged, I'll talk to Addis.'

'Good luck,' Sally told him.

'Thanks,' he replied. 'When he finds out he's taken Anna, I'm going to need it.' He disconnected the phone from the laptop and headed for the lifts that would take him to the heights of the south tower and Addis's office. A few minutes later he was standing in front of Addis, who was sitting at his desk reading from an open file. After a few seconds, he closed it and looked up at Sean.

'I've got a meeting with the Commander of SO13 in about ten minutes,' Addis warned him, 'so you'd better make this quick – whatever *this* is.'

'This isn't easy to say,' Sean explained, 'but there's been a development – in the investigation.'

'A *development*?' Addis demanded. 'Well don't beat about the bush, Inspector. What is it?'

'The man we're looking for has taken Anna,' he answered.

'He's threatening to kill her unless we hand Sebastian Gibran over to him.'

Addis's jaw fell open. 'What did you say?' he asked.

'I said—' Sean began, but Addis stopped him.

'I heard,' he said, holding up a hand. 'I heard. And who did he make these demands to?'

'To me,' Sean told him. 'Just a few minutes ago.'

'How do we know he's telling the truth?'

'He sent me some footage of Anna from a phone. I have no reason to believe it's not genuine. We've been trying to get hold of Anna, but she's not answering her mobile.'

'My God,' Addis shook his head. 'I don't believe this is happening. Anna has been kidnapped by this lunatic – from under our very noses?'

'There was nothing to make us suspect she was in any danger,' Sean tried to explain. 'His victim type, his method – his obsession with Gibran never suggested he would go after someone like Anna.'

'Then perhaps he's cleverer than you thought,' Addis snarled, 'and you are not as clever as you thought.'

'Maybe you're right,' Sean replied, trying not to let his frayed temper rip.

'And he seriously expects us to hand over Gibran?'

'Yes,' Sean confirmed. 'I believe he does.'

'What is he?' Addis grunted. 'Insane?'

'Very probably,' Sean answered without humour.

'Thank God the media know nothing about it,' Addis said, shaking his head. 'We'd be slaughtered.'

'Unfortunately, they do know about it,' Sean admitted. 'The footage he sent me was also sent to Jackson at *The World*.'

'Wonderful,' Addis threw his hands in the air.

'He insists we keep Jackson informed about what we're doing and that he prints it in *The World* or he'll kill Anna.'

'Are they going to release the film of her.' Addis asked, 'or print still pictures from it in their paper?'

'No,' Sean shook his head. 'I don't think Jackson would do that. He knows we need to work together or she'll die.'

'Work together?' Addis queried.

'We let Jackson run the story that Gibran's being swapped for Anna,' he explained.

'That's impossible,' Addis insisted.

'The real Gibran, yes,' Sean agreed, 'but we don't use Gibran – we use a UC who can pass as Gibran – at least from a distance.'

'And when the suspect realizes it's not Gibran?'

'It'll be too late,' Sean explained. 'He'll have to get close enough to be sure and we can have SO19 ring-fence the entire area. It would give us a decent chance.'

'But if he slips away,' Addis argued, 'and knows he's been set up, then Anna's as good as dead.'

'We need to change our mindset,' Sean told him coldly. 'It's the only way we can use the situation to our advantage.'

'Mindset?' Addis asked.

'That we're doing this to save Anna,' Sean said bluntly, though his heart didn't believe it. 'We need to consider this as a way to catch him – not to save her.'

'Jesus,' Addis stared at him. 'You want to give up on her?'

'I think we need to accept that the only chance Anna has is if we can take him out,' Sean told him. 'If we give him the real Gibran, he'll kill her anyway. If he realizes it's a trap and manages to avoid capture – again she's dead. The only way to save her is to find him and catch him – assuming she's still alive.'

'And if you do catch him,' Addis asked. 'What makes you think he'll tell us where he's keeping her? He could just leave her to die from dehydration or starvation. His last hoorah.'

'He'll tell me where she is,' Sean insisted.

'Really?' Addis questioned, interlocking his fingers. 'Once he's locked up safely in a police station with his solicitor sitting next to him?'

'I wouldn't have to take him straight to a station,' Sean reminded him. 'With a missing woman in imminent danger, I'm within my powers to question him about her whereabouts where and when he's arrested. I'll make him take me to her.'

'I see.' Addis nodded slowly. 'And how would you explain the cuts and bruises? Say he fell down the stairs? This isn't the eighties, Inspector.'

'There are other ways of making him talk,' he insisted. 'There'll be no cuts and bruises.' They stared unspeaking for what seemed an age. 'We have no choice,' Sean broke the silence. 'This is Anna we're talking about. If we don't go through with this, she'll die and he'll remain free.'

Addis drummed his fingers in front of his face for a few seconds. 'Fine,' he agreed. 'Get hold of Jackson and tell him to run the story that we're going give him Gibran. Then go see your old friends in SO10 and find a suitable UC. I'll call the Home Office and let them know we have no such intention before someone has a heart attack.'

'I'll let SO10 know what we're planning,' Sean assured him, getting to his feet. As he did, he felt his phone vibrate, warning of an incoming text message.

'I hope for both our sakes this works,' Addis told him, reaching for his desk phone.

'We'll soon find out,' Sean answered and headed for the door, speaking quietly to himself as he walked: 'One way or the other.'

David Langley rolled his car to a stop next to the concealed caravan and grabbed his rucksack from the passenger seat. He looked around him and listened for any signs of disturbance as he headed to the caravan door and unlocked the padlock. Inside, Anna writhed and struggled, trying to pull away from him, but her bindings and chain held her fast. He dropped the bag on the bed and pulled out the knife, then strode to her side and gripped her hard around the neck. He took a few seconds to imagine how much he was going to enjoy cutting her throat before pulling the tape roughly from her mouth. 'Quiet,' he warned when she cried out in pain.

'Please,' she pleaded, feeling the cold metal of the blade pressed against her cheek.

'I said be quiet,' he repeated. He gave it a few seconds and then cut her ankles free and unchained her from the cooker, lifting her from the floor and dumping her on the bed. 'You need to eat,' he told her as he rummaged in his bag, pulling out a large bottle of water and a tinfoil package. Using his knife tip, he cut a hole in the bottle top. Another rummage in his bag again located the pack of straws he'd bought on the way to see her. He put one through the hole and moved it to touch her lips. 'Here,' he insisted. 'It's water. You have to drink.' She cautiously allowed the straw between her lips and took a nervous sip. Once she was sure it was only water she drank hurriedly and deeply until he pulled it away. 'You can have some more soon,' he promised as he swapped the bottle for the tinfoil – unwrapping it to reveal two sandwiches made with cheap white bread. 'Food,' he told her. 'You need to eat.' He held the sandwich under her nose for her to smell before allowing her to take a small bite. 'Keep going,' he demanded. 'You need to eat it all – keep your strength up.' She did as she was told – taking bite after bite until he pushed the last piece into her mouth, smiling as he watched Corrigan's pet psychiatrist being fed like a child or armless cripple. Again he held the bottle and pushed the straw between her lips so she could drink while he used his other hand to pull his phone from his jacket and begin to film her. Once she'd drunk enough, he took the bottle away and lifted her to her feet, pushing her through the tight space of the caravan.

'Where are you taking me?' she broke her silence.

'You'll need the toilet,' he told her as he slid open the folding door. 'It's right in front of you,' he explained and pushed her inside the tiny enclosure.

'But my hands,' she complained. 'They're tied behind my back and I can't see.'

'You'll manage,' he dismissed her complaints and slid the door noisily shut. He took several deliberately heavy steps backwards then silently crept forward and pressed his ear close to the thin door – listening to her struggling to undo her clothing until finally he heard the sound of her urinating into the toilet. 'Are you finished?' he asked after a few seconds.

'Yes,' came her weak reply.

He yanked the doors apart and grabbed her by the hair – pulling her from the cramped space and forcing her back to the floor next to the cooker.

'Please, David,' she begged. 'Just let me go and I swear I won't tell anyone.'

'Don't move,' he ignored her pleas and went back to the bed where he recovered his knife before taking the roll of insulating tape from his bag.

'I know you have children,' she told him. 'I know you do. Please – stop what you're doing and think of your children.'

He stalled for a few seconds, staring at her. 'In time they will understand,' he eventually replied and tore a strip of the tape from the roll. He moved towards her and slapped the tape over her mouth just as she was about to reply. She tried to speak through her tears and the tape, but he dragged her up against the cooker and chained her to it. 'I'll bring more food and water soon,' he told her before packing up his rucksack and leaving the caravan without looking at her again.

Sebastian Gibran sat in his room inside Broadmoor maximum security hospital staring out of the window at the rain falling outside. The simple furnishings were not what he'd been used to on the outside, but they were pleasant enough, as was the room – like a cut-price hotel room, only bigger and lighter – a far cry from the sort of room he would have been locked in if he'd been found guilty of his crimes and sent to Brixton or Wandsworth prison, instead of being declared insane. Here his door would usually have been left unlocked, although the eyes of the staff and CCTV constantly watched him and the other patients, but this morning he along with everyone else had been locked inside their rooms. Medication, therapy and discipline usually kept the hospital quiet and tranquil, except for occasional outbursts of violent insanity from individuals, but today the entire institution seemed disturbed, as a cacophony of screams and shouts permeated from every room. Above the bedlam he heard the turning of the lock in the door behind him – his eyes shifting towards the sound although his head and body remained rigidly still. Moments later he sensed the door opening and another presence in the room. He breathed in their aura and their scent and immediately knew who it was. 'Nurse Rollins,' he said without looking. 'How kind of you to check in on me.'

'I'm checking in on everyone,' the burly nurse who accompanied Gibran to all his appointments replied. 'Something's got the wildlife excited.'

'Indeed it has,' Gibran answered, staring calmly out of the window.

'All except for you,' the nurse said. 'Any idea what's going on?'

'Ah,' Gibran sighed, nodding his head. He considered killing the burly nurse – to punish him for his foolishness in entering his room alone – smash his head on the floor until his brains spilt from his skull, but the unfolding game was too interesting to risk missing. The nurse would live – at least for one more day. 'Their insanity has made them perceptive to things you can only imagine. They all sense it. It has them very agitated. I fear you'll have your work cut out, these next few days.'

380

'Why?' the nurse asked. 'Why are they so *agitated*?'

'The coming of a man who would be king,' Gibran answered.

'What the hell's that supposed to mean?'

'Never mind,' Gibran told him. 'Now, is there anything else I can do for you, Nurse Rollins?'

'Yes,' Rollins answered. 'You're being moved to solitary confinement.'

'May I ask why?' Gibran enquired.

'All I've been told is it's for your own safety,' Rollins replied. 'You need to pack some things – toiletries, clothes and you might want to take some of your books. I don't know how long you're going to be there for.'

'Of course,' Gibran calmly agreed. 'I'll just need a few minutes.'

Sean and Sally knocked on the front door of an attractive terraced house in Chiswick, West London. After a short wait, it was opened by a short stocky young woman with long blond hair wearing an inexpensive suit. They all immediately recognized each other as being police, but Sean showed her his warrant card anyway. 'DI Sean Corrigan. SIU.'

Sally kept her warrant card in her pocket. 'DS Sally Jones from the same.'

'Sir. Sarge,' the woman acknowledged them. 'DC Annie Doyle. Wandsworth CID – family liaison officer until someone tells me different. You'd better come in.' She stepped inside, allowing them to enter the spacious hallway. Sean scanned the walls, stylishly decorated with prints and paintings, along with framed photographs of Anna with her husband. His mind flashed back to guilty memories of the brief moment three years ago when he and Anna had entwined their limbs together in her office as they kissed – both wanting more until Anna had stopped it going too far. 'Husband's in the kitchen – Charlie,' Doyle explained. 'Upset and confused.

381

Says his wife was working with the police. Says she was working with you.'

'She was,' Sean admitted. 'She is.'

'So you know her husband?' Doyle asked.

'No,' Sean answered. 'We've never met.'

'Lead the way,' Sally intervened.

'Down here.' Doyle led the way deeper into the house until they all emerged into a modern, open-plan kitchen bathed in light from every angle and fitted with every appliance imaginable. In all the time he'd known Anna, Sean had never seen inside her house – not even in a photograph. So this was how she lived: surrounded by the trappings of wealth in a beautiful house twice the size of his own. Would she have ever seriously considered giving all this up to have a chance with him? Anna's husband stood as soon as they entered. 'Mr Hadfield,' Doyle said, nodding towards Sean and Sally. 'This is DI Corrigan and DS Jones from the Special Investigations Unit. They need to speak with you.'

'You're the ones she's been working with,' Hadfield practically accused them before they could speak. 'I thought she was safe,' he continued, his face tense with fear and anger. 'She said she was safe and now she's missing and nobody will tell me a damn thing.'

'I promise I'll tell you everything,' Sean promised, 'but we need to ask you some questions first.'

'Questions?' Hadfield complained. 'Why do you want to waste time asking me questions? You just need to find her.'

'Please,' Sean pleaded. 'We're as desperate to find her as you are. Believe me.'

Hadfield eyed them suspiciously for a few seconds. 'Fine. Ask your questions.'

'When was the last time you heard from her?' Sean began.

'Yesterday morning. She left to go to Scotland Yard about seven thirty.'

'No phone calls after that, no texts?' Sean checked.

'No,' Hadfield shrugged. 'She knew I had a busy day of surgery ahead and I rarely bother her when she's at work.'

Sean couldn't help but wonder what kind of relationship they had if they rarely contacted each other during the day, then remembered that he and Kate didn't either. 'So nothing since yesterday morning?' he clarified. 'Nothing at all?'

'No,' Hadfield shrugged, looking slightly awkward. 'Nothing. Look, we don't live in each other's pockets. We both have pretty demanding jobs.'

'I understand,' Sean played along, 'but weren't you concerned when she didn't come home last night?'

'I didn't get home until late myself,' Hadfield explained. 'After midnight. I went straight to bed. It's not unusual for Anna to come home very late. Especially since she's been working with you. When I woke up this morning and she still wasn't home I began to become concerned, but before I could start making phone calls your colleagues arrived and told me that she was missing.'

'Can you think of anything she may have said?' Sean dug deeper. 'Was she concerned about anyone? Anyone giving her a hard time? Did she feel she was being watched or followed?'

'No,' Hadfield shook his head. 'Definitely not. She would have said.'

'Someone at work then?' Sean persisted. 'A patient that may have concerned her?'

'We didn't discuss her patients,' Hadfield insisted. 'Client confidentiality. If you want to know about her patients you need to speak to her secretary, Lizzie.'

'I have people on their way to see her now,' Sean told him, 'but for the moment is there anything you can think of that was unusual or strange. Anything out of the ordinary that's happened recently that we need to know?'

'No. Except that she was working with you again. Now

you said that if I answered your questions you'd tell me everything. I want to know everything.'

'The man we're looking for,' Sean explained, 'the man Anna was trying to help us find, has attacked three people that we know of so far. I'm afraid the people he attacked were killed.'

'No,' he shook his head frantically. 'No. She's not dead.'

'No, she's not,' Sally quickly intervened. 'We know she's not dead.'

'I don't understand,' he said, his eyes filling with tears, 'what are you telling me?'

'We believe that the man who killed those three people has taken your Anna,' she explained. 'He sent us some video footage of her being held somewhere – possibly a boat or caravan, but she was alive and appeared uninjured.'

'Do you know anyone who owns a caravan or boat or anything like that?' Sean asked. 'Anyone who knows Anna?'

'No,' he shook his head. 'We're not into that sort of thing.'

'OK,' Sean let it go, sure he couldn't help. 'We're checking everything we can,' he tried to reassure him.

'I understand,' Hadfield said, 'but you still haven't told me why he's taken Anna.'

Sean took a breath. 'He's making demands.'

'Demands?' Hadfield asked. 'What demands? Money?'

'No,' Sean explained.

'Then what?' Hadfield demanded.

'He wants us to release an inmate from Broadmoor,' he elaborated.

'Broadmoor?' Hadfield questioned. 'Who?'

'Sebastian Gibran,' Sean admitted.

'My God, I've heard of him,' he replied, sounding shocked. 'He's insane. He's a murderer. What the hell has he got to do with Anna?'

'We don't know,' Sean lied.

'But if you release him, he'll let Anna go?' he asked.

'That's what he's saying,' Sean answered.

'Why does he want him freed?'

'We're not sure,' he lied again.

'Christ,' Hadfield said, running his hands through his hair.

'We're doing everything we can to find her,' Sean tried to assure him.

'Just bring her back to me,' he pleaded.

'I will,' Sean told him. 'I promise. For now, DC Doyle will stay with you. As soon as we have any news, we'll be in touch.'

'You should have protected her,' he accused them. 'She should have had a bodyguard. She's not a cop, yet you let her help you find these animals without any protection. If she hadn't been helping you, she would never have been taken.'

'We had no idea she was in danger,' Sean tried to explain. 'If I had – I'd have never left her alone.'

'But you did leave her alone,' Hadfield twisted the knife, 'and now this madman has her.'

'Yes,' Sean admitted. 'Yes, he does, and now I need to find him.' He spun on his heels and headed towards the hallway.

'We'll do everything we can,' Sally told him. 'Anna . . . Anna is my friend,' she added before she walked from the kitchen followed by Doyle. When they reached the front door, Sean turned to Doyle and handed her a business card.

'You need anything, call me,' he told her as she took the card from him. 'If he thinks of anything I need to know straight away. I'm a little short on Family Liaison Officers at the moment, but when I can free one up I'll get you relieved.'

'Don't worry about it,' Doyle assured him. 'I'd rather see it through, if that's all right.'

'Fine,' Sean nodded. 'I'll speak to your DCI and get it sorted out. Welcome to the SIU.'

He set off towards the car in silence.

'You can understand why he's angry,' Sally said.

Sean was about to answer when his mobile rang. He leaned

against the car, wrestled the phone from his belt and checked the caller ID. It was Donnelly.

'I'm at Anna's office,' Donnelly told him. 'Talking with her secretary, Lizzy.'

'And?' Sean hurried him.

'Anna came here yesterday about four o'clock to see a client,' he continued. 'He was the only client she saw.'

'Do you have a name?' Sean asked, the excitement swelling in his chest.

'Aye,' Donnelly answered. 'David Langley.'

'Previous?' Sean hurriedly asked.

'No,' Donnelly answered. 'Nothing. Looks like he's clean.'

'False name?' Sean checked.

'Not according to Anna's secretary,' Donnelly explained. 'Langley was referred to her by his GP, who he's been with for years, and then there are National Insurance numbers and NHS patient numbers. All very difficult to falsify. It looks like Langley is who he says he is. And then there's the CCTV.'

'CCTV?' Sean repeated.

'Aye,' Donnelly told him. 'The underground car park where Anna left her car is covered by CCTV. We've had a look at it. A red Vauxhall Vectra enters the car park about two hours before Anna is taken.'

'*Our* Vauxhall Vectra?' Sean interrupted.

'Could be, but it's on different plates,' Donnelly explained. 'The driver looks like our man, though: tall, slim, hood pulled up so he can't be identified – carrying a rucksack. So he parks up and makes his way out of the car park back into the street. About an hour and forty minutes later he returns and hides behind a pillar right next to Anna's car. Twenty minutes after that Anna enters the car park and makes her way to her car, only she can't get in the driver's door because he's blocked it, so she goes around to the passenger's side and that's when he jumps her.' Suddenly Donnelly stalled.

'Go on,' Sean encouraged him.

'Next bit's not going to be easy for you to hear,' Donnelly warned him.

'I need to know,' Sean insisted.

'Aye,' Donnelly agreed. 'Aye, I suppose you do. He steps out from behind the pillar and . . . and he hits her in the jaw. He hits her hard. She goes straight down. Unconscious.'

'Christ,' Sean said, closing his eyes, trying to stay focused on the investigation instead of letting his feelings for Anna and his fears for her now overwhelm him.

'He drags her to the boot of his car and uses a roll of tape to secure her hands and feet and he tapes her mouth and eyes too.'

'Bastard,' Sean muttered, opening his eyes and staring up into the winter sky.

'He then lifts her into the boot, gets into the car and drives off,' Donnelly continued. 'But here's the thing – you need a special token to exit the car park – to get the shutter up – so he must have had one. Anyone can enter, you just press the button, but you can't get out without a token.'

'How do you get a token?' Sean asked, squinting with concentration.

'You collect one from whoever you're visiting and slot it into the machine to exit,' Donnelly told him. 'Anna's secretary kept some for Anna's clients.'

'Are they timed and dated?' Sean asked.

'No,' Donnelly answered. 'They're reusable. Once a week the caretaker empties the machine and returns the tokens to whoever they belong to.'

'Shit,' Sean complained.

'There's something else,' Donnelly told him. 'This David Langley guy – Anna's secretary tells me he didn't use a car yesterday. He has on previous visits, but yesterday he was on foot. She let him in through the external intercom, so whoever was driving the Vectra, it doesn't look like it was him.'

'Maybe,' Sean partially agreed. 'We need to speak to him anyway.'

'Naturally,' Donnelly conceded. 'What you want me to do now?'

'Seize all CCTV from the block,' Sean instructed, 'and any from outside. It may show us something we haven't thought of yet.'

'Will do,' Donnelly agreed. 'And the Vectra?'

'Probably false plates again,' Sean admitted, 'but run them through the PNC anyway and speak with the owner. You got an address for Langley?'

'Aye,' Donnelly replied. 'Home and work.'

Sean glanced at his watch. This time of day, Langley was most likely at work. 'Text me both,' he told him. 'Sally and I'll go pay him a visit. There may be more to him than first appears.'

'Aye,' Donnelly agreed. 'If we're lucky.'

'Keep me informed,' Sean told him and hung up. 'Come on,' he said to Sally and started to climb into their car.

'Where we going?'

'Get in,' he told her. 'I'll explain on the way.'

Addis sat at a table in the restaurant of the Dean Street Town House in Soho – an exclusive and expensive establishment. He'd swapped his uniform for a dark grey tailored suit and looked much like any other executive that haunted the trendy establishment. He looked up from his glass of ice-cold water at Geoff Jackson sitting opposite him.

'Interesting place to meet,' Jackson said. 'Thought this place was for the artistic types – actors, movie people – that sort.'

'I know a lot of people,' Addis told him. 'Many of whom owe me a favour or two. Let's just say I called in one of those favours, so we could meet somewhere a bit more private.'

'Very nice it is too,' Jackson replied, 'but couldn't we have spoken over the phone?'

'I don't like to handle sensitive business over the phone,' Addis explained. 'Sometimes face to face is better, don't you think?'

'I thought I'd be dealing directly with DI Corrigan,' Jackson ignored the question, knowing that Addis was letting him know he didn't trust him.

'DI Corrigan's busy with other matters relating to the investigation,' Addis explained, 'and I thought it was time you and I talked.'

'So,' Jackson spread his arms wide, 'here we are.'

Addis leaned forward and lowered his voice. 'We know you have the hostage footage of Dr Ravenni-Ceron.'

'It was me that told Corrigan. So what of it?'

'I need your word that you won't release it to anyone in any way,' Addis insisted, 'and I mean *anyone.*'

'I came by the film in the normal pursuit of being a journalist,' Jackson pushed back, unwilling to be intimidated by anyone, even Addis. 'It's protected journalistic material. I could use it if I wanted to. You couldn't touch me.'

'Don't quote the law to me, Jackson,' Addis warned him. 'Trust me – the law is very, very grey and I'm an expert at exploiting those grey areas. You'd be surprised how many people live in the grey world. I should imagine some very senior people connected to your newspaper can be found there who wouldn't want to appear to be morally compromised. It would be unfortunate if I had to speak to them.'

'I'm not going to use the footage,' Jackson told him, swallowing his anger. 'Unlike some people, I know the difference between what's wrong and what's right. The only person I ever put in harm's way is me. You should have researched me properly, Mr Addis. I handed you that celebrity paedophile ring on a plate, but I never made a penny out of it. You should have seen what I was being offered to write the book or help make the documentary. So don't preach to me about morals. I'm an investigative journalist. I expose the truth even when the establishment doesn't want me to. Can you say the same?'

'Sometimes it's my job to protect the establishment,' Addis replied, 'but perhaps not today.'

'What do you want from me?' Jackson demanded.

'Your cooperation,' Addis smiled. 'I need you to run the story that we are preparing to exchange Gibran for Dr Ravenni-Ceron.'

'You'll never be allowed to do that,' Jackson argued. 'Even Gibran has human rights. It's impossible.'

'And if I was to tell you we *are* going to make the exchange?' Addis asked.

'I wouldn't believe you,' Jackson answered.

'But you'd run the story?'

'No,' Jackson insisted. 'I'm not knowingly going to lie. I know you're not going to exchange Gibran for Ceron.'

'That's what I thought,' Addis said, smiling and reaching for a silver pot on the table. 'Coffee?'

'No thanks,' Jackson replied, not wanting to be in Addis's debt for so much as a cup of coffee.

'Very well,' Addis continued as he poured himself a cup.

'So what now?' Jackson asked.

'You say you won't knowingly lie to your readers,' Addis reminded him.

'No,' he confirmed. 'No I won't.'

'But that's exactly what I need you to do, Mr Jackson,' Addis told him calmly.

'What are you talking about?' Jackson demanded.

'I need to be able to trust you,' Addis replied and sipped from his cup. 'Can I trust you, Mr Jackson?'

'Depends what with,' he answered.

'An innocent woman's life,' Addis put the hook in. 'You see, we've no intention of handing over Gibran to anyone, but we can use it to try and trap the man we're looking for and release Dr Ravenni-Ceron.'

'How are you going to do that?' Jackson asked. 'You going to use a double for Gibran? Try and draw the killer in close enough to make a grab for him?'

'You don't need to know the details,' Addis told him. 'You just need to run the story that the exchange is genuine. Make the killer believe it's really going to happen. And when it's all over, I'll personally give you full disclosure on how the operation unfolded – as much detail as I can. You'll have complete exclusivity.'

'So, lie to my readers?'

'Not really,' Addis argued. 'You'll be part of the bigger story and when it's all over you can tell your readers everything – how you and *The World* helped capture a killer and save an innocent woman.'

'It's my job to report the news,' he said. 'Not become part of it.'

'But you don't always stick to those rules, do you, Mr Jackson?' Addis reminded him. 'Your dangerous liaisons with Jeremy Goldsboro, for example.'

'That was different,' Jackson insisted.

'Barely,' Addis smiled.

Jackson was quiet for a long while, considering. 'I'll need to be there for the arrest.'

'Difficult,' Addis told him. 'There'll be armed officers involved. I'll try to get you close, but I can't promise anything. What I can promise is that the arrest and release of Dr Ravenni-Ceron will be filmed, and the footage can be sent to you within minutes of it being taken.'

Again, Jackson thought for a long time. 'You're going to be under a lot of pressure once I run the story.'

'Only from a few do-gooders,' Addis smiled. 'I can handle them. It's not as if the masses will be up in arms. They'd no doubt welcome Gibran being handed over to save an innocent woman. Poetic justice and all that.'

'OK,' Jackson finally agreed after another pause for

thought. 'Fine. I'll run the story and you guarantee me exclusivity.'

'Agreed.'

'And I get the arrest and rescue footage within minutes of real time?'

'As promised.'

'Will Corrigan be making the arrest?'

'No,' Addis insisted. 'It'll be SO19 or the TSG. Corrigan will take over after the suspect's been secured. Why do you ask?'

'No reason,' he lied. 'Just this is his investigation.'

'No,' Addis reminded him. 'This is a Metropolitan Police investigation.'

'Of course,' Jackson smiled as he got to his feet. 'Thanks for the chat.'

'Don't cross me, Mr Jackson,' Addis warned him as a parting gesture. 'That would not be wise.'

Sean and Sally entered the furniture store in Wandsworth and scanned the interior for signs of life. Towards the back of the shop they saw Langley busy with a female customer in her early forties. Even from a distance, they could see that Langley was laying on the charm and that it was having an effect on the smiling woman.

'Want to go interrupt?' Sally asked quietly.

'No,' Sean replied in little more than a whisper. 'Let's have a look around until he's finished.'

'OK,' she agreed. 'We looking for something specific?'

'Anything out of place. You'll know it when you see it.'

'Fair enough,' Sally shrugged, 'but he might not want to admit he saw her yesterday. Some people are very private about receiving counselling,' she told him. 'What if he says he never saw her? You going to arrest him?'

'Maybe,' he answered.

'Then you must think he could have been involved,' she insisted. 'Despite what Dave told you about the car.'

'I just want to speak to him,' Sean assured her. 'See how he reacts.'

'Well, now's your chance,' she told him, nodding towards Langley as the woman turned away from him, heading towards the exit, watched all the way by Langley. He didn't seem to notice them until she was gone – the smile falling from his face for a second as he stared straight at Sean as if he was seeing an unwelcome person from his past, but within a few seconds the smile was back as he approached them.

'Good afternoon,' he greeted them. 'Are you looking for something in particular?'

'Nice-looking woman,' Sean said, looking over his shoulder at the door the female customer had just walked through.

'Excuse me?' Langley asked.

'Your customer,' he explained, trying to keep Langley off balance. 'She was nice-looking.'

'Yes,' Langley smiled. 'I suppose so. Sorry, but do I know you? You look very familiar.'

'I don't think so,' Sean answered, convinced there was more to Langley than a salesman with an eye for pretty women and that the game between them had begun.

'I'm sure I recognize you,' Langley insisted, his eyes narrowing as he pretended to try and remember where from. 'Of course,' he suddenly beamed. 'I've seen photographs of you in the newspaper. You're a detective, right?'

'Detective Inspector Corrigan,' Sean replied. 'Special Investigations Unit.' He pulled his warrant card from his coat's breast pocket, flashed it and quickly put it away again.

'DS Jones,' Sally introduced herself without bothering to show her identification. 'From the same.'

'Yes,' Langley nodded. 'You're investigating the one who's killing the homeless people?'

'They weren't all homeless,' Sean corrected him.

'No,' Langley accepted. 'I don't really know much about it, to be honest. Only what I hear on the news or see in the papers. So, what brings you to my store? Has something happened around here?'

'Your psychiatrist,' Sean told him while trying to read the significance of every word Langley said. 'Dr Ravenni-Ceron.'

'Anna,' Langley said, shaking his head. 'What's Anna got to do with anything?'

'She's missing,' Sean played along.

'Missing?' Langley acted confused. 'What do you mean missing?'

'As in she hasn't been seen since leaving her office yesterday,' Sean answered.

'I saw her yesterday,' Langley admitted. 'I had an afternoon appointment at her office. She seemed fine.'

'She was fine,' Sean told him, 'but she hasn't been seen since shortly after you left.'

'Do you think something's happened to her?' Langley's face was a picture of concern. 'Has this got something to do with the man who's been killing people? The man you're investigating?'

'What was your relationship with Dr Ravenni-Ceron?' Sean tried to move on and keep Langley unbalanced.

'Business-like,' he answered, spreading his arms as if it should have been obvious to them. 'She's my counsellor. I've been having some . . . difficulties, and she was helping me. We had no personal relationship, if that's what you mean.'

'So why were you seeing her?' Sean asked, knowing Langley didn't have to answer if he didn't want to.

'I don't believe I have to tell you,' he smiled. 'What's discussed between a doctor and patient is confidential, isn't it?'

'Do you have something to hide?' Sean pushed, hoping for a reaction that could tell him what he needed to know about the man in front of him. For a moment Langley was stony-faced – emotionless and lifeless, but suddenly he returned to the cooperative, friendly guy he wanted them to believe he was. 'My wife and I split up a few years ago,' he explained. 'I'm a single man. I have my job and my kids. My wife burnt me pretty badly. I've had some trouble dealing with the marriage break-up. Depression. Anxiety. My GP said I should speak to someone, so I did.'

'Anna?' Sean clarified.

'Yes,' he shrugged.

'What made you choose her specifically?' Sean continued.

'Great reviews,' Langley assured them. 'She was highly recommended.'

'And you've seen her how many times?'

'Yesterday was my sixth consultation,' he answered, sounding slightly confused.

'And you were seeing her privately?' Sean clarified.

'Yes,' Langley shrugged. 'Meaning?'

'Must be very expensive,' Sean said, looking around the smallish shop. 'Why didn't you see someone through the NHS and save yourself a small fortune?'

'The NHS has a six-month waiting list, Inspector,' Langley answered. 'I wasn't in a position to wait six months.'

'Or maybe you went private so you could choose to see Dr Ravenni-Ceron?' Sean accused him.

'And why would I want to do that?'

'So you could get to know her. Get to know her office and her movements.'

'You haven't told me what's happened to her.' Langley ignored Sean's accusations.

'I'm sorry, we can't,' Sally intervened. 'It's confidential.'

'Well,' Langley smiled, 'I hope she's all right.'

'Me too,' Sean said, his eyes locked with Langley's. 'How did you get to Swiss Cottage? Drive?'

'No,' Langley replied, still calm and in control. 'I took a bus to East Putney tube station and the underground from there.'

'What bus?' Sean hurried him, hoping for a stutter or a mistake.

'The 317,' he answered without hesitation. 'And then the district line to Earl's Court, where I changed to the circle line to Baker Street and another change to the Jubilee Line to Swiss Cottage.'

'Long journey,' Sean pointed out. 'Couldn't you find someone closer?'

'It's not that far,' Langley smiled, 'and I wanted the anonymity of seeing someone who wasn't local. I didn't want to risk my wife finding out and using it as a reason to deny me access to my children.'

'We understand,' Sally tried to soften the questioning while Sean stared long and hard into Langley's eyes looking in vain for a glimmer of something. He began to think that either his first instincts about Langley were wrong or he was so polished and convincing that he could persuade anyone he was merely a forty-something divorcee looking to get his life back on track.

'We have to check these things out,' Sean eventually told him. 'Just in case.'

'Of course,' Langley replied, nodding his head in understanding. 'Just in case.'

'One last thing,' Sean asked him. 'Do you own a car?'

'No,' Langley replied, shaking his head. 'Not much point in London any more.'

'OK,' Sean finished, knowing further questioning wouldn't help him be sure of Langley's guilt or innocence. Not this time. 'Thanks for your time. Sorry if some of the questions were a little personal.'

'No need to apologize,' Langley told him. 'I mean, you have to be sure, don't you? Absolutely sure.'

Sean stared at him hard, trying to work out what Langley was trying to say to him. Or was he mocking him? 'We'll be in touch,' he eventually said. 'If you think of anything, you can contact us through Scotland Yard.'

'Of course,' Langley smiled.

'Thanks again,' Sally told him before following Sean out of the store and towards their car. 'Gave him a bit of a heavy ride,' she complained. 'You actually think he could be our man?'

'Maybe I just didn't like him,' he answered.

'Why not?' she asked. 'Seemed like a decent guy – co-operative. Didn't even get stroppy when you were giving him a hard time.'

'I had the feeling he was trying to manipulate us,' Sean warned her. 'Turning on the charm when he had to. The same way the man we're after does. Remember, he gets to know his victims first. Wins their trust.'

'Jesus,' Sally exclaimed. 'You do like him for it.'

'Maybe,' he admitted. 'I'm not sure.'

'You can't arrest him,' Sally insisted. 'You've got nothing on him.'

'I know,' he agreed. 'Maybe a surveillance team. It could lead us to Anna.'

'You haven't got enough to get a surveillance team authorized,' Sally argued. 'I mean, what have you got? He saw Anna yesterday sometime before she was taken. And he was on foot, remember? That won't persuade many.'

'Maybe I can convince Addis,' he replied.

'You're going to need a surveillance team for the decoy operation you want to try,' she reminded him. 'Addis isn't going to give you a second one to follow this guy around.'

'I guess not,' he reluctantly agreed. 'Get hold of DVLC and see if there are any vehicles registered to Langley's address.'

'We usually give them a vehicle and they give us a name and address,' Sally reminded him.

'See if they can do it the other way round,' he insisted.

'OK,' she agreed. 'What next?'

'Only thing I can do,' he told her. 'I go see Gibran.'

Sally's hand immediately went to her chest and the wounds

that lay beneath her clothing. 'I can't see him,' she insisted. 'I'm sorry. I just can't.'

'No problem,' Sean told her. He knew that Gibran would only seize the opportunity to torture Sally about what he'd done to her. 'I'll take Dave.'

'Fine,' she said, sighing with relief, 'and remember, this is Anna we're trying to find. We have to tread carefully. Do things by the book. We don't want to spook anyone. If we do, there's no telling what he might do to her.'

'This one doesn't spook,' Sean told her, 'but if he hurts her – when I find him . . .'

'Put your feelings to one side, Sean,' she warned him. 'If we're going to find Anna then we need you thinking straight. Revenge can wait for another time.'


Geoff Jackson went to one of the last remaining public phone kiosks in Wapping. It wasn't far from his office and he'd used it many times in the past when he couldn't trust his own mobile phone or the landline on his desk. The meeting with Addis had left him feeling that precautions were necessary. He only wished it had been an old-style booth he could have sheltered from the biting wind in, but the kiosk would have to do. He pressed the numbers he'd memorized into the phone and waited for an answer. A long time and several curses later, someone spoke on the other end.

'Broadmoor Psychiatric Hospital.'

'Yeah,' he replied. 'I need to speak with a patient. Sebastian Gibran. He's kept in the Personality Disorder Directorate.'

'Access to patients in the Directorate is restricted,' the male voice told him. 'You'll need permission from the board of directors.'

'Listen, I have permission from the board. My name is Geoff Jackson. I'm a journalist from *The World* newspaper and I've been doing a series of interviews, but now I need to speak to him on the phone. It's urgent. Check with the

Medical Director – Dr Rachel Thorpe. She'll confirm I have access to Gibran.'

'You'll have to wait,' the voice told him.

'Fine,' he agreed. 'I'll hold.' A second later he was listening to a crackling instrumental version of 'Bridge Over Troubled Water'. 'Come on,' he complained after waiting for more than a minute.

'Hello,' the voice came back on the line.

'I'm here,' Jackson told him.

'Unfortunately, Mr Gibran has been moved to an isolation room,' the voice explained. 'I'm afraid it won't be possible for you to speak to him today.'

'You don't understand,' Jackson warned him. 'It's vitally important that I speak to him right now. I know you can get a phone to him. Dr Rachel Thorpe. Speak to her. She'll authorize it.'

'Very well,' the voice told him. 'You'll have to hold again.'

'Dr Rachel Thorpe,' he reminded him. This time he was subjected to the muzak for even longer, shuffling from foot to foot in an effort to keep warm, constantly muttering to himself as he waited, praying he'd be put through. 'Come on, come on.'

'Hello,' the voice returned.

'Yes, yes,' he replied. 'I'm here.'

'I'm putting you through now,' the voice told him. 'It's a direct line to Mr Gibran's room.'

'Fine,' Jackson agreed. A second later he was listening to the ringing tone, then the familiar voice spoke.

'Mr Jackson,' Gibran greeted him. 'These are interesting times.'

'Excuse me?'

'First I'm moved to an isolation room and now I'm receiving a phone call from you.'

'Do you know why you've been moved to isolation?'

'Something to do with our mutual friend,' Gibran told him.

'Has anyone spoken to you?'

'No,' Gibran answered, 'but I detect the hand of someone I haven't seen in quite some time.'

'You mean Corrigan?'

'The very same,' Gibran replied. 'Have I made our friend angry?' he asked cheerfully. 'Has he threatened to kill me?'

'Listen, there are a lot of things happening out here. I wouldn't be surprised if you get a visit from someone very soon.'

'Corrigan?' he asked, the anticipation thick in his voice.

'Yes,' Jackson confirmed. 'No matter what he says – no matter what he suggests, go along with it. Cooperate.'

'Cooperate,' he repeated. 'I'm intrigued.'

'Play along and it could be to your advantage,' Jackson tried to entice him.

After a few seconds of silence, Gibran replied, 'Very well, Mr Jackson. I'll *cooperate*.'

'Good,' Jackson told him. 'You won't—' he heard the line go dead before he could say, 'regret it'. He hung up and looked around at the few people hurrying along the freezing street – collars turned up against the wind. For a moment he was envious of their ignorance of the world that existed parallel to their own. The mean, ugly world where monsters that looked like men killed innocent people simply because they were in the wrong place at the wrong time. But as quickly as the thought came, it disappeared. The dark world was where he thrived. He pulled his coat tight and hurried back towards his office.

Hour after hour, Anna waited for sounds of approaching footsteps or the creak of the door opening, unsure what she feared most – the continuing silence or his return. If the silence was never broken then she knew she would die of dehydration, but if it was it could mean he'd returned to kill her. She knew he'd almost certainly never let her go – not

400

without dooming himself to many years in prison. Terrified as she was, her ability to read people like Langley hadn't deserted her: she knew his best chance of avoiding being caught would be to kill her. He'd crossed the line of no return. Unless she escaped or was rescued, she faced certain death. For the first time in her life she longed to hear the sound of approaching sirens. Living in London, she heard their screaming wail dozens of times a day without ever thinking about them, but now she prayed to hear their sound at least one more time.

Chained to something that felt like cold heavy metal and with her eyes, mouth and hands taped, she was deprived of any senses except smell and hearing. She had become attuned to every sound, from the wind in the trees outside to the noise of her own movement reverberating in this enclosed, barren place. The hours of blackness had fuelled her fear to the point of panic. She took a breath through her nose and twisted her head as far as she could until her cheek rested against the smooth metal surface behind her. She moved as much as she could, trying to find a corner or protrusion she could catch the tape on, but there was nothing.

She took another deep breath and pushed hard with her legs, raising her face higher along the metal panel until at last she reached something that felt like a handle. In desperation, she started to scrape her temple backwards and forwards on the edge of the handle, praying it would catch before her legs gave way and she collapsed to the floor. Just as they were about to fail her, the tape caught and pulled away – only a few millimetres, but enough to encourage her and fill her legs with a new-found strength as she repeatedly scraped her eyebrow across the handle until her blindfold came away from one eye, enough for her to see for the first time since he'd taken her. Now that she could see what she'd been using to peel the tape away she was able to improve her technique, but she was still only able to uncover one eye. It was enough.

Exhausted, hungry and burning with thirst, she allowed herself to sink to the floor again and take stock of her situation and surroundings.

She saw the bigger picture first: she was being held in an old caravan. The fact that she'd heard no signs of life meant she was somewhere far from any campsite; even in winter there'd be someone around. Next she saw that she was chained to a small cooker, but that it was a fixed appliance and any attempt to rip it free would be futile. After that she looked at her ankles and wrists, which had been bound together with thick insulating tape, and again she knew that trying to free herself would be a waste of time and energy. Finally, she started to see the smaller details. The caravan was old, dating back to the seventies, but the duvet on the small bed was new and clean. The electric heater that had kept her from freezing was a modern design, as were the lights that had been wired into a new-looking battery, so either he still used the caravan regularly, or he'd prepared it just for her. She took a deep breath at the thought of him getting it ready – planning how he would keep her there until he got what he wanted.

*What he wanted*, she repeated in her mind. What did he want? If he was going to kill her, wouldn't he have done it by now? Tortured her, raped her, mutilated her and killed her? But everything he was doing said he wasn't interested in her – that she was being used to get him what he really wanted. And what he wanted was Sebastian Gibran. He was using her to blackmail Sean into giving him Gibran. She felt a moment of relief until she realized it meant nothing. Whether he had Gibran or not – he'd still kill her.

Depression swept over her until something caught her eye, distracting her – photographs of a middle-aged man who was vaguely familiar with a boy in various stages of youth who she also thought she somehow recognized. Her eyes flicked from one photograph to another until she recognized the boy when he was a teenager. It was Langley. And the man who looked a lot like the boy had to be his father.

Most of the pictures appeared innocent enough – a boy and his father with arms around each other's shoulders – but some were more sinister. The boy drinking beer from cans alongside his approving father. Others of them in the forest crouched over dead rabbits and squirrels, each brandishing evil-looking hunting knives, while others depicted both proudly showing off their bows and arrows. Only these were unlike any she'd seen, more compact and curved, one way then the other, with multiple strings and a system of circular pulleys on the tip of each end. They looked more like militarized weapons than something used for target practice or hunting.

The thought of Langley killing animals with his bow and then skinning them with a knife sent panic ripping through her. She thrashed against her restraints wildly until she was exhausted and bruised, her attempt to free herself completely futile. She would have to think of something else or be killed in the woods, like the other animals speared and skinned by Langley.

Sean and Donnelly parked in the car park outside Broadmoor maximum security psychiatric hospital and looked up at the foreboding red-brick building, the main entrance an arc above which the famous clock tower was perched, flanked by two towers peppered with tall, thin, arched windows, most of which were covered by lattices of white bars. The entire entrance stood behind a security gate made from a solid metal frame and wire mesh.

'Jesus,' Donnelly complained. 'I hate this place.'

'Been a long time since I was last here,' Sean said, looking up at the clock tower.

'Not long enough,' Donnelly moaned. 'Place gives me the creeps.'

'It's better on the inside than it is on the outside,' Sean reminded him.

'Aye,' Donnelly agreed. 'A prison on the outside and a hospital on the inside.'

'Something like that.'

'Well, the sooner they build the new hospital and knock this place down, the better,' Donnelly insisted.

'Come on,' Sean told him. 'Let's get this over with.'

Thirty minutes later, having cleared the scanners and metal detectors and various levels of security, they were with the medical director, Dr Rachel Thorpe, in her office. She continually pushed her short ash blond hair behind her ears as she re-read the email she'd received from Sean only a short time earlier. When she'd finished reading, she removed her designer spectacles and looked across the desk at them. Sean studied her attractive, fine-boned face and guessed her to be in her fifties.

'I'm not sure,' she told them. 'I only received your request to see Sebastian less than an hour ago. I really don't feel I've had the time to properly evaluate its possible emotional impact on him.' Her educated Home Counties accent suited her appearance perfectly. 'You were, after all, the officer who arrested him.'

'I'm aware of that,' Sean answered, 'but a woman's life is at stake.'

'I'm not sure,' she hesitated. 'You have the time it takes to reach his cell to persuade me. I'll take you there myself. We can talk as we walk to save time.' She pushed her chair away and was immediately on her feet and heading for the door. Sean and Donnelly followed her lead – scrambling after her in an effort to keep up. 'We've done as you've asked and moved him to an isolation room in a separate area of the Personality Disorder Directorate. No other patients know where he is or could contact him even if they did.'

'Good,' Sean told her.

'But you still haven't told me the nature of this threat to Sebastian's life,' she reminded them, 'let alone what this unfortunate kidnapped woman has to do with him.'

'The man who's taken the woman,' Sean explained, 'has also killed several other people. Now he's making demands.'

'And this relates to Sebastian how?'

'He's demanding we hand Gibran over in exchange for the woman,' Sean answered.

'What?' she asked, stopping in front of the security check at the entrance to the isolation area and handing over her identification tag to one of the two men in prison officer's uniform. 'Why Gibran?'

'He's obsessed with him,' Sean replied. 'Wants to be like him. Wants the infamy.'

'You know I couldn't possibly authorize such an exchange?' she insisted. 'I'm not sure anyone could – not even the Home Secretary.'

'We're aware of that,' Sean assured her.

'Then why do you need to see Sebastian at all?' she asked.

'As I explained in the email,' he reminded her, 'when we receive a credible threat to someone's life we are legally obligated to inform that person of the risk.'

'And that's the only reason you want to see him?' she checked.

'There are other things I need to tell him,' he admitted. 'Operationally sensitive things he needs to be aware of.'

'Such as?' she enquired.

'I can't tell you,' Sean insisted. 'It's confidential.'

The guard handed her back her security tag and looked at Sean and Donnelly. 'They're police officers,' she told him. 'They have clearance.' He nodded and waved them through the body scanner. Everything they possessed that could have set it off was safely locked away in reception. 'Are you asking Sebastian to cooperate in some way?' she asked as they entered the deserted isolation area.

'Not cooperate,' he assured her. 'Just not to be obstructive.'

'I don't see how he could be,' she argued, 'given he's in a maximum security psychiatric hospital.'

'With Gibran,' Sean explained, 'it's always best to be sure.'

'Indeed,' she agreed. 'Very well. You may see him, but not for long. I'm guessing I don't need to remind you how dangerous he can be, given that you arrested him?'

'We know what he's capable of,' Sean answered.

'All the same,' she said, 'please stay alert at all times and keep your distance. He's not restrained in any way, so his nurses will remain with you throughout the visit.'

'But we have confidential matters we need to discuss with him,' Sean argued.

'The staff have all signed confidentiality contracts,' she assured him. 'They won't repeat anything they hear.'

'I need to be alone with him,' Sean argued.

'Out of the question. Sebastian's assessments are . . . inconclusive, to say the least. Until we know his true state of mind, it's best to assume he represents a significant danger to others.'

'We'll bear it in mind,' Donnelly told her as they reached a door at the end of the corridor, two muscular male nurses standing outside with their arms folded like nightclub bouncers. Thorpe nodded once to them and they stepped aside.

'He's in here,' she told them as one of the nurses half turned and looked through the door's window before taking hold of the key on a chain attached to his belt and unlocking the heavy door. He pushed it wide open and stood aside so they could enter. Thorpe entered first followed by Donnelly. Sean took a couple of seconds – afraid that Gibran would use his insightfulness to dig deep into his own character. He took a deep breath through his nose and stepped into the room. Gibran sat with his back to them, looking out of the window. Sean didn't need to see his face to know without any doubt it was *him*. He felt the same malevolent presence he'd sensed the last time they'd met.

'Sebastian,' Thorpe addressed him respectfully. 'There are some people here to see you.'

'Detective Inspector Corrigan,' Gibran announced, putting emphasis on every word, as he spun his desk chair around to face them. He stared straight at Sean. 'I genuinely thought I'd never see you again, at least not on this side of the wall.' His glance shifted to Donnelly: 'And I see you've brought your trained monkey along with you.'

'Let's try to keep this civilized,' Sean told him. 'There are things we need to discuss.'

'I'll leave you gentlemen alone now,' Thorpe interrupted, 'but the door will remain open and the nurses will wait outside. They'll show you back to my office when you're done.' She marched from the room.

'So,' Gibran asked, 'what brings you here after all this time?'

'I told you: we have things to discuss.'

'Such as?'

'Such as the fact we believe there's a credible risk to your life.'

'In here?' Gibran questioned. 'I don't see how.'

'The man you've been talking to Geoff Jackson about,' Sean explained, 'he's taken a woman and is demanding we hand you over in exchange for her life.'

'Has he now?' Gibran smiled. 'What woman?'

'I can't tell you that,' Sean insisted.

'Then this conversation is over,' Gibran threatened. 'I shall have to ask Mr Jackson instead.'

Sean knew it was only a matter of time before Gibran found out anyway. 'Dr Ravenni-Ceron.'

A smile spread across Gibran's face. 'Well, well. Your very own tame psychiatrist. How very embarrassing. Tell me – was she assisting you with the case?'

407

'Yes,' Sean admitted.

'Not very good at protecting the women in your life, are you, Inspector? Gibran mocked him. 'First Sergeant Jones and now the good doctor. How is she anyway?'

'None of your fucking business,' Donnelly snapped.

'A typical response,' Gibran goaded him. 'How you'd like to hand me over to this admirer of mine, but we all know you can't.'

'You're right,' Sean confirmed. 'We can't.'

'Then we have nothing to discuss,' Gibran insisted and turned to look out of the window.

'We can't be sure he's working alone,' Sean told him. 'We have to consider the possibility he's working with someone here inside Broadmoor. Another patient. A member of staff. Which means you could be at risk – which means we have to inform you of that risk. It's the law.'

'And since when do you have such high regard for the law?' Gibran asked, spinning back to face him. 'I wouldn't be in here now if you hadn't *planted* evidence in my home.'

'That's an allegation you've made before,' Sean reminded him, 'and one that I deny.'

'What's the matter, Gibran?' Donnelly joined in. 'Don't you like it when someone else doesn't play by the rules?'

'Tell me,' Gibran ignored Donnelly and addressed Sean, 'why did you come to tell me this yourself? Why not send one of your minions?'

'Because you've been talking to Jackson,' Sean explained. 'Saying less than complimentary things about the man we're looking for – shifting his focus on to you.'

'And you want me to stop?' Gibran assumed.

'No,' Sean countered. 'We want you to continue.'

'Why?' Gibran asked suspiciously.

'Because it may assist our efforts to catch him,' he explained. 'Efforts that do not involve you being exchanged for his hostage.'

'Shame,' Gibran smiled. 'I would have enjoyed some time alone with our mutual friend.'

'Just keep talking to Jackson,' Sean told him. 'That's all you need to do.'

'So,' Gibran worked it out, 'you want me to give the impression that I will indeed be exchanged for the woman – that you'll spirit me away in the middle of the night and deliver me to him like a pig to the slaughter?'

'Something like that,' Sean admitted, knowing it would be counter-productive to lie to him now he had caught a scent of the truth, 'but you don't need to make him believe anything. Jackson will take care of that. I just need you to know it's not true.'

'I see,' Gibran nodded. 'So Jackson is cooperating with you. Tell me – is he going to splash news of my intended exchange across the front of that rag he calls a newspaper?'

'Don't believe what you read,' Sean told him.

'And why should I help you?' Gibran asked. 'Why shouldn't I contact my solicitor and have them tell a rival newspaper Jackson is printing lies? I owe you nothing.'

'You're not helping me,' Sean reminded him. 'You're just not obstructing us.'

'Seems like the same thing to me,' Gibran argued.

'I can speak to Dr Thorpe,' Sean bargained. 'Have your privileges increased.'

'I already have most privileges,' Gibran told him. 'You're not selling this very well, Inspector.'

'There's another reason,' Sean replied. 'The longer he's out there, the more infamous he becomes. Soon people will be talking about him and not you.'

'Trying to appeal to my vanity, Inspector?' he asked, his head cocked to one side like an inquisitive bird. Sean didn't answer. 'Very well,' Gibran continued. 'You have my word I won't interfere in your operation to catch this insignificant individual, providing you answer one question honestly.'

Sean felt his heart sink. He knew Gibran was about to stretch his tendrils deep into his mind probing for weaknesses. 'Fine,' he agreed. 'One question.'

'Why did you really come here to see me? And no more lies about "legal obligations" and "operational necessity". You came to look at me, didn't you? To remind yourself that you really are special enough to catch a natural-born killer? Think carefully before you answer. If you lie to me, I'll know.'

'Yes,' Sean answered, not sure he was telling the truth. 'You're right. I came to look at you.'

'Only trouble is, you didn't catch me,' Gibran said through straight white, gritted teeth. 'Did you?'

'I've answered your question,' Sean ignored the bait. 'We're done here. Goodbye, Sebastian.' He turned and headed for the door, closely followed by Donnelly.

'I can't help but feel our paths will cross again one day,' Gibran called after them. 'Only next time I'll be ready. You won't get lucky twice, Inspector.'

As they passed the burly nurses they heard the heavy door closing behind them and the sound of large locks sliding into place. Sean kept walking at a pace fast enough to make it difficult for Donnelly to keep up.

'He still bears a grudge then,' Donnelly smiled.

'It would appear so.'

'What was all that about?' Donnelly asked. 'Your paths crossing again?'

'It's nothing,' Sean dismissed it. 'He's insane, remember.'

'I'm not sure about that,' Donnelly replied.

'Gibran's never getting out,' Sean told him, in hope more than belief. 'We won't be seeing him again. Ever.'

# 16

As soon as Sean arrived back at Scotland Yard, he headed for the SO10 office on the fifth floor. He knew the inauspicious office well from his days as an undercover officer – having sat in the cramped backroom many times as he was briefed on his latest infiltration or sting operation. Few people who saw it would have guessed it was the vital hub of covert operations across London and the Southeast as well as much further afield. He arrived to find the familiar counter blocking his entry and the same old placard warning *Entry strictly for SO10 personnel only*. He looked into the office beyond and saw the familiar face of DI Arif Chopra sitting at one of the few desks, which like the others was covered in out-of-date computers and clutter. Chopra continually stroked his long beard as he studied yet another request for the deployment of a UC.

'You need a shave and a haircut,' Sean called over the counter.

'Sean,' Chopra greeted him. 'I wouldn't mind losing the beard, but I'll keep the hair,' he added, pushing his fingers through his long grey-speckled black hair. 'Let yourself in.'

'Thanks.' Sean lifted the hatch section of the counter and entered, closing it behind him. 'Backroom?' he asked, looking in the direction of the infamous cupboard.

'No need,' Chopra told him. 'There's no one else around. They're all out on jobs. Take a seat.' Sean did as he was asked. 'Haven't seen you in a while.'

'Haven't had the need for SO10 for a while,' he explained. 'It's all been pretty straightforward.'

'Straightforward?' Chopra asked. 'That's not what I've heard.'

'Don't believe everything you hear.'

'No,' Chopra agreed, fixing him with his infamously intimidating deep brown eyes and the stone-faced expression that had scared many a criminal into making a mistake.

'You know why I'm here?' Sean asked.

'Addis gave me a heads-up.' Chopra tossed the file he was holding on to his desk. 'Can't say I like what he told me.'

'I wouldn't ask if there was a better way,' Sean assured him. 'I've got a few leads – a few ideas, but nothing solid – nothing I can get warrants for.'

'Just your instinct,' Chopra said, well aware of Sean's capabilities.

'Something like that,' he admitted.

'Yeah, but this plan of yours,' Chopra complained. 'You want me to deploy a UC to act as a madman to catch another madman – expose him to fuck knows what. You even have a journalist involved, and not just any journalist, but Geoff bloody Jackson from *The World*. Do you know how many SO10 operations he's compromised in the past?'

'I can imagine.'

'The man's got more informants than Special Branch. Probably got a few inside Special Branch, come to think of it. And with the type of jobs you get, you can be sure he'll be trying to tap-up someone on your firm.'

'I'll bear it in mind,' Sean replied, thinking of information leaking from SIU.

'And yet you want to work with him?' Chopra checked. 'You trust him?'

'Of course I don't trust him,' Sean told him, 'but the

suspect's calling some of the shots on this one. If he thinks we're cutting Jackson out of the loop, he'll kill the woman. I need the suspect to believe we're going to give him Gibran. Jackson's an important part of making that happen. I need him to run the headline.'

'Well, if I'm going to have one of my UCs waiting around to be grabbed or worse by your man, then the plot better be spot on,' Chopra warned. 'I don't want him any more exposed than necessary.'

'That could be a problem,' Sean admitted. 'We'll suggest somewhere, but he almost certainly won't agree to it. He's too careful for that. He'll want to decide where and when.'

'I can't deploy someone if you can't guarantee the plot,' Chopra told him. 'You know that.'

'He's going to go for somewhere rural,' Sean argued. 'I'm sure he is. As soon as we know where, we can have an inner ring of SO19 and an outer one of TSG – all wearing camouflage. As soon as he walks on to the plot we'll grab him.'

'And his hostage?' Chopra reminded him.

'Let me worry about that,' Sean insisted.

Chopra slumped back in his chair, chewing over the plan in his mind. 'I don't like it, Sean.'

'We have to try it,' Sean pleaded. 'It's the only chance I have of catching him quickly and finding Dr Ravenni-Ceron alive.'

'She may already be dead,' Chopra reminded him.

'No,' Sean told him. 'He'll want to keep her alive until he gets what he wants. He knows we'll continue to ask for proof of life.' Chopra shook his head, unconvinced. 'Arif, please. I need your help. Anna's one of mine.'

'OK,' Chopra sighed. 'Talk to SO19 – they have a few plots already researched for this sort of thing – then get them to liaise with me. I'll try to find you a suitable UC who's mad enough to take the job, but I'm making no promises. No guarantees.'

'Just do your best,' Sean told him, holding out his hand to shake on the deal. Chopra accepted it. 'Thanks,' Sean said, getting to his feet. 'I'll be in touch.'

Sean took the stairs, climbing two flights and taking the narrow corridor that led to the main office of the SIU. It was a noisy hive of activity, with most of the team present, everyone talking on phones or frantically typing at computers. He hoped one of them could come up with some lead that would allow him to find the killer without having to resort to a risky and dangerous UC operation with someone else's neck on the line instead of his own.

He grabbed Zukov. 'Any luck with the car?'

'Boss, there are thousands of them,' Zukov complained, 'and we don't even know what we're looking for.'

'You're looking for anything,' Sean told him. 'Chase it up, will you.'

Next he saw Jesson standing at his desk on the phone. He went and stood beside him until he hung up. 'Boss?' Jesson asked.

'What's happening with the Oyster card enquiries?'

'We know pretty much all the movements of the first two victims for the two weeks leading up to their deaths. We're still working on Witney Dennis, but so far there's nothing of interest – no shared routes or destinations linking her to the other two.'

'What about buses in and out of Roehampton the night Dennis was killed?' he pressed.

'That's a big job, boss. It'll take time.'

'We don't have time,' he snapped, striding across the office in search of Maggie O'Neil. He found her sitting at her desk, rubbing the stress from the back of her neck as she stared at her computer screen. 'Maggie,' he got her attention. 'How we getting on with the CCTV?'

'Most of it's been processed,' she informed him, 'but it's mainly footage of a man in a plain hooded top. We've released

414

the images to the media, but it's unlikely anyone will be able to recognize him from the CCTV.'

'Someone must have an idea who he is.'

'That's half the trouble. You know how these appeals go: most of London seems to think they know who it is. We've had hundreds of calls to the information line giving us names. Anyone who knows someone they don't like who wears a hoodie has called us. They're just trying to spoil someone's day.'

'But in amongst them could be the one we're looking for.'

'I'm running all the names through the intelligence system, but nothing interesting yet. If I find anything, I'll let you know straight away.'

'OK,' he sighed in frustration and was about to leave when he remembered. 'I have a name for you,' he told her. 'David Langley. That name comes up, you drop everything and call me.'

'Is he a suspect?' she asked, surprised that Sean suddenly had a name he was interested in.

'Not yet,' he told her, 'and keep it to yourself. I don't want anyone to know I'm looking at him.'

'No problem.' She didn't question his reasons for requesting secrecy; she knew that once someone became an official suspect, they would be more restricted in what they could and couldn't do.

'Thanks,' he whispered, and headed back to the sanctuary of his own office only to be intercepted by Sally.

'Doing the rounds?' she asked.

He knew she must have been watching him. 'Just staying on top of things.'

'And the UC operation?'

'It's on,' he told her. 'So I need you to get hold of SO19 and the TSG. Tell them what we're planning and find out if they have a plot we can use. If they do, we need to know where it is.'

'You think he'll let us pick the venue?'

'No,' he admitted, 'but we need one ready just in case. Get them to liaise with DI Chopra in SO10. He'll be running the UC side of things.'

'Are you sure this is a good idea?'

'We've run out of time, Sally,' he insisted. 'We have to go for the exchange or Anna is as good as dead. And we can't use Gibran, so what choice do I have?'

'Keep looking for something that'll lead us to him,' she urged. 'You said it yourself – he's connected to Anna in some way. He could be a patient of hers.'

'Listen,' he told her, frustration finally getting the better of him as he spun to face the rest of the team. 'Listen up, everyone. We've been trying to find this son of a bitch for almost two weeks now and still we have almost nothing. If we can't find him within the next twenty-four hours, some unfortunate UC is going to be standing in a forest, waiting for this bastard to sneak up behind him and stick a knife in his back. So if you don't want that to happen, you'd better start doing a better job than you've done so far. Now get on with it.'

The team stood frozen, staring back at him blankly.

'I said, get on with it!' he shouted.

Like machines that needed time to warm up, they returned to their tasks, slowly working themselves back up to normal speed.

Sean turned away in disgust and stormed back into his office, leaving Sally to pick up the pieces. Embarrased by his outburst, he slumped in his chair, rubbing his throbbing temples as he stared at the phone attached to the locate/trace equipment, praying it would ring. 'Shit,' he cursed under his breath and tried to think straight. There was one last thing he could try – one throw of the dice before they committed to the high-risk operation. He had to go and see David Langley. Alone.

\* \* \*

416

Less than an hour later, Sean stood outside an oppressive grey low-rise block of flats in Wandsworth that looked like it had been thrown up in the sixties or seventies on the edge of a sprawling thirties red-brick estate. It was one of the last areas of now affluent Wandsworth that had yet to become gentrified. He'd searched the small car park, but there was no sign of a red Vauxhall Vectra. Now he examined the list of names lined up next to the numbered doorbells on the intercom, some neatly typed, others handwritten. But there was no name next to the one he was interested in – often a sign that the occupant wasn't planning on staying long or hadn't accepted their situation. He stood with his face close to the intercom and pressed the button for flat 12, listening to the ringing tone, similar to a phone's, until it cut off. Undeterred, he pressed it again and waited. This time, after a few seconds, a tinny-sounding voice leaked from the small speaker.

'Yes,' was all it said, but he was sure it was the man he'd come to see.

'David Langley?' he asked. 'It's DI Corrigan. We spoke earlier, at your shop.' This was greeted by silence, which told Sean that Langley had not anticipated him calling at his home. If he was the man he'd been looking for, it was the first time he'd managed to be a step ahead.

'What do you want?' Langley finally replied.

'I have a couple of questions,' he answered, imagining Langley desperately looking around his flat for anything incriminating he might have left on show.

'I've already answered your questions,' Langley argued.

'There were some things I forgot to ask,' he lied, enjoying the concern in Langley's voice – a far cry from the polished act he'd convinced Sally with earlier in the store. 'It'll only take a few minutes.' More silence. 'Can we discuss this inside?'

'Of course,' Langley regained his composure. 'Come on up. Second floor.'

A second later the buzzer sounded and he pushed the door

open – the mixed scents of the communal hallway immediately washing over him. As he climbed the stairs, he reminded himself not to jump to conclusions purely because he'd taken a dislike to Langley. If the furniture salesman was his man, it was vital that he didn't scare him away from the trap that was being set. His priority should be to bait that trap, to do whatever he could to make it irresistible.

On reaching the second floor he walked along the narrow, dim corridor until he found Langley standing in his open doorway waiting for him.

'Inspector Corrigan,' he smiled politely. 'Would you like to come in?'

'That would be best,' Sean replied, images of sharp weapons waiting in ambush around the flat flashed through his mind. He needed to be ready for anything.

Langley stepped aside to allow him to enter. As Sean made his way in, the hairs on the back of his neck stood on end. When he heard the door shut behind him, he positioned himself side on to Langley so he would be less vulnerable to an attack from behind, without appearing too defensive. 'This way,' Langley said as he moved past him, slightly brushing against him as he led the way into a poky kitchen and living area. 'Can I get you a drink?' he offered.

'No thanks,' Sean replied, looking around Langley's living space – neat, tidy, ordered and uncluttered, adorned with a few framed photographs of Langley with his children.

Langley noticed him looking around.

'It's not much,' he shrugged, 'but it's fine for me. So,' he said, sitting down, 'what is it you wanted to see me about? Please – take a seat.'

'I'm good standing,' Sean replied. 'Like I said, I have a couple of questions I forgot to ask you earlier.'

'How did you know where I live?' Langley changed the subject.

'Dr Ravenni-Ceron's records,' Sean answered.

'I see.' Langley smiled. 'What about patient confidentiality?'

'I had a production order,' Sean explained. 'Wasn't too difficult to persuade the judge to allow us access to her records – given she's the one who's missing.'

'But you must have had my telephone number too.' Langley's smile remained fixed in place. 'Why didn't you call me?'

'I prefer the personal touch,' Sean told him. 'Too much policing these days is done down the phone or on a computer. I like to see people when I'm talking to them. Besides, it was on my way home,' he lied.

'Oh,' Langley said, 'and where is home for you?'

'Morden,' he answered, looking hard into Langley's eyes for signs he knew he was lying. The killer had followed him to the church in Dulwich. Maybe on another occasion he'd followed him home.

'Really?' Langley asked, unsmiling.

'Really,' Sean assured him.

'Anyway,' Langley moved on. 'Your questions?'

Sean continued to probe Langley's calm exterior: 'When you arrived at Dr Ravenni-Ceron's office, did you see anyone hanging around? Outside or possibly inside? Someone who looked out of place.'

'Not that I remember,' Langley shook his head.

'Perhaps when you parked your car in the underground car park?' Sean tried to make him slip up.

'I told you,' Langley answered calmly, 'I took a bus to East Putney, then the tube.'

'Sorry,' Sean lied. 'I forgot.'

'Hardly surprising,' said Langley. 'You must ask a lot of people a lot of questions.'

'What about during your other visits?' Sean persevered. 'Ever take your car?'

'No,' Langley answered, his head slightly cocked to one side. 'I told you, I don't have a car.'

Sean smiled slightly. 'My mistake.'

'Anything else?' Langley asked, impatient to be done with the charade.

'You're sure your relationship with Dr Ravenni-Ceron was purely professional – a doctor–patient relationship?'

'I'm sure.' His smile stiffened a fraction.

Sean made a show of looking around the room. 'Nice-looking kids,' he changed tack. 'Yours?'

'Of course,' Langley told him.

'They don't live with you?' he tried to rattle him.

'No,' Langley answered calmly.

'Your wife?' he asked, nodding to the sole picture that included an attractive woman.

'Ex-wife,' Langley replied without emotion. 'The children live with her.'

'Shared custody?' Sean kept it up.

'I'd like more,' Langley admitted, 'but my ex-wife likes to be difficult.'

'Did she move away with them?' he asked, working towards finding out where they lived.

'No. She kept the family home.'

'Where's that?' he probed, keeping his tone casual.

'Earlsfield,' Langley told him after a pause.

'Nice,' he said. 'Kids still use your surname or did she change it to hers?'

'They use both,' he replied.

Sean decided not to push any more. If he wanted to speak to the ex-wife, he'd have to find her with the information he had. 'Got a couple of kids myself,' he told him. 'Must be difficult for you, not seeing them every night.'

'I don't suppose you do either,' Langley countered. 'Given your line of work. I imagine your children are in bed before you get home, most nights?'

'Why did she leave?' Sean asked, ignoring Langley's question.

'She found out I was seeing someone else,' he admitted. 'Someone at work.'

'I see,' Sean nodded as if he was being understanding.

'Look,' Langley told him, suddenly getting to his feet and taking a few steps towards the fridge. 'My wife and I splitting up . . .' he started to explain as he pulled a beer from the fridge. 'Do you want one?'

'No,' Sean shook his head. 'Driving.'

'Right,' Langley said. 'Anyway, my wife and I splitting up – it was my fault. I was an arsehole. I was seeing other women when I should have been getting home to help with the kids. She found out and threw me out. I ain't complaining. I got what I deserved.' Langley played the honest, fundamentally flawed, Jack-the-lad routine to perfection. Almost well enough to disarm Sean. He needed to try to unbalance him again.

'You don't own a car, but do you have access to a car?'

'No,' Langley shook his head. 'You seem obsessed with cars, DI Corrigan.'

'We believe a red Vauxhall Vectra may have been involved in Dr Ravenni-Ceron's disappearance,' Sean told him. 'Does that mean anything to you? Anyone you know drive a red Vectra?'

'Not that I'm aware of,' Langley shrugged.

'Maybe you've seen a car like that outside Dr Ravenni-Ceron's office?' he continued to try to rattle Langley.

'It's busy out there. I don't think anyone could hang around in a car for long without causing traffic chaos. They'd be noticed.'

'No,' Sean agreed, trying to think of more questions to test Langley with, although he was beginning to doubt his earlier instinct. He felt like an intruder in Langley's home, instead of an investigator questioning a viable suspect. 'Maybe not.'

'I googled you,' Langley told him. 'After you left my store. I hope you don't mind?'

'No,' he shook his head. It had happened plenty of times before. He knew it didn't mean anything.

'Store was quiet, so I thought I might as well,' Langley explained. 'You caught that Sebastian Gibran, didn't you?'

Sean felt his heart miss a beat. 'That's a matter of opinion,' he managed to reply.

'I know a bit about him,' Langley went on. 'Someone at work gave me a book about him. Can't remember who wrote it now. It was an interesting read. Is it true you think he may have killed many more people you'll never know about?'

'We know about them,' Sean answered. 'We just can't prove it was him who killed them.'

'Fascinating,' Langley said, 'but I don't suppose it matters, given that he's locked up for the rest of his life.'

'He's not,' Sean corrected him. 'He's not in prison. He's in hospital.'

'You mean Broadmoor?'

'It's a psychiatric hospital,' Sean told him, 'where he's being *treated*.'

'So he could be released if he's no longer considered to be insane?'

'Technically,' Sean answered. 'Yes.'

'Incredible.' Langley smiled. 'And I see you caught some others too.'

'Some,' Sean confirmed.

'It must be *difficult*, dealing with these weirdos and lunatics all the time. Trying to find them and then interviewing them. Must change the way you look at the world.'

'Not really,' he told him. 'It's my job.'

'But if you're going to find them,' Langley insisted, 'then surely you need to work out why they're doing what they do. Their motive.'

'That's part of it,' Sean admitted, uncomfortable with having the tables turned on him, answering questions instead of asking them. Suddenly he regretted having come to see

Langley alone. He wanted to be far away from him, even if he was the man he'd been searching for. Langley had the upper hand, and Sean knew it. If this was the man who had Anna, then one wrong move, one wrong word, and Sean could be signing her death warrant. It had been a mistake to come to his home. He'd hoped to learn something, but now it was Langley who was toying with him like a cat with a mouse. Langley had Anna. Langley held all the cards.

'And after years of trying to work out *what* they're thinking,' Langley continued, any trace of a smile now gone, 'surely at some point you start to *think* like they think?'

'Maybe a part of you does,' Sean admitted, in an attempt to take some control back, 'but only enough to use it to find whoever I'm looking for. They always seem to assume you can't predict what they're going to do next, but I can.'

'Is that so?'

'Yes,' Sean warned him.

'By thinking like them?'

'Yes,' he said again. 'If I have to.'

'So,' Langley continued, 'if, say, someone has taken Dr Ravenni-Ceron against her will, what do you suppose their motivation could be? What are *they* thinking?'

'I don't know,' he replied, knowing that if Langley was the killer he hunted, he already knew he was lying. 'If indeed she has been taken against her will, then unfortunately she's in the hands of some sick sexual deviant who can't get it up unless he's carrying out some sort of perverted act.' He waited for Langley's reaction.

'Well then, let's hope that's not the case,' Langley answered with a look of concern.

'Let's,' Sean echoed.

'Are you sure her disappearance isn't connected to some other crime or crimes you're investigating?' Langley asked. 'I've seen some pretty nasty things in the news the last few weeks.'

'Such as?' Sean encouraged him.

'I can't remember the details,' Langley replied. 'Like I said – this sort of thing doesn't interest me. Someone cutting people's throats, was it?'

'It's not connected,' Sean kept up the untruths, aware that he was getting dangerously close to interviewing Langley, which meant he should arrest, caution and take him to a police station where he could speak to a solicitor. Otherwise he would risk losing anything he confessed to on a technicality. 'That's a separate matter.'

'One you're investigating?' Langley continued the duel.

'Yes,' Sean told him what he already knew, 'although I didn't want the case,' he added.

'Oh?' Langley couldn't help himself. 'How come?'

'To be honest,' Sean baited him, 'it's a bit beneath the SIU.'

'SIU?' Langley kept up his facade of ignorance.

'Special Investigations Unit. We specialize in difficult cases, finding particularly dangerous individuals like Sebastian Gibran. This guy's just another sexual predator. Was probably abused as a child and now he's got a chip on his shoulder. Doesn't need SIU to find this loser.'

'Loser?' Langley repeated, anger flashing in his eyes before he regained control. 'Well, for a loser, he seems to be proving difficult to catch.'

'That's probably exactly what he thinks,' Sean moved his piece on the chessboard. Despite Langley's impervious exterior, Sean was sure he could hear his heart beating hard. He'd learnt everything he needed to: if Langley was the killer of Tanya Richards, William Dalton and Witney Dennis, and the kidnapper of Anna – then he *would* walk into the trap he'd designed for him. His ego wouldn't allow him to walk away. 'Anyway,' he began to plot his exit. 'It's getting late. I should leave you in peace.'

'No need to worry about that,' Langley told him. 'I've enjoyed the company. An interesting conversation.'

'It was,' Sean agreed.

'Let me show you out,' Langley said, getting to his feet.

'I can let myself out.'

'No, no,' Langley told him. 'I need to lock the door behind you anyway.'

'Fair enough,' he said, and followed Langley from the kitchen-cum-living area into the small hallway, remaining alert lest Langley should slip a knife from somewhere and turn on him. But all he did was open the front door and step aside to allow him to pass into the communal corridor. Sean turned to face him. 'Good night, Mr Langley.' He waited for some reaction that would confirm this was the man who'd carried out such acts of brutality and cruelty. That behind this calm, affable exterior was the monster he sought. But Langley merely smiled and said, 'Good night, Inspector. Perhaps we'll meet again sometime?'

It was almost nothing, but it was enough for Sean to be all but sure Langley was indeed the killer. For a second he considered arresting him there and then. That would give him the power to search the flat. But if he found nothing, the decoy trap would be blown and Anna would be as good as dead while Langley would walk away laughing at them.

'Perhaps,' he said, turning away and heading off down the corridor, listening to the sound of his own footsteps reverberating off the walls until he heard Langley's front door closing. He stopped and looked back at the flat for a few seconds. 'Who are you?' he whispered to no one before turning away again and heading towards his car and home.

# 17

Sean walked into his office, dropped that morning's edition of *The World* on to his desk, and stripped off his coat and jacket. The front-page headline told him that Jackson had done as he'd asked, but now he wanted to take a few minutes to read the piece in full. He sat at his desk, smoothed the paper out and started reading. Jackson had done well. The story was convincing and he'd even thrown in a few photographs of a concerned-looking Gibran – taken some years earlier, but the killer wasn't to know that. He tapped one of the photographs several times, then jumped to his feet and moved to his doorway ready to ambush whoever walked past first. Maggie O'Neil was the unlucky victim.

'Boss?' she asked, knowing that some task was coming her way.

'I need you to do something for me,' Sean told her. 'Something I don't want shouted about the office.'

'Sure,' O'Neil agreed, looking around to make sure they weren't overheard.

'I need you to find somebody.'

'OK,' she nodded, wondering what was coming next.

'It's the ex-wife of that guy David Langley I asked you to look into,' he explained. 'They used to live together in a house in Earlsfield until she chucked him out, but she and their two kids still live there. Sounds like it all got a bit messy, so Family Court may know the name. The kids use the Langley surname, but they use the mother's too. Dad works for a furniture store called Harper's. The ex is probably late thirties to early forties.'

'That's it?' O'Neil asked.

'That's it,' he confirmed.

'OK, I'll do my best.'

Sean left her to it and headed back into his office. He snatched up his phone and dialled a number.

'SO10,' the voice answered.

'Ash, it's Sean. You seen today's edition of *The World*?'

'Got it in front of me now,' Chopra told him. 'Your friend Jackson's done a good job.'

'He's not my friend,' Sean corrected him. 'How's the rest of the planning going?'

'Good: I've found you the perfect UC to play decoy – an ex-Commando who thinks triathlons are fun. Your man tries anything he knows about a thousand ways to kill him with his bare hands.'

'Sounds good,' he agreed. 'And SO19?'

'They've been in touch,' Chopra confirmed. 'They have a plot in mind, if you can persuade your man to use it.'

'I'll try,' Sean promised, images flashing through his mind: Langley, knife in hand, closing in on the UC. 'But I can't guarantee it.'

'SO19 will not like it if the target chooses the plot,' Chopra warned.

'If it happens, I'll give them as much notice as I can as to where it's going to be,' he tried to assure him. 'It's the best I can do. I know everybody likes things set in concrete, but we're all going to have to be a bit more fluid this time. Our man's resourceful and clever and he needs to be caught. This is our best chance.'

'I hear you.'

'Thanks,' he told him, 'and Ash . . .'

'Yeah?'

'I've got a feeling he's going to call very soon. Make sure your people are ready.'

'We'll be ready.'

Once he'd hung up, Sean sat in silence for a while, trying to calmly run through all the possibilities in his mind. He couldn't afford to let his suspicions about Langley run away with him. To give the decoy operation the best chance of success, he needed to be ready for anything, and that meant he couldn't assume he knew the identity of the man who'd be walking into the trap.

He stared into the main office and watched Sally and Donnelly arrive for work within minutes of each other. This time last week, Anna would have been right behind them, her raven hair wrestled into a manageable mass, the scent of her perfume and the soft reflection of the world in her dark eyes. Fear for her swarmed over his skin and pulled him closer to the darkness that always swirled close by. For a second he remembered the taste of her lips – then he shook the memories away and turned his attention to the phone rigged with technical equipment, willing it to ring. He'd drifted into a near-trance when an unfamiliar ring tone broke through to him. It was the covert phone he'd given the killer the number of. With a sense of desperate urgency, he grabbed it from his desk. The display showed a number neither he nor the phone recognized. He took a deep breath and answered. 'Hello.'

'Sean,' the strained, artificial voice greeted him cheerfully. Despite the disguise, he was sure he recognized it – the tone and rhythm, the pace and intonation. The voice had a face to it now, no matter how hard he tried to be open-minded. 'I thought I'd use this number to call you on. I hope you don't mind. I thought it would be more . . . *private.*'

'If it suits you better,' Sean kept it polite – remembering his visit to Langley's flat the previous night, neither loathing him nor liking him, just two men pitched against each other by fate. One driven by madness or nature to kill, and one whose job it was to stop him.

'I read *The World* today,' he moved on. 'Jackson would have me believe you're actually going to hand over Gibran in exchange for the woman.'

'Anna,' Sean snapped, trying to stop him from dehumanizing her. 'Her name is Anna. And it's true – but first I need proof she's still alive, or the deal's off.'

'I don't have to prove anything,' he insisted. 'It's you who has to prove you're telling the truth. How do I know you're really going to hand him over? How did you get permission?'

'We have the Home Secretary's authority,' he lied, but the silence at the other end told him it wasn't enough to convince him. 'And Gibran has agreed to it. He wants it to happen.' He was met with more silence, but he knew he'd said the right thing – possibly the only thing that would convince him. 'It's not like we have to worry about public opinion,' he added. 'Handing over a psychopathic homicidal killer to save an innocent woman – the public will practically demand it.' There was yet more silence and then he spoke again.

'I know you'll try and trap me,' he sneered, 'but it won't work. I'll take him from right under your noses and you won't know I've been.'

'It's not a trap,' Sean tried to persuade him. 'We give you what you want and you give us Dr Ravenni-Ceron.'

'Once I have Gibran, she'll be released,' he promised. 'You have my word. Headley Lane, Surrey Hills,' he told him. 'Park in the car park outside the Surrey Outdoor Learning and Development Centre and wait for my call. Take this phone with you and don't be late. Be there by two p.m.' The line went dead.

'Shit,' he cursed, picking up his desk phone and dialling the SO10 office.

'SO10,' Chopra answered.

'Ash, it's Sean. It's on,' he told him, as he searched Google Maps on his mobile for the location. 'Two p.m. today in Surrey. Looks like a rural location.'

'The target's picked the plot?'

'Yeah, he already had somewhere lined up. Gave me the details then hung up before I could argue. You'd better give SO19 the good news.'

'They won't like it.'

'I don't like it either,' he bit back, 'but we don't have a choice. If they're unhappy, tell them to speak to Addis.'

'OK,' Chopra knew when he was beaten. 'What's the location?'

'An outdoor learning centre in Surrey. I'll text you the details.'

'Fine,' Chopra said. 'I'll get things moving.'

Sean hung up and headed to the next-door office where Sally and Donnelly waited.

Sally registered the urgency in his face. 'Developments?' she asked.

'Meeting's on today,' he told them. 'Two p.m. in Surrey Hills.'

'Who chose the location?' Sally questioned.

'He did,' Sean admitted.

'Great.' Sally rolled her eyes in disapproval.

'It was always likely to be the case,' he reminded her. 'We'll just have to deal with it.'

'What's the score?' Donnelly joined in.

'We're to wait in a car park until he calls me.'

'And then?' Sally asked.

'I assume I'll be given instructions,' he answered.

'He'll have the upper hand,' Donnelly stated the obvious.

'And he'll probably switch venues on us too,' Sally voiced

what they all knew. 'Keep us moving around so we can't get set.'

'If he does, so be it. For now, we have to follow his instructions.'

'I don't like any of this,' Sally complained.

'Jesus Christ, Sally – none of us like it. But it's not about what we like, is it? It's about catching this bastard and bringing Anna back alive.' He stared her down, preventing further dissent. 'Get everything ready. We don't have long.'

He left them, closing the door behind him, something he almost never did. Back in his own office, he slumped in his chair and spun it around so his back was facing the Perspex wall that separated him from Sally and Donnelly's office. Using the covert phone, he dialled another untraceable number. After a few rings, Addis answered. He sounded guarded, not his usual brash self.

'Hello,' was all he said. No mention of name or rank.

'It's me,' Sean told him, equally cautious.

'Something happened?'

'The meeting's on,' Sean told him. 'We have a location and a UC.'

'You didn't need to use this phone to tell me,' Addis replied.

'I know,' Sean answered.

'Something else then,' Addis guessed.

'We need a back-up plan,' he explained. 'In case something goes wrong. Something no one else knows about. Just you and me.'

'You have something in mind?' Addis asked.

'Yes,' Sean told him. 'Yes, I do.'


David Langley sat at his desk in the Wandsworth store, his hand resting on the warm mobile phone as he stared out of the small window on to the street beyond, where pointless people flowed like columns of ants – their lives of little worth – tiny, unimportant cogs in some greater machine. But not

431

him. He was different. Special. A man apart from the masses. And after what he was about to do, he would be more feared and respected than any of his kind. Even Gibran. He would be remembered for decades – if not longer. Corrigan thought he was so clever, coming to his flat to try and panic him, but he knew nothing. Corrigan was nothing. He thought he could catch him in his foolish trap, but soon he would learn how wrong he was and the world would see that David Langley was too clever and too powerful to be caught. Soon the whole world would know his name.

# 18

Sean sat in the back of the unmarked car with the handcuffed undercover officer while Sally sat in the driver's seat constantly looking around and checking her mirrors for any signs of life. Donnelly and Zukov were parked next to them in another unmarked car. There were no other police vehicles to be seen – SO19 and some TSG units having arrived much earlier in more unmarked vehicles which they'd parked well away from the outdoor centre before making their way on foot to the surrounding countryside. They were impossible to see, but Sean knew they were there. He glanced down at the hand-cuffs around the UC's wrists.

'You sure they're OK?' he checked.

The UC flicked his wrists and the cuffs popped straight open. 'Done it dozens of times,' he smiled. 'Bit of a party trick of mine.'

Sean looked him up and down, struck by how much he looked like Gibran, especially from a distance. He even sounded like him. 'What do you do when you're not on a deployment?' he asked.

'Three-area TSG,' he answered. 'It's entertaining enough.'

'I'm sure it is,' Sean agreed. 'Do you have a name you use?'

'Frank,' the UC told him. 'I usually use Frank.'

'What time is it?' Sally asked, nervously.

Sean checked his watch. 'Almost two.'

'He's supposed to call,' she complained.

'He said he'd call at two,' he reminded her, 'so that's when he will call. Not a minute earlier or a minute later.'

They sat in a tense silence until the mobile phone rang. 'Here we go,' Sean said into the radio that he knew all the units hidden in the area would be listening to, then he answered the phone. He put it on speaker and kept the radio close so everyone could hear what was being said. 'Hello.'

'Sean,' the voice greeted him cheerfully. 'I'm so glad you could make it and you've brought so many friends with you. So many policemen with guns,' he told them, making every-one's hearts freeze. 'And I see you have the person I asked for.'

'Where are you?' Sean tried his luck.

'Now, now, Sean,' he laughed. 'I'm not likely to tell you that, am I? You and Gibran need to take a little walk now – get some fresh air.'

'Where we walking to?'

'Through the car park and into the woods,' the voice demanded, 'and remember – do exactly as I say or you'll never see your precious psychiatrist alive again.'

Sean looked at the UC who gave a resigned shrug, as if it was just another day at the office. Sean sighed, stepped from the car and went around to the other side where he opened the door for Frank and helped him out like he would have done for any prisoner. Sally took hold of Frank's other arm – constantly looking around for a surprise attack until the voice from the phone stopped them all in their tracks.

'Just you and Gibran, Sean,' he demanded. 'No one else.'

Sean and Sally looked at each other. 'Wait here,' he told her.

'This is a bad idea,' she argued.

By now Donnelly and Zukov were also out of their car and moving towards them. 'Wait there,' Sean stopped them. 'Everybody wait here. Gibran and I go alone. We don't know if we're being watched.' He heard unpleasant laughter coming down the phone.

'You are being watched,' the voice told him. 'You and Gibran alone or I'll know.'

Sean scanned the car park, the rear of the outdoor centre and the surrounding woods, but couldn't work out where his tormentor was hiding. 'Fine,' he agreed. 'Just me and Gibran.'

'Good,' the voice approved. 'Very good. Now walk.' Sean and Frank did as they were told, leaving the others looking anxious in the car park. 'Quite a trap you've set for me,' the voice chatted casually. 'I've really no idea how I'm going to slip away *this* time. Have you considered that I may have a sniper rifle?' he asked.

'I've considered it,' Sean admitted.

'That I could blow Gibran's head apart any moment I choose? Maybe yours too?'

'I don't think you will, though,' Sean answered.

'Why?' he demanded.

'Not personal enough,' Sean told him. 'You like it *personal*.'

'Ah, you know me so well, Sean,' he mused. 'You see, when you're using a knife, it feels like part of you – an extension of your own hand. I'm sure our special guest has told you all about that. But some *animals* are too dangerous to try and kill with a knife. You have to be prepared to use something a little less personal and a lot more effective.'

'I don't understand,' Sean replied.

'You will, Sean,' he assured him. 'I promise you will.'

'Where's Dr Ravenni-Ceron?' Sean changed the subject.

'Safe,' he answered.

'Is she close by?' Sean tried to find out as much as he could as they entered the woods, moving around the trees, trying not to trip on the roots and fallen branches, their eyes searching for any place the suspect or an SO19 officer could be hiding.

'Close enough,' he assured him.

'How will you hand her to us once you have what you want?'

'I'll hand her to *you* personally, Sean,' he answered. 'You deserve the glory.'

'It's not about glory,' he told him. 'She's an innocent woman. I just want her to be safe. To send her home to her husband.' He was trying standard tactics to make it as hard as possible for the hostage-taker to harm their prisoner, but in his gut he knew it would have no effect on a man who'd already shown how much he enjoyed the kill.

'Innocent,' he laughed quietly. 'Nobody is innocent any more. This is a sinful world, Sean.'

He was burning with the desire to challenge him as to whether he knew Anna, to tell him that he knew he was David Langley, but daren't – not until he was safely ensnared in the trap. Instead all he said was, 'Maybe.'

'Who knows how many people she trampled over to get where she was,' he accused her. 'Success doesn't come without casualties. She's no more *innocent* than you or I, Sean.'

'I don't know about that.'

'Stop,' the voice demanded without warning. 'Stop right where you are.' Sean did as he was told, his heart pumping as he held on to Frank's arm. Was he closer than either of them imagined? Had he seen it wasn't Gibran?

'What do you want me to do now?'

'I want you to wait, Sean,' said the voice.

'Wait for what?'

'For me to call you, of course.'

'Wait,' he tried to stop him, but it was too late. He was gone.

\* \* \*

Geoff Jackson was finishing lunch in his Soho flat with his girlfriend Denise and pretending to listen to her excited chatter about her afternoon audition, but his mind was fixed on Corrigan, Gibran and the trap being set for the killer. He wouldn't believe Corrigan wasn't planning to double-cross him until he had the exclusive in the bag and his book publisher's tongue and chequebook hanging out for the paperback.

'Shit,' Denise's loud cursing broke through his obsessive thoughts. 'I'm going to be late. You don't mind, do you?' she asked, looking down at the detritus of their meal.

'No problem,' he told her. 'I got it. You go.'

'Oh, thanks, Davey,' she grovelled. She always called him *Davey* when she needed something. 'Wish me luck.'

'Good luck,' he did as he was told and watched her grab her handbag and fly out of their small flat.

As soon as she was gone he breathed a sigh of relief and looked down at the mess that remained of lunch. 'Fuck that,' he said to himself and gathered his belongings before heading for his office. He needed to check on Corrigan. He locked the door to his flat and skipped down the stairs, but as soon as he opened the communal door leading to the street, a dark, hooded figure pushed him back inside and pinned him to the wall, flashing a knife in front of his face and pressing it to his throat. He could feel the power of his faceless attacker and knew there was no point struggling.

'Take my wallet,' he pleaded. 'Here,' he began to loosen his watch. 'It's a Rolex. It's worth a lot.'

'Don't you know who I am, Mr Jackson?' the voice came from the darkness of the hood.

Immediately his head cleared and he realized whose knife it was pressed to his throat. He closed his eyes and tried to make peace with the fact he was about to die. 'Yes,' he answered, nodding slowly. 'I know who you are.'

'Good,' the voice from barely visible lips told him. 'Then you know that if you lie to me, I'll kill you?'

'Yes,' he replied, sensing a glimmer of hope that he might yet survive. 'I understand.'

'And your slut girlfriend too,' the faceless killer told him. 'If you lie, I'll come back and I'll rape her and I'll cut her into pieces and she'll know it's because you lied to me.'

'I won't lie to you,' he promised. 'I won't lie.'

'Corrigan,' he said, focusing Jackson's thoughts. 'Is Corrigan trying to set me up?' Jackson didn't answer immediately, but as the knife pressed harder into his throat he remembered how much he wanted to live.

'It's not Gibran,' Jackson told him. 'They're using a decoy who looks like him to trap you.'

'Of course they are,' he nodded slowly. 'Whose idea?'

Again Jackson didn't want to answer, but the feel of his own skin beginning to split persuaded him otherwise. 'Corrigan's,' he spluttered. 'It was Corrigan's idea.'

'Well done,' he politely thanked him, easing the knife from his throat slightly, 'but you really shouldn't listen to everything Sebastian Gibran tells you about me. He knows nothing. You should be more careful about what you put in your newspaper, Mr Jackson. I'd hate to have to come back and *discuss* it with you again.'

'And Corrigan?' he managed to ask. 'What're you going to do about Corrigan?'

'Corrigan's a fool,' he answered. 'Right now he thinks I'm hiding in some wood in Surrey, watching his every move. He thinks he's set a trap for me, but it's me who's set a trap for him.'

'I don't understand,' Jackson admitted.

'You don't have to,' the face deep in the darkness of the hood told him. 'Goodbye, Mr Jackson.' A second later he was through the door and had disappeared into the street. Jackson realized that his attacker had been bearing his weight as his

438

own legs had turned to jelly. Now he began to slide down the wall, taking gulps of air to try and control his breathing and slow his heart rate.

'Jesus Christ,' he groaned as he sat on the floor, realizing how close he'd come to being killed. 'Jesus Christ.' But within a few seconds his instincts kicked in and fired his mind into action as he searched for his phone. He immediately found the contact he was looking for and called the number, cursing as he waited for it to connect. 'Come on,' he complained. 'Answer the fucking phone.'

Sean and Frank stood in the woods, still in the exact spot they'd been in when he'd hung up. The sound of the trees swaying in the breeze mixed with the occasional alarm call of a blackbird. They constantly looked around themselves, knowing that an attack could come from anywhere.

'Maybe we should get out of here,' Frank suggested. 'Could be your target got spooked by something.'

'No. He'll call back. Even if something's scared him off, he'll call back.'

'We've been standing in the same place for a while now,' Frank advised him. 'We're sitting ducks waiting here.'

Sean nodded and reluctantly raised his personal radio to his mouth and pressed the talk switch. 'All units, this is DI Corrigan. We've lost communication with the target. We'll give it a few more minutes before calling it a day.'

'All received,' a crackly voice replied through the radio. 'We have you in our sights, but no other sign of life, over.'

'All received,' Sean acknowledged and put the radio back in his coat pocket just as his personal mobile began to ring. 'Shit,' he cursed as he struggled to pull it from his belt and check the caller ID. It was Jackson. He fumbled to answer it. 'Jackson. This better be important.'

'He knows it's a trap,' Jackson replied breathlessly.

'What?' Sean demanded. 'How?'

'He came to my building,' Jackson explained. 'The man you're looking for. He jumped me as I was leaving. He had a knife.'

'That's not possible,' Sean insisted. 'He's here somewhere, watching us.'

'No,' Jackson told him. 'He's here. In London. He just wanted you to think he was there. He made me tell him the truth.'

'Christ,' Sean shook his head in desperation. The covert phone in his other hand began to ring. 'I've got to go,' he said without explanation and hung up, quickly swapping phones. 'Hello.'

'You lied to me, Sean,' the voice told him calmly, without a trace of anger or bitterness.

'Wait,' Sean pleaded. 'Jackson doesn't know what he's talking about. We only told him that to keep him quiet. If he knew we really were willing to give you Gibran, he would have been making all sorts of demands.'

'But I told you to tell him the truth,' he reminded him, 'so if you lie to him, you lie to me. You were never going to hand over Gibran, were you, Sean? You were trying to trap me, and now Anna will die so that next time you won't be foolish enough to try anything stupid again. Next time, you will bring me Gibran.'

'Wait,' Sean told him, wandering away from Frank and lowering his voice so he couldn't be overheard. 'I can't bring you Gibran. It's impossible.'

'Then more innocent people will die until the public demand that you give him to me.'

'I have a better idea,' Sean spoke fast before he could hang up. 'Why bother with Gibran when you can have the man who caught him? I'll meet you wherever you want and I'll come alone. Just don't hurt her.' There was silence at the other end of the line. 'Imagine how famous you'll be – the man who killed the cop who caught Sebastian Gibran and

The Jackdaw. People will be talking about you for years. There'll be books. Films.'

The agonizing silence dragged on until finally he spoke: 'Very well, Sean. We'll do it your way. But if I suspect you're not alone, a lot of people are going to die – starting with Dr Ravenni-Ceron.'

'Alone,' he assured him. 'I promise.'

'Follow the A3 to the Esher bypass,' he instructed, 'and then take the A244 north for two miles until you enter the forest. Keep driving until you see the sign for Arbrook. Stop at the sign and wait for me to call. Be there in two hours.'

'Wait,' Sean tried to stop him again, but he was gone. 'Shit.'

'Problem?' Frank called over to him.

'No,' Sean lied. 'You can stand down. The target's not coming.'

'How do you know?' Frank asked.

'Because he just told me,' he answered, already walking back towards the car park – swapping his phone for the radio. 'All units, stand down,' he spoke into the mouthpiece. 'All units, stand down.'

'Received,' a mechanical voice acknowledged.

'For Christ's sake,' Sean complained as he felt his mobile vibrating in his pocket. 'What now?' He stuffed the radio into his coat and retrieved the phone. The caller ID showed the number was *withheld*, which usually meant it was a call from a police number.

'Boss,' the caller began. 'It's Maggie.'

'What is it?' he asked impatiently.

'That woman you wanted me to find,' she explained, 'the one in Earlsfield. I found her. Name's Emma Hutchinson. Lives there with her two kids. You want the address?'

'Yeah,' he told her. 'Text it to me.'

A few seconds later he emerged from the trees into the car park where Sally and the others were waiting for him.

441

'What's going on?' Sally demanded.

'He knows it's a trap,' he explained. 'He was never here. He was in London – watching Jackson.'

'What?' Sally asked, incredulous.

'He jumped him outside his flat and threatened him with a knife,' he elaborated. 'Jackson told him we were setting him up.'

'Oh that's great,' Sally said, shaking her head in disbelief. 'I told you this was a bad idea. And Anna? What happens to her now?'

'We keep looking for her,' he answered, trying to hide his true emotions and the deep sickness he felt in his stomach. 'Go with Dave,' he added. 'Take Frank back to the Yard with you. I need the car.'

'Where the hell are you going?'

'To follow a lead,' he told her.

'Alone?'

'It's better I go alone. I need you and everyone else back at the Yard checking everything we've got so far. And get Jackson in for a full debrief.'

'Fine,' Sally reluctantly agreed.

Sean looked at the text he'd just received on his phone: Langley's ex-wife's address. Two hours until he had to be in Esher. With full lights and sirens, he could make it to Earlsfield and then to the meeting point in time. The A3 would speed him in and out of London. He climbed into the unmarked car and started the engine, but before he drove away he tugged the covert phone free, selected a name and began to type a text message: It's me. He waited for a reply. A few seconds later an incoming message bubble appeared:

Problem?

We need to try what we discussed.

Then do what you have to do. And delete these messages.

Sean knew the person on the other end had gone. He pressed the *edit* icon, selected the messages and pressed delete.

He tossed the phone on to the passenger seat and sped from the car park.

David Langley let his car roll to a stop outside the caravan. He turned the ignition off and stepped out into the cold of the forest. At this time of year, it would be dark soon. After visiting Jackson, he'd taken the tube from Leicester Square to Waterloo station then caught a fast train to Esher and picked up his car from the station car park where he'd been leaving it since taking Anna. From there, it was a relatively short journey to the caravan and his hostage. He walked slowly towards the caravan, enjoying the breeze on his face and the memories of spending time in the woods with his father, hunting for whatever they could track and kill – his father smearing blood on his face the first time he ever managed to take the life of a forest animal. But now he tracked and killed much larger, more dangerous game. He unlocked the padlock and yanked the door open, making his prisoner squirm and kick as she tried to escape him. He climbed inside and stood astride her, looking around until he found the water bottle with the straw in he'd left behind. Lifting it from the shelf, he ripped the masking tape from Anna's mouth, making her scream with pain. The sound reverberated around the tiny space; he waited for silence to return and touched the straw protruding from the bottle to her sore red lips.

'Drink,' he told her. 'You're dehydrated.' She twisted her head away from whatever she felt touching her. 'You must drink,' he insisted.

'David,' she pleaded, barely able to speak. 'Please. Just let me go.'

'I can't do that,' he replied calmly. 'I still need you.'

'Why?' she asked – her tears finding a way through the tape that covered one of her eyes. 'Why are you keeping me here?'

'Insurance,' he smiled. 'Someone's coming, you see. A dangerous man. A man only a fool like Sebastian Gibran would ignore. But I'm no fool. Best to keep you around a while longer. I see you've managed to pull the tape loose. No matter. Drink.'

She took a few sips – lubricating her mouth and slightly improving her voice. 'Why is he coming?' she asked.

'Because he thinks he can save you,' he explained without emotion. 'He thinks he can save everyone. But soon he won't even be able to save himself.'

'Sean,' she said quietly as she realized who he was talking about. 'What . . . what are you going to do to him when he arrives?' she stuttered.

'I'm going to hunt him and I'm going to kill him,' he told her. 'Then I'm going to take his teeth and nails.'

'Don't do this,' she pleaded.

'I'm afraid I must. And when I've killed him, I'm going to kill you too.'

'No,' she begged as he pulled the roll of masking tape from his rucksack and tore off a fresh strip. 'Please don't do this.'

'But I have to,' he explained as he slapped the tape hard over her mouth and smoothed it down. 'You have such pretty teeth.'

Sean pulled up outside the smart terraced house in Earlsfield, Southwest London, that had once been Langley's family home. Now it was home to his ex-wife and children only. He could feel Langley's bitterness at having to swap this comfortable house for his small, unpleasant flat in the worst part of Wandsworth. He abandoned his car in the residents-only parking bay and knocked on the front door – ignoring the doorbell, as cops so often did. He could hear the sounds of children coming from inside and the door was opened seconds later by an attractive woman in her mid-thirties, with

444

olive skin and straight short brown hair. She was quite petite, no more than five foot four inches tall.

'Yes?' she asked, with a slight London accent.

He showed her his warrant card, which she examined far more closely than most while he introduced himself. 'I'm DI Sean Corrigan from the Special Investigations Unit of the Metropolitan Police. I need to speak to you about your ex-husband, David.'

'David? Why would the police want to speak to me about David?'

'Can I come inside?'

'I'm not sure,' she told him, looking back over her shoulder. 'The kids, you understand.'

'You have a room we can use,' he persisted, 'where they won't hear us?'

'Look, what's this about?'

'I'm investigating a very serious series of crimes,' he explained. 'David's name has come up during the course of that investigation. I think you could help me clear a few things up.'

'But David and I have been divorced for a couple of years now,' she argued. 'I don't see how I can help.'

'It shouldn't take long,' he encouraged her.

She looked him up and down. 'OK. Fine. You'd better come in.' She opened the door wide to allow him to enter. 'In here,' she told him, pointing with her head to the doorway immediately to her right.

'Thanks,' he nodded as he walked into the room that clearly served as an office and temporary adult retreat.

'Kids,' she shouted into the kitchen-living area. 'I've just got to talk to somebody about something for a minute, all right? I'll be in the front room if you need me.' She listened for a response, but was happy enough when she received none. 'So,' she turned to face him. 'What do you want to know?'

'I want to know more about David,' he confessed.

'Why?' she asked. 'Is he in trouble?'

'Would you be surprised if he was?'

'Look,' she told him. 'I'm busy with the kids. Why don't you just tell me what you want?'

'I need to know if he is what he seems,' he explained, 'or is there another side to him.'

'You've met him then?' she smiled.

'Yes,' he admitted.

'Put on the charm, did he?' she asked. 'His friendly, man-about-town routine. Convincing, isn't he?'

'But you know another David?' Sean pressed.

'Why're you asking me about this?'

'Because you probably know him better than anyone,' he told her. 'You were married to him.'

'Yes,' she agreed. '*Was* married to him.'

He glanced at his watch. The meeting time was a little more than an hour away. 'Why did you break up?'

'Let's just say we were no longer compatible.'

'In what way?' he kept on. 'It could be important.'

'Has something happened to David?'

'Not yet,' he told her, 'but something could, if I can't find out a few things I need to know.'

'Like why we split up?' she questioned.

'It could help eliminate him from our enquiries,' he explained.

'Or it could implicate him.' He didn't reply. 'What is it exactly you're investigating anyway? You didn't say.'

'No I didn't,' he agreed, 'because I can't. But it is serious. I'm trying to stop more people getting hurt. You don't owe him anything.'

'Bloody right I don't,' she said, folding her arms across her chest.

'Then tell me why you left him.'

'I was young,' she began, shaking her head in surprise at her own past. 'We met in a nightclub in London. An *eroticism* night – you know, everyone in bondage and leather. I was into that stuff back then and so was Dave. Am I shocking you, Inspector?'

'No,' he lied. 'I've been doing this job a long time. It takes a lot to shock me.'

'Really?' she looked him up and down. 'Anyway, I suppose we fell in love, or maybe it was never really more than lust, but we were into the same things, if you know what I mean.'

'I understand,' he assured her. 'So what went wrong?'

She took a deep breath. 'Dave started going too far. His role-plays were becoming more violent – mostly simulated, but I wasn't into his ideas.'

'Ideas?' he asked.

'Simulated rape,' she explained. 'Strangulation. And then he put a knife to my throat while he . . . Anyway, I pulled back from it all. I guess I grew up, but Dave still wanted to experiment – to be more and more . . . out there. When I refused, he turned to other women. Eventually I found out and threw him out.'

'How did he take it?' Sean dug deeper.

'Badly. There were some threats and lots of arguments over the kids, but it calmed down eventually. He still turns up at school without permission sometimes though. He's been warned about it.'

'Has he been arrested?'

'No,' she replied. 'Like I said – just warned.'

Sean had heard enough – almost. 'Does David have a car?'

'Yes,' she answered. 'Why?'

'What type?' he asked, his chest pounding.

'A Vauxhall,' she replied. 'A Vectra, I think it's called.'

'What colour? he pressed.

'Red,' she told him, 'but what's his car got to do with anything?'

For a few seconds it felt as if his heart had stopped beating and his blood had stopped flowing. 'You sure?' he checked.

447

'Yes. I still get the occasional parking ticket for it in the post.'

'Sorry,' he shook his head, confused. 'The tickets come here?'

'Yes,' she shrugged.

'Then the car's registered to this address?'

'Probably,' she admitted. 'It was our old family car.'

'Can you remember the number plate?'

'No,' she shook her head. 'I never knew it in the first place.'

He had everything he needed. 'OK. Thank you,' he told her. 'I'll leave you to get back to your kids.'

'Are you going to tell me what this is about?' she asked as he headed for the door.

'I will,' he assured her. 'In time. Goodbye, Ms Hutchinson.'

He waited until he'd seen her close the front door behind him before taking out his phone and calling Donnelly's number.

'Guv'nor,' Donnelly answered.

'Did you check with DVLC for vehicles registered at Langley's home address?'

'Aye,' Donnelly answered, 'but there weren't any. Dead end, I'm afraid.'

'Because it's registered to his ex-wife's address.'

'How do you know?' Donnelly asked.

'I've just spoken to her,' he admitted. 'Langley owns a red Vauxhall Vectra. She confirmed it.'

'Shit,' Donnelly cursed.

'It's him,' Sean told him. 'David Langley's the man we're looking for. He took Anna.'

'What do you need me to do?' Donnelly asked.

'Get warrants for his flat and his work. Search them both.'

'You think Anna could be at one of them?'

'No,' Sean dismissed it. 'She won't be there.'

'How can you be so sure?' Donnelly asked, his voice laced with suspicion.

448

'I just am.' Sean checked his watch. He didn't have time to explain.

'Where are you?' Donnelly pressed him.

'I . . . I can't tell you that,' he answered.

'Boss,' Donnelly asked nervously. 'You're not planning on doing something stupid, are you?'

'You just have to trust me,' he tried to reassure him. 'It's the only chance Anna has.'

'Boss,' Donnelly appealed to him, but Sean hung up and turned his phone off to avoid the barrage of calls he'd undoubtedly receive from Donnelly and Sally. What he had to do could only be done alone.

# 19

Sean drove fast along the A244, the blue light swirling on the roof of his car. He'd turned off the screaming siren that had cleared the traffic on the A3 so he could approach in silence. The blue lights were enough to warn the light traffic of his speeding presence. He glanced at the clock on the dashboard. The two hours were almost up. He squinted at the darkening road ahead of him until at last, he spotted the sign for Arbrook, Langley had told him to expect and hit the brakes hard as he pulled over on to the side of the road. He looked at the covert phone on the seat next to him, his heart thumping in his chest as he thought of Kate and his daughters. He took out his own mobile and turned it back on. Once it was alive he called Kate's number and waited for her to answer.

'Sean,' her voice spoke to him, sounding concerned. 'Everything all right?'

'Just thought I'd call,' he told her, trying to sound casual.

'Not like you to call from work,' she reminded him. 'Are you sure everything's all right?'

'Of course,' he lied. 'I wanted to talk to you, that's all.'

'OK,' she continued, growing ever more suspicious. 'What about?'

'I . . . I have to do something,' he confessed. 'It's important.'

'What?' she asked cautiously. 'What do you have to do?'

'I can't tell you,' he answered, 'but I'll be fine.'

'OK,' she said, 'then why are you telling me this?'

'Because,' he continued, trying to stop his voice from betraying his fear, 'I wanted to tell you that I love you. And the girls. I love you all very much.'

'What's going on, Sean?' she demanded. 'You're not going to do something stupid, are you? Please tell me you're not putting yourself in harm's way again.'

'No,' he lied, making his stomach tighten to the point where he felt sick. 'Just something I have to do.'

'Come home to us, Sean,' she pleaded. 'Just come home to me and the girls.'

'I will,' he promised her, without knowing if he could keep his promise. 'Once I've done what I have to do, I'll come home. I promise.'

'Sean,' she appealed to him. He could hear the tears choking her.

'I have to go now,' he told her, struggling to breathe properly.

'Sean,' she said again, but he couldn't think of anything to say. He hung up and turned the phone off, sadness overwhelming him. He knew he had to somehow bury his feelings as deep as he could and force himself into action. At that moment the covert phone began to chirp and vibrate. He steadied himself and answered. 'Hello.'

'I'm so glad you could make it, Sean,' the same lifeless voice greeted him. 'I was beginning to think you weren't coming.'

'You can see me?' Sean asked.

'There's a dirt road to your right. Can you see it?'

'I see it.'

'Drive slowly along it until I tell you to stop. If you're being followed, I'll know.'

'I'm not being followed,' he assured him – pulling off the main road and rolling his car slowly along the dirt road.

'Good,' he told him. 'Keep driving.'

'Is Dr Ravenni-Ceron nearby?' he asked.

'Oh yes,' he gleefully answered. 'Very close.'

'Can I see her?'

'Once I've taken care of a few things,' he replied.

'Things?'

'You'll see.'

'I know it's you, David,' Sean tried to shake him.

'Of course,' Langley laughed slightly.

'I've told others.'

'Naturally.'

'They'll come for you,' he warned him.

'None of that matters now,' Langley told him. 'We're almost at the end.'

'End of what?'

'Don't you know?'

'No,' Sean lied.

'After today, the world will take notice. I will have achieved all I set out to achieve.'

'I saw your ex-wife,' Sean again tried to rattle him. 'Emma. Right before coming here. She told me about you. About why you split up.' There was no reply. 'Must have hurt – her getting the house and the kids?'

'None of them matter any more,' he answered, but the bitterness was thick in his voice.

'Your children don't matter?' Sean pushed. 'I don't believe you. Is that what this is all about – making Emma pay? Or are you just a sexual deviant who has to use violence to get a hard-on?'

Silence. Followed by the sound of laughter leaking down the phone. 'Very good, Sean. You really are very good. Now stop the car.' He did as he was ordered. 'Turn off the engine and the lights. Time for you to take a walk. Get out of the car.'

Reluctantly, he did as he was told. 'I'm out. What now?'

'Keep following the track,' he answered.

'OK,' Sean agreed and began to walk. The light was fading

fast so he unclipped his Maglite torch from his belt and shone it on the path ahead.

'I see you brought your torch,' Langley mocked him. 'If it makes you feel . . . *safer.*'

'It's dark,' Sean said. 'I can't see the track without it.'

'Keep your torch,' Langley dismissed it, 'but you should know, I virtually grew up in these woods. I don't need light to know where I am. My father taught me how to train my eyes to see in the dark.'

'Really,' Sean replied. 'What else did he teach you?'

'He taught me how to move without noise through the trees,' he hissed. 'How to catch birds and squirrels with my bare hands without them knowing I was there. So imagine how easy it is for me to hunt a man.'

'Is that why I'm here?' Sean asked. 'So you can hunt me?'

'Did you really think I'd walk into your pathetic trap?' he ignored the question. 'I knew you'd never give me Gibran. I just used him to throw you off the scent. Send the dogs running in the wrong direction while you ran towards me. Alone. I always knew you would. It was simply a matter of creating the right conditions, choosing the right bait. You're so predictable, Sean. Can't you see it was never Gibran that I wanted? It was you. And now we're here. Just the two of us. How it should be. I started seeing Anna weeks before I even killed my first. I took my time, learning her movements, working out how she could be taken – and you never suspected a thing. I knew that once I had her, you would do as I said. Gibran is an irritation, sniping from his padded cell, but once I'm finished even he won't dare question my supremacy. And what about you, Sean? The famous DI Sean Corrigan. Frankly, you've disappointed me – so easy to make you think exactly as I wanted you to think. That night I followed you – made you fear for your wife, did it? Your children? Tell me – did you have nightmares about me coming into your house? Going to the rooms where your children sleep?'

Sean closed his eyes against the memories of the nightmares Langley described.

'I was never coming to your house, Sean,' Langley mocked him. 'It was all part of my plan to make you look the other way – to worry about protecting your family while Anna was left all alone and vulnerable. Do you know how easy it was to lead you by the nose?'

'So now what?' he asked, sick of listening to Langley congratulating himself. Desperate to stand in front of him. Face to face.

'Keep walking,' Langley told him. 'Soon you'll come to a clearing.'

'And then?'

'You'll see.'

'And Anna? You need to prove to me she's still alive.'

'I don't need to prove anything,' Langley told him.

'But that's not true though, is it?' Sean argued. 'This is all about you proving yourself. About you wanting to be something special. Only you're not. You're just another madman I need to lock away.' Sean waited for a reply as he sensed the trees thinning ahead of him, but he heard only the sound of the leaves rustling against the darkening sky. After several more steps he found himself in some sort of a clearing.

'Do you see it?' Langley suddenly spoke and made him jump slightly – sending his pounding heart into almost uncontrollable palpitations.

Sean arced the beam of his torch right to left until he thought he saw a shape – some sort of building perhaps, but it had become almost part of the forest. Tentatively, he moved a little further forward then stopped, cautious about being out in the open. He moved the light back and forth over the structure until he realized what it was. *The caravan.*

'Well?' Langley prompted. 'Do you?'

'I see it,' he answered. 'Is she inside?'

'Why don't you go and find out for yourself?'

He took a step forward but once again stopped himself. He took two steps back, deciding it would be safer to make his way around the outskirts of the clearing to the caravan, so he could use the trees as cover should Langley have a shotgun or other firearm. But Langley's voice in the phone destroyed his plan.

'No, no, Sean,' he demanded. 'You must walk across the clearing – so I can see you. So I know there's no tricks.' Sean swallowed hard and stepped carefully into the clearing once more, half expecting an old bear trap to snap closed around his ankle – metal teeth biting to the bone. But nothing happened.

'Do you know what a compound bow is?' Langley asked.

'No,' he admitted.

'It's like any other bow,' Langley explained, 'only it's re-curved and compact – for extra power.'

Sean scanned the floor with his torch for signs of traps. 'I see,' he answered.

'The arrow from a compound bow travels at one hundred metres per second,' he continued, 'whereas the speed of sound is three hundred metres per second, which means if you're lucky enough to hear the arrow being released you have two-thirds of a second to react or you'll be hit by a fibreglass arrow tipped with a metal hunting point the size and weight of a bullet from a .44 magnum. One arrow is enough to bring down a fully grown stag. So, how are your reactions, Sean?'

He sensed, rather than heard, a disturbance in the flow of the air around him – as if it was being torn open by an alien object travelling dangerously fast towards him. Within a split second he knew what was happening and threw himself to his right on to the leaf-covered ground. He rolled over twice, scrambled to his feet and ran hunched over and into the imagined safety of the trees as another bolt flew over his head and disappeared into the darkness. Langley had managed to fire two arrows in little more than four seconds. Sean clicked his torch off, straightened and sprinted into the darkness counting for three seconds before ducking behind a tree – expecting another arrow to fly close by or stick rigid into his hiding place, but none came. For the first time, he realized he'd dropped the covert phone. 'Shit,' he whispered a curse, as he imagined Langley close by, circling through the woods, ready to take aim with the lethal bow.

'You dropped your phone, Sean,' he called from somewhere in the darkness. 'Never mind. I think we've said all we need to say to each other anyway – don't you?'

Sean didn't reply, focusing instead on listening for the sound of footsteps on leaves or a breaking twig. He heard nothing.

'You should know,' Langley added, his voice seemingly coming from a completely different place, 'those first two arrows were warning shots. Something to get you running. Wouldn't have been very fair of me to shoot you down where you stood. Not very sporting. Ah, I see you now.'

Sean pushed himself off the tree and ran almost blindly into the dark woods – branches lashing at his face and hands as he fled. But the arrow moved so much faster. First he felt an excruciating stinging pain which soon turned to a far worse paralysing ache in his right thigh. He managed to take a few more steps before falling head first to the ground, scrambling behind another tree to inspect the damage to his leg. Instead of an arrow lodged in the flesh he found a deep cut the full length of the outside of his thigh. He clamped his hand over the wound. It was only a temporary solution, but if he took the time to tear some material from his coat and bandage it properly, Langley would find him and would be unlikely to miss at point-blank range. Images of murder victims he'd found decomposing in woods flashed in his mind. Was that what was to become of him – another corpse in the forest, waiting to be found by someone walking a dog?

'I know where you are,' Langley's voice drifted towards

him. He couldn't tell where, but he sounded close. 'Time to die.'

Sean hauled himself up against the tree and tested whether his leg could take any weight – the trauma of the arrow ripping away flesh having left the muscle convulsing and deadened. He swallowed hard against the pain, but he could move freely enough. He took three short breaths and burst into the woods ahead, darting between the trees for protection. Another arrow screamed past his head as he jinked left – running for a few seconds before taking cover behind another tree to rest his leg. The effort of running had increased the blood-flow from the wound.

If he could go no further, at least he could make sure Langley's reign ended too, Sean unclipped his own mobile phone from his belt and turned it on, using his bloodied fingers to type a text to Sally – all the while listening for the sounds of approaching death.

In woods off the A244. Stop by sign for Arbrook and walk into forest. Follow dirt track to clearing. Langley's caravan is there. Be careful. He's armed with a hunting bow. I'm wounded.

He pressed send and immediately turned the phone off again for fear of a ring or text tone betraying his position.

'You can't get away,' Langley's voice, closer now, warned him. 'How long shall we keep this game going for? Long enough for you to think about what I'm going to do to the beautiful Dr Ravenni-Ceron – just before I slit her throat and watch her bleed to death?'

Sean closed his eyes, trying to block out the ugly images invading his mind. 'No,' he whispered to himself.

'Your arrogance amazes me, Sean,' Langley mocked him from somewhere in the darkness. 'Just because you're a cop, you think no one can touch you or anyone around you –

even after Gibran opened up your little pet, Sergeant Jones. Again I will succeed where Gibran failed. Your pet won't survive this time, Sean.'

Sean counted the seconds of silence that followed. When he spoke again, Langley's voice seemed to come from a totally different location. 'What are you going to do, Sean? You can't run forever.'

He was right and Sean knew it. He had to do something other than just running and hiding. His eyes were much better adjusted to the dark now as he began to search the forest floor for something he could use as a weapon. He found a fallen branch – about three feet long and six inches in diameter. It would be enough. Next he looked at the blood coming from his wound. Most of it was running down his blood-soaked trousers, but he found if he allowed it to pool in his hand he could dribble it on the floor and leave a trail that he hoped a hunter as experienced as Langley would follow. He stayed in a crouched position as he slowly moved forward, dribbling the blood on the ground as he went, always expecting to be knocked off his feet by a steel-pointed hunting arrow. When he judged he'd gone far enough, he started backtracking, walking backwards so his footprints wouldn't betray him, dropping more blood on the ground. After about eight feet he took a big side-step, crouched behind a large tree trunk and waited – the branch clutched in both hands.

'I can smell your blood,' Langley said as he moved through the trees somewhere close by. 'I once tracked a wounded deer for miles through these woods. It had lost a lot of blood by the time I found it. I finished it off by cutting its throat with the same knife I used on the drug-addicted beggar and the two whores. The same knife I'm going to use on you, Sean.'

He almost gasped as the shadow of Langley moved past him, unaware of his presence as he tracked the trail of blood along the forest floor. Sean was close enough to be able to hear him breathe – close enough to reach out and touch him. But the angle wasn't right for an attack and Langley had the bow held in front of him, primed and ready to fire, so he stayed hidden. He watched until Langley reached the end of the trail and came to a halt, looking from side to side in confusion, his back to Sean.

Sean eased himself silently to his feet, the wind rustling the leaves covering his movement, as he took two steps forward to make sure his leg would work and then sprinted the short distance between them – bringing the branch crashing down over Langley's head before he could react. He heard the *thwack* of an arrow being released and watched as Langley staggered backwards and fell to the ground. He half expected to feel the searing pain of an arrow embedded in his body somewhere, but he felt only exhilaration when he looked down at Langley, who was now sitting on the ground, both hands wrapped around his left thigh and the arrow that had entered it dead centre. He guessed it had become stuck in Langley's femur.

Langley looked up at him and made a desperate attempt to grab the bow that lay next to him, but Sean kicked him hard in the head and Langley fell away holding his bleeding nose while Sean leaned forward and grabbed the bow, tossing it into the trees. Now he turned his attention back towards Langley, but as he reached for him he saw the moonlight reflecting off the blade of his knife and jumped clear as Langley slashed at him. The knife was so sharp it took a few seconds before the pain registered and he grabbed at his hip. He'd been cut again, but the blade had deflected off the bone, leaving only a superficial, but painful, wound. Langley struggled to try and get to his feet, but the arrow through his leg made it impossible. Instead he thrashed around hopelessly on the ground – swiping at Sean with his knife. Sean simply stayed out of range, enjoying Langley's helplessness. Eventually he tired of the game and pulled out his metal telescopic truncheon, flicking his wrist to extend it before taking a step forward and smashing its down across the hand that held the knife. Langley dropped the knife and let out a high-pitched scream that echoed around the trees. Sean kicked the knife away and leaned over Langley, pulling his hood down, grabbing him by the collar and twisting it tight – using it as a ligature that made it difficult for him to breathe. He could see Langley's face turning red as the blood supply was stifled. Panicked, he tried to pull Sean's hand away, but it was useless. He stared into Sean's face, his eyes shining with hatred.

'Please,' he managed to say through his gasping throat.

Sean held on to him for a few more seconds then released him and pushed him back into the ground. 'You're not worth it,' he told him, before grabbing him under his armpits and dragging him screaming in pain to the nearest tree where he pulled out his handcuffs and fastened one side around Langley's wrist. He pulled one arm back around the tree, then the other, and handcuffed Langley's wrists together.

He recovered his torch and used it to find the knife, then cut a strip of material from his own coat that he wrapped tightly around his wounded thigh. He ignored the wound to his hip – his only thought now to find Anna as he tried to suppress the rising fear he may already be too late.

'What about me?' Langley asked through his pain – looking at the arrow embedded in his own thigh.

'The arrow will stop the flow of blood,' Sean told him coldly. 'You won't bleed to death.' He turned away and started limping back towards where he believed the caravan was, but the sound of Langley's laughter stopped him. 'What the fuck you laughing at?' he demanded.

'You'll see,' he smirked. 'You'll see.'

Sean had felt almost nothing when he'd ended Langley's reign, but his words now filled him with dread. What would he find inside the caravan? What had Langley left for him? What unimaginable things had he done to Anna? He limped as fast as he could through the woods – assisted by his torch, but hindered by the sharp branches that again lashed at his face while hidden tree roots tripped him and brought the return of the searing pain to his thigh. 'Fuck,' he cursed as he stumbled on until at last he reached the clearing. Pinpointing the caravan with the torch, he dragged his limp leg across the clearing and grabbed the handle of the door. He was about to open it when some instinct told him to stop. Was that what Langley was laughing about? Some booby-trap device rigged to the handle – a home-made bomb or another bow ready to fire an arrow into his chest the second he opened the door?

'Anna,' he shouted at the caravan. 'Anna, it's me. Sean.' But he was met by silence. Even if she was inside, he knew she'd be gagged to keep her from calling for help – assuming she was still alive. 'Shit,' he cursed quietly and began to turn the handle slowly, ready to jump clear the millisecond he suspected something was wrong. Nothing happened. He pulled the door gently towards him and although he could feel it give, it was old and stiff – almost impossible to only open slightly. 'Shit,' he cursed again and yanked the door. He held it to stop it opening further and used the light of the torch to check it for trip wires or other signs of danger, but again he found nothing. Next he shone the light inside the caravan itself, looking for threats and signs of life, but he could see neither. 'Anna,' he called out again. 'Anna – are you inside?' He was greeted by silence, so he opened the door inch by inch until it was fully open, allowing him to lean inside and pan his torch around the interior. He saw bedding and a water bottle, a rucksack and a plastic box of something wrapped in tinfoil, but there was no Anna. 'Shit,' he repeated. 'Shit.'

He climbed into the caravan and started to search every place she could be hidden. It was obvious she'd been there, but he'd moved her somewhere else. 'Son of a bitch,' he muttered to himself just as he heard Langley's laughter winding its way through the trees – like the laughter of an evil spirit come to haunt him – to torment him in his failure. But Langley didn't know him as well as he thought, otherwise he wouldn't have laughed – he would have hidden in silent fear – afraid that his laughter would release the deep darkness that lived in Sean – the darkness that Gibran had recognized the first time he'd met him.

'Langley,' he roared, bursting from the caravan, striding back through the forest with barely a limp – the pain in his leg all but forgotten as rage took control of him and drove him towards the laughter – the clawing branches doing nothing to slow him until he reached Langley, still handcuffed to the tree.

'Where is she?' he asked, sounding far calmer than he was.

Langley's head rolled towards him. 'I don't know what you're talking about.'

'Anna. Where is she?'

'I told you,' he spat. 'I don't know what you're talking about.'

'You're going to tell me where she is,' he warned, but Langley failed to recognize the danger.

'I'm injured,' he whined. 'Get me a fucking ambulance.'

'That's not going to happen,' Sean told him, 'but you are going to tell me where she is.'

'Just get me the fucking ambulance,' Langley demanded.

'OK, I'll get you an ambulance – after you tell me where she is.'

'Fuck you,' Langley laughed at him. 'She can rot in the woods for all I care.'

Sean slowly crouched down next to him and gently brushed Langley's hair from his face. Too late, Langley realized the threat as Sean punched him hard in the thigh directly next to the arrow. Langley screamed like an animal in pain. The pain was so intense it left him almost unable to breathe, somewhere between consciousness and unconsciousness. It was a while before he was able to speak again. 'Stop. Just stop,' he pleaded. 'You can't do this. You're a cop. You have to get me medical attention. I have rights. You have to interview me.'

'Tell me where she is,' Sean demanded through gritted teeth. He punched Langley again in exactly the same place, once more filling the woods with the sound of his screams – the blood on Sean's fist looking like black oil in the darkness.

'You can't do this,' Langley complained once the pain had subsided enough to allow him to talk. 'You can't do this.'

'If you want it to stop, tell me where she is.'

'She's dead,' Langley spat, his mouth twisting into a faint, ugly smile. 'I cut her throat and watched her bleed to death – then I dumped her body where she'll never be found.'

'You're lying,' Sean accused him. 'I know you're lying. You kept her alive in case you needed something to bargain with – until you were sure you had what you wanted.'

'Did I?' Langley said, wincing from the pain.

Without warning, Sean stamped his heel on to Langley's wound and pressed down with all his weight – oblivious to Langley's screams and struggles to free himself. 'Tell me where she is and this will stop,' he promised. 'Only you can make this stop.'

'Stop. Please stop,' Langley begged, but Sean kept his heel on the wound, twisting it deeper and deeper into the thigh. 'All right,' Langley finally submitted through his tears. 'All right.' Sean lifted his foot, but kept it menacingly hovering above the wound. 'I'll tell you. She's about two hundred metres north of the caravan – tied to a tree.'

'If you're lying . . .' he warned.

'I'm not,' Langley groaned. 'That's where you'll find her.'

'Alive?'

'She was when I left her.'

'Then you'd better pray she still is.' He began to walk away back towards the caravan.

'Wait,' Langley stopped him, speaking breathlessly. Sean turned and looked down on him. 'You never asked me why I did it,' he told him. 'Don't you want to know why I did it?'

'I already know why you did it,' Sean told him. 'Because you couldn't stand being a nobody. A wife and children who left you. A job going nowhere. A life going nowhere, so you did the only thing you could think of to make you famous. You killed innocent people.'

'No,' Langley argued, shaking his head. 'You're wrong. I've had images of doing what I did in my head since I was a teenager. It was my destiny.'

'Those were just intrusive thoughts,' Sean shouted at him. 'You could have got help.'

'Help?' Langley laughed softly. 'Why would I want someone to take away the best thing in my life?'

'Jesus Christ,' Sean shook his head. 'I've had enough of you mad bastards. I've had enough of all of you.' He turned away and started trying to find his way back to the caravan.

'They'll all remember me anyway,' Langley called after him. 'Just because you caught me changes nothing. The whole world will remember me now.'

'I don't think so,' Sean whispered to himself as he carefully picked his way through the trees and branches until he stumbled into the clearing and began to look in every direction. 'North,' he said aloud. 'Where the hell is north?' Suddenly he remembered his mobile phone and grabbed it from his belt, his fingers fumbling to turn it back on, relief washing over him as the screen lit up. A second later it began to vibrate and chirp with missed calls and texts from Sally and others desperate to contact him. 'Shit,' he cursed under his breath. Their calls and messages would have to wait until after he'd found Anna. He searched the phone's icons for the compass app. Seconds later he was heading due north, scanning from left to right and back again as he walked, always wary of a trap, a snare or tripwire, searching every tree for signs of life – or death.

Suddenly he thought he heard something scampering across the leaf-strewn ground. He told himself it could have been an animal or bird, but as the beam of his torch got ever closer to the source of the sound, it became louder and more human – like someone struggling on the ground. He broke into a slow run, getting closer and closer to the noise until his torchlight fell on to the figure of a woman sitting chained to a tree – her eyes and mouth covered with silver insulation tape, her wrists and ankles bound with the same. Her heels tried to get purchase on the slippery ground when she heard him approaching – no doubt fearing it was Langley returning to inflict more misery and pain, or worse. As he drew nearer, he knew it was Anna. He spoke to her before attempting to touch her.

'It's OK, Anna,' he told her. 'It's me, Sean. You're safe now.' For a second she froze, seemingly unable to believe what she was being told, but then she started struggling again, as if she didn't trust him. 'I need to remove the tape from your eyes,' he explained. 'Try and hold still,' but she carried on struggling. He tried to hold her head as still as he could while gently peeling the tape from her eyes. She stopped struggling and blinked against the torchlight even though he made sure it was pointing away from her. 'I need to do your mouth now,' he told her. This time she nodded. Carefully he peeled the tape away, allowing her to take great gulps of air as soon as it was gone. He gave her time to recover then untied her wrists. As soon as she was free she threw her arms around him and pulled him close – holding him so tightly he thought she'd never let go.

'Langley?' she suddenly asked in panic.

'It's all right,' he assured her as he worked at freeing her ankles. 'He can't hurt you now. He's back over there a way. I handcuffed him to a tree. Are you OK?'

'Yes,' she answered, wide-eyed and frightened. 'Thirsty.' As her eyes adjusted to the light she saw the blood flecks on his face and heavier staining on his hands and clothes. 'What happened?' she asked, her voice coarse with dryness.

He tugged his coat off and draped it over her. 'It's a long story,' he answered, reaching for his phone. 'Another time. Let's get you out of here.' Before he could make a call, the phone started to ring in his hand. The caller ID told him who it was. 'Sally,' he answered.

'Jesus Christ, Sean,' she exploded. 'What the hell is going on?'

'You get my text?'

'Yes,' she replied. 'We're on our way now, but the locals and traffic should get to you first.' She took a deep breath. 'Jesus, Sean. What have you done?'

'I've found Anna,' he told her. 'Alive with no serious injuries.'

'And the suspect?' she asked, having to raise her voice to be heard above the screaming sirens.

'In custody.' Suddenly it was all he could do to get the words out. A wave of nausea and light-headedness hit him as the adrenalin faded and his wounds began to bite.

'David Langley?'

'Yes,' he confirmed. 'It's Langley.'

'OK,' she calmed down. 'What do you need?'

'Separate ambulances,' he explained. 'One for Anna and one for Langley.'

'He's injured?' she checked.

'He's got an arrow stuck in his thigh.'

'A what?' she asked.

'Long story,' he told her as he heard sirens approaching in the distance.

'Sean,' she replied. 'The team's pretty pissed off with you right now. People are beginning to think you don't trust them.'

'Langley had the upper hand. Manipulated the whole thing. I had no choice but to come alone.'

'I don't understand,' Sally admitted.

'It doesn't matter now,' he insisted. 'It's over. It's all over.'

It was past midnight when Sean limped back into the main office of SIU. There were nods from members of his team and one or two of them asked if he was OK, but he detected an unusual frostiness. He sought the solitude of his own office and flopped into his chair to examine the dressing around his thigh – his trousers in shreds where the paramedics had gone to work.

'You all right?' Sally appeared, standing by his door. 'Shouldn't you be in hospital?'

'I discharged myself,' he told her. 'They stitched it. It'll be fine now.'

'Then go home,' she ordered.

'I can't go home,' he insisted. 'There's too much to do.'

'Does Kate know what's happened?'

'Not exactly,' he admitted. 'I spoke with her. Told her I'm OK.'

'Jesus, Sean. Go home. We can handle it for now,' she told him. 'You should go and get some rest.'

'I'm fine,' he insisted. 'Where's Dave?'

'At the caravan. They've found Langley's car. We've got two other teams searching his flat and store.'

'Anything?'

'Not yet. They would have only just got started.'

'I should go and check on them.'

'I don't think that's a good idea,' she told him, stepping into his office and closing the door.

'Oh,' he asked. 'Why?'

'People think you don't trust them, Sean,' she explained. 'Your own team think you don't trust them.'

'Of course I trust them,' he argued.

'You disappeared on us,' she reminded him. 'Didn't tell a single person you were going after Langley. Didn't even tell anyone you considered him a viable suspect.'

'I told Dave.'

'Barely,' she replied. 'He told me about what happened.'

'I wasn't sure the first time I met him,' he said, too late realizing his slip.

'The first time?' she seized on it. 'You mean you met him again, before running off to the woods for some kind of showdown?'

'I went to his flat,' he confessed.

'Without telling anyone?'

'I wanted to see how he'd react,' he tried to explain.

'When?' she pressed.

'Last night,' he told her.

'And then you knew it was him?'

'He was very convincing,' he answered, 'but yes – I had a feeling it was him.'

'And still you didn't tell anyone?'

'I had nothing,' he argued. 'Only a feeling. It was better to let the operation run and try and catch him that way.'

'But why, Sean?' she pleaded with him. 'Why all the secrecy?'

He sighed deeply before answering. 'Because Jackson knows too much.'

'What's Jackson got to do with it?'

'He knows things,' he explained. 'Things that could only have come from within the unit.'

'You think there's a leak inside SIU?'

'It looks that way,' he shrugged. 'That's why I had to act alone. I couldn't risk Jackson finding out what I was doing and sticking his nose in where it doesn't belong.'

'And you thought this leak could be me?' she accused him.

'No,' he assured her. 'I knew it wasn't you.'

'Then why didn't you tell me what you were doing?'

For a few seconds he was speechless. He had no answer to

her question. 'Because I was worried you might accidentally tell someone who would tell someone else who *could* be our leak. And I couldn't risk you trying to stop me from going alone. It was Anna's only chance. You know how it works.'

'I wouldn't have told anyone,' she dismissed his excuse. 'And I wouldn't have tried to stop you – not if you truly believed it was Anna's only hope. You know what I think? I think you wanted to go alone. You used the fact there might be a leak to justify it. You wanted to be alone with him – face to face. Just the two of you. I think you enjoyed it.'

He stared at her blankly, trying to work out if she was telling the truth or if she was wrong, but he couldn't be sure of either. 'That's ridiculous,' he finally managed to answer.

'Is it?' she asked. 'I'm sorry, Sean, but I'm beginning to think I should speak to Addis. You can't just do whatever you like. There are rules and laws – there to keep everyone safe and convictions secure.'

'That won't do you any good,' he told her with a heavy sigh.

'What?' she asked, her eyes narrowing with suspicion.

'I said it won't do you any good,' he repeated.

'Why?' she demanded.

'Because Addis knew what I was planning. He won't admit to it officially, but he knew. After Anna was taken, I spoke with him,' he admitted. 'I told him that I believed I was the one Langley was after and the only way to get Anna back was to allow me to meet him on his own. Later, when we were waiting in the car park with the UC, I sent a text to Addis – to a phone nobody knows exists, telling him an opportunity had arisen that would allow me to meet Langley alone. Addis approved it. We used untraceable covert phones so that if something went wrong it could never be traced back to Addis. There was no paper-trail.'

'My God,' Sally shook her head. 'I don't know who's worse. You or Addis.'

'I just wanted to get Anna back alive,' he tried to explain. 'Addis wanted the same.'

'Please tell me you didn't know he was going to take her,' Sally demanded. 'Just tell me you didn't know he was going to Anna.'

'Of course I didn't,' he insisted, although doubts now seeped into his exhausted mind. 'How could I have known that?'

'I don't know, Sean,' she answered, 'but with you – like this – anything's possible.'

'You know what,' he told her, his head throbbing as painfully as his leg. 'I think I will go home. You can brief me in the morning on the searches before we interview him.' He stood and unhooked his spare set of clothing from his coat stand. 'I need to take a shower. I'll see you tomorrow, Sally.'

Sebastian Gibran sat alone in his isolation room watching the news on television. There was only one story dominating the airwaves – the capture of the man who had killed three people in London and the rescue of a woman he'd taken as a hostage. He listened to the female reporter broadcasting live from a road in Surrey on the edge of a forest. Apparently the suspect was wounded, but alive. The police would only say that the arresting officer was a senior detective from the Metropolitan Police's Special Investigation Unit, who had single-handedly tracked the killer to the remote spot near Arbrook, where he'd also discovered a woman allegedly kidnapped by the man now in custody. The officer was believed to be injured, but not seriously.

'Well, well,' Gibran said to himself smiling. 'Detective Inspector Corrigan gets his man again. Now maybe I'll get the chance to meet this killer of yours after all.' He leaned closer to the television – the smile gone from his face – his straight white teeth disappearing behind blood-red lips. 'Maybe one day, Corrigan, we'll meet again too.'

# Two Weeks Later

Sean sat alone in his office in Scotland Yard ploughing through lab reports and CPS demands about the Langley case. The Senior Prosecutor was most unhappy about some of the allegations Langley had made against the police, including torture and interviewing him without cautioning him or allowing him access to a solicitor. Sean wasn't worried. With regards to the caution, it was his word against Langley's. As for the torture – he'd been sensible enough to clean most of the blood from his shoe before bagging it as evidence. Interviewing him without a solicitor and away from a police station was never an issue. It was necessary to find and save Anna. He almost looked forward to lying in court just to see the look on Langley's face.

His team had calmed down too, although he had some bridges to build – particularly with Sally. Anna was still away with her husband. He'd talked to her briefly, but the conversation was awkward – as if Anna, in some small way, suspected her kidnap had been part of Sean's greater plan.

He pushed the paperwork aside and leaned back in his chair, rubbing at the stiffness in his neck and trying to ignore the pain in his thigh. When his desk phone rang, he grabbed the handset. 'DI Corrigan,' he answered, but no one spoke, although he could immediately sense some malevolence seeping through the phone. 'Hello,' he encouraged the silent caller. After a few seconds he was sure he could hear unsteady breathing. 'Is anybody there?' He was about to hang up when a man's voice finally spoke.

'Detective Inspector Corrigan?' the softly spoken voice asked – sounding nervous and afraid.

'Who is this?' Sean demanded.

'I've . . . I've just killed someone,' he confessed.

'Listen,' Sean warned him. 'I don't have time for this. You could get in a lot of trouble making nuisance calls to the police.'

'It was my first time,' the voice told him, 'but it won't be my last. It was so wonderful. So much better than I had even dared to imagine. There was so much blood. I never knew a person could have so much blood inside them.'

'Who is this?' Sean repeated.

'I don't know when I'll kill again . . . Perhaps next week. Perhaps next year. I haven't decided yet. It depends how I *feel*. But when I do I'll be sure to call you and let you know. I don't think you'll ever catch me though. Not even you. I have to go now.'

'Wait,' Sean pleaded.

'Cromer House on the Lisson Grove Estate in Paddington,' he told him. 'Number three. Ground-floor flat. You'll find her body there. Goodbye, Inspector.'

'No. Wait,' Sean tried to stop him, but he heard the line go dead. 'Hello,' he said forlornly into the empty phone. 'Hello.'

# Acknowledgements

I would like to say thank you to my agent Simon Trewin at William Morris Endeavour, for his continued advice, support and seeking of new opportunities. To Sarah Hodgson at HarperCollins for another really fantastic edit. To the sales and marketing teams as well as Jaime Frost for her work on the publicity side.

Luke Delaney